Praise for
THE THERAPIST

"The plot twist will come as a surprise and keep you flipping through the pages until the very end."

—*Mystery and Suspense*

"Psychological thrillers don't get any better than B. A. Paris's scorching *The Therapist,* one of those books that make you want to draw the blinds to make sure nobody's peeking inside."

—*The Providence Journal*

"There's plenty of guessing and twists in this story of obsession that will leave readers wondering who to trust." —*The Parkersburg News and Sentinel*

"A delicious web of lies." —Jane Corry, bestselling author of *My Husband's Wife*

"Tense and compulsive." —Louise Candlish, bestselling author of *The Other Passenger*

"Suspicion, betrayal, and dark secrets abound in this tense story—all hidden just beneath the surface of a seemingly perfect suburban life." —T. M. Logan, author of *The Vacation*

Praise for
THE DILEMMA

"An all-encompassing, tightly plotted novel of psychological suspense." —*Kirkus Reviews*

"[An] evocative drama. Welcome to B. A. Paris's dilemma. It's the kind of book you can read cover to cover in one sitting, eager to see how the characters' impossible choices play out." —*Star Tribune*

"The phenomenal B. A. Paris has done it again! I devoured *The Dilemma* in one sitting—it grabbed me from the very first page and wouldn't let go until I'd finished. Secrets, guilt, shame, and heartbreak—this story has it all in spades." —Sandie Jones,
New York Times bestselling
author of *The Other Woman*

Praise for
BRING ME BACK

"[Paris] builds a nice plot and brings some originality to the old 'good sister, bad sister' character dynamic." —*The New York Times Book Review*

"A twisty and seductive new psychological thriller you won't want to miss." —*Bustle*

"Paris once again proves her suspense chops with this can't-put-down psychological thriller." —*Library Journal* (starred review)

"An outstanding Hitchcockian thriller . . . Paris plays fair with the reader as she builds to a satisfying resolution. Fans of intelligent psychological suspense will be richly rewarded." —*Publishers Weekly* (starred and boxed review)

"A daring, stay-up-all-night love story. This should be next on your reading list if you love to read thrilling love stories." —*The Washington Book Review*

"We're in a new golden age of suspense writing now because of amazing books like *Bring Me Back,* and I, for one, am loving it." —Lee Child

Praise for
THE BREAKDOWN

"A story with a ratcheting sense of unease—a tale of friendship and love, sanity and the terrible unraveling of it." —*USA Today*

"In the same vein as the author's acclaimed debut, *Behind Closed Doors,* this riveting psychological thriller pulls readers into an engrossing narrative in which every character is suspect. With its well-formed protagonists, snappy, authentic dialogue, and clever and twisty plot, this is one not to miss."

—*Library Journal* (starred review)

"This psychological thriller is even harder to put down than Paris's 2016 bestseller debut, *Behind Closed*

Doors; schedule reading time accordingly. . . . A skillfully plotted thriller. With two in a row, Paris moves directly to the thriller A-list."

—*Booklist* (starred review)

"British author Paris follows her bestselling debut, 2016's *Behind Closed Doors*, with another first-rate psychological thriller."

—*Publishers Weekly* (starred review)

"B. A. Paris has done it again! *The Breakdown* is a page-turning thriller that will leave you questioning the family you love, the friends you trust, and even your own mind." —Wendy Walker, author of the *USA Today* bestselling novel *All Is Not Forgotten*

Praise for
BEHIND CLOSED DOORS

"Making her smash debut, Paris [keeps] the suspense level high. In the same vein as *Gone Girl* or *Girl on the Train*, this is a can't-put-down psychological thriller."

—*Library Journal* (starred review)

"Debut novelist Paris adroitly toggles between the recent past and the present in building the suspense of

Grace's increasingly unbearable situation, as time becomes critical and her possible solutions narrow. This is one readers won't be able to put down."

—*Booklist* (starred review)

"A gripping domestic thriller . . . The sense of believability and terror that engulfs *Behind Closed Doors* doesn't waver." —Associated Press, picked up by *The Washington Post*

"*Behind Closed Doors* takes a classic tale to a whole new level. . . . This was one of the best and [most] terrifying psychological thrillers I have ever read. . . . Each chapter brings you further in, to the point where you feel how Grace must feel. The desperation, the feeling that no one will believe you and yet still wanting to fight because someone you care deeply about will get hurt." —*San Francisco Book Review*

"Paris grabs the reader from the beginning with a powerful and electrifying tale. *Behind Closed Doors*, a novel sure to make one's skin crawl, also reveals no one truly knows what does go on behind closed doors." —*New York Journal of Books*

ALSO BY B. A. PARIS

THE THERAPIST

B. A. PARIS

St. Martin's Paperbacks

This is a work of fiction. All of the characters, organizations, and events portrayed in this novel are either products of the author's imagination or are used fictitiously.

Published in the United States by St. Martin's Paperbacks, an imprint of St. Martin's Publishing Group.

THE THERAPIST

For information, address St. Martin's Publishing Group, 120 Broadway, New York, NY 10271.

www.stmartins.com

Library of Congress Catalog Card Number: 2021006611

ISBN: 978-1-250-87563-1

Our books may be purchased in bulk for promotional, educational, or business use. Please contact your local bookseller or the Macmillan Corporate and Premium Sales Department at 1-800-221-7945, ext. 5442, or by email at MacmillanSpecialMarkets@macmillan.com.

Printed in the United States of America

St. Martin's Press hardcover edition published 2021
St. Martin's Griffin edition published 2022
St. Martin's Paperbacks edition / April 2023

10 9 8 7 6 5 4 3 2 1

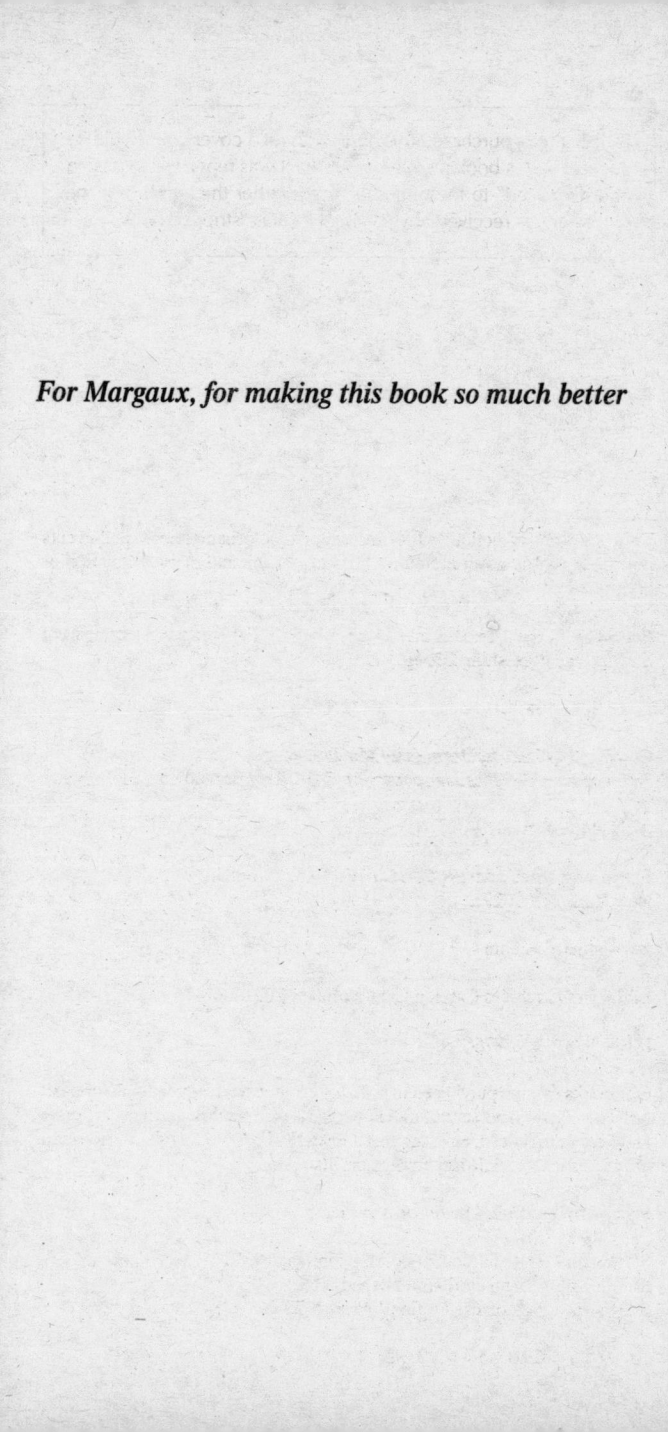

For Margaux, for making this book so much better

PAST

My office is small, perfect and minimalist. It's decorated in calming shades of gray, with just two chairs: a cocoon-style gray one for my clients and a pale leather one for me. There's a small table placed to the right of my chair for my notepad, and on the wall, a line of hooks to hang coats, and that's it. My relaxation treatment room is through a door on the left. The walls there are the palest of pinks and there are no windows, just two ornate lamps that cast a golden glow over the massage table.

Through the slatted blind shading the window of my office, I can see anyone who comes to the door. I'm waiting for my new client to arrive, hoping she'll be punctual. If she's late—well, that will be a black mark against her.

She arrives two minutes late, which I can forgive. She runs up the steps, looking around her anxiously as she rings on the bell, her shoulders hunched up around her ears, worried that someone might recognize her. Which is unnecessary, because there is no plaque on the wall advertising my services.

I let her in, tell her to make herself comfortable. She sits down in the chair, places her handbag at her feet. She's dressed in a navy skirt and white blouse, her hair tied back in a neat ponytail, as if she's come for a job interview. She's right to treat it as such. I don't take just anyone. The fit has to be right.

I ask her if she's warm enough. I like to have the window open, but spring hasn't quite shifted into summer yet and I've had to put the heating on. I gaze out of the window, giving her time to settle, my attention caught by an airplane trailing through the sky. There's a polite cough, and I turn my attention back to my client.

I angle my body toward her and, in full therapist mode, ask the standard questions. The first meeting, in some ways, is the most boring.

"This doesn't feel right," she says, when I'm only halfway through.

I look up from my pad, where I've been taking notes.

"I want you to know, and remember, that anything you say in this room is confidential," I tell her.

She nods. "It's just I feel incredibly guilty. What could I have to feel unhappy about? I have everything I want."

I jot the words "happiness" and "guilt" on my pad, then lean forward and stare directly into her eyes.

"Do you know what Henry David Thoreau believed? 'Happiness is like a butterfly; the more you

chase it, the more it will elude you. But if you turn your attention to other things, it will come and sit softly on your shoulder.'"

She smiles, relaxes. I knew she'd like that one.

ONE

The sound of excited voices draws me away from the box of books I'm unpacking. It has been so quiet all day that it's hard to believe I'm actually in London. Back in Harlestone, there would have been familiar external noises: birds, the occasional car or tractor, sometimes a horse going past. Here, in The Circle, everything is silent. Even with the windows open there's been only the occasional sound. It isn't what I was expecting, which I guess is a good thing.

From the upstairs window in Leo's study, I look down to the road outside. A woman with a white-blond pixie cut, wearing shorts and a vest top, is hugging another woman, tall, slim, with coppery red hair. I know the smaller woman is our neighbor, I saw her late last night outside number 5, pulling suitcases from the back of a car with a man. The other woman I haven't seen before. But she looks as if she belongs here, with her perfectly fitting navy jeans and crisp white T-shirt hugging the contours of her toned upper body. I should move away, because if they look up at the house, they might see me standing here. But my need for company is too strong, so I stay where I am.

"I was going to call in on the way back from my run, I promise!" the small woman is saying.

The tall woman shakes her head, but there's a smile in her voice. "Not good enough, Eve. I was expecting you yesterday."

Eve—so that's her name—laughs. "It was ten in the evening by the time we arrived, way too late to disturb you. When did you get back?"

"Saturday, in time for the children going back to school today."

A sudden wind rustles the leaves of the sycamore trees, which line the square opposite the house, and snatches away the rest of her reply. It's very pretty here, like a movie set depicting an enviable life in the capital city. I didn't really believe places like this existed until Leo showed me the photos and even then, it had felt too good to be true.

My attention is caught by a delivery van coming through the black gates at the entrance to The Circle, directly opposite our house. It turns down the left side of the horseshoe-shaped road and drives slowly around. Leo has been filling our new home with things I'm not sure we need, so it could be for us. Yesterday, a beautiful but unnecessarily large glass vase arrived, and he spent ages wandering around the sitting room with it in his arms, trying to find a place for it, before finally depositing it by the French windows that open onto the terrace. But the van continues past and comes to a stop at the house on the other side of us, and I move nearer to the window, eager to catch a glimpse of our neighbors at number 7. I'm surprised when an elderly man appears on the driveway. I don't know why—maybe because The Circle is a newish development in the middle of London—but I'd never considered older people living here.

A few moments later, the van drives off and I look back to where Eve and the other woman are standing. I wish I felt confident enough to go and introduce myself. Since we moved in ten days ago, I've only met one person, Maria, who lives at number 9. She'd been loading three little boys with the same thick dark hair as their mother, plus two beautiful golden Labradors, into a red people carrier. She'd called "hello" to me over her shoulder, and we'd had a quick chat. It was Maria who explained that most people were still away on holiday, and would only be back at the end of the month, in time for school starting again in September.

"Have you met them yet?" Eve's voice pulls my attention back, and from the way her head has turned toward the house, I realize she's talking about me and Leo.

"No."

"Shall we do it now?"

"No!" The force of the other woman's reply has me stepping back, away from the window. "Why would I ever want to meet them?"

"Don't be silly, Tamsin," Eve soothes. "You're not going to be able to ignore them, not somewhere like this."

I don't wait to hear the rest of what Tamsin says. Instead, my heart pounding, I escape into the shadows of the house. I wish Leo was here; he left for Birmingham this morning and won't be back until Thursday. I feel bad, because a part of me was relieved to see him go. The last two weeks have been a bit intense, maybe because we haven't got used to being with each other yet. Since we met, just over eighteen months ago, we've had a long-distance relationship, only seeing each other at weekends. It was only on our first morning here, when he drank straight from the orange juice carton and put it back in the fridge, that I realized I don't know all his quirks and habits. I know that he loves good champagne, that he sleeps on the left side of the bed, that he loves to rest his chin on the top of my head, that he travels around the United Kingdom so much that he hates going anywhere and doesn't even have a passport. But there's still so much to discover about him and now, as I sit at the top of the stairs in our new home, the soft gray carpet warm under my bare feet, I already miss him.

I shouldn't have been eavesdropping on Eve's conversation, I know, but it doesn't take the sting out of Tamsin's words. What if we never make friends here? It was exactly what I was worried about when Leo first asked me to move to London with him. He promised me it would be fine—except that when I suggested having a housewarming for everyone on the street so that we could meet them, he wasn't keen.

"Let's get to know everyone before we start inviting people over," he'd said.

But what if we don't get to know them? What if we're meant to make the first move?

I take my phone from my pocket and open the WhatsApp icon. During our chat, Maria had offered to add me and Leo to a group for The Circle, so I'd given her both our numbers. We haven't messaged anyone yet and Leo had wanted to delete himself when notifications kept coming in about missed parcels and the upkeep of the small play area in the square.

"Leo, you can't!" I said, mortified that people would think he was rude. So he'd agreed to mute the group instead.

I glance at the screen. Today, there are already twelve new notifications and when I read them, my heart sinks a little more. They are full of messages from the other residents welcoming each other back from holiday, saying they can't wait to catch up, see each other, start yoga, cycling, tennis again.

I think for a moment, then start typing.

Hi everyone, we're your new neighbors at number 6. We'd love to meet you for drinks on Saturday, from 7 p.m. Please let us know if you can come. Alice and Leo.

And before I can change my mind, I press send.

TWO

"There you are," Leo says, coming into the kitchen, a stack of dirty glasses in his hands. He puts them down next to the sink, pushes his hair from his forehead. "Are you coming out to the garden? You're missing all the chat." He raises an eyebrow. "I'm currently being warned about our bins being visible on the drive on collection day, not tucked away at the side of the house."

"Wow," I say, smiling. "I wouldn't even know what to say to that." I open a bag of crisps, tip the contents into a bowl, rescue a couple that spill over the edge. The scent of truffle, artificial, catches my nose. "I'll join you as soon as everyone has arrived, I promise. Someone needs to be here to answer the door."

He eyes the bowl doubtfully. "What flavor are those?"

"Try one."

He takes one, crunches it in his mouth and wrinkles his nose.

"Dead bodies," he says. "It tastes of dead bodies."

I laugh, because I get what he means. They're pungent, earthy. He takes another bite and grimaces exaggeratedly, and I'm glad he's finally relaxed. He'd been annoyed when I told him I'd gone ahead and invited people for drinks. I'd sprung it on him on Thursday evening, when he came back from his three days in Birmingham. It had been another scorching day and he'd looked hot, and cross.

"I thought we'd agreed to wait," he'd said, tugging at the neck of his shirt.

Guilt had me reaching for a bottle of wine, hoping to pacify him.

"It's only for drinks," I told him, knowing I needed to avoid the word "party."

"Who have you invited?"

I handed him the bottle while I dug in the drawer for the corkscrew. "Just the people from here."

"What—everyone?"

"Yes. But the people from number 3 can't come and only Maria or Tim from number 9 are coming, so that's twenty-one at the most."

"When is it?"

"Saturday."

"This Saturday?"

"Yes."

He'd been silent all evening and yesterday, he'd gone to see Eve's partner, Will. I watched from the window as they talked on the doorstep, worried he was telling Will there'd been a mistake and that we had to cancel. But when he came back, he said he was going out to buy beer and champagne, and I'd breathed a sigh of relief.

"How's the champagne going?" I ask now. "Will we have enough?"

"Not at the rate I'm drinking it!"

Recognizing Eve's voice, I look over Leo's shoulder and see her standing in the doorway, an empty glass in her hand, a pink flush staining her cheeks, matching the pink tips she's added to her white pixie cut. "It's delicious! I'm not sure Prosecco is going to cut it for me in the future."

I met Eve properly the day after I overheard her and Tamsin talking outside my window, and I instantly liked her. It wasn't just that—unlike Tamsin—she seemed eager to get to know me and Leo, it was also that she was warm and caring, understanding that it wasn't easy moving into a street where everyone already knew everyone else. She and Will only moved to The Circle eighteen months ago, so things are still relatively new for her too.

Leo turns. "Has everybody arrived, Eve, do you think? Alice is worried she won't hear the bell from the garden."

"Will's just arrived, his rehearsal ran over, so I think everyone is here, except Maria and Tim," she says. "But didn't I see a message on the WhatsApp group saying they have babysitting issues?"

I take three bottles of champagne from the fridge and hand one to her, two to Leo. "Yes, Maria said that one of them would come along if they could."

Eve laughs. "They have three boys, so that could explain their babysitting issues. Lovely, but noisy."

"Edward and Lorna aren't here either," I say, now

knowing the name of my elderly neighbor, and his wife. "I went over to introduce myself, and to make sure they'd seen the invitation, and they said they weren't sure they'd be able to come."

"I'm not sure parties are their kind of thing," Eve says doubtfully. "I honestly don't think anyone else will come now, but why don't you leave the door ajar?" Eve hugs the bottle to her chest like she's scared someone will steal it. "Then if Tim or Maria come along, they can let themselves in."

I hesitate a moment. Back in Harlestone, I wouldn't have a problem leaving the door open, but living in a city is different. Sensing my unease, Leo kisses the top of my head.

"It's fine," he says. "We're in a gated street, no one can get in unless they're let in."

I give him a smile. He's right, and anyway, I need to shake off my preconceptions about living in London. I go through to the hall, but before I can unlatch the door, there's a ring on the bell. "I'll be out in a minute!" I call over my shoulder to Leo. "I'll just get this."

I open the door to a tall, good-looking man dressed in smart chinos and a beautiful linen jacket. He's standing a few steps back, looking down at me from slightly hooded, deep-set gray eyes.

"You must be Tim," I say, smiling. "I'm Alice—come in."

"Hi, Alice, lovely to meet you."

He steps into the hall, ducking his head below the glass pendant lightshade. For a moment, neither of us speaks.

"Did you know the house before?" I ask, breaking the silence.

"No, not really. I know you've had some work done, though."

"Only upstairs. We created a bigger bedroom by knocking down a wall."

"Sounds fascinating. I'm trying to imagine it." He looks toward the stairs. "At the front or the back?"

"The back. I can show you if you like," I add with a smile, because it isn't the first time I've traipsed up the stairs this evening. All twelve houses in The Circle were originally identical, although some have been extended since. People are interested to see how we've used the same space.

"Great, I'd love to see it," he says, following me up.

"So, Maria drew the short straw," I say, when we reach the landing.

"Sorry?"

"She got to stay home and look after the boys. She said you were having trouble finding a babysitter."

He nods. "That's right, we couldn't. Beginning of the school year, so I guess they prefer to catch up with friends."

I open the only door on the right-hand side of the landing. As he follows me in, the sound of people chatting and laughing in the garden floats in through the open windows.

"Amazing," Tim says, looking around. "I don't think I've ever seen such a big bedroom."

"It was Leo's idea," I say. "We didn't need three bedrooms, so he had two of them knocked into one."

"I hope this doesn't give Mary ideas."

"Mary?" I can hear Eve's infectious laugh and suddenly, I'm desperate to get out there and be part of it. "I'm sorry, I thought your wife was called Maria."

He smiles. "She is, but I call her Mary. It started off as a joke because she went to a convent school, and it kind of stuck." He looks at the wardrobe, which runs half the length of the wall opposite the windows. It's extra deep and has beautiful wooden-slatted doors. "I wouldn't mind a wardrobe that size."

I laugh and he moves out of the room, letting me go past him down the stairs.

"Thank you," he says gravely when we get to the hall. "For the grand tour."

I point toward the garden. "Everyone is outside, so grab a glass and help yourself to anything you like. I'm just going to close the door."

I take a moment to breathe in the quiet air at the front of the house before going to the garden. As I pass the kitchen, I see Tim at the sink, filling a glass of water from the tap. I want to tell him that there's chilled, bottled water in the ice-bin outside but I can see Leo waving at me, so I start to weave my way through the throng of people. He's standing with Will, who is gesticulating theatrically with his hands as he explains something to Leo. Will is an actor, a rising star and, with his thick dark hair, roman nose and chiseled lips, on his way to becoming a rising heartthrob. Eve complains that they can't go out without him being recognized, but I can tell she's secretly thrilled.

As I get nearer, they're joined by Geoff from number

8, who's divorced, and—no, I can't remember the name of the other man with the tawny hair. He came with Tamsin, so I'm a bit wary. To be honest, after what I'd overheard, I was surprised when she eventually replied to my invitation on the WhatsApp group and said she and her husband—Cameron? Connor?—would see us on Saturday. Maybe Eve persuaded her to come.

I smooth my white sundress self-consciously, scanning the garden for someone standing on their own. But there are only groups of people who've known each other for years and are happy to catch up with each other after the holidays. I'm a stranger at my own party, I realize.

"Alice, over here!"

I see Eve standing on tiptoes, waving in my direction. Grabbing a bowl of crisps from the table, I make my way over.

"Nice dress." Looking up, I see the man with tawny hair standing in front of me. Judging from the four glasses he's holding in one giant hand, he's going to get refills.

"Thanks." I give him a smile. "I'm sorry, I didn't catch your name."

"Connor. I'm Tamsin's better half." His voice has the trace of a Scottish accent.

"Well, I haven't met her properly yet, but I'll keep that in mind when I do," I say.

He laughs and moves away.

Creep, I think, watching him go. Then I feel bad, because he was only having a joke.

I carry on to where Eve is standing with her friends

and I could swear Tamsin's eyes narrow a little when she sees me.

"We were just saying how brave you are, moving in here," she says, and gets a nudge from Eve in return. With corkscrew curls framing her face and her pale green eyes, Tamsin really is stunning.

I give her a smile. "I'm sure I'll get used to it. Especially with lovely neighbors like you," I add, in an attempt to get her on my side.

She frowns and I sense it then, she doesn't like me. My heart sinks. Maybe Tamsin is one of those women who guard their friends jealously and my remark has made me seem presumptuous in thinking I can join their group. I need to take things more slowly.

"Why don't you get a drink?" Cara, a pretty brunette says. I know she came with Paul but I can't remember what number they live at. Two, maybe? She dips her hand into the bowl I'm holding. "These crisps are delicious. Where did you find them?"

"From the delicatessen in Dean Street," Tamsin says, beating me to it. She gives a tight smile. "I've bought them there before."

The rest of the evening passes in a whirlwind. By the time the last guests have left, I feel more at home than I thought I would.

"Everyone is so friendly," I say to Leo as we stack glasses into the dishwasher. "We should start having people around to dinner in small groups so that we can talk to them properly."

He raises an eyebrow. "Let's take the time to work out who everybody is first."

"I already know who everybody is," I tease. "Did you meet Cara and Paul from number 2? They seem really nice."

He straightens up. "I'm sure they are. But don't make snap judgments about people, Alice. And be careful what you share about yourself. I don't want this to be like Harlestone."

I stare at him, thrown. "Why not?"

He pulls me toward him, wanting to take the sting out of his words.

"Because I don't want anyone knowing our business. We're fine on our own, Alice." He kisses my mouth. "We don't need anyone else."

THREE

We've had a lazy Sunday morning, staying in bed late before going out to the garden, where we're lying side by side on wooden loungers under an orange parasol that Leo found in the garage. The air is heavy with the heady smell of jasmine and the book I was reading is lying on my chest. I turn my head lazily toward Leo. He's checking messages on his phone and, sensing my eyes on him, he looks over at me.

"Paul has invited me to play tennis with him next weekend," he says. "And Connor has messaged to remind me about a Residents' Association meeting on Thursday." He puts his phone on the grass and reaches for my hand. "Luckily, I'm not sure I'll be back from Birmingham in time."

"I can always go," I murmur, closing my eyes at the feel of his touch.

"I think it's more of a man thing."

My eyes fly open. "Wow, I didn't realize we'd regressed to the 50s by moving in here."

He grins and rolls onto his side, his blue T-shirt exposing a line of skin at the top of his shorts. "Don't blame me. From what Connor said, everyone goes back to his for whiskey after. He's a whiskey trader and has an amazing collection, apparently."

"And women don't drink whiskey," I say, dryly. I lean toward him and give him a kiss, happy to see him so relaxed. "When do you think your work in Birmingham will be finished?"

"In another few weeks, I hope." He smiles. "I can't wait to be able to come home to you every evening. Ever since you reversed into the front of my car at those traffic lights, it's all I've ever wanted."

I can't help laughing. "Good try. We both know that it was you who smacked into my car."

"I did not *smack* into your car!" he protests, but he's laughing too. "I bumped, and it was a very small bump."

He's right, it was such a slight bump that I decided not to bother getting out of the car to check it for damage, mainly because it was a horribly wet January day. But he had come to my window and knocked on the glass, gesturing at me through the rain to open my window.

"I'm so sorry," he said, drops of water rolling down his face. The lights had by this time turned to green and as the cars began to pass around us, he bent closer and I found myself looking into brown-green eyes that managed to be both admiring and apologetic at the same time.

"There's no harm done," I told him. "Really, I hardly felt it."

"There might be harm done," he replied. "I must have damaged your car at least a little bit."

"Honestly, it's fine." I liked the way his hair, damp with rain, clung to his forehead, the hint of stubble on his chin, and began to wish he had done some damage, so that I'd have a reason to carry on the conversation. Maybe I should check. I unbuckled my seatbelt. "If it will put your mind at rest, shall we have a look?"

I walked to the back of the car, the collar of my coat pulled up against the rain, and bent to inspect the bumper. There was only the smallest of marks and I couldn't swear that it hadn't already been there because a few weeks before, I'd backed into my friend Debbie's horse-trailer.

"There might be some internal damage that you can't see, so shall I give you my details in case your bumper falls off further along the road?"

I smiled. "If you insist."

"I do." He took a card from his wallet and handed it to me. "And can I insist that you give me your details, in case your bumper does fall off, and you're too polite to tell me?"

Leo Curtis, I read, looking at the card. Risk-management Consultant.

"I don't have a card but I can give you my cell phone," I told him.

He called me that night.

"I just want to make sure you don't have late-onset whiplash."

"I'm fine, the car's fine," I reassured him.

"Then perhaps we can celebrate that fineness together," he suggested, making me laugh. "Can I take you out for dinner?"

"I think that might be a bit difficult," I said regretfully.

There was an embarrassed pause. "I'm sorry, I should have guessed—"

"No, that's not what I mean," I interrupted hurriedly. "It's just that I presume, from your card, that you live in London. I live in East Sussex. Meeting for dinner won't be easy."

"Don't worry—have car, will travel. Tell me, is there a wonderful restaurant not too far from where you live where I could take you to apologize for crashing into your life?"

"Believe it or not, there is."

And that had been the start of it all.

Now, Leo nods toward my cell phone. "Anyone message you, or am I the favorite?" he jokes, which niggles a bit but only because of how unfriendly Tamsin was.

"Just one from Cara thanking us for last night, which is lovely of her as she already posted a message on the WhatsApp group—as did everyone else. They're obviously very polite here. Did you see all the 'New Home' cards we got? I put them in the sitting room, along the mantelpiece."

"Yes, I saw them. I suppose they'll be there for weeks," he adds with a smile, referring to the way I keep birthday and Christmas cards on display for ages.

"I know it's weird, but people generally put a lot of

thought into choosing cards so I can never bring myself to throw them straight into the bin." I give my body a stretch, then stand up.

"Where are you going?" he says, reaching a lazy hand toward me.

"To make a salad to have with the steaks."

He gives a contented sigh. "Sounds wonderful."

I'm woken by a sudden movement, Leo sitting upright in our bed.

"Who's there?" he shouts, his voice loud in the quiet of the night. It's late, the shadows sitting heavy in the dark of our bedroom.

"What's the matter?" I whisper. It feels like I've only been asleep for ten minutes. What time is it, anyway? I try and pull him back down but he shrugs me away impatiently.

"There was someone here." His voice is sharp, urgent.

"What?" My heart jumps. I sit up, wide awake now, adrenaline surging. "Where?"

"Here, in the bedroom." He fumbles for the switch on his bedside lamp, and the artificial white light momentarily blinds me. I blink rapidly a few times to refocus my eyes, then scan the bedroom quickly. There's noone there, just the built-in wardrobes with their slatted doors and the chair in the corner of the room, piled with our clothes from the day before.

"Are you sure?" I ask doubtfully.

"Yes!"

I raise myself onto one arm and squint through the

partly open door into the bathroom, my mind already visualizing someone hiding in the shower, a long-bladed knife held high above their head. Leo throws the covers back, startling me, and swings his legs from the bed.

"Where are you going?"

He stands naked, his body tense. "To put the light on in the hall."

He reaches through the partially open bedroom door and flips the switch on the wall. I listen for the sound of someone leaving the house in a hurry, disturbed by the light now flooding the landing and stairwell. But there's nothing.

"Shall I call the police?" I ask, grabbing my phone from its charging pod.

"Wait a moment. I want to be sure before we do anything," he says. "I'm going to check the other bedroom."

I get out of bed and grab my cotton dressing gown. I feel less vulnerable now that I'm covered, but my heart is racing as I move to the door behind him.

"I'm coming with you."

"No. Stay here, and if you hear anything, call the police."

"Wait." I hurry to the bathroom, quickly checking there's no one there, and grab a can of hairspray. I pry the lid off and hand it to him. "If you see someone, spray this in their eyes to disable them."

At any other time, he'd laugh at this, a stark-naked man with a hair product as a weapon. But he takes it, holding the can by his side, his finger on the nozzle as he moves along the landing. I watch as he searches the guest bedroom, then his study, anxiety prickling my skin, my phone primed to dial 999.

"Nothing," he calls. "I'll check downstairs."

"Be careful!" I wait a moment. "Can you see anything?" He doesn't answer, so I move to the banisters and look down to the hall below, where he's disappearing into the sitting room.

He's back in a few minutes. "The windows and doors are still locked and nothing seems to have been disturbed."

"Did you actually see someone?" I say as we go back to our bedroom.

"Yes . . . no . . . I don't know," he admits. "It was just a feeling I had, of someone being in the room."

"It could have been a dream."

He looks a bit sheepish as he puts down the can of hairspray. "It probably was. Sorry. I didn't mean to scare you. What time is it, anyway?"

I check my phone. "Three-fifteen. You'd better get some sleep, you need to be up in three hours."

We climb into bed and soon, he's asleep. But I lie awake, grateful that Leo is here beside me, remembering all the times I'd start awake in my cottage, disturbed by the noises that would echo through it at night. I love that I have him to share things with, that I no longer have to face everything alone. Leo bumping into the back of my car was the best thing that had happened to me for years.

"Do you know, that's the first time you've shown the slightest bit of interest in anyone," Debbie had said, when I told her what had happened.

She was right. I was thirty-five, and although I'd had three fairly long relationships, they'd all come to an end, not in an abrupt manner, but in a slow, I'm-not-actually-sure-where-this-is-going kind of way. I'd begun to think that I wasn't cut out for long-term relationships and although there was a slight sadness that I might not find someone to spend the rest of my life with, it had never become a serious preoccupation of mine. But once Leo was in my life, everything changed.

After six months of the weekend commute, because Leo lived at his flat in London during the week and only came down to Harlestone at weekends, we both began to want more. One evening, we went out to dinner, and when he ordered champagne, my anxiety levels quickly rose at the thought that he might be about to propose. We had never talked about getting married and I didn't want to spoil things between us by telling him that I needed time to think. As the waiter struggled to get the cork out, I wondered if maybe I should say yes. Spending the rest of my life in Harlestone with Leo suddenly seemed a lovely prospect.

"Alice, I want to ask you something," he said, once the champagne had been poured. "I want to be able to see you all the time, not just at weekends." He took a deep breath. "Will you move in with me?"

Move in with him? Did he mean in London?

"I thought for a moment that you were going to ask me to marry you," I joked to hide my confusion.

He reached for my hand. "I love you, but I've never believed in marriage and I'm not going to start now, not at my age. I've never known a happy one and it's just a piece of paper anyway. It wouldn't make us love each other more, how could it?"

"That's not what I meant," I said, taking a sip of champagne. "I'm happy not to get married. But when you say move in with you, do you mean to your flat?"

"Yes."

I couldn't give him the answer I knew he wanted. Even though I was sometimes lonely in Harlestone, it was all I knew. I'd only ever lived in Harlestone. My friends were there. My life was there.

"Can I think about it?" I asked.

"As long as you don't take too long to decide," he said, smiling. "I want us to be together all the time, not just at weekends."

I managed to avoid the subject of moving to London until six months ago, when Leo's work began to take him to the Midlands. He didn't exactly give me an ultimatum but when he asked if I would consider moving north, I knew I had to give a little if I wanted a future with him, which I did. I could do my job anywhere but he couldn't, and if we moved to London, I could still get to Harlestone relatively easily from Kings Cross. But I needed some green around me so we agreed that he would sell his flat, and I would sell my cottage, and we'd find somewhere near a park with a garden. That way he could work out his current contract in the Midlands by spending Monday to Thursday in Birmingham, and Friday to Sunday in London with me. A new home for us, a new life for me.

My mind flits to what Leo said after the party last night, about us not needing anyone else. It honestly never occurred to me that he would want us to be together twenty-four/seven. It's true that he's a very private person, and extremely good at deflecting attention away from himself when questions become too personal. When I say that people are interested, he says they're intrusive.

"Who was that?" I asked him one Friday afternoon. I'd been at the window of my cottage in Harlestone, waiting for him to arrive from London. Because of the terrible weather conditions—there had been some snow, which had turned to ice—he had left at midday, and as he got out of the car, a woman had appeared from seemingly nowhere and had begun speaking to him. Leo had tried to get away but the woman had been insistent, and I was sure I heard him telling her to leave him alone.

"Someone wanting to know what it was like to live in the village," he'd said when I asked him about her, sounding more annoyed than he should have. We were in the early stages of our relationship, and I wondered fleetingly if she was an ex-girlfriend. But Leo, I realized quickly, hated anyone invading his personal space. It's why he doesn't have any close friends, apart from Mark, who he met a couple of years ago when he did some work for his company. Which is why I feel guilty, because I don't agree that we don't need anyone else. I love Leo, but there are other people I need in my life, like Debbie and my other friends in Harlestone. They are my family and I already miss them. Luckily, here in London, I have Ginny, Mark's wife, who has become a good friend and only lives a few miles away, in Islington. And hopefully, I'll make some new friends here in The Circle.

I flip my pillow over and give it a thump to flatten it, then turn and look at Leo, his head half-buried under the covers, and realize something that I've never realized before, which is that family-wise, I'm all he's got. He's estranged from his parents and from the little he told me about them, they weren't exactly the best role models.

He murmurs restlessly in his sleep and I feel a sudden rush of love. It's not surprising he wants some stability in his life. Someone he can depend on.

FOUR

"I'll see you on Thursday," he says the next morning, lifting me off the kitchen chair and giving me a kiss. "Be careful, won't you? Make sure you lock the doors at night."

"There was no one there," I remind him, pressing my face into his shirt and breathing in the scent of him. "We checked."

He rests his chin on the top of my head for a moment. "I know. All the same, be careful."

I pull at his tie, bringing him down for a last kiss. "Love you."

In the hall, he picks up his bag and with a wave, disappears through the front door. It slams shut behind him and I listen to his footsteps receding down the drive until I can no longer hear them. For a moment, the silence is absolute and my mind flicks to the thought of someone here, a stranger watching us as we slept. It's only as I stand there, shrouded in perfect stillness that a thought slams into my head.

I don't like this house.

I'd been on holiday in Venice with Ginny when Leo called to tell me about a house he'd visited.

"It's perfect," he said, and I could hear the relief in his voice, because we had viewed at least twenty by then. "Tell Ginny she was right about Ben. He's brilliant, he's found us exactly what we need. The perfect house."

Ginny looked up from the magazine she was reading and I gave her a thumbs-up. Before we'd left for Venice, Ginny had told Leo to go and see Ben, the estate agent who had found her and Mark their dream home a few months earlier.

"In what way is it perfect?" I asked Leo, because it seemed too easy. Too good to be true.

"I took some photos, I'll send them to you now."

"It looks big," I said a couple of minutes later. And way too expensive, although I didn't say it aloud. I carried on swiping through photos of a large white house with a front garden that opened onto a private road. It was at the polar end to my little cottage in Harlestone.

"It has four bedrooms, three upstairs and one down, and two bathrooms." Leo explained.

"Four bedrooms! Leo, we don't need four bedrooms."

"Yes, but there's stuff we can do, like use the down-stairs one as a second study."

I looked at the next photo. "Aren't there any fences between the houses?"

"Only at the back. Take a look at the other photos. It's a gated estate of twelve houses so it's really secure. And there's a lovely square in the middle, the houses are built around it."

I swiped through more photos, showing Ginny as she sat next to me. Each house had been built to the left of its plot, with a garage and driveway on the right separating it from its neighbor. The square, enclosed by black railings, was beautifully laid with flowerbeds, benches and paths, with a small play area in a corner for children. It looked better than anything we'd seen. But it was light years away from what I knew—and what I was comfortable with.

"I'm not sure I want to live on an estate," I said, stalling.

"It's not your ordinary estate; it's quite exclusive."

"Where is it?"

"Near Finsbury Park."

That puzzled me. We had previously excluded Finsbury as being out of our league.

"Isn't Finsbury too expensive for us?"

"That's the thing. The house has been unoccupied for a while, so Ben thinks I could get it for the same price as I'd get for my flat. It means you wouldn't have to sell your cottage in Harlestone, Alice."

"I don't mind," I protested. "I expected to."

"I know. But I also know how much it means to you. That's what I've wanted all along, to find a house that I can buy without you having to sell yours." He paused.

"You could rent it out for say, six months and then if you find that you don't like living in London, you'll still have your cottage in Harlestone to go back to."

"That sounds a bit ominous," I said, moving away from Ginny and walking into the bedroom. I waited until I'd closed the door behind me. "What are you saying, Leo? That you don't think we'll last more than six months?"

"No, not at all. It's just that I know you're worried about moving to London and I thought it might make it easier for you if you knew your cottage was there, waiting in the background, in case you ended up really hating it here. A safety-net, so that we could re-think our future plans, if we had to."

Tears had filled my eyes. The thought of selling my cottage had been heartbreaking, and I'd tried desperately to keep those feelings from Leo, obviously without success. And he was right, it would make it much easier for me to move to London if I still had my cottage.

"Why are you so good to me?" I asked.

"Because I love you. So, shall I go ahead and make an offer? I'd like to get it in today."

"I'll call you back within the hour," I promised.

I took my time scrolling through the photos again. Ginny loved the house and pointed out that it wasn't far from where she and Mark lived.

"At least you won't have to cross the whole of London to come and see me," she said, reaching for her wide-brimmed sun hat and cramming it on her head. "Come on, let's go for a glass of wine to celebrate you finally moving to London."

"I haven't said yes to the house yet," I reminded her. Because there was something that was niggling me. If I didn't sell my cottage, it would be Leo's house, not our house. Did it matter, though? I thought back to what he had said about us not getting married. Would we love each other more if we co-owned a house? The answer had to be no, so I called Leo back and told him to go ahead.

I finally saw the house a week later. I realized what Leo meant by exclusive when he had to type a code into a pad to open the black wrought-iron gates that stood at the entrance to The Circle.

"Each house is linked to the entrance by video, so no unwelcome visitors can get in," Leo explained.

The first house, number 1, was on the left of the main gate and the last, number 12, was on the right. Ours— number 6—was halfway around, directly opposite the gate, with the square in between.

"What do you think?" Leo asked as we got out of the car.

I'd taken in the white walls, the red-tiled sloping roof, the neatly cut lawn, the concrete driveway, the paved path that led from the drive to the front door. It looked the same as all the other houses.

"It's like a clock of houses," I said, smiling to hide the uncertainty I felt.

There was a spacious hallway, a rather grand dining room on the left—which I earmarked at once for a library—which led, through double doors, into an open-plan kitchen that ran the length of the back of the house. To the right of the hallway, there was a spacious sitting room and behind it, a ground-floor bedroom with an en-suite shower room. A staircase to the right of the front door led upstairs to an open landing with three bedrooms, a bathroom and a study.

"I thought we could turn the downstairs bedroom into a second study, then we'd be able to have one each," Leo explained.

"Good idea, as long as I can have the one downstairs," I said, kissing him. "I love the idea of being nearer the kettle."

"No problem for me to have this one." He opened one of the doors on the other side of the landing. "This is the biggest bedroom."

"Nice," I said, looking round the bright and airy room.

"Yes, but the room next door has the en-suite. Come and have a look." I followed him in. It was a little smaller than the previous one but still large. "I thought we could knock the two bedrooms into one to make one big bedroom and an en-suite," he explained. "It would still leave us with a guest bedroom for when Debbie comes to stay."

"Sounds good," I said, moving to the window so that I could see the garden. It was early May, and a beautiful Laburnum was in bloom. There was also what looked like a cherry tree and I could see raspberry canes along the left-hand fence.

"It's beautiful," I said, captivated. "Really lovely."

He came to stand behind me and wrapped his arms around me. "I can see us sitting out there on a summer evening with a glass of wine," he murmured.

His breath was warm on my neck and I instinctively tilted my head. "Me too."

He turned me in his arms so that he could see my face. "Does that mean you like it, then?" he asked, his brown eyes searching mine.

"I love it," I said, mentally crossing my fingers, because I didn't love it, not really. But I would learn to love it, for his sake. It would grow on me.

Except that it hasn't.

FIVE

I sit cross-legged on the kitchen floor, thinking about the inner voice which had told me with such intensity, just moments ago, that I don't like this house. It's not true, not really. There are things that I love, like my downstairs study. It has the palest of pink walls, a color I never thought I'd like, but which I do, and an en-suite, because it was destined to be a bedroom. The desk that once belonged to my father stands in front of the window and in the corner, there's a sofa bed that came from Leo's flat. I also love the kitchen, with its pale marble worktops and white Bulthaup units—or at least, I will once I've finished jazzing it up a bit. It's too neat and clinical for me at the moment, all clean lines and everything hidden away in clever cupboards. So, I don't hate the house, it's more the atmosphere that I don't like.

Maybe it's just that there's no atmosphere; the house was only built five years ago, whereas the cottage where I was born and brought up, and where I lived until a few weeks ago, is two hundred years old. I'm so grateful I was able to keep it. I did as Leo suggested and it's rented for six months to a lovely couple from Manchester, who want to give country living a try.

I glance at the photographs spread on the floor in front of me. They are mostly of Debbie and my other friends back in Harlestone, but there are also some of me and Leo, taken during a week's holiday in the Yorkshire Dales. Reaching out, I pick up one of the other photos, a headshot of my sister. I stare at it for a moment, then reach for another photo, this time of my parents and sister, taken on the day of her graduation, and raise it to my lips, pressing it there, my eyes closed, remembering. I can't believe that I'm actually going to put these two precious photos on the fridge, where my eyes will automatically be drawn to them every time I open or close the door. And the eyes of other people, who might ask about my family, because then I'll have to explain. It's why I usually keep photos of them hidden away in the bedroom. But this move to London is a new start for me in more ways than one.

Moving to a kneeling position, I begin to fix the photos to the upper door of the fridge-freezer, using tiny magnets to keep them in place. When there's no space left within reach, I get to my feet and continue adding photos until the whole of the door is covered. I stand back to admire my handiwork, and the two of my sister and parents leap out at me from among the others. I look around the kitchen; it still needs more color so I fetch a pile of cookbooks from the dining room, which I've lined with bookshelves. As I pass the sitting room,

I glance through the door and smile when I see that Leo has laid the "New Home" cards face down on the mantelpiece, his little joke after our conversation yesterday.

Back in the kitchen, I stack the cookbooks along the worktop. Later, I'll cut some flowers from the garden and put them on the table, in the red gold-lipped jug I found in a charity shop.

I'm still not dressed so I go upstairs, pausing when I get to our bedroom, still thrown by the size of the room. With the last of the boxes unpacked, and Leo gone, it seems sparser than usual. Overwhelmed by a sudden need to get out of the house, I look through the pile of clothes neatly folded over the back of the chair for my white sundress. The forecast for the rest of the week said to expect cooler temperatures, so today is probably the last time I'll be able to wear it. But it's not there. I know it's not in the laundry basket because I wanted to get another day's wear out of it. I must have put it back in the wardrobe.

I reach into its vast interior and look through the clothes on the rail. I still can't find my dress so I pull out some blue shorts and a vest top, noticing that my neat rows of shoes on the wardrobe floor have become jumbled up. I bend to straighten them, wondering if I could go and see Eve. She blogs for a living, mainly about beauty products, and works as much or as little as she wants each day.

"The perfect job," she told me that first day, when she came over to thank me for the invitation I'd posted on the WhatsApp group. "I'm so grateful to my sister; she's the CEO of BeautyTech and she was the one who suggested I start a blog. I write about something I love, I get to test amazing products, I'm given so many freebies that my shelves are overflowing—remind me to give you some—and I can fit it in around the rest of my life. We're lucky to be able to work from home, don't you think, Alice? I even blog from my bed sometimes!"

I could only agree. I work as a freelance translator and although I usually translate sitting at a desk, I often do the reading part of my work in bed, especially in the winter. Like Eve, I love what I do and don't miss having colleagues, or commuting. I also like that it varies in intensity. I'm in a lull at the moment, waiting for a book to come in from the Italian publisher I work with. I've enjoyed having a couple of weeks off, especially as the months leading up to the move were intense. But I need to start working again, before the boredom that I can already feel creeping up on me takes hold.

I leave the bedroom and as I walk past Leo's study, I see that his office chair has been left at an angle. I go in, lay a hand on its back and spin it around so that it sits in line with his desk. As I glance out of the window, I realize that I can see every single house in The Circle from where I'm standing. Their windows look back at me like eyes, and I give an involuntary shiver. Is that why they built the houses in a circle, so that everyone can watch each other?

Downstairs, I find my keys and slip on my sneakers. I'm not going to disturb Eve, she's probably busy. I have legs, I can go for a walk. I explored the area just outside The Circle with Leo but we never made it to Finsbury Park.

Crossing over the road outside, I cut through the square to the main entrance, which takes me all of five minutes, and that's walking slowly. It's lovely, though. With its benches and play area, it's perfect for both children and older residents. Something for everyone; that's the beauty of the place. But the play area, complete with swings and slides, is definitely in need of a few coats of paint, which explains the messages Leo and I saw on the WhatsApp group about maintenance.

I don't know London at all, and the cacophony of car horns and sirens that hits me as soon as I leave The Circle is overwhelming. The overcrowded streets and people jostling to get past are also new to me and I realize how cocooned I've been in Harlestone, where the loudest noise are the combine-harvesters reaping crops in the surrounding fields during early summer. Still, there's something invigorating about the buzz, the feeling that I'm part of a bigger picture, and I quickly pick up my pace to match that of the Londoners. With the help of Citymapper, I make my way to Finsbury Park. By the time I arrive, I feel as if I've completed an assault course.

In Harlestone, I can walk for hours over the fields without meeting anyone. It only takes me an hour to walk around the park but I'm pleased to have somewhere I can go without fear of being run over. Also, I need to stop comparing my life before, and my life now.

I arrive back at The Circle, and as I tap the code in at the side gate, the main gate opens and Maria's people carrier drives through. She waves, so I turn right, walking past numbers 12, 11, and 10 until I get to number 9.

"Hi, Alice!" she calls, as she gets out of the car. "How are you? Have you settled in?"

"Yes, more or less. I've just been for a walk."

"It's beautiful today, isn't it? I didn't have any appointments this afternoon so I decided to leave work early and pick up the children from school." Two boys scramble from the car while she lifts out the littlest one, who must be about three years old, and slides the heavy door shut. "Go on, into the house, boys. Ask Daddy to get you some juice."

"I'm sorry you couldn't come on Saturday night," I say, walking down the drive toward her.

She gives me a rueful smile. "Me too." She has the gentlest of faces, with wide brown eyes and high cheekbones. "The babysitters we usually use deserted us."

"Yes, Tim said. It was nice that he was able to come."

"Tim?" A frown creases her forehead. "I don't think so. He was here with me and the boys. Unless he went over to yours, once I'd gone to bed."

"He must have done, because he was definitely there."

She shakes her head in amusement. "Cheeky sod. He never said anything to me about it." Grabbing her handbag from the floor of the passenger seat, she moves to the door and shouts into the hall. "Tim, you never told me you went to Alice and Leo's on Saturday!"

"Hold on!" he calls back. "I can't hear what you're saying."

"Selective hearing," Maria mouths as he comes to stand in the doorway beside her.

"Sorry, what did you say?" He looks over to where

I'm standing. "Hi," he says. "Are you our new neighbor?"

And I find myself staring at a man I've never seen before.

SIX

The weirdest of feelings comes over me, a sense that something is about to happen that I'm not going to like.

"But—you're Tim?" I say, confused.

He laughs. "I was last time I looked."

"But not the Tim who came to the house on Saturday." I turn to Maria. "Well, that explains it, it was another Tim."

"I didn't think he'd have sneaked out without telling me."

"Sneaked out where?" Tim asks.

"To Alice and Leo's, on Saturday."

"I didn't."

"I know you didn't. But there was someone called Tim, and Alice assumed it was you."

I look at this Tim, registering the differences. He's not quite as tall, not quite as slim and not quite as dark-haired as the man I saw. Or quite as good-looking. And he's wearing a striped rugby shirt, which I can't imagine the other Tim wearing.

"Is there another Tim living in The Circle?" I ask. "With a wife called Maria?"

"Not that I know of," Maria says. "Unless someone new moved in over the summer. Wow, imagine having our name doubles living here!"

"She might be known as Mary rather than Maria. Maybe there's a Tim and Mary?"

Tim shakes his head. "Are you sure he introduced himself as Tim?"

"Yes." I laugh to hide my uneasiness, because it's just occurred to me that the man never actually said his name was Tim. I'd said "you must be Tim" and had let him in without waiting for him to say whether he was or not. And what about him calling his wife Mary rather than Maria? Was that because he'd misunderstood what I'd said and had looked for something to cover the slip he'd made?

"How old was he?" Maria asks.

"It's difficult to say—early forties, maybe?"

I tell them as much as I can about the other Tim but they can't come up with anyone who fits his description.

There's a crash from inside the house. "Better get back to the boys," Tim says hastily.

"It'll be someone's brother, or someone who just happened to walk in off the road and slip through the gate behind someone," Maria says. "Since Will was in that television series, there've been a couple of instances where fans have got in."

"He didn't look like a fan."

Realizing I'm being boring, I decide to stop talking about the man who gate-crashed the party. But I can't get him out of my mind, so during my fifty-yard walk home, past numbers 8 and 7, I call Leo.

"Did you speak to someone called Tim on Saturday evening?" I say, after I've asked him about his day.

"I don't think so."

"Could you try and remember whether you did or not? It's important."

There's a pause. "I don't remember a Tim. Why?"

I see Geoff coming across the square with two bags of heavy shopping and give him a wave. "Because a man called Tim came along and I thought it was Maria's husband from—"

"It couldn't have been," Leo interrupts. "I saw him this morning as I was leaving and he apologized for not being able to come."

"I know, I was just talking to him." I stop at the bottom of our drive and dig in my pocket for my keys. "The thing is, there doesn't seem to be another Tim living here." Tucking my phone under my chin to unlock the front door, I launch in to an explanation of the conversation I'd had with the stranger.

"Wait a minute," Leo says when I get to the end. "He didn't actually say his name was Tim? You said 'you must be Tim' and that was it? He never actually said that he was?"

"He didn't say that he wasn't," I say defensively, stepping into the hall and kicking off my trainers.

"And the thing about his wife—you said Maria and he said Mary?"

"Yes."

"What did he look like?"

"Tall, dark hair, gray eyes, smartly dressed," I recite, padding to the kitchen in my bare feet, the wooden floor deliciously cool beneath my feet. "Does it ring any bells?"

"None at all. Maybe you should ask around. He must have spoken to someone at the party. How long did he stay?"

I take a carton of juice from the fridge, pausing a moment to acknowledge the photo of my sister and parents. "I don't know. I left him to get a drink while I closed the front door. I saw him in the kitchen but I didn't see him after that. Are you sure you didn't see him in the garden?"

"Yes, I'm sure. I hope he didn't go upstairs. There's a lot of confidential stuff in my office."

I want to lie but I can't. "Not by himself, no."

"What do you mean?"

I reach into the cupboard for a glass and pour juice into it. "Just that I showed a few people around."

"What! Why?"

"Because they were curious to see the work we'd had done."

"For God's sake, Alice, I can't believe that you showed a bunch of strangers around our house!" He can't hide his exasperation and I can picture him running a hand through his hair, almost as if he wants to tear it out in frustration at my naïvety. "How do you know that this man didn't go snooping around once he was on his own?"

"He didn't," I protest.

"You said you didn't see him again. Maybe that's

because he was upstairs, having a good look through everything."

"He wasn't the type. He looked—I don't know . . ."

"There isn't a type! Have you checked if anything is missing?"

"No—"

"Well, maybe you should make sure your jewelry and credit cards are still there."

Worry starts to take hold. "I'm sure everything's fine," I say, making an effort to sound upbeat to de-stress him. "He's probably a friend of someone who lives here. Maybe he was staying with them or something."

"Wouldn't he have said?"

"I'll ask around," I tell him, wanting to be off the phone.

"Call me later. If you don't find out who it was, we should probably tell the police."

I hang up and run upstairs, propelled by the thought of the man being in the bedroom. Hurrying over to the dressing table, I check that my jewelry is there—it is— and that my credit cards are still in my bag, which has been on the shelf in the wardrobe since I put it there on Saturday evening; they are. Everything is exactly as it should be. But I can't relax and I know I won't be able to until I find out who the man is and why he gate-crashed our party.

It's seven in the evening when I decide to go and see Eve and Will. Someone must know who the man was, if anything he would have needed a code to get into The Circle. But Eve's car isn't in the drive and when I knock on their door, there's no answer, so I carry on walking around The Circle anti-clockwise, disrupting people's dinners and television programs. Some kindly invite me in but I stay on the doorstep and quickly explain about the man who turned up uninvited on Saturday, asking if anyone spoke to him. But nobody has.

"Are you sure he wasn't a figment of your imagination?" Connor asks with a slow drawl when I get to number 11 and describe the tall, dark, good-looking stranger that I'm trying to trace. Tamsin, standing next to him, doesn't exactly smirk but a half-smile plays on her lips and my cheeks heat with embarrassment.

The people at number 10 don't remember seeing our gatecrasher, neither does Geoff at number 8, and I'm halfway up Lorna and Edward's drive when I remember that they didn't come on Saturday. But worried that they'll have seen me from their window, I ring on their doorbell anyway.

"I hope you don't mind if I don't invite you in," Edward says, when he opens the door. With his shock of white hair neatly parted to one side and blue eyes undimmed by age, he is still a handsome man. "We haven't been well and we wouldn't like you to catch anything."

"Oh, I'm sorry," I say, feeling bad for disturbing them. "Can I do anything to help?"

Edward shakes his head. "We'll be right as rain in a couple of days. It's just a touch of flu."

"We're sorry we couldn't make your party," Lorna says, appearing behind him, patting her neat bob—the same white as her husband's—self-consciously into place. "Did you enjoy it?"

"Yes, very much, thank you." I pause and they both smile at me expectantly. "There was something strange though," I say. "I discovered earlier that one of the men who turned up shouldn't have been there."

"Oh?" Edward says.

"I thought he was Tim from number 9," I explain. "But I saw Tim earlier and realized my mistake. So now I'm curious as to who he was . . . Leo is worried and wondering if we should call the police. But I'm sure there's a simple explanation," I say hurriedly, because Lorna's face has bleached almost as white as her hair.

She raises a hand and clutches at the string of pearls looped around her neck.

"He said he was a friend of yours," she says. Her voice is strangely strangled, and I worry for a moment that she's pulling too tightly on the pearls. "And that you weren't answering the intercom. That's why I let him in."

The confusion on Edward's face quickly turns to shock. He stares at his wife, as if he can't quite believe what she did. Now Lorna's face floods with color. "I'm so sorry, I didn't realize you'd only invited residents."

"It's fine," I reassure her quickly. "It's actually a relief to know how he got in. But could you tell me exactly what he said?"

"He said he'd been invited for drinks at number 6 but that you probably couldn't hear the intercom because of the noise."

"Did he mention us by name?"

She takes a moment to think about it. "No, he just said for drinks at number 6. I've never let anyone in before, not without checking first. I can't imagine why I did this time." She looks guiltily at Edward and he nods, agreeing that it's the first time she's ever acted so imprudently.

"I'm sure it's all fine," I say again.

"Let us know if you find out who he was," Edward says, already closing the door.

"I will."

But there's only Eve and Will left to ask. I check their drive; Eve's car is there, so I go straight round.

SEVEN

Eve stops chopping a bunch of leafy coriander and turns to me, the knife in her hand.

"Nobody remembers him at all?"

I shake my head in frustration. "I've been all the way around The Circle. You and Will are my last hope."

"You said he was tall?"

"Yes, taller than Tim."

"And he said he was Tim?"

"He didn't say that he was or wasn't. I presumed he was, because we'd been talking about either him or Maria coming. The only thing I know is that he's not from The Circle."

Eve puts down the knife and wipes her hands on a towel. "Sounds like a gate-crasher to me," she says, laughing.

"You don't have to sound so cheerful about it."

"Sorry. It's just that I kind of admire gate-crashers, especially if they manage to get away with something big. As long as they don't do any damage, or steal anything." She looks at me. "Did he?"

"No, but that's not the point. We didn't invite him so he shouldn't have been there."

"Me and Will gate-crashed a wedding once," she says. "It was amazing. We were having a drink at a hotel and we were surrounded by this huge wedding party—there must have been at least two hundred guests. Then someone came in and called everyone through to help themselves to an enormous buffet. It was the summer and we could see people carrying their plates out to these white-clothed tables which had been set up outside. We watched for a while and it seemed to be very casual; there were no set places, people just sat where they wanted. So we tagged onto the end of the line, filled our plates high with food and plonked ourselves down on a table where there were three older couples."

"You didn't!"

"We did. We didn't feel bad as they seemed relieved to have us making up the numbers at their table. When they asked us how well we knew the bride and groom, we said, almost truthfully, not very well at all. It turned out that they didn't either. They were neighbors of the bride's parents and they sort of hinted that they'd only been invited out of politeness, because they were neighbors, not because they were good friends. And we definitely livened up their evening so didn't feel we'd done any harm. Besides we were hungry, and very young. We probably wouldn't do it now."

"I'd never be brave enough," I say. "But, our mystery man—what would his motive have been for gatecrashing a drinks evening? He would only have got a sausage roll and a few crisps out of it, and he didn't even get those because no one remembers seeing him in the garden. I saw him getting a drink of water from the tap in the kitchen but I doubt that thirst was his motive for turning up uninvited."

"Are you sure nothing was taken?"

"Pretty sure. Nothing major anyway. My jewelry and credit cards were still there when I checked and there doesn't seem to be anything missing from the house. We don't have anything valuable anyway."

"Did he go upstairs?"

"Yes, but only because I offered to show him the work we had done."

Eve pauses at this and rubs her hand across her forehead. "Did you stay with him all the time?"

"Yes—but I suppose he could have gone back up when I was outside. Leo is really annoyed because he has sensitive work-related stuff in his office."

Eve picks up the knife and goes back to the coriander. "I'll ask Will if he remembers a stranger at your party. He'll be here in a minute. Have you eaten? Would you like to stay for dinner?"

I get reluctantly to my feet. "That's lovely of you, it smells delicious. But I'd better phone Leo back. And go through the house again, just to make sure nothing is missing."

* * *

I check that our computers, tablets, and valuables are where they should be, but before I can call Leo, Ginny calls me.

"How did your drinks evening go?" she asks.

"Really well. I managed to meet just about everyone who lives in The Circle. The best thing is, there are quite a few couples who seem to be the same age as us. Eve and Will are younger, but the others seem to be in their late thirties, early forties. Next time you and Mark come over, I'll invite them round so that you can meet them." I pause. "I managed to make an enemy, though."

"Oh?"

"Not really an enemy but she didn't seem to like me very much. A beautiful redhead called Tamsin. I think she thinks I'm going to muscle in on her friendship group. She's friends with Eve, and as Eve lives next door, maybe she's worried we're going to be popping in and out of each other's houses all day long."

"I suppose you're going to have to be a bit careful about already established friendships," Ginny says. "Especially in a small community like The Circle."

"You make it sound like a sect."

"Maybe it is," she whispers dramatically.

She's joking, but it doesn't stop a shiver running through me.

"Everyone seemed really interested in the work we had done upstairs," I say.

"I'm not surprised. It's lovely. Leo did a really good job."

"What about you, did you have a good weekend?"

"Mark had a round of golf with Ben, so it was very good."

I laugh. Ginny and Mark work together, so are pretty much together twenty-four/seven and Ginny has been trying to get Mark to play golf each weekend so that she can have some "me-time." She's roped in the services of Ben, who, as well as being an amazing estate agent, is also an amazing golfer.

"And will that now become a weekly thing?" I ask.

"I hope so," Ginny says fervently. "You can't believe how good it was to have some time alone in the house."

"I've got a bit too much of that at the moment."

"You'll be fine once you've settled in."

"I hope so."

I don't mean to sound despondent but Ginny picks up on it straightaway. "Is everything all right?"

"It's just that I really want to start making friends here but Leo thinks we should take our time. He wasn't too pleased when I went ahead and invited people over for drinks. And then I let a gate-crasher in so he's even less happy with me now."

"Ooh, tell me more. I'm intrigued!"

I tell her about the man who nobody remembers speaking to, and the more I talk about him, the more uneasy I feel.

"Sorry, Ginny, but I really need to call Leo," I say. "At least I'll be able to tell him how our gate-crasher got in."

"No problem. Give him my love."

* * *

I call Leo and tell him what Lorna told me.

"Well, that's one part of the mystery solved," he says. "Although we still don't know why he turned up." He gives a sigh of irritation. "I really can't believe you showed people around the house."

"Sorry," I say guiltily. "But all your client files are locked away in the filing cabinet, aren't they?" I add, wondering if that's why he won't let it go.

"That's not the point."

"Do you think it might have been something to do with your work, then?"

"I'm a consultant, not a spy." His voice has an edge to it. "Look, I don't want to worry you, but have you got your keys?"

"They're in my bag. Why?"

"It's just that—well, you know I heard someone in the house last night? I was wondering if it might be linked to our uninvited guest."

I feel a prickle of alarm. "I thought we agreed that there was no one there."

"I know. And if you have your keys, it's fine. I've got mine and they're the only two sets that were in the house during the party, so it's not as if one of them has gone missing."

"And we have a mortice lock on the inside of the front door, so nobody can get in anyway," I point out. "Unless you to forgot to lock it before we went to bed?"

"No, I don't think I did. But make sure you lock it

tonight, Alice. And carry on asking around, will you? We need to find out who that man was."

"Will do."

But there isn't anyone else to ask. The mystery man has slipped away as easily as he slipped in.

EIGHT

I gather my pillows and quilt together and carry them upstairs, slightly embarrassed at having slept in my study for the last two nights. But when it came to going to bed on Monday evening, I couldn't bring myself to sleep in the bedroom alone. It wasn't just that Leo had thought there was someone in the house the previous night, it was also the knowledge that we'd had an uninvited guest. Feeling safer downstairs, I pulled out the sofa bed and slept there.

I re-make our bed, because I can't sleep downstairs forever, and go to my wardrobe for a pair of jeans. As I take them from the shelf, I see my white sundress, the one I'd wanted to wear on Monday, wedged between two other dresses. I take it out, glad to have found it. If I add a cardigan, I'll be able to wear it today. As I slip it over my head, the slight scent of washing powder tickles my nose; despite having worn it at the party, it still feels fresh and clean.

The mail comes as I'm having breakfast, bringing a

copy of the novel I've been commissioned to translate from Italian into English. I like to read books through twice before I start translating, making notes as I go, so I take it through to the study and curl up on the sofa, glad that I'm going to be able to get back into my usual routine of working from nine to seven, four days a week. Until now, I've given myself Fridays off so that I could have three-day weekends, but with Leo working from home on Fridays, I'm going to take Thursdays off instead.

It's hard to concentrate at first, because my mind is still preoccupied by our gate-crasher, wondering if we'll ever be able to find out who he was. And more importantly, why he turned up, because that's what's bothering me most.

Toward the end of the morning, when I'm quite a few chapters in, I hear voices in the road outside. Closing my book, I go through to the sitting room and from the window, see Eve standing in front of the small black wrought-iron gate that leads into the square, chatting to Tamsin and Maria who, judging by the numerous bags they're carrying, look as if they're on their way back from the local shops. I watch enviously as they laugh together at something Eve has said. A wave of loneliness hits; I want so much to be part of their group that before I can stop myself, I'm heading out to join them.

I walk down the drive and wait to let a supermarket van pass. It stops in front of Lorna and Edward's and I cross the road behind it, giving a wave to Edward as he comes out of his house. The three women are no longer laughing but are huddled together, the way people do when they're talking about something serious, something secret. I curse my bad timing. I don't want to interrupt them—but it's too late. Maria has seen me.

"It's amazing that it doesn't seem to bother her," Tamsin is saying as I approach.

"I'm beginning to wonder if she actually knows," Eve replies.

"Of course she does," Tamsin scoffs.

Maria looks up brightly and I realize that they were talking about me.

"Hi, Alice, how are you?"

"Fine, thanks," I say, smiling at her.

Eve and Tamsin turn quickly. They're both wearing dark sunglasses and I feel even more intimidated at this visual barrier between me and them.

"Alice!" Eve cries, as if she hasn't seen me for months. She pushes her sunglasses on top of her head and her pixie cut splays out on each side. "What have you been up to?"

"Reading. I heard voices and thought I'd take a break."

"What are you reading?"

"A book I have to translate."

"Into which language?" Maria asks.

"English, from Italian."

"Impressive."

"Will's grandmother is Italian and he's trying to teach me so that I can speak to her, as she doesn't speak any English," Eve says. "I'm not managing very well."

"You should try Russian. It took me ages to be able to hold a conversation."

Eve looks at Maria in awe. "I didn't know you spoke Russian."

"I do, but not very well. I'm not fluent or anything."

I turn to Tamsin, aware that she's been silent. Today she's wearing pale blue jeans and an orange T-shirt, which on any other redhead would look weird. On her, it looks great. "How about you? Do you speak any languages?"

"No." Her voice is curt.

"Right." She might not like me but she's bordering on rude. I look at her appraisingly. She's stunningly pretty but there's an air of sadness about her. Suddenly, I want to find out more about these three women.

"I was wondering—would you like to come in for a coffee instead of standing in the road?" I ask. "Unless you have work to do?"

"I don't!" Eve says. "Not today."

Maria smiles. "Me neither, so that would be lovely."

"I can't." Tamsin lifts her arms to show her bags of shopping. "I need to go and put this away. But I'll see you two later."

I know I shouldn't take it personally. But I do.

By the time we're halfway through a pot of coffee, I'm getting a real picture of who my new neighbors are. Eve and Will have known each other for twenty years and they're thirty-one now.

"We got together at our school's theater club," Eve explains. "He didn't want to join at first because it was mainly girls. But as we were friends, he began to tag along with me and suddenly everyone realized that he had this amazing talent. Except he wouldn't do anything about it until I persuaded him to audition for RADA—and he only agreed because I refused to go out with him unless he did."

"I love that story," Maria says. "Tim and I met taking our rubbish bins out at uni."

Maria and Tim are in their late thirties. Tim is a qualified psychologist, working part-time while he undergoes further specialist training in psychotherapy, and Maria is a speech therapist, working four days a week until Luke, their youngest son, starts at nursery.

"I work every day except Wednesday," she explains. "It's lovely to have a day off in the middle of the week. It means I can go to yoga with Eve and Tamsin, and pick the boys up from school afterward. Tim does the school runs otherwise."

"I never work Wednesdays either," Eve says. "If I did, I'd never see Maria."

I mentally move my day off from Thursday to Wednesday. The yoga class sounds fun.

"That's funny, Wednesday is my day off too," I say with a smile.

I ask about Tamsin and Connor. They're the same age as Maria and Tim and, as I already knew from Leo, Connor is in whiskey, selling high-end brands to rich clients. Tamsin, who used to be a model—no surprise there—is now a stay-at-home mom.

"She's also a mathematical genius," Maria says. She's dressed from top to toe in black and with her dark hair, she looks amazingly dramatic. "She does all these online courses and once she's passed her exams, she's going to set herself up as an accountant."

"Wow," I say, impressed. "I'd love to have a mathematical brain."

"So, have you found out any more about the mystery man?" Eve asks, reaching for a biscuit.

"No. I'm trying not to let it bother me but what I regret most is the effect it's had on Lorna, because she was the one who let him in. It's really shaken her."

"That's a shame." Worry chases Eve's smile away. "She and Edward don't need any more stress in their lives. Do you know about their son? He was killed in Iraq. He was their only child, which makes it somehow worse."

"How awful," I say, shocked. "It must have been terrible for them."

"They lived on the coast—Bournemouth, I think—but they moved here three years ago," Maria says, taking up the story. "Lorna told me that as time passed, the memories dragged them down more, and they wanted a fresh start. They chose London because they loved going to the theater and visiting museums and, because of their advancing age, they'd found the traveling up and down from Bournemouth more difficult. And they were fine for a while, they were really sociable and went out quite a bit, just as they'd planned. But then the whole thing of losing their son caught up with them and they've become near recluses. It's sad really, because they never go anywhere now, not even shopping. They get everything delivered, even their clothes. It's as if they've lost all their confidence."

"Or their will to live," I say quietly. I catch them exchanging uneasy glances and decide to get it out there. "It's just that I know what it's like to lose someone you love. My parents and sister were killed in a car accident when I was nineteen. I kind of lost the will to live for a while afterward."

"Oh Alice, that's awful," Eve says, reaching for my hand. "I'm so sorry."

"My sister was only twenty-two. She'd been on vacation in Greece with her boyfriend, and my parents had gone to fetch her at the airport."

"I can't imagine what it must have been like." Maria's eyes are full of sympathy. "How did you cope?"

"I had my grandparents to think about. I had to be strong for them, and they had to be strong for me. We pulled each other through."

As I refill their mugs, I'm secretly glad Tamsin didn't join us. It's why, when Maria mentioned the yoga class, I didn't say anything to make her think I was fishing for an invitation to join them, even though I'd like to. I don't want to get Tamsin's back up even more. Anyway, didn't Leo warn me not to rush headlong into friendships?

"Sorry, Alice, but I have to go," Maria says, bringing me back to the present. "Yoga is at two o'clock and I need to run home and grab my leggings. Eve, I'll meet you outside."

"It's our Wednesday ritual," Eve explains, once Maria has left. "We have our yoga class and then I go with Tamsin and Maria to fetch their children from school. If the weather's nice, we stop in the square so that the kids can have a play. Then we go back to someone's for tea."

"It sounds lovely," I say wistfully.

Eve opens her mouth and I think for a moment that she's going to ask me to join them. "Have you ever done yoga before?" she asks instead.

"Never." I give her a tentative smile. "Maybe I'll join you when the new term starts in January."

Eve leaves, and I watch from Leo's study as she and Maria walk across the square to meet Tamsin. It was a lovely break and I'm happy to get back to reading my book. I'm so engrossed in the story that when there's a ring on the doorbell, I jump in alarm. I close my book quickly, hoping it's Eve, asking me to join them in the square. I glance at the time on my cell phone; it can't be Eve, it's just before three so they won't have finished their yoga session yet. Maybe it's Lorna, or Edward.

I push my phone into my back pocket and open the door.

He has his head turned away from me, looking toward the square, but there's no mistaking him. Instinct has me quickly slamming the door, but not so quickly that I miss his look of surprise as he turns to face me. I back away, my heart racing. Why has he come back?

The doorbell rings again. I leap forward and latch the chain into place.

"Ms. Dawson?" His voice comes through the door.

"If you don't go away, I'll call the police," I say tersely.

"I really hope you won't. Ms. Dawson, my name is Thomas Grainger and I'm a private investigator looking into a miscarriage of justice. My client's brother was accused of a murder he didn't commit."

"I don't care, I'm still going to call the police. You entered my house illegally last Saturday!"

"Actually, you invited me in."

"Only because I presumed you were someone I'd invited!"

"You asked me if I was Tom, which I am, except nobody really calls me that."

"I said Tim!"

"I'm not sure you'd be able to prove that in a court of law." There's a smile in his voice and I feel my guard lowering a little. "Could I ask you to open the door? I really do need to speak to you and I can't have a conversation through a block of wood."

Reluctantly, I open the door but keep the chain in place. He peers at me through the gap, bending his knees slightly so that I can see his face. Behind him, the road is empty.

"Thank you." He takes a card from the inside pocket of his jacket and holds it out to me. "As I said, I'm a private investigator and I'm looking into the murder of Nina Maxwell."

I don't take the card, I can't. Just hearing the name sends my mind spinning. It might have happened over a year ago, but I'll never forget the murder, because my sister was called Nina.

It's always the same. If I meet someone called Nina, I automatically want to be their friend. If I read something about someone called Nina, I'll take their story to my heart. That's how the death of my big sister, who

I idolized, affects me. She lives on in the lives of other women called Nina.

It takes me a moment to let go of the memories that crowd my brain.

"Nina Maxwell?" I say. "I don't understand. What has her murder got to do with me?"

A slight frown crosses his face. "Nothing, other than this is where it happened."

I stare at him through the gap. "What—here, in The Circle?"

His frown deepens. "No, here in this house."

I shake my head. "No. There must be some mistake. She didn't live here, not in this house. We would have known if she had, the estate agent would have told us."

"I'm not sure—"

"I'm sorry," I say, cutting him off, hating the way he's making me feel. "You've made a mistake. Maybe Nina Maxwell did live somewhere in The Circle but it couldn't have been here. We wouldn't have bought the house if there'd been a murder here. And we would have known, because the estate agent would have told us."

I begin to push the door shut but he holds my gaze.

"I'm afraid there's no mistake, Ms. Dawson. This is where Nina Maxwell lived." He pauses. "And where she died."

NINE

For the second time in the space of a few minutes, I slam the door in the man's face. My legs shaking, I sit down on the stairs.

"I'm sorry." I jump at the sound of his voice coming through the door. I thought he'd gone. "I know this must have come as a shock."

"Go away, or I really will call the police," I say angrily.

"All right, I'm leaving now. But could I ask you to do something? First of all, google the murder. And secondly, call your estate agent and ask him why he didn't disclose details of it when you bought the house." There's a sliding noise as his card is pushed through the letter box. "If you feel able to speak to me again, please contact me at this number. Both I, and my client, would be very grateful."

His footsteps retreat down the path. Nailed to the stairs by a creeping dread, I can't move. What if it's true? I take my cell phone from my pocket and type

"Nina Maxwell murder" into my search engine. I look at my screen, where several links to news reports have come up. I open the first one, dated 21st February 2018, and see a photo of a pretty, blond-haired woman with laughing brown eyes, a gold chain just visible around her neck. I recognize the photo; it was all over the media in the weeks following the murder. My heart in my mouth, I scroll to the article underneath.

A thirty-eight-year-old woman has been found murdered in London. Police were called to a house in The Circle, an exclusive residence in Finsbury Park, at approximately 9.30 p.m. last night, where they discovered the body of Nina Maxwell.

Nausea swirls in my stomach. I force myself to read the article again, my eyes sticking on the words "The Circle," hoping that if I stare at them long enough, they'll disappear. But they don't, and although there's no mention of the house number, the possibility that Nina Maxwell was murdered here, in the house where I'm living, is terrifying. A memory from the time of the murder comes to me—a cordoned-off house with bouquets of flowers placed respectfully on the pavement outside. Was it this one?

I push myself up from the stairs, grab my keys and open the front door, half afraid I'll find the private investigator on the doorstep. Thankfully, there's no sign of him. Or of anyone else. I step outside, feeling horribly exposed. But I can't stay in the house, not now.

I cross over the road, push open the gate to the

square and sink onto the nearest bench, my mind still reeling. I don't know why I feel threatened. Thomas Grainger has been perfectly pleasant on the two occasions I've spoken to him. It's not *who* he is that frightens me, I realize, but what he said. How come he knows a murder was committed in the house where Leo and I are living, and we don't? How come Ben didn't tell Leo?

I find the contact details of Redwoods, the estate agents, and call them.

"Can I speak to Ben, please?" I ask, when a woman answers, trying to hide my agitation.

"I'm afraid he's away for a few days." She sounds bored rather than sorry.

My heart sinks. "When will he be back?"

"Monday. Can I help? I'm Becky, I work with Ben."

I hesitate, tempted ask her if she knows anything about a murder in the house that Leo bought through them. Surely everyone who works in the agency would have to know its history, if it included a recent death?

"My name is Alice Dawson," I say, deciding to go for it. "My partner, Leo Curtis, recently bought a house in Finsbury through Ben—number 6, The Circle. I was wondering—I heard a rumor that something happened in the house back in February last year. Someone said a woman died there?" I can't bring myself to say the word murdered.

There's a long pause, which I don't like. "I'm afraid you'll have to speak to Ben, Ms. Dawson."

"That's exactly what I want to do. Can you give me his cell number, please?"

"I'm sorry, I can't do that. But I can ask him to call you as soon as he gets back on Monday."

"Yes, please do."

I cut the call, feeling stupidly close to tears. I rub my eyes angrily, but I can't stop my increasing horror at the thought of our house being the scene of a murder. Becky might not have confirmed it but she hadn't denied it. Rage begins to build up inside me. How could Ben have kept it from us? He told Leo that the house was cheaper than its market price because it had been standing empty for over a year. Leo would have asked why, and Ben must have lied, or avoided giving him an answer. Leo is going to be devastated. If it's true, we're going to have to start house-hunting all over again.

My mind races ahead—Leo will put the house back on the market and we'll move into temporary accommodation while we find somewhere else to live. Or, better still, move back to my cottage. I quickly extinguish the tiny spark of happiness that the thought of going back to Harlestone brings. It seems misplaced among the reality of the murder and anyway, my cottage is rented out for another five months.

I want—need—to speak to Leo, but when I call his number, it goes through to voicemail. I wait a few minutes, then try again, but he still doesn't pick up. I want so much to get to the bottom of it that I decide to call the estate agents back and insist on having Ben's cell number. But something occurs to me. What if he wasn't obliged to tell Leo about the murder? Bringing up my search engine again, I type *Do estate agents have to disclose murder at a property?* A helpful article comes up but as I start to read it, my gratitude turns to dismay. It seems that although most estate agents would mention it, there's no obligation to do so.

Stunned, I lean back against the bench. I can't believe that Ben was so unscrupulous. Even if he wasn't obliged by law to tell Leo, what about his moral obligation? He was recommended to us by Ginny and Mark, he and Mark have become friends. I need to warn them about him.

I send Ginny a message **Can you talk?** Ginny, being Ginny, is able to tell from those few words that something is wrong and calls straightaway.

"Alice, what's up? Are you all right, is Leo all right?"

"Yes, we're both fine. But Ginny, I need your advice. Actually, I need to speak to Ben. Do you have his cell number, by any chance?"

"Mark does. Why—is there a problem with the house or something?"

Surprise jolts through me. "How do you know?"

"I don't." Ginny sounds puzzled. "But if you want Ben's number, it must be to do with the house, because why else would you want to talk to him?"

"Yes, it is about the house. I've just found out that a woman was murdered here, at number 6." Just saying it makes the horror come back and I grip the wooden bench with my free hand, grounding myself.

"What?" I can hear the shock in Ginny's voice. "Did you say a woman was murdered in your house, the house Leo just bought?"

"Yes."

"Are you sure?"

"Yes, I checked. Do you remember the Nina Maxwell murder? The woman who was killed by her husband?"

"Didn't he commit suicide?"

"Yes, I think so. This was their house, Ginny, this is where it happened. I checked the news reports, they mention The Circle, they don't say what number but it was here, I know it was."

"Alice, that's awful, I'm so sorry!"

"It must be why the house was empty for so long, why nobody wanted to buy it. I don't blame them, I don't want to stay here now, I can't bear to be in the house. I'm sitting in the square and even that's too close. Ben should have told Leo, but he didn't."

"But—I don't understand. Wouldn't he have been obliged to?"

"Apparently not, I checked."

"Perhaps he didn't know."

"I think he must have."

The gate clangs open and looking up, I see Geoff closing it behind him as he comes into the square. He's wearing his usual outfit of shorts and a baggy shirt, except that he's added a peaked cap to protect his balding head from the sun. He gives me a cheery smile and for a moment, I'm tempted to jump up and ask him if he knows anything about the murder. Instead, I smile back, keeping my head bent low over my phone so that he'll realize I'm on a call.

"I can't believe Ben wouldn't have told you," Ginny is saying. "I don't know him that well—Mark knows him better than I do—but I can't imagine he would be so dishonest."

"That's why I need to speak to him," I say as Geoff walks past. "I called his office and they told me he's away for a few days. But this is important. Could you get his number from Mark?"

"I'll call him now. Do you want me to call Ben for you?"

"Would you?" My voice breaks. "It's just that she was called Nina. If you could find out if he knew, I'll take it from there."

"Of course." Ginny's voice is full of sympathy. She never knew Nina but she understands why I'm extra upset. "I'll call you back."

It seems an eternity before my phone rings again, an eternity where I feel completely alone, because Geoff has long since gone and there's no one else around. Then, just as my phone starts ringing, I see Eve, Tamsin, and Maria come through the gate at the other end of the square with a group of chattering children. About to take the call, I shift quickly on the bench, turning my back to them, hoping they won't see me and decide to come over. But when I check the number, it's not one that I know. I stare at the screen, hating the effect it's having on me, the way it's making my heart race. What if it's the private investigator?

I press the green icon, accepting the call.

"Ms. Dawson?" It's a man's voice and I'm about to cut him off when I realize it isn't Thomas Grainger.

"Yes," I say curtly, because it has to be Ben.

"Ms. Dawson, it's Ben Forbes, from Redwoods. I've just had Ginny on the phone and I wanted to call you myself. I hope that's all right?"

"Yes, it's fine, I just want to get to the bottom of this, I want to know how we've ended up living in a house where a woman was murdered."

"I know it must have come as a shock to you," he says, echoing Thomas Grainger's words.

"You can say that again," I say fiercely, because it's obvious he knew. "Surely you should have told Leo, even if you weren't legally obliged to?"

"Can I ask how you found out?"

"A neighbor told me," I invent, because he doesn't need to know about the private investigator. "Anyway, why does it matter how I found out? We should have found out from you."

"Can I ask—have you spoken to Mr. Curtis?"

"No, he's at work. He's going to be devastated, because there's no way we can live here now. I hope you realize that."

"I think you should call Mr. Curtis, Ms. Dawson."

"I will, once I know why you didn't tell him about the murder."

"I'm sorry, Ms. Dawson, but Mr. Curtis already has the facts. He knew the history of the house before he made his offer. He knew why it had stood empty for over a year, why it was cheaper than it should have been." He pauses, giving me time to absorb what he's saying. "When he came back with his offer, I asked him if he was sure you were all right with it, because although we had a few couples who agreed to view the house, they said they wouldn't feel comfortable living there. Mr. Curtis assured me that you were fine with it, that you were willing to overlook its history because it meant you'd be able to keep your cottage—in Sussex, I believe?" Another pause. "I'm sorry, Ms. Dawson, but you really need to talk to Mr. Curtis."

TEN

I'm so numb with shock that I barely hear my cell phone ringing. It's Ginny. I don't take the call, I can't. My mind is too busy stumbling over what Ben told me.

I can't believe it. I can't believe that Leo went ahead and bought the house despite knowing about the murder, it seems too incredible. How could he be all right with it? How could he think, even for a minute, that I'd be all right with it? He knows how squeamish I am, how I can't watch a film without leaving the room as soon as I sense something bad is going to happen. Which must be why he didn't tell me, because he knew I'd refuse to live there. What makes it worse is that he lied to Ben about having told me. And what makes *that* worse is he told Ben that the reason I didn't mind living there was because I wouldn't have to sell my cottage. How could he? He's made me out to be both insensitive and mercenary, and I hate him for it. At least Ben knows the truth now. But it only makes me feel marginally better.

I can't understand Leo's motivation for not telling

me. He must have known I'd find out eventually. Is that why he didn't want to have people over for drinks, in case someone mentioned the murder? And why had no one mentioned it, why had neither Eve or Maria, or anyone else at the party said anything?

Because they couldn't, I realize dully. They presumed that I knew, that I was fine about it. They were hardly going to introduce it into the conversation—*So, Alice, what's it like living in a house where a murder took place?* I remember Tamsin's comment at the party about me being brave. She hadn't been referring to my move from the country to London, but my move into a house with a terrible past. And then, this morning, the conversation I overheard when I went to join them. What had Tamsin said? I close my eyes and her voice comes back to me. *"It's amazing that it doesn't seem to bother her."* And Eve's reply—*"I'm beginning to wonder if she actually knows."*

I feel a rush of gratitude toward Eve, for realizing that maybe I'm not as heartless as everyone must think. I'm surprised she's been so friendly, surprised the people here have been generally welcoming. Maybe some of them were secretly judging us for buying the house but the majority had seemed interested—

Oh God. I lean forward, my head heavy in my hands. I had paraded people through the house, I had taken them upstairs. What must people have thought? The ones who had been eager to see the bedroom—was that because the murder had taken place there?

My phone is still in my hand so I google the murder again and find an article written four days after Nina

Maxwell's death. There are more details: her body was found in her bedroom, tied to a chair. Her hair had been cut off and she had been strangled. *A man has been arrested and is helping the police with their inquiries,* the article finishes.

Bile surges in my throat. I knew how Nina Maxwell had died, it had haunted me for months after. But to see it written in black and white—I fight down the nausea, channeling it instead into anger at the people who had wanted to see the bedroom where it had taken place. Tamsin and most of the women hadn't accepted my invitation to show them the renovations, it was mainly the men who'd been interested. Eve had already been upstairs, not at the party, but the day she came over to introduce herself, and I'd dragged her to the bedroom to show her our huge wardrobe. She had held back at first and I'd put her hesitation down to a desire not to appear nosey.

"Alice?" Lifting my head, I see Eve walking down the path toward me. "What are you doing sitting here?" A frown furrows her brow. "You're shivering! Is everything all right?"

"No, not really."

"Are you ill, do you need me to call someone?"

"No, I'm fine. Well, I'm not fine, obviously," I say, trying to joke. "But I'm not ill. I just feel so humiliated, so angry!"

"Angry is good," Eve says, coming to sit next to me. The smell of her perfume—Sì, by Armani—is oddly comforting. "Much better than ill, or sad. Why don't you tell me what's happened?"

"I've just found out that our house," I thrust my hand toward it, "was the scene of a brutal murder." I look at her in anguish. "I didn't know, Eve. Leo knew but he didn't tell me."

"Oh, Alice." The sympathy in Eve's eyes is also comforting. "I was beginning to think that you might not know. At first, I thought you were one of those people who are able to compartmentalize things, who are able to say 'that was then, but this is now.'"

"I could never be that insensitive. I'm surprised you could bring yourself to talk to me. I'm surprised anyone could talk to me when I didn't acknowledge the murder, not even to say how sorry I was that you had all lost your neighbor."

"No one was judging you, Alice."

"I think Tamsin might have been."

"Well, maybe. A bit. Nina was her best friend, so it's understandable." She pauses a moment. "The first time she saw you, she thought for a moment that you *were* Nina. She was standing at her bedroom window and she saw you crossing the square. You're about the same build as Nina was and from that distance, she could only see your long blond hair. It gave her a bit of a shock."

I nod distractedly. "But why weren't people judging me?" I ask. "Shouldn't they have been?"

Eve pushes her hand through her hair. "I think everyone was just relieved that the house had been sold, that it was going to be lived in and not standing empty. It had become a bit of a shrine, I suppose, and some of the children began to say it must be haunted, and their parents didn't want them believing that it was. When we heard that someone had bought it, it was as if a breath of fresh air was coming to The Circle. At last, we were going to be able to move on." She looks at me earnestly. "People are grateful, Alice. We see it as a new beginning."

"Maybe, but we're not going to be able to stay here now. At least, I'm not. It obviously doesn't bother Leo."

"He told Will it was why he wanted to change it around upstairs, get rid of the room where it happened. He said he wanted to make it easier for you to live there."

"Insinuating that I knew about it," I say, digging in my pocket for a tissue. "And of course, nobody dared mention the murder on Saturday, even though there were plenty who were eager to see where it had taken place. You'd have thought at least one person would have asked me if I was OK living with the ghost of a murdered woman."

Eve looks uncomfortable. "I might have had something to do with that. Leo told Will he'd appreciate it if no one mentioned the house's history in front of you as you were obviously sensitive about it. Will told me and I sort of spread the word."

A memory comes back, of Leo going to see Will, the day after I told him I'd invited people for drinks. "I can't believe it!" I say, my anger coming back. "He really didn't want me to find out, did he?" I look at her, hoping she'll be able to give me an answer. "I can't understand it, Eve. He's never done anything like this before, he's never kept anything back, he's never not told me the truth. And he must have known that I'd find out eventually. It's not the sort of thing that can be kept a secret."

"How did you find out?" Eve asks, reaching into her bag and bringing out a peaked cap, and using it to fan herself.

"I got a phone call," I say, hoping she didn't notice my slight hesitation. "From a reporter." I'm not lying to her because I'm almost sure that Thomas Grainger is a journalist, and changed his job description to private investigator to make it sound more palatable.

She jams the cap on her head, not caring that her sunglasses are caught under it. "What did they say?"

"She asked me how it felt to be living at the scene of a brutal murder," I improvise, changing the pronoun to move further away from the truth. "When I said that I didn't know what she was talking about, she told me to google Nina Maxwell." That part at least is true. "So, I did."

"What an awful way to find out."

I shake my head slowly. "I can't believe Leo knew." The memory of how I accused Ben of not telling Leo makes me flinch internally. "Leo told the estate agent that I was fine with it because, with the house being cheaper, it meant I could keep my cottage in Harlestone. He made me sound completely heartless."

She tries to hug me but because of the way we're sitting on the bench, it's awkward, and I realize that I don't know Eve, not really. Do I even know Leo?

"What are you going to do?" she asks.

"I need to speak to Leo but I don't want to call him, I need to see his face. He's back tomorrow evening so

I'll have to wait until then. But I can't stay in the house, so I'll go to a hotel." I turn to her. "Can I ask you a favor, Eve? I need to get a couple of things from the house, would you come with me? I know it's stupid but I feel a bit funny going in there now."

"It's not stupid and of course I'll come with you. And you don't need to go to a hotel, you can stay with me and Will."

I falter at this, suddenly unsure of what I want. "Are you sure?"

"Sure I'm sure!"

"I don't need much, just some pajamas, a toothbrush and a change of clothes. And my book and laptop."

"Come on then."

On the doorstep, I hand my keys to Eve. She unlocks the door and goes into the house, while I wait on the doorstep, dread cramping my stomach. I don't know what I'm expecting. For it to be different, I suppose. At least to feel different. But it doesn't, it feels just the same, so I go in.

Eve stoops to pick up something.

"Someone's card," she says, handing it to me without looking at it.

"Thanks." I tuck it in my pocket and wait while she takes off her cap, shoves it into her bag, then kicks off her trainers. I slip mine off and follow her upstairs to the bedroom. She walks straight in but I stop in the doorway.

She holds out her hand to me. "It's just the same as before, Alice. Nothing has changed."

I take a steadying breath and look around the room. She's right, it is the same. The patterned curtains are still billowing in the breeze, just as they were this morning. My hairbrush is still on the dressing table, the clothes I wore yesterday are still draped over the chair. But—

"I can't be here," I say, overwhelmed by a feeling of mounting panic. Going over to the chest of drawers, I grab a pair of pajamas and some underwear then run out of the room, away from the evil I can feel seeping into my pores.

ELEVEN

"Here." Eve holds out a mug of tea. "Drink this, and then we'll open a bottle of wine."

"Sorry. I don't know why I made so much fuss about being in the bedroom." Curled up on the pale leather sofa in her sitting room, my feet tucked under me, I realize she deserves the truth. "Actually, I do. My sister's name was Nina, so anything to do with anyone called Nina always affects me more."

She gives me a hug. "Oh, Alice, I'm so sorry."

"If my sister had lived, she would have been the same age as Nina Maxwell. I know it sounds horribly dramatic but it makes me feel as if my sister has been killed twice over."

"That, coupled with Leo not telling you about the murder, would be enough to make anyone freak out," she says. "It's a lot for you to cope with."

A glass of Chablis later, I'm beginning to feel better. "What was she like?" I ask.

"Nina?" Eve takes a sip of wine. "I didn't get the

chance to know her well because we only moved here five months before she died. She was lovely, quite spiritual. As well as being a therapist, she was also a qualified yoga instructor." She smiles. "She started our yoga group and after she died, we carried on with it, in her memory."

I like that Nina Maxwell enjoyed yoga, because my sister had too. She had tried several times to get me to go to her class with her, but I'd always had something to do. After, I wished so much that I'd gone, even once. I also like that Nina Maxwell was a therapist; it seems she was a caring person.

"And her husband?"

"The nicest man you could hope to meet. From what I knew of him, anyway. But you never really know, do you?"

"You must have been shocked when he was arrested for her murder."

Eve reaches toward the low glass table that is neither round nor square but an indeterminate shape, and picks up her glass. "Everyone was." She takes a sip of wine. "We couldn't believe it, we thought it was a case of 'it's always the husband until they find the real culprit.' But then we heard he'd committed suicide."

I remember what the investigator said about a miscarriage of justice. "And that made you think he must have killed her?"

"Yes."

"But why?" Eve looks suddenly uncomfortable. "I'm sorry to ask all these questions," I say. "I'm just trying to understand. But if you prefer me not to ask, that's fine."

"No, it's OK. It's actually a relief to be able to talk about it to someone who wasn't here at the time. It's sort of become a taboo subject." She pauses, thinking about my question. "Apart from there being no signs of a break-in, there were several reasons why we believed Oliver must have killed her. First, the fact that he committed suicide made us think that he couldn't come to terms with what he'd done, because he truly loved Nina—that's what's so tragic. And other things came to light which made us think it was not just possible, but probable."

"What things?"

"The first was that he lied about the time he got home that night." She frowns, catching herself, then looks at me apologetically. "Actually, it doesn't feel good to be repeating things I only heard second or third hand. As I said, I didn't know Nina that well. Tamsin knew her better than I did. And Lorna was the one who witnessed everything." Putting her glass back down, she reaches for the bottle of wine. "Here, let me top up your glass for you."

Although I'm curious, I'm happy not to talk about the murder. I also respect her for not wanting to gossip.

"Shall we watch a film?" Eve suggests. "Something light to take your mind off things for a while?"

"Good idea," I say.

"I don't suppose you want to watch *When Harry Met Sally,* do you? I've only ever seen it once."

I laugh. "Why not? I could do with something lighthearted."

* * *

Although my mind keeps wandering back to the murder, the film keeps us occupied until Will comes home.

"Please tell me you're not hungry," Eve says, jumping to her feet and giving him a kiss. "Alice and I have been chatting. She's going to stay the night, isn't that nice?"

I can see her signaling to Will with her eyes to make him understand that there's been a bit of a crisis.

Will shrugs off his backpack and puts it down on the floor "Very," he says, smiling at me. "And yes, I'm hungry, I always am after rehearsing all day. Have you two eaten?"

"No," Eve says mournfully. "Not even a bag of crisps."

"Then how about I make a big bowl of pasta?"

She flings her arms around him. "I was hoping you'd say that." She turns to me. "Will makes the best pasta in the world. His great-grandmother passed down her recipe for the most delicious sauce. You're going to love it!"

"Except that if I make it from scratch, it will take two hours," Will points out.

"Oh yes, I forgot about that." Eve looks so crestfallen that I laugh. "All that simmering to reduce down the tomatoes."

"Exactly. So, I'll make a carbonara, if we have bacon."

Eve beams at him. "We do. Would you like a glass of wine to drink while you're cooking?"

"No, don't worry, I'll get myself a beer." He heads to the kitchen. "See you in about twenty minutes."

The sound of my cell phone ringing sends me into a panic.

"It's Leo. I can't speak to him, not yet."

"Then don't," Eve says. "Send him a text and tell him you're having dinner with us and that you'll speak to him later. That will give you time to work out what you're going to say."

"Good idea," I say, immediately feeling calmer.

Eve gets to her feet. "I'll lay the table while you do that," she says, giving me space. "Come when you're ready."

I message Leo and when he sends back a cheery **OK, have fun!** I immediately feel guilty that he has no idea of what I'm going to be saying to him when we speak. I remind myself that it's not my fault, that he's the one who hasn't been upfront but it only makes me feel slightly better.

The good thing about the houses in The Circle being built to the same model is that I know exactly where Eve and Will's kitchen is. As I walk down the hall toward it, I can hear them talking quietly together and guess that Eve is telling Will why I'm there.

"Can I help?" I ask, pushing the door open.

"Only by joining me in another glass of wine," Eve says, taking a fresh bottle from the fridge.

They've made a breakfast bar where we have our table. I heave myself onto a steel bistro-style bar-stool, watching as they move around the kitchen together, Will nudging Eve every now and then, pretending that she's getting in his way. I smile, thinking how good they are together, and then think about me and Leo.

Are we good together? I used to think so. Now, I'm not so sure.

We move to the table and while we eat steaming bowls of delicious pasta, I wait for Will to say something about what has happened, and I wouldn't mind, because maybe he'd have some insight into Leo's psyche, come up with an explanation as to why he decided to keep something so major from me. But although I've relaxed a bit, because Will is brilliant at making me laugh, he doesn't mention Leo or the murder at all.

Later, as I lie in their pretty guest room, I remember, not long ago, talking to Leo about one of my friends, who had just found out that her husband had gambled all their money away.

"You should have seen her, Leo, she's so broken. She doesn't know what to do, whether to stay with him or leave him. She says all the trust has gone."

"What would you do if you were in her place?"

"If I couldn't trust you, I couldn't be with you. And if I couldn't be with you, life wouldn't be worth living." I had stared deep into his eyes. "Do you see how much I love you?"

Back then, I never imagined those words would come back to haunt me. But they have, and worried about the conversation I'm going to have to have with Leo, I'm unable to sleep. He must have thought it strange that I hadn't called him back but maybe he fell asleep before he realized. Remembering that Ginny called several times, I scrabble on the floor for my phone and send her a holding message:

Leo knew about the murder, Ben told him.
I'm with Eve and Will next door. I'll call you
tomorrow xx

I manage to chase Leo from my mind but he's replaced by Nina Maxwell. It's hard to stop myself from
thinking about what she must have endured but I eventually manage to force my thoughts away from her
death, toward her life, and fall asleep wondering what
sort of person she was.

PAST

"How are you?" I ask, smiling. This is her eighth session and we've been making excellent progress.

"I'm good," she says. "I'm feeling much more positive about everything."

It's true that this is the most relaxed I've seen her. She was still wearing classic skirts and formal shirts at her fourth session. Today she's wearing a pleated skirt that comes to just above her knee. Her hair is tied back, as usual, but if the last few sessions are anything to go by, it will soon be loose around her shoulders.

"Excellent," I tell her. "I take it you've had a good couple of weeks?"

"Yes." She raises a hand and pulls the elastic from her ponytail. "I've spent a lot of time thinking about what we talked about last time," she says, swishing her head from side to side, settling her newly released hair around her shoulders.

I nod approvingly. It's taken a while, but at our last session, she finally accepted that her husband is at the root of her problems and that the only way forward, if she is to gain some inner peace, is to leave him. I wait for her to expand.

"You were going to speak to your husband," I prompt, when she doesn't say anything. "Could that be the reason you're feeling better?"

She nods. "We had a long discussion, and it made me realize something. He's not the reason for my unhappiness."

I stifle a sigh. It is not my place to show disappointment, but it's there, nonetheless. I draw my notepad toward me. "During our last session, you had concluded that he is," I say, consulting the notes I'd made. I pause. "You had also made the decision to leave him."

"I know. But everything's different now. I'm not unhappy anymore. I don't think I ever was, really."

The sun is bright today, despite it being cold outside, and through the blinds, lines of light run across her face in perfect blocks.

"I think we need to explore the reason for your change of heart."

"I think it's just that I came to my senses." She smiles across at me. "And I have you to thank for that."

"Oh?"

"Yes. You said honesty was the best policy so I told Daniel how I felt—not that I wanted to leave him, but that I was unhappy—and he said that I wasn't unhappy, I was bored. And I realized that he was right." She fiddles with the tiny silver J, which hangs from the clasp of the white-gold Omega watch on her wrist. "I've never thought about getting a job because financially,

I haven't needed to. It means I have too much time on my hands—too much time to think, too much time to focus on myself when I should be looking outward, channeling my energy into helping others. Daniel suggested that I do some voluntary work and he's already put me in touch with a couple of organizations." She laughs. "I told you he was perfect."

"That's progress indeed," I say, smiling.

"I guess I'm going to have to stop these sessions," she says. "I feel guilty for never having told Daniel about them and I'm not sure I really need them now. On the other hand, I don't want to undo all the good work we've been doing by stopping abruptly." She looks at me anxiously. "What do you think?"

"I think a few sessions of the relaxation therapy we discussed during our first session would be a good way of transitioning out of therapy. Is that something you think you'd like to consider?"

She nods happily. "Definitely. Relaxation therapy is something that Daniel will understand."

"Good." I hate losing clients when I've put so much work into them. I check the time on my watch and stand up. "We have time for one now, if you like."

TWELVE

"Stay as long as you like," Will says the next morning, taking his plate and coffee cup from the breakfast bar and putting them into the dishwasher. "Just pull the door behind you when you leave."

"Thanks," I say gratefully.

"Are we leaving together, Eve?" he asks, pushing his shirt, which he'd been wearing loose for breakfast, into the waistband of his jeans. "Because I need to go now."

Eve slides off her bar-stool and looks anxiously at me. "Are you sure you don't want me to cancel my mum? She won't mind."

"No, it's fine, I need to think about what I'm going to say to Leo."

"Then yes, Will, I'm coming with you." She gives me a quick hug. "If you need me at all, just call. You have my cell phone."

"And we're both here this evening," Will adds, picking up his backpack.

"Thank you. You've both been so kind."

Eve hovers. "Will you be all right?"

"I'll be fine. I have work to do."

But I'm too wound up to concentrate on the book I'm meant to be reading. And hurt. And insecure. For Leo to have lied to me, and about me, makes me wonder what else he might have hidden from me. I actually know very little of his life before we met. I know that he left home at eighteen because of his difficult family background and drifted from one low-paid job to another, until he realized that education was the answer to his problems. He studied hard and worked for a couple of investment management companies before setting himself up as a freelance consultant in risk management.

Needing something to do, I open my laptop and then pull out the business card Eve passed to me when she took me back to the house last night. I hold it tightly along the edges; the font is black in a block print: THOMAS GRAINGER. I type "Thomas Grainger, Private Investigator" into my search engine, to see if he's legit. To my surprise, he is. His website is professional and discreet and his offices are in Wimbledon. I put the address into my phone. With new motivation, I begin to research Nina Maxwell's murder. I want to know everything there is to know although I'm not sure why. Maybe it's my subconscious telling me I'll feel better if I have all the facts. Something to do with feeling in control, instead of completely out of control.

I read article after article, making notes as I go, but I don't learn much more. She was killed at around 9 p.m.

Her husband called 999 at approximately 9:20 p.m. to say that he'd come home from work and had found her dead in the bedroom.

My stomach churns when I remember Leo's insistence on knocking the two bedrooms into one. "I want to change things around a bit up here," he'd said. *I bet you did,* I think resentfully. *I bet you wanted to change things around so that when I eventually found out about the murder, I wouldn't be able to freak out about sleeping in the same bedroom, because essentially, it wouldn't be the same.* Except that essentially, it is.

According to one of the more detailed reports, there had been a struggle during which Nina Maxwell had put up a valiant fight before being rendered unconscious, then tied to a chair with belts from bathrobes belonging to her and her husband. As far as I could see, everything pointed to her husband being the killer.

A text arrives: **Hope to be home by 7. I've got the Residents' Association meeting tonight so I'll only have time for a quick dinner. Can't wait to see you xx**

I text back: **Message me when you arrive at Euston.**

Had he noticed that I didn't put my usual two kisses? When he texts from Euston at six forty-five, I take my courage, laptop, book and bag in my hands, and go home.

Home. *This is my home now,* I remind myself as I put the key in the door. In the few weeks that I've been here, I've made it our home, mine and Leo's. What's going to happen if I can't bring myself to stay here?

In the hall, I try to think about the happy times Nina Maxwell must have had in this house. Because she must have been happy; she'd had friends and from what Eve had said, her husband was lovely. Except that he had ended up killing her. From the photos I've seen of him during my research and the testimonies I've read, he didn't seem capable of murder. But then, not many people do.

Determined to think of them as Nina and Oliver, rather than victim and perpetrator, I walk around the house using memories of my sister and her boyfriend to picture their life together. I imagine them in the kitchen, chatting as they made dinner, then curled up on the sofa in the sitting room, watching a film, Nina's legs hooked over Oliver's, living a perfectly normal life until something terrible had changed their lives forever. Just as it had my sister's.

By focusing on Nina and Oliver as people, I manage to lose some of the anxiety that has gripped me since yesterday. Wanting to test myself, I move toward the stairs. I'm fine when I get to the landing, fine when I go into the spare bedroom; it's just a bedroom. But when I push open the door on the other side of the landing and peer into the room beyond, all I can see is what I've tried to block from my mind—Nina's lifeless body tied to a chair, her long blond hair strewn on the floor around her. The image is so vivid I can hardly breathe. Slamming the door behind me, I hurry downstairs, clutching dizzily onto the handrail. Aware that Leo will be arriving at any moment, I go to the kitchen and scoop water from the tap onto my face, then sit down at the table, waiting to find out how it is that I'm living in a house where a woman was murdered.

*   *   *

I don't have long to wait before I hear Leo's key in the door, his footsteps in the hall, the thump of his bag as he lets it drop to the floor.

"I'm home!"

The soft brush of material as he slips his jacket from his shoulders, the chink of coins as he hangs it over the newel post, the whip of his tie as he pulls it from under his collar, the sigh as he eases his neck—I hear them all.

"Alice, where are you?" he calls.

I can't see the frown that crosses his face at the silence that greets him, I can only imagine it. He walks across the hall and into the kitchen, his shoes still on his feet, the frown still on his face, which quickly turns to relief when he sees me sitting at the table.

"There you are," he says, a smile in his voice. He bends to kiss me and I twist away from him.

"What's the matter?" he asks, alarmed.

"Who are you, Leo?"

The color drains from his face so fast that my instinct is to jump up and make him sit down. But I stay where I am and watch dispassionately as he grabs hold of a chair, leaning heavily on it as he tries desperately to recover his composure.

"How could you? How could you keep something so—so terrible, so horrible, from me?" I say, frustrated that I can't find anything better than "terrible" or "horrible" to describe what happened upstairs. "How did you think I wouldn't find out?"

"Who told you?" he asks, his voice so low I have trouble hearing him.

"A neighbor." I don't care that I'm lying. I'll tell him about Thomas Grainger once I've got to the bottom of his deception.

He looks up, shock visible beneath the anguish on his face.

"A *neighbor* told you?"

I hold his gaze. "Yes."

"But—" He runs a hand through his hair, keeping hold of the chair with the other. "Which neighbor?"

"What does it matter who it was?" I say impatiently. "How could you lie to me, Leo?"

"I—I—" He sounds close to tears and I feel a twinge of alarm, and also a little ashamed. He must have been living in dread of me finding out. But I can't forgive him, not yet.

"What's almost worse is that you lied *about* me, not just to me."

"What do you mean?" he mumbles.

"You insinuated to Ben that I was fine about living here, because it meant that I could keep my cottage in Harlestone."

He stares at me for so long that I think he's going to deny it, or tell me that Ben misunderstood. After what seems an eternity, he pulls out the chair he's been holding onto, and sinks onto it.

"I'm sorry." The relief on his face tells me he's glad it's out in the open.

"What were you thinking? Were you hoping that I wouldn't find out?"

He studies his hands. "No, I knew you would. I was hoping that you wouldn't before I could tell you."

"And when were you going to tell me?"

"I—I just wanted you to be a bit more settled here."

"Why?"

"So that you'd find it harder to leave. It's why I didn't tell you before I bought the house. I knew you would refuse to live here and"—he raises his eyes to mine—"I really wanted to."

"So much that you were willing to overlook that a woman had died here?"

"It's not the same house, Alice. It's been redecorated and renovated, and I've changed the layout upstairs."

I slam my hand down on the table. "It's exactly the same house! I don't understand how you can't see that! It's still the house where a murder took place!"

He gives a helpless shrug, which does nothing to calm me. "Then maybe it's just that I'm able to live with that. I know it might sound callous, but it doesn't really bother me. And I remember you saying once, when someone pointed out that people must have died in your cottage, given that it's two hundred years old, that it wouldn't bother you if they had."

"There's a huge difference between someone dying peacefully in their bed of old age and being brutally murdered at thirty-eight years old!"

"We can't always know the history of the houses we live in. Somebody might have been murdered in the cottage in Harlestone."

I hate that he has a point.

"I mean, if somebody called you tomorrow, and said, 'Hey, I've just discovered that fifty years ago, somebody was murdered in your cottage,' would you leave immediately and never spend another day there?"

I hesitate. I love my cottage. Noticing, he leans forward.

"You would still stay there, wouldn't you? You wouldn't sell up."

"Yes, actually, I would. I'd put it on the market. Even fifty years is too close."

"I don't believe you," he says, rubbing his face with his hands.

My anger flares again. "Since when has this become about me? And since when have you started not believing me? I'm not the one in the wrong, Leo, you are!"

"I know, and I'm sorry." He reaches for my hand but I move it away.

"What must people have thought on Saturday, when I offered to take them upstairs to see the changes we'd made? They thought I knew about the murder."

"I never expected you to show people around."

"That's why you didn't want to have people over, isn't it?" I stand up, needing to put distance between us. "You were worried someone would mention what had happened here." I move to the other side of the kitchen and lean against the worktop. "I don't understand, I don't understand how you thought you could get away with it."

He opens his hands, pleading with me to understand. "I wasn't trying to get away with it. I was going to tell you, as soon as the time was right."

"And until then, you didn't mind people thinking I was a callous bitch."

"I'm sure no one thought that."

"Tamsin did."

"The redhead?"

"Yes. I overheard her say that she couldn't believe it didn't bother me. I had no idea what she was talking about. Now I do."

He sighs. "What do you want to do?"

I grab a cloth and start wiping the worktop, which is already clean. "I can't stay here, not now."

"We could go and stay in a hotel for few days."

"And then what? Come back here and pretend the murder never happened?"

He flinches. "Not that it never happened, no. But maybe accept that it happened, and move on. I think you should give the house a chance, Alice."

I stop wiping and turn to look at him. "What do you mean?"

He leans forward, fixing me with his eyes. "Make new memories for it. Be happy here."

Resentment bursts out of me. "Be happy here? How can I?" I throw the cloth angrily into the white enamel sink. "She was called Nina, Leo!"

"I know, and that's another reason I hesitated about telling you." His voice, quiet and reasonable, is designed to calm me. "I was worried that, just when you'd decided to try and let go of the past by leaving Harlestone, it would bring everything back. You've done so well by actually agreeing to move here. Can't we build on that?" He waits for me to speak but I can't because what he said about making new memories for the house has struck a chord. He rubs at his face again. "What do you want to do? Do you want to go back to Harlestone? Do you want me to put this house up for sale and rent a flat in London while I wait for it to be sold? Because that's what I'd have to do. I couldn't take all that traveling from Harlestone to Birmingham each day so I'd have to live in London during the week and see you at the weekends—sometimes, occasionally, just like we did before we moved here. Is that what you want?"

He sits there, waiting for my answer, the fine lines around his eyes deeper than before. But I can't give him one. I want everything he suggested and none of what he suggested. I don't want to stay—but I don't want to go. I want him to leave—but if I'm going to stay here in the house, at least tonight, I don't want to be alone. The only thing I'm sure about is that, for the moment, I don't want to be anywhere near him. Or anywhere near the room upstairs.

I move toward the door. "I don't know what I want," I say, my voice tight. "And until I do, I'll be sleeping in my study."

It's only when I'm making up the sofa bed that I realize I didn't ask him why he wanted the house so much.

THIRTEEN

"Why did you want this house so much?" I ask Leo the next morning. We're standing in the kitchen. It's spotless, because neither of us bothered to eat last night and the early morning light is bouncing off the pale marble surfaces.

"Sorry?" He looks tired, but not as tired as I do.

"Yesterday, you said that the reason you didn't tell me about the murder before moving in was because you knew I'd refuse to live here and you really wanted this house. I'm asking you why you really wanted this house. It's a nice house but not so nice that anyone with a conscience would overlook a murder." I know I'm being harsh but I barely slept and fatigue is dragging me down.

He walks over to the black and chrome coffee machine.

"Coffee?"

I'm dying for one. "No thanks."

He makes his coffee before answering my question,

as if he's hoping I'll tire of waiting. But I'm prepared to give him as much time as it takes.

"I wanted this house because it's in a secure environment," he says eventually. "I like that nobody can get in unless they live here, or they're let in by someone who lives here. It makes it safer. And because I could afford it. I'd never have been able to afford it if it didn't have a past."

"Since when have you become security conscious?"

"Since I started getting harassed by clients."

"I wasn't aware you'd been harassed by clients."

He glances at me. "That's because I chose not to tell you."

"I know you had unwanted calls," I say, remembering the times he answered his phone only to hang up straightaway, and the way he sometimes stared at the screen before deciding not to answer, then telling me it was a wrong number. "I didn't realize they were from clients. But nobody actually came to the door, did they?" I pause as a memory resurfaces. "Except that woman, the blond one, in Harlestone. I asked you about her at the time and you told me she wanted to know what it was like to live in the village. Was she one of your clients?"

"No," he says. "The point is, if a client had wanted to find out where I was, they could have. I've never given anybody your address but if somebody had turned up in Harlestone looking for me, every single person in the village would have taken them right to your front door and on the way, told them what I'd had for dinner the previous evening."

There's something about his reasoning that doesn't ring quite true. He's not telling me everything—but what is it that he's holding back?

"But this—The Circle—is a small community in the same way that Harlestone is," I say, perplexed.

He gives a tired sigh. "That's exactly why I chose it. I would have preferred an anonymous block of flats with a built-in security system, something like I had before. But you made it clear you weren't going to live somewhere like that so I looked for a way to keep both of us happy. Here we have the intimate set-up that you prefer and the security that I need. It's a compromise, Alice, another damn compromise."

"Isn't that what relationships are about?" I say, stung. "Compromise?"

He takes his cup from the machine. "I'll let you have your breakfast in peace. If you want to talk, I'll be in my study."

Tears sting my eyes. I'd lain awake most of the night and I still don't know what to do. I'm tempted to go back to Harlestone but if I do, I'll have to ask Debbie if I can stay with her for the next few months, because I can't move my tenants out without notice. But where will that leave me and Leo? He's right, we'd have to go back to how we'd managed before, only seeing each other at weekends when the whole point of moving to London was so that we could spend more time together. And I can't get what he said about making new memories for the house out of my mind. It's created a feeling of obligation that I resent, because if I don't take up the challenge, I'll feel as if I'm turning my back, not just on Nina Maxwell, who I feel bound to in some inexplicable way, but also my sister.

"I meant to ask." His voice comes from behind me and turning, I see him standing in the doorway. "You said a neighbor told you about the murder. Was it Eve?"

"No."

"Who was it, then?"

I have no choice. I have to tell him what I told Eve.

"It wasn't a neighbor, it was a reporter," I say, horribly aware that there are too many lies creeping into our relationship.

"A reporter? You mean, a journalist?"

"Yes."

"Did they come here?"

"No, it was a phone call."

"A man or a woman?"

"A woman."

He rakes his hair, a sign that he's riled. "Did she say which newspaper she was with?"

I turn to the coffee machine and start pressing buttons. "No."

"Didn't you ask?"

"No, I was in too much shock to care."

"Did you get her name?"

"No."

"What did she say, exactly?"

"She wanted to know what it was like to live in a house where someone had been murdered." I stop abruptly, wondering if he's noticed that I used almost the same phrase as he did when he told me about the woman who came to Harlestone—*She wanted to know what it was like to live in the village.* Which means we're both lying.

"Did she say anything else?"

"No." I look at him curiously. "Why?"

"No reason."

He leaves and I sit down at the table. Something isn't adding up. Leo seems paranoid about my fictitious reporter. And his behavior yesterday when I first confronted him had been over the top. He'd looked as if he'd been about to pass out. But his reason for not telling me—that he wanted this house because it provided him with security—doesn't stand up.

I go to my study, closing the door behind me. Since last night, it has become not just my workplace, but my haven. The bed is now a sofa again, the quilt folded neatly into the bottom of the cupboard, because I can't work in a mess. I sit down at my desk. I need to call Ginny, and a message has come in from Eve, checking that I'm all right. I text Eve back and tell her I'm fine, and that I'll see her after the weekend. **If you need me before then, just let me know xx** she replies and I feel lucky to have made a friend so close to home. Home. Again, the word resonates in my brain. Can it ever be my home now?

I call Ginny.

"How are you?" she asks.

"Not good."

"Did you speak to Leo?"

"Yes, he said he didn't tell me because he really wanted the house and he knew I wouldn't want to live here once I knew about the murder. He was right about that." I pause. "It's the reason he gave for wanting the house that doesn't ring true. He told me it was because it's in a gated residence and nobody can get in unless they are let in by a resident. He said he'd been harassed by some of his clients."

"Do you mean he's received threats of some sort?" Ginny asks.

"I don't know. He's never mentioned being harassed to me. I know there were some phone calls that he didn't answer, or where he hung up straightaway. And once he got annoyed with a woman who tried to speak to him outside the cottage in Harlestone. He said she wasn't a client, but he was more annoyed about it than he should have been."

"How have you left it with him?"

"Well, I slept on the sofa bed in the study and I'll be sleeping there again tonight."

"I'm really sorry, Alice."

"Thank you, but it's fine. Or it will be."

I hang up, wondering if it will ever be fine between me and Leo. I know I'll never be able to sleep in the bedroom again, not now that I know what happened there. That in itself isn't a problem as we can move into the guest bedroom, and Leo can put his gym equipment in our bedroom instead of in the garage, where he usually works out. But for the moment, I can't think about sharing a bed with him. And why is Thomas Grainger investigating the murder, anyway? He said he was working on behalf of his client, and then something about their brother being accused of a murder he didn't commit. His client must be Oliver's brother or sister, which makes me slightly dismissive about his miscarriage of justice claim. It's normal for close family members not to believe their loved ones are capable of murder. It doesn't mean they didn't do it.

I search on my phone for the screenshot I took of Nina's photo. Her long blond hair is gathered into a messy bun and thin gold hoops hang from her ears. She looks happy and carefree and I'm hit by a familiar wave of sadness.

"Who killed you, Nina?" I murmur. "Was it Oliver?"

She stares back at me, a smile at the corner of her mouth. *That's for you to find out*, she seems to be saying.

I study her photograph, looking for a trace of my sister. There isn't; my Nina was darker than this Nina, darker than me. My sister who wanted me to be called Nina like her. She was three when I was born and very insistent, so my parents told her she could choose my name. She chose it from her favorite book, *Alice in Wonderland*.

The rest of the weekend passes with me and Leo avoiding each other, moving to different areas of the kitchen if we happen to be there at the same time and being extra polite, like two almost-strangers. When he tells me that he's off to play tennis with Paul, I have to hide my surprise. In his place, I'd be too embarrassed to show my face. But then I realize that apart from Eve and Will, no one from The Circle knows that he didn't tell me about the murder.

I use the time to catch up on the work I didn't do on Thursday and Friday, and by the time Sunday evening comes around, I've finished the first read-through of the book.

I'm pulling out the sofa bed when Leo knocks on the door.

"Thank you for not leaving," he says, helping me move the cushions.

"I still might. I haven't decided what to do yet."

He nods. "I'm going to commute to Birmingham this week, so that you won't be alone in the house at night—if you decide to stay," he adds.

"Thanks," I say, because I'd forgotten that I was meant to be by myself until Thursday. We make up the bed and I close the door behind him, struck by the irony of the situation. This was meant to be a new start, a chance—once his current contract was finished—for us to live as a normal couple where, after a day's work, we would meet again in the evenings—every evening—to chat about our day face to face. Even if we can get over this, what if it doesn't work out? What if we find we can't live together day after day? Maybe our relationship only worked until now because we lived apart for most of the time.

I'm almost asleep when I remember I need clothes for the morning. Since Friday, I've lived in clothes pulled from the ironing basket but they're now back in the wash. My clean ones are in the bedroom, where I don't want to go.

I text Leo.

Before you leave, please get me some clothes
from the bedroom and leave them on the chair
in the hall. My white shorts, my red dress, a
pair of jeans, two white T-shirts, two navy
T-shirts and four sets of underwear. My white
sneakers and the blue sandals with the gold bar.
And socks. Thanks.

I turn off my phone and go back to sleep.

FOURTEEN

I wake in the night, my heartbeating hard against my ribs. Something woke me, I don't know what. I lie without moving, holding my breath, my body tensed, trying to work it out. And then it comes to me. There's someone in the room and I know instinctively that it isn't Leo.

There's no light near me, the nearest lamp is on my desk. I'm too scared to move, too scared to open my eyes. My eyes dart around under my closed lids. Where are they? Shouldn't I be able to hear them breathing, detect some sort of movement? There's nothing, just a feeling that someone is watching me. Then, when the effort of not moving, not breathing, becomes too much, the sense of someone being there leaves me.

My held-in breath whooshes from me, a shuddering gasp in the suffocating silence of the night. I wait for my heartrate to slow, then move my legs from under the covers. I feel too vulnerable to leave my bed so I stretch my arm toward my desk and turn on the lamp. The weak yellow light doesn't reach into the corners of the study but I'm able to see that there isn't anyone there. The door is slightly ajar, and I can't remember whether or not I closed it before going to sleep.

I get out of bed, about to call for Leo, then stop. I can do this myself. My heart in my mouth, I switch on the light in the hall. Taking a deep breath, I walk through the downstairs rooms with pretend confidence, giving myself courage, turning on lights as I go. There's a neat pile of clothes on the chair in the hall; Leo must have brought them down once I was asleep to save him doing it in the morning. I continue upstairs, checking his study and the guest bedroom. The door to our bedroom is shut. I put my hand gently on the handle and push it open. It creaks slightly and I hold my breath, expecting Leo to wake up, ask who's there. But there's no sound. I peep in; he's sleeping soundly, his breathing deep and regular.

I'm going back downstairs when I see it, a white rose cut from the garden lying on the window sill next to the front door. I smile grimly to myself, amazed that he thinks I can be won over so easily. I carry it through to the kitchen, open the bin and dump it inside.

Back in bed, I leave the light on and my door half-open so I'm not in complete darkness. I expect to have trouble getting to sleep but suddenly, it's morning and Leo has already left for Birmingham.

The next morning, a text comes in from Eve—**Coffee?** I check the time; it's already nine o'clock but I can start work a bit later today. I go straight over. She comes to the door dressed in white running gear, eating toast spread thickly with peanut butter.

"I did a five-mile run this morning, so I'm allowed," she says, offering me her plate. "And you're allowed, because you had a crap weekend. Or maybe you didn't?"

I take a piece of toast and follow her to the kitchen. "It was crap on the Leo front but the upside was that I managed to get a lot of work done. It took my mind off everything, which was good."

"You were able to stay in the house, then?"

"Yes, but I slept downstairs, in my study."

Eve puts her plate down, hoists herself onto the worktop, then picks up her plate again.

"How did it go with Leo?"

"We're keeping our distance while I try and work out how I'm feeling. I'm so confused about everything. I feel I should be running away from the house, maybe even running away from Leo. But he said we should create new memories."

She tilts her head to one side, looking at me. "How do you feel about that?"

"I'm not sure. This might sound strange, but since Leo said that, I've begun to feel as if I owe it to Nina to stay. I feel drawn to her in some way. When I went back to the house on Thursday, I could almost sense her presence, I could see her in the sitting room with Oliver, see them together in the kitchen. And when I think how she must have suffered," I add quietly, "any hardship that I might be feeling is nothing in comparison. Maybe Leo is right, maybe the only way to rid the house of the evil that happened there is to create new memories."

"Good vibes chasing away bad ones doesn't sound strange at all," Eve says. "Don't you want to sit down?"

"Sorry," I say, realizing I've been pacing the kitchen. I pull out a chair. "Leo should be staying in Birmingham until Thursday, like he usually does, but he's going to come home every evening so that I won't be alone at night."

"That's good of him."

"What would you do, Eve, if you were in my place?"

"I think if I was kind of managing, which you seem to be, I'd stay for a while, see how things pan out."

"I'd feel much better if I could go and see everyone here and explain that I didn't know about the murder before moving in. But I suppose that would be kind of weird."

"If you really want it out there, I could tell Tamsin and Maria and they could tell their neighbors, who would tell theirs, and before you know it, it will be common knowledge," she says. "Would you like me to do that?"

"Yes, please. I really need people to know I'm not callous." A new thought comes to worry me. "But what will people think when they know that I know about the murder and am able to carry on living in the house, at least for the moment?"

"They already thought that you knew, and the only thing they thought was that you were incredibly brave. So that's what they'll continue to think, that you're brave. And not many people would be able to afford to move out and rent somewhere else to live while the house is being resold, so they'll understand that too. Your cottage is rented out, it's not as if you can go back there. Anyway, why do you care what people think?"

"I don't want to be shunned when I've only just arrived here."

Eve bursts out laughing. "You're not going to be shunned!"

"So, if I invite you, Tamsin and Maria to lunch on Wednesday, before you go to your yoga class, will you come?" I say, surprising myself, because I hadn't actively thought about inviting them over.

"Sure we will! We came to your drinks evening, didn't we?"

"I'd like to invite Cara but I don't think she's around during the day. Did she say she works for Google?"

"Yes, she's a software engineer. She works crazy hours so you'll only be able to get hold of her at weekends."

"Just the four of us, then."

I leave soon after. Eve told me I could work at hers but if I'm to stay here, in this house, I need to get used to being alone. "What would you do, Nina?" I murmur to the photo of my sister pinned to the fridge. "Would you stay or would you go?" But there's no answer, just the absolute stillness of an empty house.

Instead of doing a second read of my book, I decide to start translating straightaway. Translating requires focus and right now, I need to be able to concentrate on something other than the murder.

The day passes surprisingly quickly. When Leo arrives home, he goes out of his way to apologize, to try and make good the harm he's done.

"Your hair looks nice," he says, referring to the way I've plaited it to keep it out of my way while I'm working.

"Thanks."

He sighs. "Tell me how I can make it up to you."

"I don't know, I don't even know if you can. How can I trust you if you're able to keep something so momentous from me?"

What I hate most is that I feel I'm being unfair. But expecting me to fall into his arms, say I forgive him, is too much. He offers to make me dinner and when I refuse, he eats quickly and disappears to his study. He doesn't mention the rose I threw in the bin so maybe he didn't see it.

The house is quiet, too quiet. Realizing I didn't tell Leo that I thought there was someone in the house last night, I'm tempted to go after him. But I don't want him to think that I'm using it as an excuse to start a conversation. Anyway, there wasn't anyone there, it was just the murder playing on my mind.

FIFTEEN

I leave it to Eve to invite Maria and Tamsin to lunch and the three of them arrive together, turning up at twelve with flowers from Maria's garden and a bottle of wine. They're all wearing shorts and T-shirts, which makes me feel overdressed in my mid-length flowing skirt.

"Come in," I say, moving back to let them past.

Eve and Maria walk straight in but Tamsin hovers uncertainly outside the door and for a confused moment, I think she's having reservations about having lunch with me.

"Sorry," she says. "It's just that this house always reminds me of Nina."

"Of course." I nod sympathetically, wanting to reach out and hug her. But she steps quickly inside.

"How are you?" Maria asks, giving me a hug. "It must have been such a shock, finding out about Nina like that. I can't imagine how you must have felt."

"Angry and scared," I say, leading them out to the

garden. "I wanted to leave, I didn't think I'd be able to stay."

"But you're still here," Tamsin says pointedly.

If anyone is going to judge me, it's Tamsin.

I turn to her. "Yes, I'm still here. For the moment." I smile tentatively. "I was hoping you might tell me about Nina. I'll never be able to sleep in the bedroom upstairs again but if I knew she'd had some happy times here, it might help me feel less anxious."

Tamsin's face softens. "She had lots of happy times here."

"Shall we chat over lunch?" Eve says. "It's just that we need to leave here by twenty to two for our yoga class."

"Yes, I know," I say. "I've made a salmon quiche and salad, and there's strawberries for dessert. I hope that's OK?"

Maria smiles. "Sounds perfect to me!"

It's one of those beautiful mid-September days, with the sun warming the garden. A gentle breeze carries the heavenly scent of brightly colored phlox to where we're eating on the terrace, adding to the impression that we're still in summer. There's so much I want to ask them about Nina but I curb my impatience and ask instead about Maria's children, and Tamsin's two little daughters, Amber and Pearl.

"I love their names," I tell her.

She smiles. "Thanks. You'll have to join us on a Wednesday afternoon, then you can meet them in person."

"I'd like that," I say, pleased that the invite has come from her. "I've only ever seen them from afar."

I wait until they sit back, their empty plates in front of them.

"I know Nina was thirty-eight and Eve told me that she was a therapist, but that's all I really know about her," I say.

Tamsin brushes a couple of crumbs off her immaculate white T-shirt. "She loved her job, she loved helping people. She had time for everyone, you could always go and see her if you had a problem. She helped me so much."

"And Oliver? What did he do?

"He worked for a shipping company," Maria says. "I'm not sure what his actual job was but he traveled abroad quite a bit."

"And they were happy together?"

"Yes, very."

"Except—" I hesitate. "He killed her."

Tamsin glares at me from across the table. "Who have you been talking to?"

"No one," I say hastily. "I only know what I read in news articles."

"Isn't that enough?"

I flush, embarrassed at the sudden change in atmosphere, as if the temperature has suddenly dropped ten degrees.

"I'm just trying to understand the sort of person she was," I say, trying to get things back to how they were. "Eve mentioned that she was quite spiritual and that she started your yoga group. Did she have any hobbies?"

It doesn't work. "Why does it matter?" Tamsin says coldly. "It's hardly important now."

I hate playing the sister card but I can't think of any other way to get her on my side. I push back my chair. Eve turns worried eyes on me.

"It's OK," I say. "I'm just going to get the strawberries. I'll take the plates through at the same time."

In the kitchen, I deal with the plates, take the strawberries from the fridge, and the photo of Nina from the door.

"Did Eve tell you about my sister?" I ask Tamsin, putting the strawberries down in front of her and going back to my seat.

She shifts awkwardly. "Yes, she did. I'm sorry."

"This is a photograph of her," I say, holding it out.

Maria reaches over and takes it. "She was beautiful."

"Can I see?" Eve asks. She looks at the photo then looks up at me. "She has the same eyes as you."

"Yes," I say. I turn to Tamsin and Maria. "Eve probably told you that my sister was called Nina. I know it's stupid, but since she died, I have this need to know about other Ninas."

"It's not stupid," Maria says. She smiles. "I don't know about your Nina but our Nina loved taking impromptu photographs. It could be quite annoying sometimes because she would get you at your worst moment, when you were eating, so your mouth was open, or full of food."

"Or when you'd had a bit too much to drink, so you'd have that glazed look in your eyes and a red nose," Eve says, miming the pose and making me laugh.

"But she also took some beautiful photos." Maria looks across the table at Tamsin. "I have some lovely ones of the children, you do too, don't you, Tamsin?"

"Yes." To my dismay, Tamsin's eyes fill with tears. "I still miss her."

"I'm sorry," I say guiltily. "I shouldn't be asking you about her. It's just that I want—I don't know—to make her real, to have a sense of who she was, I suppose. It might help me decide whether to stay or not."

Tamsin fishes for a tissue and blows her nose. "I hope you do. It's nice to have the house lived in again instead of it being like a mausoleum."

"Thank you," I say, because it had sounded genuine.

"Eve said you found out about the murder from a reporter?" Tamsin adds.

"Yes, that's right."

She picks up her bag and rummages inside, drawing out a new packet of tissues. "What did she say, exactly?"

"She asked me how it felt to be living at the scene of a brutal murder," I say, remembering what I told Eve, because I don't want my lie to come back to bite me.

"And that's all she said?"

"Yes. I told her that I didn't know what she was talking about and she advised me to google the Nina Maxwell murder."

"Did she give you her name, or tell you which publication she was with?"

"No." Tamsin's questions make me uncomfortable. Does she know I'm lying?

"So how do you know she was a reporter?"

She does know I'm lying. "I—I don't know, I just presumed that she was. Who else could she have been?"

"Tam," Maria says gently. "Stop. You're making Alice uncomfortable."

"Sorry. It's just that I hate the thought of someone poking their nose in, dragging it up again when we've only just managed to put it to rest."

"Let's talk about something else," Eve says brightly. "Like Christmas, or Halloween, or Maria inviting us to supper on Friday." She looks over at her. "Isn't that right, Maria?"

Maria laughs. "Thanks for reminding me. Tamsin, Alice, are you free Friday evening? I mentioned supper to Eve yesterday and she and Will can make it, so I hope you can too." There's no reply from Tamsin; she's lost in thought. "Tamsin, are you and Connor free on Friday?" Maria says again, more loudly this time.

"What?" Tamsin shakes her head quickly as if to clear it. "Yes, why?"

"For supper at mine."

"That will be lovely, thank you."

"What about you, Alice, are you and Leo free?"

"I think so."

"Why don't you let me know once you've spoken to him?"

"I'll ask him tonight," I promise.

They leave soon after and while I tidy up, I think about Maria's invitation. I'd love to go because I don't want to miss the chance to see the friendship group that Nina and Oliver were part of in action. I want to observe the dynamics between the couples, see how they interact with each other, get to know them a little better. There are things I don't fully understand, like their insistence that Nina and Oliver were blissfully happy. If they were, why did he kill her? Remembering what Eve had said about Lorna witnessing everything, I decide to go and see her.

In the study, I swap my T-shirt, which I managed to spatter with dressing, for a clean one, grab my keys from the table in the hall, throw open the front door—and find myself looking straight at Thomas Grainger.

SIXTEEN

I've startled him as much as he's startled me. His arm, which he'd raised to ring the doorbell, drops quickly to his side. He takes a step back, as if he's expecting me to verbally attack him.

"Ms. Dawson, I'm sorry." He raises his hands in a backing-off gesture. "I'll leave, it's fine."

"Wait a minute." He stops, his body half-twisted toward the drive. "You said you were investigating Nina Maxwell's murder."

He turns back to face me. "That's right."

"Why now, more than a year after she died?"

"I've been investigating it since her husband committed suicide. But I had to put it to one side because I couldn't get the information I wanted. I'm a private investigator, so persona non grata as far as the police are concerned."

"What information do you want?"

He finds my eyes, holds my gaze. He had done exactly the same thing last time, I remember. I want to look away but I can't. There's something mesmerizing about them.

"I'm afraid I'm not prepared to discuss anything on the doorstep."

It's now or never. If I don't invite him in, he won't come back. I open the door wider.

"Thank you." He steps into the hallway. "I really appreciate you agreeing to let me talk to you." I take him through to the sitting room, wondering what I'm doing letting a stranger into my house. He might be dressed smartly—a casual, lightweight suit and open-necked pale blue shirt—but he could still be a murderer. He could be Nina's murderer. I take my phone from my pocket, hold it in my hand. I offer him a chair but I stay standing by the door. If I need to make a quick exit, I can.

"I'd like to apologize again for the shock you must have got last week when I told you about the murder," Thomas Grainger says. "I had no idea you didn't know."

"I realize that."

"I hope it didn't cause any trouble."

"None at all." I'm not about to tell him that Leo kept it from me and that we're barely speaking. "My husband and I are deciding what to do." He doesn't need to know that we're not married either. "We're not sure how we feel about living here now."

"I can understand that."

"I think you should start at the beginning. How did you know we were having drinks here?"

"I'm afraid I can't tell you that."

"Why not?" He looks steadily back at me. "Are you in touch with someone from here?"

"No, absolutely not." He waits for me to move on and when I don't, he nods. "Let's just say that I found out through the invitation you posted."

It takes me a while. "You've hacked the WhatsApp group?" He doesn't confirm or deny it and I'm not even sure a WhatsApp group can be hacked. I don't press him any further because he wouldn't tell me anyway. "So why did you decide to crash it?" I say instead.

"It was unethical of me, I know. But I've been trying to gain access to the house for over a year now. I posed as a potential buyer once but the estate agent stayed with me the whole time, so I was unable to do what I'd hoped to do, which was take a look at the room where the murder took place. Without a general idea of the layout of the place where a victim died, it's hard to offer an alternative version as to what might have happened that night." He gives a slight smile. "The fact that I was shadowed during my visit only strengthened my belief that my client's brother wasn't responsible for Nina Maxwell's murder. I'm convinced the agency had instructions from the police to keep a close eye on anyone who showed an interest in the house."

My curiosity aroused, I move to the chair nearest the door and perch on it. "Why would they do that?"

"Perhaps they were hoping the real killer would return to the crime scene and somehow give himself away."

"But the police believe that the killer is dead, don't they? That it's a closed case."

"Not according to my source." He sees my frown. "Yes, it's true, every private investigator has a source somewhere in the police, just as a journalist does. Often the same one. And my source tells me that the investigation is still ongoing." He pauses. "Can I ask if your experience was the same when you visited the house?"

"My husband visited it without me. I only saw it after he bought it." He tries to hide his surprise but he's not quick enough. "So, our drinks evening?"

"I thought I'd be able to pass unnoticed." He gives a slight smile. "It didn't occur to me that you had only invited people from here. Once I realized, I left."

"Well, my next-door neighbor, the lady who let you in, is elderly and she's been badly affected by all this. She was very upset when she learned that you weren't a friend of mine."

"I'm sorry. Again, I'd imagined a big party and thought I'd be able to slip in through the gate behind someone."

"How did you get in? Just now? You didn't disturb my neighbor again, did you?"

He shakes his head. "I intended to ring your intercom in the hope that you would agree to listen to what I had to say. But there was someone in front of me and he let me in. I wanted to tell him that he should be more careful but I suppose that if he'd been playing by the rules, he would have had to slam the gate in my face, and most people aren't like that, they're too polite. Last time I came to see you I walked in through the main gate after a car." Another pause. "I don't know if you or your husband are on a residents' committee or anything but perhaps you should mention it, and maybe change the code. I was able to see the code he typed in over his shoulder."

"I'm sorry, but I still don't understand what you're doing here."

He shifts on his seat. "Believe me, I wouldn't be troubling you if time wasn't running out."

"What do you mean?"

A shadow clouds his face. "My client isn't in good health. She's determined to clear her brother's name while she can." He stops and I can see that he's having some kind of internal struggle. "I was at university with Helen," he says, giving up the struggle. "I never really knew Oliver because he was five years younger than us, but even back then I knew how much he meant to her. When she said she didn't believe Oliver was responsible for Nina's murder, and asked me to help her, I felt I couldn't refuse."

I nod sympathetically, desperately sorry for Oliver's sister.

"Why is Oliver's sister persuaded that it wasn't him who killed Nina?" I ask. "Nobody wants to think the worst of someone they love. Maybe she just doesn't want to believe that her brother was capable of murder."

"That's what I thought at first. I hate to say it but I was—and this sounds awful—humoring Helen by agreeing to look into the murder, because in my experience, it bore all the hallmarks of a typical crime of passion. But many people have testified that Oliver Maxwell was the gentlest, kindest of men and that he adored Nina. The cynics point to his suicide and say that he killed himself because he couldn't cope with what he'd done. Those that knew him take it as a testimony of his broken heart. Not only couldn't he bear to live without her, he also couldn't bear to live with the violence of her death."

So which camp did that put Eve, Tamsin and Maria in, I wonder? They had known Oliver, they had told me he was the loveliest of men. Yet they believed that he killed Nina. Why was that?

"Wait a minute—did you say 'crime of passion'?" I say, realizing.

"Yes." He pauses. "Apparently, Nina had been having an affair."

I stare at him. "An affair?"

He leans forward in his seat. His skin is pale, almost translucent, providing a marked contrast with his dark hair.

"Yes."

"But—who with?"

"That's what I'm trying to find out."

"Why?"

"Because I think he might be responsible for her murder."

My mind reels. "Did the police know she was having an affair?"

"Yes."

"Then they must have found out who he was and eliminated him from their inquiries."

"That's what you would have thought," he agrees.

"I suppose if Oliver knew Nina was having an affair, he had a motive to kill her."

"Except that, according to the people who knew him best, he would never have harmed Nina."

"I'm not sure why you think I can help you. I've only just moved here—as you know," I add pointedly.

"It's exactly for that reason that I'm asking for your help," he says earnestly. "When Helen first asked me to look into the murder, I tried to speak to people here myself. But I came up against a lot of—not hostility, exactly, but tight lips. It's why I didn't hang around at your drinks evening. When I looked through the kitchen window and saw that the people you'd invited were the people I had tried to talk to, I thought it wiser to leave before someone recognized me." He pauses. "You didn't know Nina, you don't really know anyone here yet, which makes you impartial. I know this is a lot to ask but—if you happen to hear anything—you know, in conversations with the neighbors—perhaps you could let me know?"

I stand up. "I'm sorry, I couldn't do that."

He gives a small smile. "Of course." He gets to his feet, holds out his hand. "Thank you for your time. Goodbye, Ms. Dawson."

His handshake is strong, dependable. It makes me feel that I can trust him but, at the same time, I'm disappointed that he wanted me to betray the confidences of the people I'm hoping will be my friends. Given the circumstances, I suppose it's understandable that he wants to get closure for Oliver's sister before it's too late. He strikes me as the sort of man who would do a lot for a friend—but not someone who would give that friend false hope, or take on a lost cause. He admitted that at the beginning, he was only humoring Oliver's sister.

What made him change his mind?

SEVENTEEN

I've barely begun working when the highlighter I'm using dries up on me. I know Leo has some in his study so I force myself upstairs. Living with Nina's ghost isn't easy. I pause, one foot on the next step. *Living with Nina's ghost.*

After my sister died, there were times when I felt she was with me, times when I could feel her presence, especially in the quiet of the night or when I was feeling particularly low. It was as if she was letting me know that I wasn't alone. I hadn't been particularly spiritual before but, intrigued, I began to read about life after death and, because of what I had experienced in relation to my sister, I came to accept that sometimes, our spirit lives on, particularly when a person dies unexpectedly before their time. One of the things I read was the belief that if a death was violent, the spirit of that person might wait around until their murderer was brought to justice. It had particularly marked me because I hadn't sensed my sister's presence since the day her case was brought to court, and although I hadn't been satisfied with the outcome, maybe my sister had been, which was why she had left. What if Nina Maxwell's spirit is living on, here in the house, waiting for justice to be done?

The study on the first floor is Leo's space and I'm always surprised at how tidy it is. There's nothing on the desk apart from a wooden ruler and a couple of pens. I pull open the drawers that run down each side of the desk. The bottom one on the left-hand side is jammed full of pens, pencils and highlighters. I choose a yellow one and, as I take it out, the back of my hand brushes against something taped to the underside of the drawer above. Curious, I push the jumble of pens and pencils to one side and unpick the tape with my fingers. There's something metal underneath. I let it fall into my hand and see a tiny key, which I recognize as coming from one of those metal cash boxes that I used to save money in as a teenager. I turn it over, inspecting it. If Leo has gone to the trouble of hiding it, there must be something he doesn't want anyone, including me, to find. Was that why he was so jittery when I told him I'd taken people upstairs to see the work we'd had done?

I turn to the gray metal filing cabinet that stands in the corner, where Leo keeps his client files. I tug at the top drawer but it doesn't open. Neither do the other three; all the drawers are centrally locked. Puzzled, I go back to the desk, looking for another key, running my hand along the underside of each drawer in case Leo has hidden that one too. When I don't find anything, I search the rest of the study.

I empty the pen holder on the desk, run my fingers over the little ridge above the doorway and come away with nothing but dust. I get down on my hands and knees and look under the desk, hoping to find the key to the filing cabinet taped somewhere on its underside. I turn Leo's chair upside down, check behind his computer, under the keyboard and then repeat the whole process. But I can't find the key. Frustrated, I stick the tiny key back where I found it and go back to work.

While I'm on my lunch break, I remember that before Thomas Grainger turned up yesterday, I'd been on my way to see Lorna. It's early afternoon, so I'm not worried about her and Edward being in the middle of lunch. But no one answers my knock and I don't like to insist, because they might be having a nap. I turn to go home and see Will standing at the bottom of the drive, on his way out.

"Hi, Alice!" he calls. "How are things?"

"Oh—you know. I was hoping to see Lorna but she doesn't seem to be in."

"I'd suggest going to see Eve but she's at her mum's. She'll be back around five, if you're looking for company."

"Thanks, Will."

He gives me a wave and I turn back to the door, because I can hear a lock being turned. The door opens, the chain still in place.

Lorna peeps at me timidly through the gap.

"It's only me," I say cautiously. "I didn't mean to disturb you."

"I wasn't going to answer but I heard your voice." She stares for a moment, as if deciding whether or not to let me in. She doesn't seem to want to and I'm about to apologize and tell her I'll call back another day when she begins removing the chain, slowly, as if she's hoping I'll get fed up waiting and go away.

"Are you sure?" I ask doubtfully, when she finally opens the door.

"Yes, come in. It's just that Edward isn't here and I'm always more careful when I'm on my own."

"That's very wise. How is he?"

"Much better, thank you." She opens a door to the right and I follow her in to a cozy sitting room.

"This is lovely," I say, admiring the delicate pastel tones. There's the beautiful scent of lavender and I trace it to a crystal vase, sitting on a low table. Like ours, her sitting room looks onto the square and from the window, I can see our driveway perfectly.

We sit down.

Lorna gives me a nervous smile. "Would you like a cup of tea?"

"No, thank you. I just wanted to ask you something."

"It's not about letting that man into your party, is it? I don't know what came over me. I'm usually so careful."

"No, it's not about that," I reassure her, sad at how much it has knocked her confidence, because she doesn't seem quite as sharp as when I first met her, nor quite as smartly dressed. Although she's wearing her pearls, her clothes—a camel skirt and blue patterned shirt—seem hastily put together, and her hair isn't the same neat bob.

"Have you managed to find out who it was?" she asks.

I hesitate, because I know that if I tell her the truth, that the man is a private detective, she'll feel better about having let him in. On the other hand, I'd have to tell her that he's investigating Nina's murder. She would ask why, and I'd have to admit that Thomas Grainger believes Oliver was innocent. I don't want to open old wounds.

"Not yet," I say, making a quick decision. "But I'm not worried about him and I hope you aren't either. I know how upsetting it must be after what happened to Nina," I add, pleased to have found the perfect lead into the conversation I want to have with her.

Lorna raises her hand to her pearls.

"It was terrible," she says, her voice barely a whisper. "Truly terrible."

"I didn't know about it, I only found out a few days ago."

Lorna looks shocked. "Oh Alice, that's awful. But—I don't understand. Why didn't you know?"

"Because Leo chose to keep it from me. He *was* going to tell me, but he hoped that by the time he did, I'd have grown to love the house as much as he does and wouldn't want to leave."

"Do you want to leave?"

"It's so difficult. I'm not sure how I feel about the house, but I love The Circle, everyone has been so welcoming and I know I'd make friends here. I wanted to leave, but then Leo said something that I can't get out of my mind. He said that the house deserved to have new memories, happy memories." I pause, working my way through my feelings. "It's not that simple, though. Leo and I aren't really speaking at the moment because I can't forgive him for not being upfront with me before we moved in. It's all a bit of a mess, to be honest."

"I can see that," Lorna says, and I smile gratefully at her. It's a relief to be able to pour out my heart to someone with life experience who, like me, has lost someone she loved.

"I don't have any family apart from Leo," I say, on impulse. "My parents and sister were killed in a car crash when I was nineteen years old."

Lorna's hand moves to her heart.

"You lost your sister and your parents? Your poor thing, how did you cope? To lose three loved ones—it doesn't bear thinking about."

"If it hadn't been for my grandparents, I'm not sure I would have coped. They were so strong; they'd lost their only son, their only child—" I stop, halted by the look of desolation clouding her face. "I'm so sorry, Lorna, that was clumsy of me. I know you lost your son too." Lorna doesn't say anything; her fingers pluck at the material of her skirt and I hate that I've upset her. "It must have been so hard for you."

"Yes, it was," she says, her voice almost a whisper. "Any loss is terrible, however it happens."

We sit in silence for a moment. I wonder if I should leave her in peace but I want to find out what I can. "I was wondering—would you be able to tell me about

Nina? Maybe if I knew a little about her, if I could make her real to me, it would help."

Lorna eyes dart, as if she's looking for a way out. Then she nods and squares her shoulders in acceptance of my request.

"She was lovely," she says. "So was Oliver. He was like a son to us, he would help us in the garden, cut the hedges, mow the lawn, that sort of thing. That's why I still don't understand what happened, why it all went so wrong between them. One minute they were the happiest couple in the world and the next—we heard them arguing one evening, it was awful. Oliver sounded so angry, which was strange, because I'd never seen him get cross about anything. But they say that, don't they, that sometimes, when easy-going people explode—well, they really explode. Edward and I didn't know if we should go over, or call the police. We were so worried for them."

"And did you? Call the police?"

"No, because everything calmed down. Oliver was still angry but he wasn't shouting."

"Did you hear what they were arguing about?"

A frown comes over her face and I realize that, like with Tamsin, I've crossed some sort of invisible line.

"I'm sorry," I say hastily. "I don't mean to pry."

Lorna's internal struggle is visible on her face as she tries to work out how much she should tell me. Her shoulders sag.

"Edward said I shouldn't talk about it, but nobody does and somehow, it makes everything worse."

"I can understand that," I say gently. "When my sister

died, people stopped talking about her, they thought it would upset me. But it upset me more when nobody mentioned her at all, as if she'd never existed for them."

"I'm not allowed to talk about our son, or have photos of him anywhere in the house."

"That must be hard."

"It is." Tears fill her eyes but before I can say anything, she blinks them away. "But back to Nina and Oliver," she says, giving me a wobbly smile. She pauses a moment to recall everything. "I went to see Nina the next day, the day after we'd heard them arguing. I waited until Oliver had gone to work. She was in a dreadful state, very tearful. She was mortified that Edward and I had heard them fighting. She said it was her fault, that she'd been having an affair and that Oliver had found out."

"Did she say who she'd been having an affair with?" Appalled that I've been so brusque, I rush to apologize. But she takes my question at face value and carries on talking.

"No, but she said she was going to break it off with him. And then, that night, just hours later, Oliver—" She stops. "I still can't believe it."

"Maybe it wasn't Oliver," I suggest carefully. "Maybe it was the man Nina was involved with. You said she told you she was going to tell him it was over. I'm sorry, but why couldn't he have been the one to have killed her?"

She fishes a tissue from her sleeve. "Because Oliver lied to the police and that proved his guilt," she says, wiping her eyes. "I wish I'd known, I wish I'd known what he was going to tell them because—I know

I shouldn't say this—I would have lied—not lied exactly, but I would have told the police I hadn't seen anything. But when they came to see us that evening, I had no idea that Nina had been murdered and they didn't tell us. They wanted to know if we had seen or heard anything and I answered truthfully, that I saw Oliver come back just after nine o'clock and go into the house. I knew it was just after nine because we'd sat down to watch the news on the BBC news channel, like we always do at nine o'clock—they say old habits die hard, don't they, and anyway the *News at Ten* is on too late for us now—and when we heard Oliver's car, I got up and looked out of the window. I wouldn't normally have done that, not in the winter when the curtains are already drawn, but we were anxious because of the argument we'd heard the night before. I waited a moment, hoping they wouldn't start arguing again. But I didn't hear anything so I went back to the news." She stops a moment. "It must have been about half an hour later, because the news was ending, that we heard a lot of cars pull up and when I looked out, I saw it was the police. We thought that Oliver and Nina had been arguing again and that one of them, or maybe another neighbor, had called for help. To tell you the truth, we were relieved that the matter had been taken out of our hands because if we *had* heard them arguing again, like the previous night, I think that this time, we might have called the police—or at least gone round to try and calm things." She twists the tissue in her hands. "The next thing we knew, the police were knocking on the door, asking their questions. We only found out the next morning that Nina had been murdered."

"It must have been such a shock," I say gently. But lost in the past, I'm not sure Lorna hears me.

"Oliver told the police that he hadn't gone into the house, that he'd gone to sit in the square for a while. But it wasn't true."

"Could he have gone into the house and then gone straight back out again, to sit in the square?" I suggest.

Lorna shakes her head again. "If he had, he would have told the police. If I'd known he was going to say he'd gone to sit in the square, I wouldn't have mentioned seeing him go into the house. But I didn't know, I didn't know he was going to lie. And why would he have gone to sit in the square at nine o'clock at night, when it was cold and dark?"

"Did you tell the police about the conversation you had with Nina, when she told you she'd had an affair with someone?"

"Yes, and they were very interested, because it gave Oliver a motive for killing Nina."

"Didn't they consider that maybe it was the man she was having an affair with who killed her?"

She looks sadly at me. "Why would they? It was Oliver who killed her."

I nod. "I won't take up any more of your time. Thank you for talking to me."

"Do you think you'll be able to stay?" she asks. "Now that you know about the murder?"

"I don't know. My sister was called Nina and it's hard

to explain, but if I leave, it will be as if I'm abandoning her too. I know it's not healthy but I haven't let her go yet, not really."

"That's understandable."

"After almost twenty years?"

"I think time has no meaning when it comes to grief."

The gentleness in her voice brings sudden tears to my eyes and I nod, grateful that she understands.

"I'll let you know what I decide," I promise. "Everyone here has been so kind—Eve and Will have been amazing, and Maria and Tamsin are lovely too. And I still love Leo, despite everything."

"Yes—well, it's been lovely talking to you, thank you for coming by," she says. She leans in to give me a kiss, and I hear the whisper of her voice in my ear.

Startled, I pull back. "Sorry?"

Again, Lorna's hand flies to the pearls at her neck. "I was just saying goodbye." She seems flustered. "Perhaps I shouldn't have embraced you but after what you told me about your parents and sister—" Her voice trails off.

"No, no, it's fine, I thought—"

Moving back, Lorna opens the door. "Goodbye, Alice."

EIGHTEEN

Anxiety presses down as I close the front door behind me. Had Lorna really whispered *Don't trust anyone* when she'd leaned into me, or had I imagined it?

I must have imagined it because why would she have felt the need to whisper when she was alone in the house? She had told me that Edward was out. I try and recall what I was saying before she whispered in my ear. I'd been talking about Will and Eve, and I think I mentioned Maria and Tamsin, and then Leo. She couldn't have been warning me about Leo, she doesn't even know him. Had she meant Will and Eve? Maybe she had heard me chatting to Will before she opened the door. Unless she meant Maria, or Tamsin. Or no one at all, because she hadn't whispered anything.

I'm on my way up to Leo's study to watch for Edward walking back across the square, because I can't believe that Lorna would have lied to me about being on her own in the house, when there's a ring on the bell. Retracing my steps, I open the door and see Tamsin standing there, her hands pushed into the pockets of a brown leather jacket.

"Oh, hi Tamsin," I say, surprised. "How are you? Do you want to come in?"

She shakes her head. "No thanks. I just want to say that I don't think you should be upsetting Lorna by bringing up the murder again."

My cheeks burn. "I was only trying to find out a little more about Nina."

"Why?"

"Well, I—"

"Why do you want to know more about Nina?" she interrupts. "Didn't we tell you enough yesterday at lunch? What more could Lorna tell you about her than we, her friends, already have?"

"I—I was just trying to help," I stammer. "Lorna said she was glad to be able to talk about Nina."

"Bullshit." I flinch at the animosity in her voice. "Look, I understand that it must have been a shock to find out about the murder," she goes on. "And I have no idea what that reporter's motive was in contacting you. But you're going to do more harm than good if you start sticking your nose into things that don't concern you. You don't want to start alienating yourself, especially if you decide to stay here." Turning her back on me, she walks down the drive without saying goodbye.

My face burning at Tamsin's unjustified aggressiveness, I run upstairs to Leo's study and watch from the window as she walks across the square to her house. Maybe it's the truth behind her words that stings. I had upset Lorna. Losing Oliver must have been like losing her son all over again, but somehow worse, because she had been the one to pull the trigger. As she'd sat there, twisting her hands in her lap, I'd felt the weight of her guilt. But I don't like being threatened and Tamsin's visit had felt like a threat. How did she know I was asking Lorna about Nina anyway? Did she see me coming out of her house and make an educated guess?

There's still no sign of Edward. I scan the other houses and see Tim standing at the upstairs window of number 9, also watching the square. Even though I'm doing the same thing, it makes me uncomfortable to see him there. Ten minutes pass, then fifteen. A movement to the left catches my eye—Lorna and Edward's garage door swinging upward and outward. I look down and see Edward, his green gardening shoes on his feet, walking down the drive toward their wheelie bin. I watch as he takes hold of the handle and pulls it slowly back up the drive and into the garage. So, he wasn't out, as Lorna had said. Unless—her actual words had been "Edward isn't here." I had taken that to mean he was out; but maybe all she had meant was that he wasn't there in the house with her, but in the garden.

When Leo comes home, he asks me if I want something to eat. Still upset by Tamsin's visit, and worried about Lorna's warning—if that's what it was—I'm not hungry. I sit at the table and follow him with my eyes as he walks from cooker to fridge and back again, silently asking *Who are you really, Leo? How come*

I didn't know that you would ever lie to me? And more importantly—*why have you got a key taped to the underside of your drawer? What is it that you're hiding from me?*

"We've been invited to Maria's tomorrow evening for supper," I say, breaking the silence.

He turns from the cooker. "Are you sure you want me to come?"

He sounds as if he wants the answer to be no.

"It will look strange if you don't."

"If you prefer to go without me, I can always say I'm ill."

For a moment, I wonder if I should tell Maria we can't go. I can barely act normally around Leo and I don't want the awkwardness between us to spoil the evening. Also, Tamsin will be there. But I want to get to know the other couples—and I'll be doing Leo a favor if I cancel. Everyone will understand if things are a bit fraught, given that he didn't tell me about the murder.

I take out my phone. "I'll call Maria and tell her to expect both of us."

"Lovely," Maria says, when I tell her we're free.

"Can I bring anything?" I ask.

"Not at all. Is 7 p.m. all right for you?"

"It's perfect."

I hang up. "It's at seven," I tell Leo.

"Great," he says, trying to inject enthusiasm into his voice.

He doesn't try to make small-talk while he eats his dinner, just reads the news on his phone, a glass of full-bodied red wine in his hand. I don't know whether to be offended or relieved.

"I saw Lorna today," I say.

"How is she?"

"Still upset about letting someone in to The Circle on Saturday evening. I told her that I'd only just found out about Nina," I add, unable to stop myself from having a dig.

He takes a sip of wine. "Right."

"We talked about Nina and she told me that Nina had had an affair. So now I'm thinking that maybe it wasn't her husband who killed her but the person she was having an affair with."

His glass slips from his hand and crashes onto the table. Wine seeps across the wood, like blood from a wound. For a moment, we both stare at it, seemingly mesmerized. Then he leaps to his feet, grabs a tea-towel from the side and begins dabbing at the table while I move the glass out of the way.

"Sorry," he says. "My hand slipped."

I frown at the mess the wine has made, then pick up his glass and stand it on its base again. "No harm done."

"I don't think it's a good idea to gossip about the dead," he says, kneeling to mop up the wine that has spilled onto the floor. I stare at the back of his head, noticing for the first time that his hair is thinning on top. Flashes of pink skin show through as he begins to rub vigorously at the floorboards.

"Lorna wasn't gossiping, I asked her to tell me about Nina," I say.

He balls the tea-towel, walks over to the sink and puts it down on the side. Turning on the tap, he rinses his hands. "Why?"

"Because I want to know about the woman whose house I'm living in."

"Only because she was murdered," he says. "If she hadn't been, you wouldn't have been curious about her."

I glare at his back. "So, Leo, how was it for you when Ben told you that a young woman had been murdered in the house you wanted to buy? Weren't you curious? Didn't you ask any questions about her, not even ask who she was?"

He reaches for a clean towel and turns. "No, I don't think I did," he says, drying his hands carefully. "If I re-member rightly, it was Ben who volunteered her name."

"And you didn't google her to find out what had hap-pened? You were that disinterested?"

"I wasn't disinterested. I recognized her name and I knew what had happened, I remembered the case. Any-one would have remembered it, it was well-documented at the time, in the press, in the papers."

"Yet there was never any mention of her having an affair."

He puts the towel down, comes back to the table. "Maybe she didn't have one. Maybe it was just a rumor."

"No," I say. "She admitted it to Lorna." I go to refill his glass but he shakes his head.

"That must be why her husband murdered her, then. He found out she'd been cheating on him and killed her in a fit of jealousy."

"Maybe. Unless it was the other man who killed her."

He frowns. He seems on edge, but then he's never enjoyed listening to gossip. "Why do you say that?"

"Because, according to Lorna, Nina was going to tell him that it was over. And because everyone says that Oliver was the nicest man you could ever wish to meet."

"Everyone?" He pounces on the word.

"The people here! His friends and neighbors."

Leo picks up his near-empty wine glass and drains it. "If there had been anything suspicious to find, I think the police would have found it." He pushes away from the table. "I've got work to do. I'll see you later."

I listen as he goes upstairs and into his study. A moment later, I hear the screech of metal on metal and I know that sound, it's one of the drawers in the filing cabinet being pulled open. So, the key to unlock it was up there somewhere. Unless—I go out to the hall. His bag is no longer by the front door and his jacket has gone from where he usually hangs it on the newel post. Maybe he carries the key around with him. But why would he do that? His client files can't be that confidential, can they?

NINETEEN

When morning comes, I know I can't do it. I can't go to Maria's. I don't want to have to pretend that everything is all right between me and Leo and I don't want to have to face Tamsin. What if she tells everyone I've been upsetting Lorna?

"I'm going to Harlestone for the weekend," I tell Leo. "I'll be back Sunday evening."

He looks at me, surprised. "Right, OK. Are you staying with Debbie?"

"Yes. I need to get away from The Circle for a while."

"What about supper at Maria's?"

"You can go by yourself, if you like," I say, knowing that he won't.

I call Debbie.

"Are you busy this weekend?"

"Why, are you coming down? Oh God, I'm so happy, you don't know how much I've missed you! Is Leo coming? Do you want to stay here? There's plenty of room!"

I laugh, immediately feeling better. Debbie lives on

her own in a large four-bedroom farmhouse. She's never married but has had several men in her life, although she's now happily single.

"No, I'm coming on my own and yes, I'd love to stay with you."

"Even better! Not that I don't love Leo, but it means we can really chat and you can tell me all about living in London."

She makes it sound as if it's the other side of the world. But like me, Debbie was born and bred in Harlestone. She's never even been to London, preferring to stay with her horses, running her riding school.

"Is it all right if I arrive today?"

"Of course. Are you driving down?

"Yes, I'll aim to arrive around lunchtime."

"Great!"

I call Maria and am relieved when my call goes through to her voicemail. I leave a message, apologizing profusely, telling her I need a break and have decided to go away for a couple of days. She texts back ten minutes later, saying that she understands, which puts my mind at rest.

Being back in Harlestone is bittersweet. As I drive through the village, the brightly colored hollyhocks standing tall and proud like sentinels against heat-soaked walls and the huge domes of white hydrangeas peeping their heads over garden fences makes me realize how much I've missed it. So much has changed in the month I've been away. The field of yellow rape that I loved to walk through on my way to the village store has since been plowed, and I wonder who was the first to tread a new path through the heavy clods of earth.

Debbie, back from a ride on her fearsome horse Lucifer, senses my low mood. While she cleans her riding boots over a sheet of newspaper, I tell her about Leo and how he hadn't told me the truth about the house he bought.

"I can't understand it," Debbie says, her forehead creased in bewilderment. "What a thing to keep from you. No wonder you don't particularly want to go back. Even I'd feel uneasy living in a house where someone has been murdered and I've got a strong stomach." Her boots clean, she goes to the sink to wash her hands.

"And now I've started putting people's backs up by trying to find out more about the murder," I say.

Debbie turns, water dripping from her elbows. "Why?" she asks, reaching for a checkred towel.

"Because they don't like me asking questions."

"No, I meant—why do you want to know more about the murder?"

"Because it isn't as straightforward as people make out. There are rumors that there was a miscarriage of justice, that it wasn't her husband who killed her."

"Have the police re-opened the investigation, then?" she asks, checking her reflection in the pine-framed mirror that hangs on the wall. Usually wild and unruly, her auburn hair has been flattened by her riding hat, and she remedies this, using her fingers as combs.

"I don't think it was ever closed," I say.

She frowns. "But why are you getting involved? Sorry, Alice, but I can kind of understand that people don't want to talk about it. You should leave it alone, let sleeping dogs lie."

"I can't."

"Why not?"

I look away. "She was called Nina."

"Oh Alice." She comes over and sits beside me, puts an arm round my shoulder, and gives me a hug. "You need to let go."

I lower my head, ashamed. Debbie was there to witness my obsession with a mutual friend's daughter here in Harlestone, born long before my sister died, who happened to be called Nina. Although I was always fond of her, I became a little obsessed after my sister's death, buying her expensive presents and generally doting on her until her mum gently told me that I needed to stop, because it was too much. Stupidly, I had felt hurt and it had ended up spoiling our friendship.

"I'm trying," I say quietly.

"But even if there was a miscarriage of justice," Debbie points out, "it's not your place to go around asking questions, especially on the basis of a rumor."

"It's not just a rumor. I had a visit from a private investigator. He's looking into the case for Nina's sister-in-law, who is convinced that her brother was innocent."

"Well, of course she is."

"But my neighbor told me that Nina admitted to her that she was having an affair with someone. So why couldn't it have been him who killed her?"

"Didn't the police investigate him?"

"I don't know." I hesitate. "The private investigator

asked me to keep my eyes and ears open, let him know if I heard anything."

Debbie's mouth drops open. "He asked you to spy on your neighbors?"

"I refused," I say quickly.

"I hope so. If you decide to stay in The Circle, and want to be accepted—to belong—you need to keep your head down. And really, you should be focusing on you and Leo, not on the murder of someone you didn't even know," she adds gently.

We spend the rest of the weekend catching up with friends from the village, our plans for a long walk scuppered by a blast of rain and cold air that comes in from the east. It matches my mood as I drive back to London on Sunday afternoon but as I get nearer, I give myself a mental shake. Being in Harlestone, away from The Circle, has allowed me to get some perspective. If Leo and I are to get over what he did, I need to make the first move.

I park the car on the drive and go into the house. I thought Leo might have come to the door when he heard me arrive but he's nowhere in sight. I find him in the kitchen, sitting at the table, a glass of wine in his hand, his phone open on one of his news apps.

I clear my throat. "Hello."

He looks up. "Hi. Did you have a nice time with Debbie?"

"Yes, thanks. What about you, did you have a good weekend?"

"Yes, great." He raises his hands above his head,

stretching, then links them behind his neck. "I played tennis with Paul and then I spent the rest of the time watching stuff on Netflix."

He looks carefree and relaxed, and a wave of jealousy hits. I swallow it down.

"Shall I make dinner?" I ask.

"I've been snacking all day so I'm not hungry. But go ahead if you want something."

He goes back to the news, oblivious of my eyes on him, oblivious to the frustration building inside me. I'd been about to ask if I could have a glass of wine with him but suddenly, I'm furious. How dare he sit there as if he doesn't have a care in the world when he screwed up so badly?

"I'm going to my study," I say.

"Don't you want a glass of wine?"

"No thanks."

"OK."

He returns to his screen, seemingly unconcerned. I watch him dispassionately for a moment.

"You can stay in Birmingham this week," I say.

His head jerks up. I've got his attention now. "Sorry?"

"You don't need to come home each evening, you can stay in Birmingham."

"But—where are you going?"

"Nowhere."

"What, you're going to stay here by yourself?"

"Yes."

He stares at me like he doesn't know me. "What about Thursday? Do I come home?"

"I'll let you know on Wednesday."

In my study, I go over everything I've learned about Nina's murder. Lorna and Edward heard Nina and Oliver arguing; the next day, Nina admitted to Lorna that she had been having an affair. That evening, according to Lorna, Oliver had come home at 9 p.m. and had gone straight into the house. Twenty minutes later, Nina was dead. That evening, according to Oliver, he had arrived at the house at 9 p.m., had gone to sit in the square for a while, and only then had gone into the house. And had found Nina dead. Which was it? Lorna was adamant about what she'd seen. So why had Oliver said he'd gone to sit in the square when he so obviously hadn't? Had he panicked and said the first thing that had come into his head? Or had he planned it out beforehand, hoping that nobody would be able to say that he *hadn't* been in the square, because nobody would be watching from their window at that time of night?

TWENTY

Leo takes a while getting ready for work the next morning, giving me time to change my mind about staying on my own. His footsteps are heavier than usual as he moves around upstairs. He's making his presence felt, showing me how empty the house is going to be without him.

He comes downstairs and drops his bag in the hall with an exaggerated thud. It's irritating, this over-the-top reminder that he's leaving for several days. It was how we were meant to be living until his Birmingham contract finished, him leaving on Monday mornings and not coming back until Thursday. Now he's perceiving it as a punishment.

I stay in bed long after he's left for work, overwhelmed by a lethargy I can't shake. The uncertainty of our situation has hit me hard. I'd been so full of hope coming here—a little nervous as to how I was going to adapt to living in London, but looking forward to being with Leo on a more regular basis. Now our relationship seems to be falling apart. Even in the aftermath of my parents' and sister's deaths, I hadn't felt this alone.

It's the need of a coffee that gets me to my feet. I carry it through to the sitting room and drink it standing by the window, watching the trees start a slow shed of their leaves. It's gone nine o'clock, I'm late at my desk. A movement catches my eye, Eve coming out of her house. She's dressed in her running gear and I'm about to knock on the window and wave when Tamsin appears behind her. I step back quickly, but I can still see them. They exchange a few words, then Eve runs across the road and into the square, leaving Tamsin standing on the drive.

Needing breakfast, I go to the kitchen, put some bread in the toaster and search the fridge for honey. A ring at the doorbell startles me; the jar slips from my hand and smashes on the floor, right by my bare feet. I stare at the shards of glass sticking to the bottom of my blue pajamas, wondering where to begin cleaning up the mess, and the doorbell rings again. Whoever it is isn't going to go away.

Stepping carefully over the broken jar, I go into the hall, open the door and come face to face with the one person I could do without seeing. Tamsin.

"Hi, Alice." In deference to the colder weather, she's wearing a white padded jacket and white suede ankle boots. She looks perfect.

"Sorry," I say, conscious of being in my pajamas. "I'm not feeling good. So, if you're here to have another go at me, I'd rather you come back another day."

She shuffles from one foot to the other. "No, I'm not, I'm here to apologize. I shouldn't have been so aggressive. I was having a bad week."

"It's fine. But as I told you, I didn't upset Lorna, she said it was a relief to talk about Nina because nobody did anymore."

Tamsin nods, and I ignore the image that comes to mind, of Lorna playing with her pearls.

"I wondered if you'd like to come for coffee on Friday," she says. "In the morning, around ten-thirty. I know you work but would that be OK? Eve will be there," she adds, as if she thinks I might not go if it's just the two of us.

I'm not keen on interrupting my working day but I can always work through lunch to make up for taking time off in the morning. "Thank you, that would be lovely," I say.

She looks both pleased and relieved. "Great! Well, goodbye, Alice, I hope you feel better soon."

I watch her as she walks down the drive.

"You look beautiful, by the way!" I call.

She turns and gives me a little wave but there's sadness on her face, as if she doesn't really believe me.

In the kitchen, I clean up the mess from the broken jar with renewed energy. It's the house that's stifling me, I realize. What I need is a blast of cold air. Half-an-hour in the garden will help. I can do some weeding. I enjoy weeding, it's the kind of task I can do on autopilot, leaving my mind free to wander.

The previous day's rain makes the weeding easier. I'm halfway up the left-hand side of the garden when

I discover a panel missing in the fence between our house and Eve and Will's. It's not a problem because the gap is partly covered by thick green foliage. I push it aside and realize that I could walk straight into their garden if I wanted to. Maybe Eve and Nina used it as a shortcut instead of walking across the driveway when they wanted to see each other. I make a mental note to ask her about it when I next see her.

My cell phone rings. I straighten up, ease my back. It's Ginny.

"Hi, Alice. I'm calling to see how you are. Am I disturbing you?"

"No, it's fine, I'm taking a break in the garden. It's lovely to be outside. How are you? Did you have a good weekend?"

"Well, I'm fast becoming a golf widow, which suits me fine. Mark and Ben spent the whole day yesterday on the golf course. Ben came back for a drink afterward, he was asking about you."

"That was nice of him."

There's a pause. "I'm actually calling because Leo called me this morning."

"Leo?"

"Yes. He said that you don't want him coming home this week, that you told him he could stay in Birmingham. He wanted me to check that you'll be all right on your own."

"I'll be fine," I say, sounding braver than I feel, because I do have a niggling apprehension about being on my own tonight.

"Would you like me to come and stay?"

"That's lovely of you, but honestly, it's fine. I need to do this, Ginny, I need to see if I can stay here. We've only been here a month, I don't want to give up yet."

"I think Leo's afraid you might give up on him."

I sigh. "To be honest, I don't know how I feel about him anymore. I still can't get my head around him lying to me."

"How about we have lunch this week? I'll take a longer lunch hour."

"That will be lovely. When were you thinking?"

"Either tomorrow or Friday."

"Tomorrow," I say, remembering coffee at Tamsin's on Friday morning. "Shall we go to the restaurant in Covent Garden where they serve that delicious monkfish? It's not too far for you, is it?"

"Neptune? I can walk there in ten minutes. I'll call and make a reservation for twelve thirty."

"Great, see you there."

The two invitations, plus the weeding, make it easier for me to get back to work. I love the story I'm translating and I become so absorbed in it that it's three o'clock before I stop for something to eat. The sun has come out and rather than head straight back to work after a sandwich, I decide to go for a walk in Finsbury Park and translate this evening instead. With Leo not coming home, I'll need something to take my mind off being alone in the house.

Half an hour later, I'm on my way, glad to be away from The Circle, from its cloying, claustrophobic atmosphere. It's the gates, I decide. They make it feel a bit like a prison. If they weren't there, The Circle would be just another street in London.

The park is glorious in its new autumn colors. I walk for an hour, trying not to think of anything much, then sit down on a bench and watch the world go by. A few people stride along, in a hurry to be somewhere, but most stroll leisurely, especially the mums with young children, or the older couples, some hand in hand. I smile, then feel a pang of melancholy. Will Leo and I ever have children, grow old together? Is it strange that we have never talked about having children? Or was it a conversation we were waiting to have once we'd settled into our new life in London?

"Alice!"

I look up and see Eve jogging toward me.

"You're not still running, are you?" I ask in pretend alarm. "I saw you leave at nine this morning."

She laughs and sits down on the bench, taking a moment to catch her breath.

"No, I ran with a friend, then went to hers for lunch. Now I'm jogging back to blog. What about you? Did you have a good weekend? Leo said you were away."

"Yes, I went back to Harlestone and caught up with some of my friends there. I felt bad about canceling on Maria at the last minute, but I needed a change of scene."

"Don't worry, she understood."

"Also, I had a bit of a run-in with Tamsin so I thought it better to keep my distance."

Eve wrinkles her nose. "Yes, she told me. If it helps, she's feeling bad about it."

"I know, she came and apologized this morning, which was nice of her. And invited me for coffee on Friday."

"Oh, good, she said she was going to. Don't think too harshly of her, Alice. Nina's death hit her hard."

"It must be dreadful to lose your best friend in such a terrible way," I say, watching a little dachshund sniffing around a pile of leaves.

"It was all the harder for her because—well, there wasn't a row, or anything like that, but I think that when we moved in next door, Tamsin felt a bit pushed out."

"In what way?"

"The thing is, I only knew that Tamsin and Nina were best friends, or had been best friends, after Nina died, when Tamsin came to see me. She was distraught, she wanted to know if she had upset Nina in any way. I asked her what she meant and she said that until a few months before her death, she and Nina had been best friends, always popping in and out of each other's houses, having supper together at weekends. Then, suddenly, everything changed. She said she'd go past Nina's house and see me chatting to her through the window, and wonder why Nina hadn't invited her to join us. I told her they were usually spur-of-the-moment coffees—you know, Nina would see me coming back from a run and shout 'want a coffee?' But there were the suppers too. We went around to Nina and Oliver's a few times with Maria and Tim, but Tamsin and Connor were never there, which was why I didn't know she and Nina were supposedly best friends. I asked Maria about it recently, asked if she knew what had happened between them and she said that she didn't. Nina had stopped coming to yoga too, and Tamsin suspected it was because she didn't want to see her." She pauses. "I really liked Nina but it bothered me afterward, to think that she was being—well, maybe a bit mean."

I nod slowly. "Was it common knowledge that Nina was having an affair?"

"Who told you that?"

Was there a slight edge to her voice or had I imagined it? "Lorna."

Eve shakes her head. "No. We only found out after." She turns to look at me. "You can understand now why we were able to accept that Oliver killed her."

Just like that, I want to ask, *without question?* "But why couldn't it have been the man she was having an affair with who killed her?" I ask instead.

Eve bends to tie her lace. "I'm sure the police looked into it," she says, straightening up again. "And if they didn't think there was anything to investigate, well, who were we to argue?"

Oliver's friends, I want to say. *You were Oliver's friends.*

"You said Tamsin was Nina's best friend. Did she know about her affair?"

"No, not back then. Nina never spoke to her about it."

"I remember Tamsin saying at lunch last week that Nina had really helped her. Did she see her in a professional capacity?"

"No, Nina wouldn't have been allowed to be her therapist, given that they were friends. Tamsin suffers from depression—I don't think she'll mind me telling you that—and I think Nina gave her advice on natural remedies, as Tamsin didn't want to take anti-depressants. Which is why it was doubly hard for her when Nina began distancing herself. Tamsin felt abandoned, and not just physically."

"Did Nina work from home?"

"No, she had an office about twenty minutes from here."

"What about Connor, what's he like?"

"Connor is Connor. He's actually all right when you get to know him. But he can be a bit insensitive, especially to Tamsin."

I don't want to pry but I'm curious. Luckily, after a drink from her water bottle, she carries on without any prompting.

"For example," Eve goes on. "After the murder, Tamsin wanted to move away. We all did; it was a natural knee-jerk reaction. A violent murder had happened in close proximity to where we were living and we were all scared. But Connor insisted they were staying and refused to even consider a possible move. If he had tried to find a middle ground, told Tamsin that yes, they could think about moving away if that was what she really wanted, she wouldn't have broken so completely. Will was brilliant, he said that we could put the house back on the market even though we'd only been here five months. Lorna especially was in a terrible state. She wanted to go and stay with her sister in Dorset, at least for a while, and Will offered to drive her and Edward there. But the next day, Edward was taken to hospital with a heart attack, brought on by the stress of the murder next door, so they hadn't been able to leave. Anyway, before anyone could do anything, Oliver was arrested, then he killed himself. And everyone began to feel safe again. The only people that did actually move away were the Tinsleys, who lived at number 3."

"Hm," I say, because my mind is still stuck on Tamsin and Nina's falling out. I don't want Eve to know that she's given me lots to think about so I look for a way to change the subject.

"By the way, I was in the garden this morning and I found a gap in the fence between our two properties."

"Gosh, I'd forgotten about that! Oliver used to lend Will his lawnmower because it was a new state-of-the-art one and they opened up the fence so they could push it through instead of having to take it around the front. You'll probably find a gap on the other side too, because Oliver used to cut Lorna and Edward's grass for them. Geoff does it now."

"He lives on the other side of them, doesn't he?"

"Yes."

"Does he live there on his own? Someone mentioned that he's divorced."

"Yes, for a few years now. I never knew his wife but Maria did, because they were neighbors. She met someone at work and that was it, marriage over." She stands up and stretches her arms above her head, easing her muscles. "Sorry, but I need to go. Do you want me to ask Will to put the panel back up?"

"No, don't, it's fine. The gap has grown over anyway.

And you never know, it might come in useful," I add with a smile.

"Is Leo coming back each evening, like he did last week?"

"No, I told him not to. It's a long journey to have to make twice a day."

"Then do you want to come and sleep at ours?"

"That's lovely of you. But if I'm to stay here, I need to get used to being in the house on my own."

"If you change your mind, just let us know. Do you want to jog back with me?"

"No, thanks, I'm not really the jogging kind."

She laughs. "Bye, Alice. It was nice talking to you. See you at Tamsin's on Friday, if not before."

I watch her thoughtfully as she runs off. I'm grateful for everything she told me but it was a huge amount of information to dump on me in one sitting. Maybe it's Eve I'm not meant to trust. And from what I'm beginning to learn about Nina—her affair, her rejection of Tamsin—maybe she wasn't as lovely as I thought.

PAST

I have a new client and a new office. It's on the first floor of an old, rickety building and I hear her running up the stairs, her feet hammering on the wooden steps. She's late.

"I'm sorry," she says, flustered. "I got lost. I haven't been living here long and I don't know my way around yet."

"It's fine," I say, giving her a smile. "You really shouldn't have run." I mean it; her cheeks are flushed and she looks slightly sweaty. Her hair is a mess, half of it still tied up, the other half falling in strands around her face.

I wait while she takes off her coat and extra-long scarf, both of them black. The dress she's wearing is also black, as are her boots. She sees me looking and gives a self-conscious laugh.

"Trying to fit in," she explains. "Most of the women here seem to wear black."

I smile non-committally and tell her to make herself comfortable, although it may be difficult in the angular chair I've chosen for this office. I ask her if she's warm enough; it's cold outside, the temperature is almost zero.

"Yes, thank you," she says.

I move my eyes to the window, giving her time to settle. The street outside is busy with the sounds of people going home after their working day.

"How are you?" I ask, once she's sitting down.

She shifts in the chair. "To be honest, I'm not really sure why I'm here. I mean, there isn't really anything wrong. I just need to talk to someone, I guess."

"That's what I'm here for," I say, putting her at ease.

She nods. "I'm not sure where to begin."

"Why don't I ask you a few questions first?"

Another nod. "Yes, of course."

I pull my pad toward me. "Before we begin, I want you to know, and remember, that anything you say in this room is confidential."

She gives a little laugh. "Good. Not that I'm going to tell you anything amazing. As I said, I don't really know why I'm here. My life is perfect. But I'm not happy. I feel terrible for saying that but it's true."

The tension in her vibrates around the room. I pick up my pen and jot down the words—"perfect" and "unhappy" then lean forward in my chair.

"Do you know what Henry David Thoreau believed? 'Happiness is like a butterfly; the more you

chase it, the more it will elude you. But if you turn your attention to other things, it will come and sit softly on your shoulder.'"

She smiles, relaxes. It always works.

TWENTY-ONE

I start awake. I'm about to open my eyes but some primal instinct tells me that I need to pretend I'm still asleep. My mind darts, trying to work it out. And then I realize; there's someone in the room.

Adrenaline surges through my body, whipping my heartrate to a frenzy. It hammers in my chest and I tell myself frantically that I'm imagining it, remind myself that last time this happened, there was no one there. But I know, with a horrible, terrible certainty, that someone is standing at the foot of my bed. I lie in a state of near-paralysis, not daring to breathe, waiting for the crush of their body on mine, the tightening of their hands around my throat. The tension is unbearable; I try to hold on to my fear but I can't.

"Go away!" The words tear out of me and I push myself up forcibly, ready to face whoever is there. The room is in darkness, panicking me further, because I had left the lamp on. I reach down, fumbling for the switch, steeling myself for a hand seizing my bare arm and pulling me from the bed. I snap the light on and scan the room, my breath coming in shallow gasps as I peer into the shadows. There's no one there. I wait, listening to every noise the house is making. But nothing sounds wrong.

I slump back against my pillow, cold sweat on my forehead, trying to slow my pounding heart. *It's all right, it's all right. Nothing happened.*

But there was someone there, I know there was. I slide my cell phone from under my pillow, tap 999, then change my mind and find Leo's number. I need to hear someone's voice and he's the only person I feel I can call at—I check the time, and when I see that it's only two o'clock, the knowledge that I still have the rest of the night to get through is devastating. It won't be light for another five hours and I'm not going to be able to go back to sleep, not now. I force myself to be calm. I'm not going to call Leo. Nothing has happened to me, nothing will happen to me now. But why would someone break into the house to do absolutely nothing? And how did they get in?

Reluctantly, I get out of bed and make the same journey through the house that I made a week ago, but with less bravado because this time, Leo isn't asleep upstairs. In the kitchen, I check the French windows. There's no broken glass, no sign of forced entry. Moving to the worktop, I grab a knife from the drawer. The knife, black-handled with a serrated edge, used for cutting lemons, will only be dangerous if I plunge it deep into someone. Which I could never do. Nevertheless, it gives me a weak kind of courage.

The windows in the downstairs rooms are intact,

nothing has been disturbed. The front door is still locked from the inside. I continue slowly up the stairs, my heartbeat increasing with each step I take. I try not to think about someone leaping out at me from the guest bedroom or the study. With those lights now on, the whole house is ablaze, except for our bedroom, the one Leo and I used to sleep in. The one where Nina was murdered. I push open the door, snap on the light and peer in. Like the other rooms, it's empty. And yet. I stand still, trying to work it out. There's a sort of presence, not a physical one, but something invisible, intangible. Something I can sense, but can't name. Slamming the door behind me, I hurry downstairs.

Somehow, I make it through the next few hours. To pass the time, I make several cups of tea and drink them in the sitting room, feeling safer at the front of the house. I want to check the street outside but the thought of seeing someone standing there, watching the house, watching me, is almost more terrifying than thinking they're inside, so I keep the curtains closed. At five, I crawl back into bed. Dawn will be breaking soon, people will be waking up, getting ready to start the day ahead. Nobody will come now.

When I wake, and think about the previous night, it's impossible to believe that it was anything but my imagination. Maybe I turned off the lamp myself, without realizing, as I descended into sleep? I walk through the house again, checking the windows and doors for the slightest trace that someone had somehow managed to get in. But there's nothing out of the ordinary.

My positivity takes a knock when I find strands of my hair on the worktop in the kitchen. Added to the ones I found in the bathroom this morning, it points to the thing I fear most, losing my hair again. Some months after my parents and sister died, my hair became noticeably thinner and when Debbie persuaded me to see a doctor, I was diagnosed with Telogen effluvium, brought on by the stress of what had happened. Barely able to eat since the accident, I'd lost a lot of weight. If I didn't want to aggravate the condition, the doctor told me, I needed to start eating healthy, balanced meals again. My hair eventually recovered, but it was a long process and, at nineteen years of age, hugely distressing.

The stress I'm feeling now, because of what happened in this house, and Leo not telling me, is nothing to the stress I felt back then. But I'm older now, my hair naturally more fragile. I twist it into a loose knot, secure it with a clip. If it's not hanging around my shoulders, I won't be constantly thinking about it.

In the fridge, I look for something for breakfast and find in the vegetable drawer, along with an overripe avocado, a bottle of expensive champagne, which Leo must have put there before he left yesterday. I'm not sure if it's for me—if, like the white rose he left me in the hall, he's trying to make up for everything—or if he put it there to drink when he's next home.

There's a message from him on my phone—**Everything OK?**—to which I reply **Everything fine.**

I go back to my breakfast but my appetite has gone, chased away by my worry over the state of our relationship. I'm glad I'm meeting Ginny for lunch, I desperately need someone to talk to.

I work for a couple of hours, then leave the house. Edward is in their front garden, tending his roses and, remembering what Tamsin said about me upsetting Lorna with my questions about Nina, I feel suddenly awkward.

"Hello!" I call, testing the water.

The smile Edward gives me puts my mind at rest. "Alice! How are you?"

I walk over the drive toward him. "I'm fine, thank you, I hope you are too?"

"Yes, yes, I can't complain. Are you going shopping?"

"No, I'm meeting a friend for lunch. How is Lorna?"

"She's very well. It was nice of you to call by the other day. She gets a bit lonely sometimes."

"I hope I didn't upset her."

"Upset her? Why would you have upset her?"

"I'm afraid I was asking about Nina and Oliver."

"Don't you worry your head. If she was upset, it was about you. She told me you lost your parents and sister?"

"Yes, that's right."

"What a shocking thing to happen. A drunk driver, was it?"

"No, just a young driver without much experience."

"Absolutely terrible for you," he says, shaking his head.

"Yes, it was. But it's in the past now."

"It doesn't do any good to dwell on the past," he

growls and I know, from the fierce look on his face that he's thinking about his son. He's of the generation where people don't talk about their emotions.

"You're probably right," I say.

He turns away. "Well, I'd best get on."

"If you need shopping or anything, I hope you'll let me know."

"Thank you, but we get everything delivered. We don't really go out anymore."

Except that he was meant to be out the other day.

I nod. "Well, goodbye, Edward. Tell Lorna I'll see her soon."

TWENTY-TWO

Ginny is already at Neptune when I arrive. She's beautifully dressed in a chocolate-brown leather skirt and jacket that I've never seen before.

"Mark's birthday present to me," she says, when I mention it.

"That's the problem with working from home," I say. "It doesn't matter what I put on in the mornings. I'd love something like that but I'd never get any wear out of it."

We have a quick catch-up while we study the menus but once we've ordered, I find myself confiding my worries to her.

"I can't work out if the reason I'm finding it hard to forgive Leo is because our relationship was already doomed before he lied to me," I say, turning my fork over and over on the white cloth. "When we only saw each other at weekends, we were on our best behavior, not wanting to spoil the time we had together. We didn't really know each other. It's only now that we're discovering each other's faults and weaknesses."

"But you love him," Ginny says.

"Yes. But I'm not sure that the love I feel for him is strong enough to overcome the negatives." I look guiltily at her. "That makes me sound horrible, I know."

"Not horrible, just honest."

"I don't want to give up on our relationship so I need to find a way forward. It's just that, for the moment, I seem unable to." I give her a smile. "Come on, let's talk about something else."

We're interrupted by the waiter bringing our food over.

"Something weird happened the other day," I say, when we've finished eating. "You know I told you that Nina admitted to Lorna, the lady who lives next door, that she'd been having an affair? When I mentioned it to Leo, he almost jumped out of his skin."

"Even I was surprised when you told me." Ginny sits back in her chair and places a hand on her stomach. "That was delicious."

"Yes, but it was more than surprise. He dropped his glass of wine, it went everywhere and—I don't know—he just seemed overly flustered."

"Strange." She laughs. "Unless he was the one having an affair with her."

"What?" I stare at her and she sits up quickly and reaches across the table for my hand, her two silver bangles jangling together.

"Alice, I'm joking! Leo didn't even know Nina."

It's too late, I can't stop the thought from flying through my mind. "What if he did? What if he did know her?"

"Stop it." She gives my hand a shake. "Don't start imagining something that didn't happen. How could he have known her?"

"I don't know. She was a therapist, maybe he was a client."

Ginny groans. "I wish I hadn't said anything. It was a joke, Alice, seriously." She picks up her menu. "Do you want dessert?"

"Sorry. No, just a coffee." I close my menu and put it down on the table. "Tamsin has invited me to hers on Friday."

"Tamsin? Your archenemy? How come? Tell me, I want to know everything."

I launch into an account of my latest conflict with Tamsin and her subsequent apology and by the time we leave the restaurant half an hour later, I can tell Ginny's relieved that I've forgotten what she said about Leo having known Nina. But I haven't, it's lodged right there in the back of my mind.

It's a direct tube ride from Covent Garden back to Finsbury Park. It's the way I came, on the Piccadilly line, but I go to the map on the wall in the Underground station, wanting to see where else I could get to. My eyes fall on Leicester Square—theaterland—and Knightsbridge, where I know Harrods is. It's also home to the Natural History Museum, another place I'm keen to visit. I follow the dark blue line past Earl's Court right to the end, amazed that I can get all the way to Heathrow Airport from practically my front door. The Piccadilly line is certainly a good line to live on. And if I change at

Earl's Court, I could go to Kew Gardens and—I follow another branch of the line—to Wimbledon. Leo and I both love watching tennis and I wonder how difficult it is to get tickets for a match there. And then I wonder if Leo and I will even last until next summer.

I'm about to turn away when I remember that Thomas Grainger's offices are in Wimbledon. I take my cell phone from my bag and find the address—26 William Street. I stand for a moment. A part of me wants to go and check out the address, just to make sure he is who he says he is, in case I ever need to call him. I don't know why I'm thinking I might need to call him—except that if there *was* a miscarriage of justice and I do hear something which could put the real perpetrator away, wouldn't it be my duty to tell him? There's something off about the way everyone was so quick to accept that Oliver killed Nina. Maybe they're protecting someone, someone from The Circle who they suspect of having had an affair with Nina. But who?

I go through the barriers and instead of heading north on the Piccadilly line, I head south toward Earl's Court, then change to the District line. I've never traveled so far on the tube by myself and when I get off at Wimbledon, I'm so out of my comfort zone that I'm tempted to go straight back home. Everyone seems to know where they're going except me.

I move to the side and use Citymapper to locate William Street. It's quite a long walk and the further I go, the more I wonder what I'm doing here. William Street is a long road of smart townhouses, most of which seem to have been turned into offices. I approach number 26; there's a discreet gold plaque on the wall and I have to go up the first two of four stone steps to read the words *Thomas Grainger, Private Investigator*. Behind the dark blue door, I can hear a murmur of voices and when they get steadily louder, I realize that someone is coming along the corridor. The thought of him discovering me on the doorstep sends me scooting back to the pavement. I just have time to hide myself in the doorway of a house two doors down when the sound of someone saying goodbye—a woman—and a man's voice answering her, reaches my ears. I bend my head over my phone, pretending to search for something, praying that the door in front of me won't suddenly open. My back is to the road and when I hear the light click of heels on the pavement, I breathe a sigh of relief. Turning my head slowly, I check number 26 to make sure Thomas Grainger isn't still there. He isn't, so I leave the doorway and see a woman, smartly dressed in a camel-colored coat, walking down the road. I need to go back that way anyway, so I follow her to the tube station, wondering what business she had with a private investigator. The majority of his cases are probably people wanting to know what their partners are up to. *Maybe I should get him to check out Leo for me,* I think, and then feel guilty.

I get home and even as I'm dialing Thomas Grainger's number, I'm wondering what I'm doing. What's the point of calling him when I have absolutely nothing to tell him? But it's too late; my call connects before I can hang up.

"It's Alice Dawson," I say, instantly recognizing his voice.

"Ms. Dawson, thank you for calling." He can't quite hide his surprise, which is understandable after I told him that I wouldn't help.

It sounds too formal. "Alice," I say. "You can call me Alice."

"And I'm Thomas."

"I'm sorry, I'm not really sure why I am—calling you, I mean." I hate that I sound flustered. "I don't have any news. I did go and see my neighbor, but she didn't tell me anything that I'm sure you don't already know. She was the one who saw Oliver arrive home on the night of the murder and—"

"I could come by tomorrow afternoon," he says, interrupting me.

My heart misses a beat. "But there's nothing really to tell. I can go over it now, if you like."

"I prefer not to talk on the phone. I'm going to be in your area anyway, so it's no trouble. Would 2 p.m. suit you?"

"Yes, but I'm not sure—"

"Thank you, Alice, I'll see you tomorrow."

I try to concentrate on my work for the rest of the day but the guilty feeling in the pit of my stomach has me constantly reaching for my phone, wanting to call Thomas Grainger and tell him not to bother coming over. Even though I'm not going to be telling him anything he doesn't already know, it feels wrong to be speaking to him. I wish I could run it by someone but I already know what Debbie would say. And I can't ask

Ginny for advice, because I still haven't told Leo that the man who gate-crashed our party is a private investigator. If Ginny knows, she might tell Mark, who would tell Leo. And I need to be the one to tell him. The reason I haven't told him yet is that I know he'll call the police, and Thomas will get into trouble if they find out he's investigating Nina's murder. And I don't want that to happen.

I work late into the evening to make up for taking most of the afternoon off and when it gets dark, still traumatized by my experience last night, I read in the sitting room with the curtains open, getting up occasionally to check what the other residents of The Circle are doing. It's comforting to see lights on, to know that even though it's late, not everyone is in bed.

By the time one o'clock comes, most of the lights have gone out and I feel nervous standing at the window in full view. There could be someone waiting in the shadows, someone who can see me even if I can't see them. Of the few lights that are still on, one comes from Tamsin's house and I like to think that she might be awake too.

When I go to bed, I leave the light on in the stairwell so that the house isn't in complete darkness. But I'm unable to relax and I know that I've been fooling myself in thinking that I can ever feel comfortable living here. Ginny had been appalled when I told her that I'd thought there was someone in the house the previous night, and had urged me to move in with her and Mark while I sort things out with Leo. I should have taken her up on her offer—and tomorrow I will. I don't know what will happen between me and Leo, the only thing I know is that I can't go on living in The Circle.

TWENTY-THREE

Thomas arrives at precisely two o'clock. I was expecting him to ring on the intercom, so it's a shock to find him at the front door.

"I thought I'd check if the entry code had been changed. It hasn't," he says, by way of explanation. He sounds disapproving.

"I'll speak to someone about it." I close the door on the cold wind that followed him in and lead him through to the sitting room. It feels rude not to offer him a coffee but I want to get rid of him as quickly as possible. Even though I managed to get through the night unscathed, I still don't want to be here. The only thing I'm hesitating about is whether to go to Ginny's, or to Debbie's in Harlestone.

"I don't have very long, I'm afraid," he says, as if he's read my mind and is putting me at ease.

"Yes, of course." I wait until he's sitting down, his phone on the table beside him. "How is Oliver's sister?"

"Health-wise, not so good. But it's done wonders for

her morale knowing that we might be able to make some progress in clearing Oliver's name. She's very grateful to you, Alice."

I frown. "As I said on the phone yesterday, I don't think I'm going to be telling you anything you don't already know. I'd hate for you, or Oliver's sister, to have false hope."

"Believe me, false hope is the last thing I want to give Helen."

I tell him quickly about my visit to Lorna.

"Did Helen—Oliver's sister—know that Nina was having an affair?" I ask.

"Not until my police source told me about your neighbors' testimony."

"Was she aware there were problems in the marriage?"

"No, but she said that Oliver probably wouldn't have told her if there had been."

"My neighbor was adamant that she saw Oliver go into the house," I say. "But what if he went in, then went out again? Maybe he heard Nina breaking things off with the man she was having an affair with, and decided to leave them to it. And then, while he was in the square, that person killed her."

"You don't know how much I'd like that to be true. But if that was the case, wouldn't Oliver have said as much to the police? He maintained that he didn't go into the house at all, even when his lawyer suggested to him that it might have been the case."

"What do you think happened?" I ask.

"I believe Oliver, because he had no need to lie. But I also believe your next-door neighbor—Mrs. Beaumont." He leans forward, fixing me with his eyes. "Think about it for a minute; she sees Oliver arrive, she sees him getting out of the car. At that moment, someone sneaks past the car and goes into the house. Oliver, about to head to the square, doesn't see that person because he's going in the other direction. Your neighbor, thinking that she's seen Oliver go inside, has stopped watching because she's anxious that he and Nina might start arguing again. It's why she doesn't see Oliver walk into the square. And as nobody else came forward to say that they saw him there—well, in the police's eyes, without an alibi, he has to be lying."

I nod slowly, realizing that what Thomas said is not possibly what happened, but probably what happened. I like that he believes both Oliver and Lorna.

"So, what we need to find out is who could have sneaked past Oliver into the house." I flush, realizing I said "we" and not "you." "The person Nina might have been having an affair with."

"Exactly."

"What I don't understand is why everyone was so quick to condemn Oliver, and why nobody wants to believe that someone else could have killed her. Do you think they're protecting somebody?"

"Yes," he says softly. "I do."

"Someone from here—from The Circle?"

"Why else would they close ranks?"

"It's true that they don't seem to like me asking questions about Nina," I say. "Tamsin especially. She was Nina's best friend and she really didn't like me going to see Lorna." I stop, realizing I've said too much.

"It's understandable, if she was Nina's best friend. Does Tamsin have red hair, by any chance?"

"Yes, how do you know?"

"Because Nina often spoke about her to Helen, but Helen couldn't remember her name and I wasn't sure which one of Nina's friends she was." He consults his phone. "There was another friend who used to go to yoga with them."

"That would be Eve, my immediate neighbor."

He nods. "Eve Jackman. Does she have a partner?"

"Yes, her husband, Will."

"I've got here that they moved in about five months before Nina was murdered."

"That's right."

He looks up. "There's another friend then, someone Nina had known for longer."

"That would be Maria. You know, married to Tim, except that he calls her Mary because she went to a convent school," I say dryly.

He gives a slight smile. "Ah yes, that Maria. Maria Conway and her husband Tim."

"Yes."

He finishes tapping into his phone and slides it into his pocket. "Thank you," he says, getting to his feet. "And once again, please don't do anything that you don't feel comfortable with. The last thing I want is to put pressure on you, so I won't be contacting you. If anything comes up and you feel able to tell me, you have my cell."

I don't bother telling him that I'm not going to be around much longer. "Give my best wishes to Helen," I say.

"I will, thank you."

I close the door behind him and lean against it, aware that the thought of not seeing him again is bothering me more than it should. There's something about him that I find reassuring. He's solid, the sort of person you could rely on if things got tough, and I wonder if his relationship with Oliver's sister is more than platonic. I go over what I told him, wanting to make sure that I hadn't said anything to feel guilty about. I hadn't repeated what Eve told me yesterday, about the falling out between Nina and Tamsin, because I'm not sure why she told me, and with Lorna's warning stuck in my mind, I prefer to be cautious. I wish I knew if she actually whispered anything. It doesn't matter, I realize, I'm leaving. But there are still a few personal ends that I want to tie up before I go.

I call Leo. He picks up straightaway.

"Alice, thank you for calling." His relief whooshes down the line and I remember that I'm meant to be letting him know if he can come home tomorrow. He's going to be pleased when I tell him that he can—but maybe not so pleased when I tell him that I won't be here.

"Why did you jump when I mentioned Nina having an affair?" I ask.

I can hear his mind adjusting itself away from what he thought I was phoning about, to why I'm actually calling.

"Because you insinuated that maybe he was responsible for Nina's murder."

"So?"

"It's just that when I played tennis with Paul on Saturday, he told me that Nina used to see quite a few of the men from The Circle."

I frown. "Do you mean in her role as a therapist? Because I don't think she'd have been able to see them in that capacity, if they were friends or neighbors."

"No, not as a therapist. She helped them out with other stuff, Will with his lines, Connor with his whiskies, that sort of thing."

"That doesn't mean she was having an affair with either of them."

"I never said she was."

"How did you come to have this conversation with Paul, anyway?"

"I just happened to ask him what Nina and Oliver were like. He said that they were both really nice people, always helping others out. Oliver used to help the older residents with their gardens, do odd jobs for them." He pauses. "All I'm saying is that a lot of people here were close to Nina, men as well as women, which is why I don't think you should be going around talking about her having an affair and then saying you think he might have murdered her, like you said to me."

"But if it was someone else who murdered her, don't you think he deserves to be brought to justice?"

"Well, yes, of course."

"Even if it turns out to be someone from The Circle?"

There's a pause and I can almost see the two deep lines between his eyes that appear whenever he frowns. "Is there something you're not telling me?"

"Just that not everyone thinks Oliver is guilty."

"What do you mean?"

I'm pacing the floor now, wondering if I should tell him about Thomas, how he's an investigator and not a reporter, and how he thinks that Oliver is innocent. But if I tell him that he's a friend of Oliver's sister, Leo will say he has a vested interest. Besides, if he asks how I met him, I'll have to tell him he's the man who gate-crashed our drinks evening, and Thomas's credibility will be less than zero, private investigator or not. And, I remind myself, it's no longer my business.

"I'm finding it hard to reconcile this image of Oliver as a paragon of virtue but also a killer," I tell him, coming to a stop by the window. Maria and Tim, on the way into the square with their boys, are chatting to Geoff at the gate. I watch for a moment. Did Nina help Tim and Geoff in some capacity too, as well as Will and Connor?

"Maybe. But I don't understand why you're getting involved." Leo interrupts my train of thought. "Unless it's because of your sister. Because if that is the reason, you need to let it go. It isn't healthy, Alice."

I hang up before he can say anything more and re-mind me what my therapist told me—that I can't live my sister's life through the lives of other women called Nina.

TWENTY-FOUR

Stay!

The soft, sibilant whisper lulls me from my sleep. Instead of feeling afraid, the lingering echo of the word fills me with lightness.

"Nina," I murmur.

The sense of her, strong, silent, acts like a balm to my troubled mind.

"I'm not going to leave you," I promise her silently. "I'm going to get to the truth. If it wasn't Oliver who killed you, I'll find out who did."

I expect her to leave. But she stays, and I drift easily back to sleep.

I wake late, luxuriating in the aura of peace cocooning my body. I search the reason for this unexpected feeling of wellbeing and remember how I sensed Nina's presence in the night. I have no trouble believing her spirit was there, that—like my sister was—she's trapped between this life and the next, waiting for justice to be done. I throw back the covers, driven by new purpose. I'm not going anywhere, I have a promise to fulfill.

My cell phone beeps, a message from Leo.

You didn't tell me if I should come home tonight. My heart sinks. I take a moment, then text him back **I'm sorry, I need more time.** I wait anxiously for his reply, feeling guilty that I don't want him here. It comes—**It's fine, I understand. I'm here if you need me xx.** Tears fill my eyes. We were good together, me and Leo.

I find myself thinking about Thomas. I've already worked out that he must be around forty-four years old and I'm still wondering about his relationship with Helen. I've noticed a tenderness in his eyes whenever he mentions her name and I can't imagine what it must be like—whether she's a friend or something more—to know that time is running out for her. Leo thinks it's only because my sister was called Nina that I've taken Nina Maxwell's murder to heart, but he's wrong. If my husband or brother was wrongly accused of murder, I'd want the truth to come out. And from the relatively little time I've spent in The Circle, I'm convinced there's a truth to be found.

I call Thomas.

"I heard something," I say.

"Oh?"

He listens while I repeat what Leo told me about Nina helping out people in The Circle, including the husbands of her close friends.

"Thank you for being so open with me," he says when I get to the end.

"The only reason I'm telling you is because something strange happened. When I was leaving Lorna's house the other day, after I'd asked her about Nina, I could have sworn she whispered 'Don't trust anyone' in my ear."

"She's probably right. The more I look into Nina's murder, the more secrets I think there are."

"Yes, but that's not the point. She told me her husband wasn't there, so I thought it was strange that she felt the need to whisper. Then, not long afterward, when I got home, I saw him coming out of the garage. So I think she might have lied. Although he could have been in the garden, because he had his gardening shoes on."

"How did Lorna seem when you spoke to her?"

"Not frightened exactly, but definitely uneasy. Maybe she was worried that Edward—if he was there—might not be happy that she was talking to me. Unless there was someone else there, someone who didn't like Lorna speaking to me." I pause. "I'm sorry, I need to go."

"Is everything all right?"

But I've already hung up, my heart plummeting at what I've just realized. Tamsin had turned up on my doorstep two minutes after I'd left Lorna's that day and had warned me against asking her questions. I thought she'd seen me come out of the house and had guessed my motive for going there. But what if she'd been there all the time? She might have gone to see Lorna to warn her against speaking to me and I had chosen that very moment to call round. Had she been listening to our conversation from somewhere close by, is that why Lorna had been so nervous? It would explain how Tamsin knew what I'd been talking to Lorna about.

I sigh, uncomfortable with the position I've put myself in. Having a foot in each camp—wanting to help Helen get to the truth behind her sister-in-law's murder, and wanting to make friends here—is becoming increasingly difficult.

Eve rings at the door.

"Come in," I say, happy to see her. Then, over her shoulder, I see Tamsin walking quickly across the square, toward her house, and my bubble of happiness bursts. Maybe Eve's visit isn't as innocent as I thought.

"How are you?" she asks, following me to the kitchen.

"I'm fine. What about you?"

She pulls out a chair and sits down. "All good. I was going to come and see you on Tuesday, toward the end of the morning, but I saw you leaving the house."

"Yes, I went out to lunch."

She nods. "With a friend?"

I laugh. "Of course with a friend. Who else would I go to lunch with?"

She shifts in her chair. "I don't know—the reporter maybe?"

I pull out the chair opposite her, playing for time. Did she see Thomas when he came by yesterday?

"The reporter?" I ask.

"Yes, the woman who told you about Nina's murder."

"Oh." There's a hair on the table and I surreptitiously sweep it onto the floor, my brain screaming *ignore! ignore!* because the more I stress about it, the more hair

I'll lose, a wretched vicious circle. "No, I went to lunch with my friend Ginny."

"Has she been back in contact with you? The reporter?" She catches my frown. "Sorry," she says, embarrassed. "Asking for a friend."

"If Tamsin isn't careful, I might think she has something to hide," I say mildly.

"It's normal that she's worried, Alice. We've only just begun to put the murder behind us and we don't want it being dragged up again." When I don't say anything, she sighs. "Look, after Nina was murdered and before Oliver was arrested," she says, choosing her words carefully, "when we'd only just found out that Nina had been having an affair, I think all her friends had a moment when they wondered if their husband could have been that person. It might only have been a moment, but it was there. And then, after we'd looked at our own husbands, we began looking at our friends' husbands and wondering if it could have been one of them. It was horrible, Alice. We were all at it, secretly trying to work out if someone from the Circle had been having an affair with Nina."

"Why would you think that?" I say, disingenuously.

She gives a little shrug. "Nina was very popular. She loved helping people and was very generous with her time. God knows how many hours she spent with Will, helping him rehearse his lines. She'd done some acting in the past, amateur dramatics, that kind of thing, and she was so happy when she discovered that Will was an actor. I'm not a jealous person and I never minded him going to see her, I was just glad that she could help him because, to be honest, I found listening to him repeating his lines a bit tedious. But, I admit, when I heard she'd been having an affair, there was that tiny moment of 'Oh God.' And although we've never discussed it, I think Maria and Tamsin probably had the same thought about their husbands."

"Why?"

"Because when Tim decided that he wanted to specialize further, Nina helped him look at various options, and it's down to her that he chose psychotherapy. And Connor was always bringing his whiskies for Nina to try because she was about the only person in The Circle who really knew about whiskey. Her parents owned a distillery before they retired and she used to joke that she was practically brought up on the stuff. She and Connor bonded over their Scottish roots, I guess." She leans forward and looks at me earnestly. "But what you have to understand is that nobody minded, not Oliver, nor any of us wives. We all loved Nina and we were glad that she had the time, with Oliver being away a lot, to help our men with their various projects. And it wasn't just men; she ran a yoga class for expectant mothers one evening a week at her house, which she started when Tamsin was pregnant with Pearl. She also ran a book club once a month. People were always in and out of her house. Sometimes Will would be there and Connor would show up with one of his whiskies so she'd call me over and the four of us would sit and chat for a couple of hours."

"You never suspected that she might have been having an affair?" I say, glad she has openly told me what Leo already had.

"Never. That's why it was such a shock."

"I can't imagine what it must have been like, everyone suspecting everyone else."

"It was terrible, especially as our first thought was that the man, whoever he was, was also her murderer. It sounds awful, but it was a relief when Oliver was charged. A terrible shock—but also a relief. We knew who had killed her, we could get on with our lives. We had nothing more to fear. If Nina had been having an affair, it didn't matter who the man was as he was no longer a suspect in her murder. It wasn't important to know his name, especially as Nina was dead. What was important was knowing that the person responsible for her murder wasn't going to come back and kill anyone else."

"You still believe that Oliver was responsible, then?"

"Yes."

"Because it's convenient to believe it." I make it a statement but I say it gently. "What if Nina's murderer is still out there somewhere?"

Eve looks uncomfortable. "I don't think he is." She takes out her phone and checks the screen. "Sorry, Alice, I've got to run," she says, standing up. "Hair appointment. See you tomorrow for coffee at Tamsin's."

Her relief at being able to get away is tangible. "Yes, see you there."

I shut the door behind her, mulling over what she told

me, more convinced than ever that Nina's murder isn't as straightforward as Eve would like me to believe. Somebody is hiding something.

But who?

TWENTY-FIVE

I'm expecting Eve and I to walk to Tamsin's house together the next morning. But when I glance out of the window I see her hurrying down her drive, as if she needs to be somewhere fast. I check my watch; it's just ten o'clock and we've been invited for ten-thirty so she must be going for a run first. Except that she isn't wearing her running gear.

I hurry upstairs to Leo's study and watch Eve as she crosses the square. When she's nearly at the end, instead of carrying on toward the main gate, she veers to the left, heading straight for Tamsin's house. Realizing that I've got the time wrong—Tamsin must have said ten, not ten-thirty—I run downstairs, find my trainers and leave the house quickly, surprised that Eve hadn't come to get me. But maybe she thought I was already there.

By running, I arrive just a couple of minutes after her. Like some of the other residents, Tamsin and Connor have enclosed their porch and as I open the outer door, I can hear her and Eve talking in the hall, on the other side of the inner door. I'm just about to knock when I hear my name.

". . . Alice actually say that the reporter hadn't contacted her again?" Tamsin is saying.

"No, not exactly."

"Did you ask her where she went on Tuesday?"

"She said she went to lunch with a friend."

"Do you believe her?"

"Yes, why wouldn't I?"

"But she didn't say that the reporter *hadn't* been back in contact with her?"

"No. She kind of evaded the question."

"I'm worried, Eve. What if she's trying to find something out?"

"Like what?"

"Like who really killed Nina."

I freeze.

"Oh Tam, you're not going to start all that again, are you?" Eve sounds as if she's stifling a sigh.

"Oliver didn't kill Nina, Eve."

My heart thuds.

"You make it sound as if you have proof." Now there's an edge to Eve's voice. "Do you, Tam, do you have proof that Oliver didn't kill her? Because if you don't, maybe you should just accept that he did."

"He used to go and sit in the square."

"Who?"

"Oliver." Tamsin sounds near to tears. "Nina mentioned it to me once, she said that sometimes, after a long day at work, he would park the car in the drive and go and sit in the square for a while, to clear his head. Sometimes, if she saw him go in, she would join him."

"But—did you tell the police?" Eve sounds scared and I take a step back, uneasy about what I might hear. I want to leave, I should leave, and come back later, once they've finished their private conversation. But I'm worried they'll hear me walking back down the drive and I can't really hear anything now that I've moved back, not clearly anyway. And then—I draw in my breath so sharply I think they must have heard me. My heart thuds again. Did Tamsin really say something about Connor having an affair with Nina? She can't have— but she must have, because now Eve is telling her that she needs to speak to him. And then she's saying something about Will, and I catch the words "see Nina" and "gap in the fence" and my mind reels even more.

"I think everyone is capable of murder, if they feel threatened," Tamsin says, her voice so shrill that I catch her words in their entirety.

I don't hear Eve's reply but then I hear my name. Thinking I'm about to be discovered eavesdropping, my heart almost stops. But instead of the inner door being flung open, their footsteps disappear down the hall and I'm weak with relief until I realize that I still need to face them. I don't know how I'm going to do it, how I'm going to sit down and have coffee with them, not just because of what I overheard but because of the shame I feel at having listened in the first place. But I have to go through with it.

I wait a moment, then wipe my sweaty palms on my jeans, take a deep breath and knock.

Tamsin opens the door.

"Sorry, I'm late," I say, panting slightly to make it sound as if I've been running.

She gives me a look, as if she knows I've been standing in the porch for the last five minutes.

"You're not late. I said ten-thirty."

"Oh, sorry." My cheeks flush. "It's just that I saw Eve leaving her house, and I thought I must have got the time wrong. Shall I come back later?"

She opens the door wider. "Don't be silly. Come in."

"Thanks."

I ease off my trainers slowly, playing for time, even more flustered now. I follow her down the hall to the kitchen. It's beautifully minimalist, all neat lines and no clutter anywhere. Compared to my kitchen, with its stacks of cookbooks lying on the worktop and a fridge-door full of photographs, it's pristine. And calming. I feel suddenly confident. I can do this.

"Hi, Alice." Eve gives me a wave. "Welcome to Tamsin's supertidy house."

"It's lovely," I say, looking around. "And admirable, considering you have two young children."

"I need the house to be tidy. It's the only thing I feel I can really control, the only thing where I'm in charge." Tamsin gives a little laugh. "The only part of my life that is mine."

There it is again, that streak of vulnerability. She comes over with a pot of coffee and I give her a smile.

"I think we all feel like that sometimes, that we've lost control. I know I did when I found out about the murder."

She stiffens, and I wish I could take the words back. I shouldn't be bringing up the murder now, not after what I just heard.

"In what way?" Eve asks, coming to the rescue.

"Everything that I thought was true, wasn't. The house wasn't what I thought it was, Leo wasn't who I thought he was. I could see the future that I'd built up in my head crumbling before my eyes. Things were happening that I had no control over. I know that sounds dramatic but it was horribly destabilizing."

"And now?" Tamsin asks. "Do you feel back in control?"

"I'm getting there. I've managed to stay in the house on my own, although I can't bring myself to sleep upstairs yet. And yesterday, I told Leo I needed space, so he's staying in Birmingham this weekend."

Tamsin raises an eyebrow. "And he accepted it?"

"Yes. For now."

She pushes a plate of homemade flapjacks toward me. "And wouldn't you rather do that—leave?"

"It's not an option anymore," I say, taking one.

"Why's that?"

"Tam," Eve warns gently.

Tamsin shrugs. "Sorry. It's not that I don't want you to stay. I'm curious, that's all. If you're sleeping downstairs, you're still not at ease in the house."

"You're right, I'm not totally comfortable yet. But I'm working on it."

Eve exchanges a quick look with Tamsin. "If that reporter contacts you again, she'll be surprised to know that you're still living there," she says.

It's clumsy, but Eve is only trying to find out what Tamsin wants to know. I decide to boot the elephant right out of the room.

"Don't worry, if I ever hear from her again, the only thing I'll tell her is to leave me alone," I say.

"So you haven't heard from her since the day she told you about the murder?" Tamsin asks.

"No."

Tension seeps out of her, relaxing her body, reminding me of a balloon deflating. She reaches for a flapjack, breaks a piece off, pops it into her mouth, then breaks another piece off, and puts that in her mouth, as if she's famished. Tamsin starves her emotions, whereas I feed mine, something I hadn't realized until now. When I think about it, there have been quite a few times when I've stood in front of the open fridge, feeding my anxiety, trying to appease it, make it go away.

There's a beautiful family photograph perched on top of a sleek gray dresser, of Tamsin, Connor and their two little daughters.

"Amber is the image of you," I say, studying it.

"And Pearl is the image of Connor," Eve says.

"Yes, I can see that, she has his eyes." I turn to Tamsin. "Your hair was much longer back then."

She reaches for another flapjack. "It used to be as long as yours but I cut it after Nina died."

"Gosh," I say.

"I'm not really sure why I did it, all I know is that it was stronger than me. Nina had had her hair cut off so maybe I instinctively thought that whoever killed her had a fetish about long hair and I was protecting myself, in case he came back and killed me. Or maybe it was just a subconscious desire to honor Nina in some way. Amber cried and cried when she saw it and I had to promise I'd grow it long again." She gives a resigned smile. "I've still got quite a way to go."

"I used to have really long hair," Eve says. "Ages ago, when I was about seventeen. I cut it because I wanted to look older. I'm too small to have long hair, it made me look like a doll. It was darker in those days too."

"Did you have it dyed white at the same time?"

"Yes. I didn't intend to but the hairdresser suggested it. Will went mad. He hated my short hair at first. Now he loves it, right down to the pink tips."

"I'm thinking of cutting mine," I say.

Tamsin frowns. "Why? It's so lovely and long."

"It's falling out. After my parents and sister died, I lost it in clumps. It was horrible, I found it really distressing. And now it's happening again."

"Is that why you've been wearing your hair up?"

"Yes."

"Is it when you wash your hair that you lose it?" Eve asks. "Because I can recommend a really good shampoo."

"No, not really. I mean, I don't notice it coming away in the shower, or even when I comb it through after—at least no more than usual. But I keep finding it all over the house, especially in the kitchen, which is just about the worst place, because it can get in the food. It won't be so noticeable if my hair is shorter. Anyway, short hair must be so much easier to maintain."

"Don't you believe it. This"—Eve points to her hair—"takes a ton of gel and a lot of patience to achieve."

I turn to Tamsin. "Eve said you used to be a model. Is that when you met Connor?"

"Yes. We met at a party during London Fashion Week. I wasn't at all interested in him, he was too brash for me, so when he asked what I was looking for in a man, I told him I wanted someone who would take me to the theater, listen to classical music with me and spend hours reading books by my side. I felt safe saying that; it was a polite brush-off because I didn't think he'd be interested in any of those things. But he told me I was in luck and a couple of days later, he sent me a ticket for *The Tempest*. I really wanted to see *The Tempest,* so I went along. Then came the concerts and the weekends away, where we would spend rainy afternoons curled up with a book. He suited me so perfectly that there was nothing to stop me falling in love with him." She takes a sip of coffee. "I should have told him that I wasn't looking for a man, then he'd have left me alone."

"But it's lovely that you both enjoy the same things," I say, surprised at the vehemence of her last remark.

She shakes her head. "We don't. As soon as we were married, the trips to the theater, the classical concerts, the books—all that came to an end. If there's something I want to see, he tells me to go with a friend." She gives a little laugh. "It's hard to realize that the man you married never really existed at all."

"I know what you mean," I say quietly, thinking of Leo. "Not that Leo and I are married."

"Didn't you want to get married?" Eve asks.

"It never really came up. Leo doesn't believe in marriage anyway. He says he's never known a happy one."

"Me and Will are happy," she protests.

"Oh, shut up," Tamsin and I say simultaneously, and the three of us burst out laughing.

Eve and I walk back across the square together, then go our separate ways. In the study, I sit at my desk. I'm meant to start working but I can't stop thinking about what Tamsin said, that Nina once told her that Oliver would sometimes go and sit in the square when he came home from work. I wish I knew if she had told the police, I wish I'd been able to hear her answer to Eve's question. But she must have told them, it would have been criminal not to. And then I remember what she said about Connor having an affair with Nina. Did Tamsin keep back information that might have helped Oliver's case, to protect Connor? Except I can't be sure she did say that he'd had an affair with Nina.

Then there was Eve's comment about the gap in the fence between our houses. Was she insinuating that Will would have been able to come and go between theirs and Nina's without being detected? And why had Tamsin said that everyone is capable of murder if they feel threatened? Did someone know that Connor, or Will, was having an affair with Nina and threatened to tell? Did Tamsin or Eve feel threatened because they thought their husband might leave them for Nina? Connor, Will, Tamsin, Eve—they could all have had a motive for killing Nina.

Suddenly ashamed at how easily I'm able to consider that one of our neighbors, all of whom have been perfectly lovely to me, is capable of murder, I lay my head on my desk with a groan. I don't even know Connor or Tim very well, my fault for not going to Maria's last Friday. I think for a moment, then lift my head from the desk and reach for my cell phone.

"I don't suppose you and Will are free for supper tomorrow evening?" I ask Eve.

"We are," she says, sounding pleased. "Is Leo coming back, then?"

"No, it'll just be me. That is all right, isn't it?"

"Of course!"

"I'm going to invite Tamsin and Connor, and Tim and Maria too. And maybe Paul and Cara," I add, remembering that it was Paul who told Leo about Nina helping her neighbors. "What do you think?"

"I think it's a great idea. Are you sure it won't be too much?"

"No, it'll be fine. I'll make something easy, like a curry."

"And Will and I will bring tiramisu, another of his grandmother's recipes!"

"Great, thank you."

Maria and Tim are free, Cara and Paul aren't, and Tamsin needs to see with Connor. She calls me back to confirm that Connor hadn't planned anything for the two of them.

"I preferred to check, in case he'd bought tickets for the theater as a surprise for me," she jokes.

"Perfect," I say, laughing. "I'll see you at seven, then."

TWENTY-SIX

In the middle of the night, I sense someone there. *It's only Nina,* I remind myself, before fear can take hold.

"I think your murderer's is still out there," I tell her. *"And I'm going to find him."* But in my mind, it isn't Nina Maxwell's face I see, it's my sister's.

I remember this when I wake up and a terrible uncertainty consumes me. Who am I doing this for? Is it because my sister never got what I considered justice for her death that I'm determined it won't be the same for Nina Maxwell? I'm not even sure what it is that I'm doing. How can I justify secretly helping to look into a miscarriage of justice when there might not even have been a miscarriage of justice?

Then a letter arrives, pushed through the door by the postman. It's so unusual to get a handwritten letter that I spend some time studying the envelope, trying to guess who it's from. I don't recognize the writing; it's slightly shaky, so maybe it's from someone elderly.

Lorna comes to mind but when I open it, and unfold the single sheet of paper inside, I understand straightway.

Dear Alice,

I wanted to write and thank you personally for accepting to listen to what he had to say regarding Oliver and Nina. I know you may not be able to help, or even wish to help. But I want you to know how grateful I am for your willingness to consider that Oliver might not be guilty, when those who knew him well were so quick to condemn him.

Please forgive me for not writing more, and for my appalling handwriting, I know that Thomas has explained my situation and that you will understand.

I sincerely hope we will get to meet each other one day.

With warmest wishes,
Helen

For a moment I wonder how Helen got my address, then remember that her brother had lived here. I feel horribly emotional as I slide the letter back in its envelope, the doubts I had about helping Thomas fading as quickly as they came. It's not as if I'm going to tell him my theories about Connor or Will, or anyone else. I'll only tell him what people have said, and leave him to draw his own conclusions. If Oliver didn't kill Nina, and someone else is murdered, I'd never forgive myself for being too afraid of upsetting people to do the right thing.

I already have most of what I need for supper this evening, because I went shopping in Stoke Newington last night. But I forgot the coriander, so I shrug on a jacket and head to the local shops.

I cross the square quickly, waving to Tim and his boys as I pass the play area. A chill wind I hadn't reckoned with drags tendrils of hair from my clip, and I button my jacket to the neck, wishing I'd worn something warmer. I'm soon at the greengrocer's, where I add a huge bunch of deep purple grapes, and some pears, apples and oranges to the coriander I need. And as I have grapes, I buy a couple of creamy cheeses at the delicatessen next door. There's a flower stall a little further along and on impulse, I buy a bunch of pale pink roses for Lorna. I'll take them round later; maybe I'll be able to catch her on her own.

Feeling the need for a coffee, I cross over to a café I've been to before. As I get nearer, I see Tamsin sitting in the window, a steaming mug in front of her. I start to move away but, suddenly aware of my eyes on her, she lifts her head. I smile awkwardly and raise my hand in a wave, as if I'm just passing by. But, jumping up, she pushes through tables and comes to the door.

"Do you have time for a coffee?" she calls over the noise of the traffic.

"Why not?" I say, glad that she's asked.

I love this café, with its vibrant hum of conversation interspersed by the hiss of the coffee machine, the clatter of crockery, the *ting!* of cutlery on plates. It's warm and crowded, but not so crowded that we can hear what the people at the next table are saying. The air is heavy with the scent of coffee and freshly baked cakes.

"You've been busy," Tamsin remarks as she takes my bags from me and pushes them under the scrubbed wooden table. "Is it for tonight?"

"Some of it is."

She nods approvingly at the roses. "I like a girl who buys herself flowers. If I didn't buy myself some, I'd never get any."

"They're not for me, they're for Lorna. She looked a bit down the last time I saw her."

"That's nice of you."

She lifts her bag onto her lap, pushes her cell phone, red leather gloves and white bobble hat into it, making room on the table, then takes out her purse.

"What can I get you?"

"Oh—thank you. Your hot chocolate looks delicious so I'll have the same, please."

She's back a few minutes later with a mug in one hand, and two plates precariously gripped in the other, each bearing a slice of cake. One is definitely chocolate but the other I'm not sure about. Coffee, maybe?

"And walnut," Tamsin says when I ask. "You choose."

"Gosh, thank you, I wasn't expecting cake. They both look amazing—why don't we do half-and-half?"

"Perfect!" There's something almost childish about her delight as she cuts each cake down the middle.

"Are we celebrating?" I ask. "It's not your birthday, is it?"

"No, but it feels like it."

"Has something happened?"

She takes her time answering. "Connor and I had a long talk last night about something that's been bothering me for a while, and well, it wasn't what I thought it was. So now I'm feeling kind of good about everything."

"That's great," I say casually. But I'm on high alert after what I overheard yesterday. "It's always good to get things out in the open, otherwise misunderstandings can build up."

She nods slowly. "I'm glad I've seen you because I feel guilty about bad-mouthing him yesterday, when you came over for coffee, especially as you'll be seeing him tonight. He's not all bad—he's a brilliant father—but we're very different people, something I didn't realize at first."

"I guess we all try to fit the ideal of the person we want to impress," I say, thinking back to what she said about Connor pretending, when they first met, to enjoy the same things as her.

"That's exactly what he said. He said he fell madly in love with me and tried to be the perfect man for me. He couldn't keep it up, that's all." She picks up her fork and breaks off a piece of the chocolate cake. "It's not just that, though," she says, pausing with her fork halfway to her mouth. "I've always suspected that he had an affair with Nina but I never dared ask him because I was afraid of what he would say, of what I might find out. Now, I wish I'd asked him ages ago and saved myself a lot of anguish." She lifts her fork the rest of the way. "This is delicious. Try it."

"So he didn't have an affair with Nina?" I ask, attacking my cake.

"No. But he wanted to."

"Oh." I put my fork down. "How do you feel about that?"

"Surprisingly fine, because it's cleared up something that's been eating away at me for a long time." She turns her plate and makes a start on the coffee cake. "A few months before she died, Nina began distancing herself from me," she says, telling me what I already know from Eve. "I thought I'd annoyed her by asking her to refer me to her therapist. She had been helping me sift through my emotions—as a friend, not a therapist—and I felt that I needed the professional help she couldn't give me. I was worried she'd taken offense, especially when she never came back with a name."

"I had therapy after my sister and parents died and I don't know if I'd have made it through without it. But—Nina saw a therapist?"

"Yes, a lot of therapists do. Some because they feel they need it, some because they believe the experience of being in therapy makes them a better therapist. I think for Nina it was a mixture of both." She stabs at her cake. "Anyway, the reason she no longer wanted to see me was nothing to do with her being annoyed with me, but because of Connor. He used to take his whiskies over for her to taste and I was fine about it, I hate whiskey so I was glad he had someone who shared his passion. But one night, he tried to kiss her. She pushed him away but the trouble with Connor is that he can't take no for an answer. When he insisted, she threatened to tell me. He begged her not to and, in the end, she agreed not to say anything. But she did a complete character assassination on him, said she despised him for even thinking he could cheat on me."

"And he took it? The character assassination?"

She looks at me appraisingly. "I know what you're thinking. You're wondering if maybe he was angry with her for what she said, and killed her."

"No, I wasn't thinking that at all," I say, my cheeks hot, and not just because I'm worried about someone overhearing our conversation, despite the distance between the tables. It's the way she said it so matter-of-factly that shocked me. Also, I can't ignore the possibility—because Lorna's words are never far from my mind—that this is another conversation that has been staged. "I was thinking that you're amazing for not minding that he kissed Nina."

She pushes her empty plate to one side and sits back in her chair. "I do mind, of course I do. But the relief of knowing that Nina only dropped me because she felt awkward around me somehow means more than knowing that Connor kissed her." She fixes me with her green eyes. "Can you understand that, Alice?"

I nod slowly. I can, because Leo lying to me, and about me, has affected me just as much, if not more, than the thought of Nina being murdered in our bedroom.

"And Connor told you all this?" I try not to sound skeptical.

"Yes."

"Well, it's great that you've worked it out between you," I say.

She nods happily. "We've agreed to start over, put it all behind us." She looks at my slice of coffee cake. "Aren't you going to eat that?"

I laugh and push my plate toward her. "Go ahead," I tell her. "I need to get going, anyway."

TWENTY-SEVEN

Leo calls me when I'm on my way home but by the time I've shifted my bags into one hand, tucked the flowers under my arm, and taken my cell phone from my pocket, his call has gone through to voicemail. I listen to his message and feel relieved when he says that Ginny and Mark have invited him for the weekend, because I've been feeling guilty about him being alone. My phone rings again and I smile when I see that it's Ginny.

I put my bags between my feet while I talk to her. "Yes, I know, Leo is spending the weekend with you," I say, because I know she'll feel that she has to tell me.

"That is all right, isn't it?" she asks anxiously. "Mark said we should invite him."

"Yes, of course, it's lovely of you."

"I don't want you to think we're taking sides."

"I don't. You said I could stay with you, remember?"

"What about you, are you doing anything nice?"

"I'm having Eve, Tamsin, Maria and their partners over for dinner. I'm doing a curry, nothing major."

"Sounds lovely."

"I have to go, I'm on the way back from the shops and it's freezing. Let's catch up after the weekend."

"Definitely! I'll call you on Monday."

I start walking again, my mind going over my conversation with Tamsin. I can understand her relief now that she knows Connor didn't have an affair with Nina, because it must have been terrible to have that hanging over her. But if she didn't tell the police about Oliver's habit of going to sit in the square to protect Connor, shouldn't she be wracked with guilt? She didn't seem to be, so maybe she did tell the police and they dismissed it. Or it's as I thought, and both conversations—the one I overheard yesterday and the one I had just now with Tamsin—have been fabricated for my benefit.

As I cut across the square to the house, I happen to look up, and see the blur of a face at the study window. My heart plummets. Leo must have come to get something before going to Ginny and Mark's. I wish he'd mentioned in his voicemail that he was coming to the house. If he had, I'd have gone for another coffee so that I wouldn't have to see him. I don't want him putting pressure on me to let him come home.

I put my shopping down in the hall, expecting him to appear at the top of the stairs.

"Leo!" I call. There's no answer so I go upstairs and push open the door to his study. It's empty. I check the guest room, because it's at the front of the house and maybe I got the wrong window, calling for him as I go. I stop in the doorway of our bedroom. It seems empty but there's something in the air—the scent of his aftershave maybe—that tells me he was here. The bathroom door is ajar. I head toward it nervously.

"Leo, are you there? You'd better not be hiding behind the door to scare me!" I try to make my voice jokey but inside I'm shaking at the thought he might jump out at me.

I give the door a shove and it smashes back against the wall with a bang. The noise ricochets through the house, a gun being fired over and over again. Stupidly, I've managed to scare myself even more.

I hurry back through to the bedroom, coming to a momentary stop when I see that the framed photograph I keep on the chest of drawers, of me and Leo in Harlestone, has been laid face down. *Pathetic!* I think, as I go downstairs, the drumming of my feet igniting my anger at the stupid game he's playing. He must have gone down to the kitchen as soon as he saw me walking across the square.

Gone completely, it seems, because there's no sign of him anywhere. I can't believe he actually left by the French windows and sneaked around the side of the house as I was going through the front door to avoid seeing me. *But didn't you want to avoid him?* a voice asks. *If you had known he was coming, you would have waited in a café until he'd left.*

The voice calms my anger. It's sobering to think that Leo doesn't want to see me any more than I want to see him.

* * *

By 7:20 everyone has arrived. Tamsin and Connor are the last; they had trouble getting the girls to bed before the babysitter arrived, Tamsin explains, giving me a kiss.

"Until I tanned their wee hides," Connor growls.

I look nervously at him, wary of the scowl on his face.

Tamsin smiles. "Don't worry, he's joking."

Connor leaves to go and talk to Will and Tim and I find myself thinking about Lorna. When I took the flowers around earlier, it was Edward who came to the door. I hoped he would invite me in, but he kept me on the doorstep, telling me that she was having a nap. Which means I'm still no nearer to knowing what she whispered, or if she whispered.

I mentioned in my text message to Tamsin and Maria that Leo wouldn't be here tonight, so there are no awkward questions. Eve and Maria are in deep conversation and I leave Tamsin to join them while I get her and Connor drinks. I don't usually make snap judgments but there's something about Connor that makes me wary. I'm surprised that he and Tamsin are a couple. She's beautiful, fragile, while there's something almost brutish about him. He's a big man, muscle, not fat. It's easy to imagine him overpowering someone.

"You seem miles away." Connor's eyes find mine and I realize he saw me watching him. I search for something to say.

"I was just wondering why you didn't ask for a whiskey, given that your job revolves around it."

"That's why I don't drink it socially. I love whiskey, but I drink too much of it for work purposes. Does Leo like whiskey?"

"Not really. He's more a G&T man."

I give him the beer he asked for and take a glass of wine to Tamsin.

"Lovely," she says, taking it gratefully.

"I'll just go and say hello to Connor, otherwise he'll think I'm ignoring him," Maria says.

Tamsin waits until she leaves. "I was telling Eve earlier about bumping into you this morning, and our subsequent chat," she says.

Her choice of words jars slightly. It's as if she wants me to know that she's told Eve I know about Connor and Nina.

"I hope you also told her about the two slices of cake we demolished."

She grins. "That too."

I look around for my glass, which I'd put down to go and answer the door. It's on the table and I go to fetch it because the more time I spend with Eve and Tamsin, the more confused I feel. There always seems to be an undercurrent of something I can't quite explain.

Still, it's a fun evening. Connor and Will are the perfect foil for each other. Will tells jokes and stories with a nervous energy and Connor's interventions are witty and ironic. He's also surprisingly laid-back. Tim is quieter, and perfectly lovely, jumping up to help me fetch and clear plates, totally at home in my kitchen, which must be the same as theirs, because he doesn't have to ask where anything is. *It's not possible that any of them murdered Nina,* I think, and again feel ashamed that I could have thought that one of them might have. Connor catches my eye and looks steadily back at me, as if he's read my mind and knows that my motive for inviting them tonight wasn't just to be neighborly. For some reason—maybe for that reason—I feel slightly afraid of him.

"Tamsin said that you found out about Nina from a journalist," he says, and the conversations that had been going on around us comes to a sudden halt.

"That's right. I'd rather have heard it from Leo, then it wouldn't have been such a shock when the reporter asked me what it was like living in a house where a murder had taken place," I say.

"Why didn't Leo tell you?" Connor's eyes are the same tawny color, I notice, as his hair. If he were an animal, he would be a lion.

"Because he knew that if he did, I wouldn't want to live here and he really wanted this house. So, in a way, he did the right thing, because once I knew, it was too late to leave."

"Why?" He's curious, not aggressive.

"Because I already felt invested in my life here. And I don't like to give up easily."

"That's good to know," he says, raising his glass toward me.

"Well, we're glad you're still here, aren't we, Will?" Eve says.

"Definitely. I can't think of anyone better to replace Nina and Oliver than you and Leo."

There it is again, the slightly awkward phrasing,

this time from Will. Or is it just me being overly sensitive?

"By the way, did you ever discover who the man was, the one who gate-crashed your party, pretending to be me?" Tim asks.

"He wasn't really pretending to be you, I don't think. He just used the fact that I thought he was you to get into the house. But no, I haven't managed to find out who he was. I'd completely forgotten about him, to be honest."

"It's strange nobody saw him," Tamsin muses.

"I don't think he stayed around long enough."

"Then what was the point of him coming along?"

I take a sip of wine to steady my nerves. "Your guess is as good as mine," I tell her.

She exchanges a smile with Eve that I don't much like. Thankfully, Connor launches into a joke and everyone relaxes into the evening again.

I don't know if it's the effect of there being so many people in the house, but later, when I close the door behind them, the silence seems heavier than usual. I stack the dishwasher, unnerved by the memory of Leo's clandestine visit. Why did he come? Was it to fetch something from the locked filing cabinet, something that he didn't want me to see? Is that why he left in such a hurry?

I delay going to bed, annoyed that Leo's secret visit has managed to destroy the relative peace of mind I'd managed to cultivate over the past few days. My dreams are a mix of him and Nina, and when I half-wake in the middle of the night, it's Leo I sense standing at the foot of my bed, not her. I go back to sleep but suddenly find myself sitting bolt upright in the bed, trying frantically to catch on to something that had occurred to me as I slept, something to do with what Ginny had said about Leo having had an affair with Nina. And then I realize—the woman who had come to Harlestone, supposedly wanting to know what it was like to live in the village, had had long blond hair.

TWENTY-EIGHT

I don't want to disturb Leo's weekend with Ginny and Mark but I'm desperate to speak to him about Nina Maxwell. My mind tells me that he couldn't have known her but my heart wonders if that was why he wanted this house so much. The thought that he didn't just know her, but had had an affair with her, won't go away and a chill goes down my spine when I remember what Thomas said, about a murderer returning to the scene of the crime. I chase the thought quickly; Leo might have concealed the murder from me but he's not a murderer.

I don't want to disturb him at work either so I wait until the end of the afternoon to send him a text.

I need to speak to you, when is a good time?

Now, he replies, and my phone starts ringing.

His eagerness is unsettling. I'm not ready, I wanted to get my thoughts in order first.

"How are you?" he asks.

"Fine. Did you have a good weekend?"

"Yes, it was good to be with Ginny and Mark. What about you, how are you getting on staying in the house by yourself?"

"I feel fine here now."

"Right."

There isn't anything particular in his voice but I don't like that a tiny part of him might be thinking that I got over my squeamishness a bit too quickly.

"Sometimes, something bad happens and then something worse comes along—like someone you trust lying to you—and the first thing doesn't seem so bad after all," I say.

He sighs. "What did you want to speak to me about?"

"Nina."

"Your sister?"

Is he doing it on purpose? "No, Nina Maxwell. Did you know her?"

"No." He sounds puzzled.

"OK, so did you ever meet her?"

"Isn't that the same thing?"

"The woman you were talking to in Harlestone one day, the blond woman who supposedly asked you what it was like to live in the village. Was it Nina?"

"What? No. Why would you think it was Nina Maxwell?"

"Did you have an affair with her?"

"Who?"

"Nina."

"Are you serious?" Now he's angry. "For God's sake,

Alice, where has this come from? You really think that I had an affair with Nina Maxwell? I didn't even know her!"

"Then who was the woman who came to Harlestone? And don't tell me she was someone who wanted to know what it was like to live in the village."

"All right." There's a pause. "She was one of the clients I told you about, who were harassing me."

"Why was she harassing you?"

His voice becomes cold. "I'm not going to explain my business dealings over the phone. Anyway, I'm glad you called. I need to get something from my study—is it all right if I come over?"

"What, tonight?"

"Yes, now."

"Aren't you in Birmingham?"

"No, I had to be in London today."

"All right."

"I'll see you in half an hour."

He cuts the call and I stand with my cell phone in my hand, thinking over the conversation we just had. There was something off about his request to come over. He tried to make it sound as if it had been in his plans all along, but it came across as a spur-of-the-moment decision, brought on by my mention of Nina. Besides, if he needed to come over, he would have called me to ask, not waited until I called him. Worry gnaws away at me. What if he *had* known Nina?

It's only a week since I last saw Leo, but he looks like someone I used to know, not because he hasn't shaved for a couple of days but because of the awkwardness between us. He's taken off his jacket and left it in the hall, as if he's expecting to stay for a while. It makes me feel that I should offer him a drink but I don't really want to.

"Hi," he says.

"Hi."

He waits and when I don't say anything more, he shrugs. "I'll go and get what I need, then."

"OK."

He returns to the hall, and I hear him rustling in his jacket. Moving quietly to the door, I see him go upstairs, two steps at a time, his wallet in his hand. A moment later, there's the familiar screech of one of the drawers in the filing cabinet being pulled open. So, he keeps the key to the cabinet in his wallet.

In his wallet. Why not in the drawer of his desk, or on top of the filing cabinet, where it would be easily accessible? Are his client files really so important that he doesn't want anyone, including me, to be able to get to them? Or is he hiding something there, something that the little key, taped to the underside of his drawer, would open?

A few minutes later, he runs down the stairs, fumbles with his jacket, then comes into the kitchen, a couple of files under his arm.

"Did you forget to take them when you came over on Saturday?" I ask.

He puts them down on the table. "What do you mean?"

"The files. Why didn't you take them with you when you were here on Saturday?"

"I was with Ginny and Mark on Saturday."

"Yes, but you came here first, I saw you in the study. And then, as soon as you saw me crossing the square you left."

He shakes his head. "Not me."

"I saw you, Leo!"

"Alice, it wasn't me, I swear."

"Where were you when you called me?"

"At Ginny and Mark's, in my bedroom." He frowns. "Are you saying you saw someone in the house?"

I think back to the blur of a face I'd seen at the window. I don't want to believe that I scared myself into thinking there was someone in the house when it was only the late-September sunshine casting its glow on the upstairs window.

"I thought I saw someone in your study, but maybe I was mistaken."

"Did you check the house?"

"Yes, and everything was fine." I decide not to mention the faint smell of aftershave in the bedroom. He's only been gone a week, it's not surprising that there are still traces of him. And maybe I knocked the photo of us over when I was vacuuming, and hadn't noticed. "But if you could check the windows, I'd be grateful."

"Sure."

He starts to head off and I feel mean not offering him a drink.

"Would you like a glass of wine?"

He retraces his footsteps. "Thanks."

I take a couple of glasses from the cupboard, find a bottle of red wine, open it, pour it.

"Thanks." He takes a sip. "I hope you were joking when you asked me if I had an affair with Nina. I didn't know her, I promise."

"It's all right, I believe you."

He pulls out a chair and sits down. "The woman who came to Harlestone—she was a journalist. She wanted to interview me about my job for an article she was writing. I'd already refused twice by phone so she thought she'd accost me in person."

"Wouldn't it have been easier to accost you at your London flat rather than travel all the way to Harlestone? How did she know you'd be there, anyway? How did she get my address?"

He takes another sip of wine. "I have no idea."

"I'm not being funny, but your job has never struck me as particularly exciting, at least not exciting enough to devote column inches to."

"Certain aspects of it are. Risk management is a hot topic at the moment."

I nod, because maybe it is.

I ask him about his weekend with Ginny and Mark and he asks about mine with the neighbors. Stupidly, I tell him that because of the face I thought I saw at the window, I found it hard to sleep.

"You shouldn't be here on your own, Alice."

"I'm fine."

He toys with his glass. "I'd like to come back."

"I need more time."

"How much more?" He leans forward, finds my eyes. "I love you, Alice. I want to be with you, not stuck in a dingy flat in Birmingham."

"You don't have to be in a dingy flat."

"That's not the point."

"It is. It's as if you're trying to make yourself as miserable as possible."

"I am miserable!" When I don't say anything, he sighs. "Do you want me to check the upstairs windows as well?"

"Yes, please."

He drains the rest of his wine. "I'll do them first."

I follow him into the hall, my arm brushing against his jacket as I stand at the bottom of the stairs. I pause, then make a split decision.

"I'll wait here in case you need anything," I say. "A screwdriver or something."

"OK."

I wait until he's disappeared up the stairs and into the guest bedroom, then wait a few minutes more.

"Is everything all right?" I call, my hand already in his jacket.

"So far. I just need to check our bedroom."

There are three windows in the bedroom, plus the one in the en-suite, which should give me enough time. I take out his wallet, open it, leaf through it quickly. At first, I think the key isn't there but then I find it, tucked in one of the two smaller slots at the front, normally reserved for stamps. I slip it into my pocket.

"All OK?" I call, pushing his wallet back into place.

"All good." My heart misses a beat—his voice is close, too close. I look up and see him standing at the top of the stairs. Can he see my hand inside his jacket? He starts coming down and I take a quick step back.

"By the way," I say, looking for something to distract him from the guilt I'm sure is showing on my face. "Did you know there's a gap in the fence between ours and Will's? Oliver used to lend Will his lawnmower and they used the gap to get back and forth between the gardens. There's one on the other side too, apparently, because Oliver used to cut Edward's grass for him."

"No, I didn't know. But it's a good idea to have them there." He pauses. "Do you think I should be offering to cut Edward's grass?"

"Eve said that Geoff does it now."

While I worry that he might need to open the filing cabinet again before he leaves—because if he can't find the key, he'll guess that I've taken it—he checks the downstairs windows.

"What time is your train back to Birmingham?" I ask, needing him to leave.

"I have to be in London again tomorrow, so I'm staying with Ginny and Mark tonight."

"They must be waiting for you to have dinner."

He gives a quick smile.

"It's all right, I'm leaving."

"I'm sorry," I say, guiltily. "I wish I didn't still feel angry with you. But I do."

I wait until he's left, then take out my cell phone and call Ginny.

"You know when you called me on Saturday to say that Leo was staying the weekend with you? Where was he when you called me?"

"Um—upstairs in his bedroom, I think. He told me that he'd left you a message to tell you he was staying with us and I realized I hadn't told you that Mark had invited him, and I didn't want you to think we were taking sides. Is everything all right? It's not because he's still here, is it? But he had to be in London today, and again tomorrow."

"No, it's absolutely fine, it's lovely of you to have him," I say.

"Are you sure you're all right with it?"

"Yes. It's just that on Saturday, I was out and when I got back, I was sure he'd been here. But he said that he hadn't, that he was at yours."

"Yes, that's right. He arrived on Friday evening and didn't go out all weekend. Mark offered to take him golfing on Saturday with him and Ben but he had work to do and spent the day in his bedroom."

"Great. Thanks, Ginny. Let's have lunch again soon."

"Call me when you know what day."

"I will."

I cut the call, feeling bad for not believing Leo when he said he hadn't come to the house. I take the key from my pocket, the one I sneaked from his wallet, and drop it into a little earthen pot that stands on my desk. I'm not going to use it, I can't. I'm not that sort of person.

TWENTY-NINE

I'm running up the stairs. I need to open the filing cabinet but I can hear someone moving silently through the rooms downstairs. I reach the study, take the key from my pocket, my fingers fumbling as I insert it into the lock. It won't turn, there's something wrong. I take the key out, try again. I need to be quick, he's checking the rooms, looking for me. The key still won't work. I jiggle it and it turns. I pull open the drawers carefully, my breath coming in short gasps, aware of soft footsteps on the stairs. The first three are full of client files. I tug the bottom one open; it seems empty but I crouch down and reach into the shadows at the back of the drawer. It's there, the metal cash box is there.

The footsteps are coming along the landing now. I close my hand around the box, lift it out, place it on the floor. The door of the guest room creaks as he pushes it open and checks inside. I don't dare breathe as I insert the tiny key in the lock. I need to hurry, he's almost here. I unlock the box; the door behind me pushes open slowly and I crouch lower, hiding myself. I lift the lid and a scream of pure terror unfurls from deep inside me. But before I can give voice to it, a hand clamps down on my mouth, silencing my scream before it's even begun.

I start awake, my breath coming in ragged gasps, residual damage from the dream I just had. I reach out a trembling hand and switch on the lamp, remembering that as I tossed and turned in the throes of my nightmare, I was aware, on another level of my subconscious, of Nina watching me. I had wanted to call out, ask her to save me from what was to come. But I hadn't been able to.

I throw back the covers and get shakily out of bed. I'm no longer sure I can do this, stay in the house by myself. The temptation to call Leo, and ask him to come home is so strong that I take my cell phone through to the kitchen with me. I'm in desperate need of a drink, something soothing, so I pour milk into a mug and find the chocolate powder. The comforting hum of the microwave soothes me and I try and recall what the metal cash box of my nightmare had held. But it's as elusive as the face of the man who stifled my scream.

I manage not to call Leo, but it's five o'clock before I feel ready to go back to bed. Although I sleep late, I'm uneasy for the rest of the day, rattled by my nightmare. The discovery of more of my hair in the kitchen, and in the bathroom, depresses me further. I'm still losing it steadily.

There's a ring on the doorbell. I go to answer it and find Eve, on her way for her morning run.

"I wanted to thank you for Saturday evening," she says. "Will and I really enjoyed it."

"I enjoyed it too," I say, smiling as she hops from one foot to another on the doorstep, already in warm-up mode. "It was lovely to meet Connor and Tim properly. Do you want to come in?"

"No, thanks, I need my run." There's a pause. "I'm not being nosy or anything, but it's hard not to see things here. Is Leo back?"

"No, he came to pick up some files."

"How is he?"

I pull a face. "Managing to guilt-trip me by feeling hard done by."

"That's not fair. He should have been upfront with you about the house in the first place."

"I know. But if he had, I wouldn't be here. I wouldn't have met you, I wouldn't have met any of you. Don't you think it's amazing, the way fate works?"

She stops moving and looks at me curiously. "Do you think it's your destiny to be here?"

"Yes. I'm a great believer that fate takes you where you're meant to be."

"For a purpose, you mean?"

"Yes, although I'm not sure what that purpose is."

"You're not trying to find the truth behind Nina's murder, then?" Behind the question, her eyes are innocent.

"But if everyone believes that Oliver killed her, surely there's no truth to be found?" I say, puzzled.

"Except you don't really believe that Oliver is guilty." *Neither does Tamsin,* I want to say, but as I wasn't meant to have overheard their conversation, I can't. "That's what I don't understand, Alice. Why do you think he didn't do it? It's not as if you knew him."

"You're right, I only know what everyone here has told me about him and that's what I find hard to reconcile: the picture you've painted of him and the violence of the crime. But I'm not trying to solve any mysteries. First of all, it's not my place, and secondly, if everyone is happy that Oliver killed Nina, there isn't anything to solve anyway."

We're interrupted by Will coming out of the house.

"Still here?" he calls over, looking at Eve in amusement. "I thought you were desperate for a run."

"I am." She starts to move off. "Bye, Alice!"

She jogs to meet Will at the bottom of the drive. They exchange a few words and she plants a kiss on his mouth before disappearing into the square. Will gives me a wave and follows at a more leisurely pace. I watch them go, acknowledging once again that the more time I spend with the people who knew Oliver and Nina, the more I feel that something is off. Eve said she knew that Leo was at the house yesterday because it's hard not to see things in The Circle. Yet Nina had apparently had an affair for several months before she died and no one, not one person, had seen someone going into her house more frequently than they should have. Which means that Nina either met up with him outside The Circle, or they were able to sneak into her house undetected—which points the finger right at Will. He'd have been able to come and go as he pleased, using the gap in the fence without fear of detection. Although Eve works from home, she goes for a run for at least an hour every morning, and spends every Thursday with her mum. If Will had wanted to, he had plenty of opportunities to go and see Nina while Eve was out.

It doesn't take me long to accept that I am the sort of person who will snoop through her partner's affairs. The key to the filing cabinet is an itch I can't get rid of. I've tried to distract myself by keeping my head down and working, but by the time I break for lunch on Wednesday, I can't ignore it any longer.

I take the key from the earthen pot and go up to Leo's study. There's no point unsticking the smaller key from the underside of the drawer in his desk if there's nothing in the filing cabinet except client files. I unlock it; the first three drawers hold exactly that—a neat row of client files lying snugly in their hammocks. I bend to open the bottom drawer and when I see that it contains client files too—not as many as the first three, because they're pushed to the back, leaving room at the front for new files—I begin to feel a bit foolish.

And ashamed. I sit down on the floor, embarrassed that a part of me had actually wanted to find something. But I need something more, because if I'm to leave Leo, I'm worried that his lie of omission, plus his lie about me—both of which have changed the way I feel about him—won't be accepted as a good enough reason, not just by Leo but by others I care about, like Ginny, Mark and Debbie. In their eyes, maybe those lies aren't so great. I still care for Leo but the trust has gone. I told him, the day we spoke about my friend, that if I couldn't trust him, I couldn't be with him. He knew, yet he still took the risk.

The bottom drawer is still open and, disheartened, I give it a shove to close it. Something shoots out from under the files; I just have time to see it before the drawer slams shut, pulling it back underneath. My heart in my mouth, I crouch down, open the drawer and reach in under the hammocks. My fingers touch something solid. I pull it toward me, expecting a book, a desk diary maybe. What I get is a black metal cash box.

I stare at it. Apart from the color—I had imagined it red, like the one I had as a teenager—it's exactly the sort of box I'd imagined the key fitting. And then I remember the nightmare I had, how the box had been black, just like this one, and how what I saw inside had caused me to scream—a scream that had been silenced by a hand over my mouth. I scramble to my feet and look nervously toward the door. Voices reach me from the road outside, a parent speaking, a child laughing in response. They calm me; it's the middle of the day, there are people around, nothing bad is going to happen if I open the box now, in broad daylight.

I unstick the tiny key from the underside of the drawer in Leo's desk, telling myself that it might not fit the lock anyway. When I lift the box from the filing cabinet, I'm surprised at how light it is. I move it a little and something slumps against the side, a small book, a diary or journal maybe. My heart thumps, Nina heavily on my mind.

I place the box on the desk and insert the key. It fits. I turn it and lift open the lid.

At first, I think it *is* a diary. But it isn't, it's a passport, one of the old blue ones that are no longer valid. I feel a rush of adrenaline. Was this Nina's? I pick it up gingerly, my fingers already shaking, because why would Leo have Nina's passport? I turn to the page where the photograph is, and forget to breathe. Taken twenty years earlier, yet instantly recognizable, it's not a photo of Nina, but of Leo. And then I see the name, and once again, the world I thought I knew crumbles around me. The passport is in the name of Leo Carter, not Leo Curtis.

I grope behind me for the chair and sit down, vaguely aware of someone ringing on the doorbell. Why would Leo tell me his surname is Curtis when in fact it's Carter? I remember then, the way he looked as if he was about to pass out, the day I confronted him about the murder, when I asked him who he was. I had meant—who was he that he could lie to me? But he must have thought I'd discovered his true identity.

The doorbell rings again, sending panic surging through me, because Leo must have noticed that the key has gone from his wallet and has worked out that I've got it. I jump to my feet; what am I going to say to him about why I took it? And then I realize—if he has a passport in a different name, he must have something to hide, something far worse than sneaking a key from a wallet.

THIRTY

I go downstairs, taking the passport with me, a sick feeling in the pit of my stomach, dreading the confrontation I'm about to have with him. I open the door and take a sudden step back. It's not Leo, but Thomas.

"Oh." I should have realized that Leo wouldn't ring on the bell, he has keys. But why is Thomas here? Did we have an appointment?

"Alice, I'm sorry to disturb you but could I come in?"

He seems almost as flustered as I feel.

"Um. Yes, I suppose so." I open the door wider, realizing how ungracious I sound. But my mind is still spinning with the discovery of Leo's passport.

He comes into the hall and I close the door behind him.

"Can I ask—did you get a letter from Helen, Oliver's sister?"

It's hard to focus. "Yes. Yes, I did."

"I'm so sorry. I saw her last week and she said she wanted to write to you. I intended to check that you were open to receiving a letter from her. But when I saw her this morning, she told me that she'd already written and had asked her carer to post it." He looks at me anxiously. "I hope she didn't put pressure on you in any way."

"Not at all," I tell him. "It was a very sweet letter. It must have cost her a lot physically to write it."

He nods. "She's so weak she can barely hold a pen. She can't hold a book either and she loves reading. Thank God for audio books." He frowns slightly. "Is everything all right? You look shaken."

"That's a good question. I don't really know." Even to my ears my voice sounds strangled. "I've just discovered something very strange."

"Is there anything I can do to help?"

"No, thank you, it's fine." I reach around him, intending to open the door so that he can leave, and find myself pausing. He's a private investigator, maybe he can help me. "Actually, do you have a minute?"

"Yes, of course."

"I really need a coffee. Would you like one?"

"I'd love one."

He follows me to the kitchen.

"Have a seat. How do you take your coffee?"

"Black, please, no sugar."

He sits down. I'm still holding Leo's passport so I put it on the table and go to make the coffee. My movements feel heavy, and I have to concentrate on getting the capsule into the machine. I take the cup over to the table, then go back for mine.

He waits until I'm sitting down opposite him, then

nods at the passport. "I haven't seen one of those for a long time."

I pick it up. "It's Leo's—my partner's. He told me he didn't have a passport and I just found this in a drawer."

"Perhaps he meant he didn't have an up-to-date passport. These haven't been in use for years."

"It's not that. It's in a different name."

He frowns. "Then—are you sure it's his?"

"It's his photo. It's the name that doesn't match." I pick up the passport and turn to the relevant page. "His surname is Curtis, here it says Carter."

"Could I see?" I hand it to him. He studies it for a moment then looks over at me. "You could always check it against his birth certificate."

"I wouldn't know where to find it."

"Hm. What about his bank cards? Are they in the name of Curtis?"

"Yes, I suppose so. I mean, I've never noticed."

"What about his mail?"

"Um, I don't know. I've never actually seen any mail for him." I look at him, worry creasing my brow. "Is that strange? We weren't living together before we moved here, he had a flat in London so his mail went there. And since we moved here—it was only a month ago but he should have received some mail here, shouldn't he?"

"I would have thought so."

I raise my cup to my lips, trying to push away the black cloud of terror looming behind my eyes. My hand is shaking so much that coffee spills everywhere.

"Sorry," I say, horribly aware of the tears pricking my eyes.

He reaches out and takes the cup from my hand, then goes over to the sink and comes back with a cloth.

"Can I make you another coffee?" he asks, mopping up the mess. "Or would you prefer some water?"

"Water, please."

He goes back to the sink and I hear the sound of running water, then cupboard doors being opened and closed as he looks for a glass. His movements are measured, giving me time to compose myself.

He brings the water over to me. "Thank you," I say, taking the glass gratefully. Our hands brush and I pull away, confused by the electricity shooting through me at the feel of his skin.

He sits down. "If I can do anything to help."

I take a shaky breath. "I think Leo might have known Nina."

He doesn't seem shocked, just looks at me intently, and it crosses my mind that maybe he's known all along that Leo knew Nina. Maybe that's why he came to our drinks evening, maybe he wanted to see up close the man he believes is responsible for her murder. Is that the reason he's been visiting me, hoping I'll let something slip? The sense of impending doom makes my heart race so fast I feel dizzy.

"Why do you think that?" he asks. His voice is calm and some of my terror subsides.

I tell him about the blond woman who turned up in Harlestone.

"And you think it was Nina?"

"I don't know. I mean, I didn't see her face or anything, I just noticed she was blond."

"Did you ask Leo about her?"

"Yes. At first he told me she was a client who was harassing him—"

"Is he a lawyer?"

"No, he's a consultant. In risk assessment."

He raises a dark eyebrow. "And he gets harassed by clients?"

"That's what he said. But later he told me she was a journalist who wanted to interview him."

"Do you remember when this was?"

"Not long after we met, so late January, early February last year." I pause, remembering that Nina had been killed at the end of February.

He nods. "Where does Leo work?" He's in full investigator mode now.

"In the Midlands. But he used to work in London."

"Do you know if he saw a therapist?"

"I don't think so. But I only saw him at weekends, he stayed at his flat during the week, so maybe he did."

He looks up then and the concern I see in his eyes makes me afraid. I can't help it; afraid for Leo, afraid for me, I feel close to tears again.

"Maybe she was just a journalist who happened to be blond," he says.

"I know. And I'm sure she was. It's just that Leo knew about Nina being murdered here before he bought the house but he didn't tell me."

This time, he can't hide his surprise. "That must have been—"

"Devastating," I finish for him.

"Did he say why he didn't tell you?"

"He said he knew I wouldn't agree to live here if I knew about the murder and he really wanted this house."

"Why this particular house?"

"For obvious reasons, it was cheaper than other properties we'd looked at so he made out that it was because I wouldn't have to sell my home in East Sussex to help buy it. But he also admitted that he wanted this house because it's in a gated residence. That's when he told me he was getting harassed by clients, something he'd never mentioned to me before." I raise my eyes to his. "I did ask him if he knew Nina. He said he didn't and I believed him. But that was before I found his passport."

"Would you like me to look up Leo Carter, see what I can find?" Maybe he sees the panic in my eyes; although I want to get to the truth, engaging a private investigator to look into the man I'd been hoping to spend the rest of my life with is a huge step. "I don't mean as a private investigator," he says quickly. "I mean as a friend. Here, now. I can google him, see if anything comes up."

"Yes," I say. "Could you?"

He takes out his phone. "There probably won't be anything," he says reassuringly.

"And if there's not?"

"Then you'll need to speak to Leo." He smiles to lessen the tension. "Maybe he just didn't like the surname Carter."

I watch, barely daring to breathe as he types into his phone. I keep my eyes fixed on his face, not on his screen, looking for a sign that he's found something. It remains immobile, professional. I'm aware of his fingers scrolling down, then stopping. He reaches for the passport, opens it to the photo page with one hand. His eyes flicker from screen to photo and back again, staying there for a while as he reads.

I'm afraid to ask. "Have you found something?"

He raises his eyes to mine.

"I think you might want to read this," he says quietly, passing his phone to me.

I look down at the screen, my heart thudding, and see a photo similar to the one in Leo's passport, along with a news story about Leo Carter being sent to prison in 2005 for two years. For fraud.

My heart slows to a dull beat, keeping rhythm with the thought throbbing in my head. *Leo went to jail?* It's so far away from what I thought that I have trouble focusing on the words in the article, something about him having been a compliance officer for an asset management company. Panic whirls in my stomach.

"I don't understand," I mutter.

He clears his throat. "Unfortunately, in my line of business, changing identity to conceal a criminal background is fairly commonplace." He pauses. "Leo didn't mention it to you?"

"No."

"You need to speak to him."

I nod. "I know."

"Then perhaps I should leave." He gets to his feet. "Please, don't get up, I can see myself out." He walks to the door, then stops. "If you need anything, anything at all, you have my number."

THIRTY-ONE

Silence shrouds me like a blanket. I sit without moving, trying to work through the emotions that assault me mercilessly, one after the other—disbelief, bewilderment, fear and anger. It's the cold that finally moves me to my study for a sweater. I can't find one so I put on my robe, tying it tightly around me.

I haven't called Leo, I couldn't bring myself to. Again, it's not a conversation I want to have with him over the phone and he's in Birmingham until tomorrow evening. I want to talk to someone. Normally, I would have called Ginny because she's nearer and could have come over. But she's too close to Leo, so I call Debbie.

"I'm so sorry, Ali," she says, stunned at what I've told her. "Coming on top of him not telling you about the murder, you must be devastated."

"I am," I say, brushing away the tears that I haven't been able to hold back. "I feel so lost. I told him everything about me, everything. I didn't hide anything, I was one hundred percent honest. That's what makes it so hard."

"I know," Debbie says. "Why don't you come and spend a few days here, clear your head a bit?"

"I'd love to, but I need to speak to Leo first. He's not back in London until tomorrow evening. I was going to ask him to go to Ginny and Mark's like last week but I'll get him to come here. He's going to think I've forgiven him for not telling me about Nina."

"Would you like me to come to you?"

"It's lovely of you to offer but I need to speak to him alone."

"Let me know how it goes and if you need anything, just shout."

"Thanks, Debbie."

It takes me a while to call Leo.

"Alice?" Once again there's that hope in his voice, that I'm calling to ask him to come back.

"Are you working in London on Friday?"

"Yes."

"Then you can come home tomorrow evening."

"Really? Brilliant. Would you like to go out for dinner?"

"No, it's fine. See you tomorrow."

"Yes—thanks, Alice."

In the morning, I find it impossible to concentrate on the translation I'm meant to be doing. My stomach jitters at the thought of seeing Leo this evening. He texts me when he arrives at Euston and suddenly, I'm scared. I have no idea how he'll react when I tell him that I know who he really is. I don't think he would harm me but who knows what he's capable of when he's already been capable of so much?

I press my face to the window and call Ginny. I haven't been out at all today. In the square, a fierce wind whips the fallen leaves into a frenzy. Under the nearest tree, a small child, his little arms outstretched, tries to catch them, and they fall around him like extra-large confetti. His parent is filming the scene on his phone. It's Tim, I realize, with his youngest son.

"Hi, Alice," Ginny says cheerfully. "How are you?"

"Leo's arriving any minute now," I say, my eyes still on the little boy.

"Yes, I know, he told me you said he could go back."

"Only to talk."

"Oh."

"I hate to ask but would you mind coming over? It's just that I might need some back-up."

"Is everything all right?"

I turn from the window. "No, not really, but I'll explain when you get here. Could you leave now? It'll give me time to speak to Leo on his own first."

"I hope it's not what I think it is," she adds sadly. "I love you both."

I want to tell her that it's worse than she could possibly imagine.

Even though I'm expecting him, the sound of his key in the lock makes me jump. There are the usual sounds from the hall: the rustle of his Barbour being shrugged off, then his jacket, the chink of coins as he throws it over the newel post.

"Alice?"

"In here."

He comes into the kitchen. He's wearing a sweater I've never seen before. He's had his hair cut and the stubble he had five days ago is thicker, almost a beard. It makes him look younger. It makes him a stranger.

"How are you?" he asks.

"Not great."

I'm sitting at the kitchen table, like I was last time, when I confronted him about the murder. His passport is balanced on my knees, out of sight.

There's a scrape as he pulls out the chair opposite me.

"Has something happened?"

Questions crowd my mind. There's so much I want to ask him, too much.

"Is there anything you want to tell me?" I ask, needing him to come clean, because then, there might be hope for us.

"Apart from being sorry I didn't tell you about the murder?"

"Yes, apart from that."

"No, I can't think of anything." He rubs his hand over his chin. "I mean, I'd like to know how much longer you're going to hold it against me, because we can't go on like this." He leans forward, his eyes pleading. "I love you, Alice. Can't we put this behind us? I made a mistake. I'm sorry. Can't that be an end to it?"

"I'm going to ask you something, and this time I'd like the truth. Do you have a passport?"

He sits back, fake puzzlement on his face. "You know I don't. I told you that."

I can't look at him, I can't believe he's thrown our relationship away.

"What about a birth certificate? Have you got one of those?"

"Yes, of course."

"Can I see it?"

"I don't have it here."

"Where is it?"

"It's in a safe, in the bank."

The pause was slight, but I noticed it. "In a safe? I didn't know you had a safe." He doesn't say anything, just stares at me mutely. "Why don't you start by telling me who you are?" I say.

"What do you mean?"

It goes on a bit too long, the pretense that he doesn't know what I'm talking about. Tired of his lies, I take his passport from my knees and lay it on the table.

"I found this in your filing cabinet."

The change that comes over him is dramatic. His eyes dart around the room, looking for somewhere to hide and, realizing that there's nowhere to go, because I'm sitting right in front of him, they come to rest on me. The panic I see in them sends waves of adrenaline coursing through my body. For one horrible, frightening moment, I think he's going to lunge at me across the table.

The silence as we stare at each other becomes

unbearable. My heart is racing so fast I think I might never be able to breathe again. Behind me, there's a tiny *drip-drip* from the tap in the sink. I focus on it, counting each drop. When I get to ten, I swallow painfully and force words out.

"Is your real name Leo Carter?"

It's there in his eyes, the knowledge that he's cornered. He puts his elbows on the table and buries his face in his hands.

"Leo." His despair makes him oblivious. "Leo," I say, raising my voice.

He lifts his head. His tear-streaked face is ashen. "You must hate me."

I can't cope with his pain. I push my chair back and move to the sink, turning the tap so that it no longer drips. "I could never hate you," I say to his reflection in the window.

He rubs at his face. "I shouldn't have lied to you, I know. But I couldn't tell you the truth, I was too scared that if I did, you wouldn't want to be with me anymore."

I turn back to him. "What is the truth?"

He sighs heavily. "When I was young and stupid, I worked for an asset management firm. I allowed myself to be influenced by a couple of guys I worked with and spent a few months in prison for fraud."

"How many months?"

"Four or five." I keep my eyes fixed on his face. "Maybe a bit more," he admits.

"I looked you up, Leo. I looked up Leo Carter. You spent two years in prison."

He shakes his head. "No. I was released early for

good behavior." I don't say anything. "But you're right, it was more than a year, I'm not sure—"

I walk over to the table, hating that he still hasn't got it. "It doesn't matter how long you spent in prison, whether it was two months or two years," I say. "What matters is that you're still lying to me."

The desperation on his face is hard to witness. "I'll tell you everything, I promise. That woman, the one who came to Harlestone, I wasn't lying, she was a journalist. She wanted to write about the irony of someone who was once convicted for fraud advising clients on risk management issues. She kept on asking me and each time, I refused, because I didn't want you to find out what I'd done." New tears fall from his eyes. "Don't you see, Alice? I've turned the bad stuff I did into a positive. I'm making amends."

"Which is great, Leo," I say. "But it doesn't change the fact that at heart, you're dishonest." I stop, struggling for the words to tell him why it feels like the ultimate betrayal. "What I can't get my head around is why you didn't tell me the truth when I told you everything about me. Everything."

"But I went to prison!"

"Exactly. You paid the price for what you did." I turn at the sound of a car pulling up outside.

"Where are you going?" he asks.

"To open the door. Ginny's here."

"Ginny?"

"Yes, I asked her to come."

"But we haven't discussed anything yet."

"There isn't anything to discuss."

"Alice, please!"

"I'm sorry, Leo. It's over."

I go and open the door. Behind me, I hear Leo sobbing and I hate myself for not being able to comfort him.

"Is Leo still here?" Ginny asks anxiously, coming into the hall.

"Yes."

"What's happened?"

"I'll let Leo tell you," I say, reaching for my coat. "It's his story, not mine." I give Ginny a hug. "I'll call you later."

In the square I sink onto a bench and let the vicious wind whip tears from my eyes.

THIRTY-TWO

Ginny calls me.

"Where are you?" she asks.

"Sitting in the square."

"Coming now."

"I can't believe it," she says when she arrives a couple of minutes later, looking as shocked as I still feel. "I can't believe Leo spent time in prison."

I shove my hands deeper into my pockets, only realizing now how cold I am. "It's why he could never admit to having a passport. He must have changed his name officially, because he bought the house in the name of Leo Curtis."

"I'm so sorry, Alice, this is awful for you."

"How is he?"

"Upset, broken."

"Why do I feel guilty?"

"Because you still care for him."

"Maybe. But I can't forgive him."

"Because of his crime? I mean, fraud is terrible but it's not as if he murdered anyone."

"You're right, he didn't. But it's not that."

"Is it because he spent time in prison?"

I nod slowly. I wish I could explain to her why it matters so much, but I can't.

"What are you going to do?" she asks.

"Go back to Harlestone, I suppose. I'll ask Debbie if I can stay with her until I can get the tenants out of my cottage." Tears fill my eyes. "Six weeks, Ginny. Leo and I barely lasted six weeks."

She puts her arm around me. "Why don't you come and stay with us for a while?"

"That's lovely of you but I'm going to ask Leo if he'll let me have the house for another couple of weeks."

"But—won't he want the house? Especially as he's going to be working in London from Monday."

"Why? Has the Birmingham job finished?"

"Yes."

"Oh," I say, deflated. "Could he stay with you for a bit, do you think?"

"Of course. But why do you need the house for another couple of weeks? It won't take you long to pack up your stuff, will it?"

"No, but I need time to work out what I'm going to do."

"Can't you do that from ours? You can stay as long as you like, you know that."

I shake my head. "I want to be here."

She looks curiously at me. "This wouldn't be about the murder, would it?"

"What do you mean?"

"Leo says you've become a bit obsessive about it."

"No, it's not about the murder." I hate that I'm lying to Ginny. "I want to be able to say goodbye to everyone properly. Anyway, I don't think it's unreasonable to ask for a couple of weeks, given what he's done."

"You're right." She links her arm through mine. "Come on, let's get you back. You're freezing."

We leave the square and cross over to the house.

"Do you think Leo will stay in The Circle?" I ask Ginny.

"I think he intends to."

It doesn't seem fair, somehow.

She leaves me in front of the house with a hug. "If you need anything, you know where I am."

Leo is waiting for me in the kitchen, leaning against the worktop. I go and lean against the sink so that I'm facing him.

"I wish there was a bigger word than sorry," he says. "But there isn't."

"I'm sorry too," I say.

"What for?"

"That it hasn't worked out."

He nods. "It's all right. I always knew this would happen once you found out."

I push myself upright. "But not if you'd been upfront with me from the beginning!" I say, upset that he doesn't seem to understand. "If you'd told me about your prison sentence when we first met, everything could have been different."

"It wasn't a risk I was prepared to take." He gives a wry smile. "I've never been able to own up to my mistakes, I've always preferred to lie my way out of trouble. At least, that's what my therapist told me."

"You saw a therapist?"

"Yes. But not anymore. My parents found her for me when I was released from prison."

Something jars. "Are you really estranged from your parents?"

He sighs. "How could I introduce you to them when I was using another name? You would have found out pretty quickly that they were Mr. and Mrs. Carter, not Mr. and Mrs. Curtis."

I don't know why I feel shocked. "Don't tell me. They're loving parents, you had a pretty decent upbringing."

He ducks his head. "Something like that."

"And they don't know about me."

"I'm sorry."

I throw him a look of disgust. "It's bad enough that you lie about yourself. But that you lie about other people—you should be back in therapy, Leo, you still need help." I pause. "Are you going to stay here, in The Circle?"

He takes a glass from the cupboard and I move from the sink so that he can get to the tap. "Yes. I told you, I love this house, despite its history," he says, his back to me.

"I was wondering—I know it's your house, but would you let me stay here a couple more weeks? I'd like a bit of time to get used to the idea of going back to Harlestone."

He takes a drink of water, then turns to face me. "I thought you'd be overjoyed to be going back."

"No, not really. It feels like a failure, to be honest."

"I'm going to be working in London from Monday. But don't worry, I won't get in your way."

"I'd like two weeks on my own. Ginny says you can stay with her and Mark."

I feel his eyes on me. "Why do you need two weeks on your own?"

"I told you, I need to get used to the idea that I'm going back to Harlestone."

There's a rattle as he places his glass in the sink. "So it's not because you're still trying to solve a murder that's already been solved?"

"I'm not trying to solve it. But as I've already told you, I don't believe that Oliver killed Nina."

"Why are you so sure that he didn't?" he asks, perplexed.

I look for something to tell him. "I read an article. Apparently, Oliver's sister has always maintained his innocence."

"Well, of course she's going to say her brother is innocent! Are you telling me that because of an article you read in a newspaper, you've decided to go on a one-woman crusade to clear Oliver's name? You should leave things alone, Alice."

"So you think it's all right that the real killer got away with it?"

He throws his hands up in exasperation. "We're not going to get anywhere going backward and forward like this. You can have two weeks and then I want my house back."

"Thank you," I say. But he's already gone.

PAST

She's late. Again.

"How are you today?" she asks, once she's sitting down.

I smile. "Aren't I meant to ask you that?"

"Therapists are allowed to have off days too, aren't they?"

The fact that she's relaxed enough to joke with me is pleasing. Could it mean that she's finally going to tell me what I've been waiting to hear?

"No, I don't think they are," I say.

She laughs.

"Shall we begin?" I pull my pad toward me. "Over the last few sessions, we've been exploring the reasons for your unhappiness. You've told me about your childhood, your teenage years, your experiences in the world of work and we came to the conclusion that all those were mostly positive experiences. I think now we need to focus on when you first began to think about yourself as unhappy."

A small frown creases her brow.

"If you remember, during our last session, we touched on your marriage as a possible source of your unhappiness," I prompt.

"The thing is, I don't think I am."

"Sorry?"

"Unhappy."

I turn my head toward the window, giving her time to reflect on what she's just said. Through the slats in the blinds, I can see brightly lit garlands strung across the street outside.

"I mean, how can I be?" she goes on. "I'm married to the most amazing man who would do anything for me, who gives me everything I want. That's what attracted me to him in the first place—that, and the fact that he was different from the men back home. He's a real gentleman." She laughs nervously. "I know that sounds old-fashioned but it's true."

I turn my attention back to her and smile. "There's nothing wrong with old-fashioned."

"I think what I've been feeling is guilt. Guilt that I have so much. That's what has been making me unhappy, not Pierre. I love him." She pauses. "You know that quote by Henry David Thoreau, about happiness being elusive?"

"Yes?"

"Do you think it's true?"

"I think it's worth careful analysis."

"Then maybe I need to turn my attention to other things."

"That's probably a very good idea."

"The only thing is, I'm not sure where to begin."
She looks across at me. "I wish I didn't feel so anxious
about everything."

I put my pen down, close my pad. "Do you remem-
ber that during our first session, we spoke about relax-
ation therapy?"

"Yes. It sounds amazing."

I stand up. "Why don't we make a start?"

THIRTY-THREE

Debbie calls me the next morning.

"How are you?"

I don't have to pretend with Debbie. "Miserable. It's over between me and Leo."

"I'm so sorry, Ali."

"The worst thing is, nobody is going to understand why I left him. As Ginny pointed out, it's not as if he murdered someone. Everyone will think I've left him because he spent time in prison—which it is. But not in the way that they think."

"Does Leo understand?"

"I'm not sure that he does. After everything I told him, I don't think he really gets it. But you do, don't you, Debbie? You know why I can't be with him now."

"Yes," she says softly. "But, you know, if you want people to understand, you could tell them. You could explain why you feel as you do."

"I can't," I say, my voice tight. "I'd rather they think I'm unforgiving."

"Have you decided what you're going to do?"

"Short-term, Leo is letting me have the house for the next two weeks but long-term, I'm not sure. Could I come and stay with you for a bit? I'm not going to be able to get my cottage back until February so I'll have to find another solution until then."

"You can stay with me for as long as you like, you know that. We're hardly going to get in each other's way here. You can have the two bedrooms at the back of the house, make one into a temporary study, and in return, you can come for a ride with me each day, on Bonnie. How does that sound?"

Sudden tears fill my eyes. "Idyllic," I mumble.

"It's going to be all right," she says.

"I hope so."

"What are you doing today?"

"I don't know. I'm not sure where to begin. I feel a bit lost."

"Then why don't you take the day off, give yourself a break? I'm sure there's plenty to do in London. You're not going to be there much longer, you should do some sightseeing."

"You know, that's a great idea," I say, feeling brighter.

We chat for a while longer. Debbie suggests that I only take what I need from the house and arrange with Leo to leave behind my personal pieces of furniture—my desk, the dressing table which belonged to my mother, my sister's bookshelf and chest of drawers, my dad's chair—until I can move back to my cottage.

"Or, if he doesn't agree, you can store them in one of the barns," she says.

"I'm sure it will be fine. I don't want to leave Leo on bad terms, I'll still want to know how he is, how he's doing." I think for a moment. "I know I said I'd be down in two weeks, but if I decide to leave before, would that be OK?"

"You can arrive tomorrow as far as I'm concerned," Debbie says cheerfully. "Today, even."

"Thanks, Debbie, what would I do without you?"

We hang up and I decide to do as she suggested. I make a list of the places I really want to see before I go back to Harlestone and start with the Victoria and Albert Museum. Just sitting on the tube surrounded by people getting on with their everyday lives makes me realize, once again, how claustrophobic living in The Circle can be for people like me, who don't have to leave it every day to go to work. For those who do, coming home at the end of the day must feel like entering a haven of calm and privilege, an oasis in the midst of a teeming, bustling city.

I force myself not to think of Leo, not to think of anything except having a nice day out. On the way home, I bump into Eve.

"Hi, Alice!" she calls. She nods at the various bags I'm carrying. "What have you been up to?"

"I took the day off and went to the Victoria and Albert, it was amazing. And then I looked around the shops in South Kensington, treated myself to a couple of things, then went to a café and watched the world go by."

"It sounds perfect."

"I'm going to do some more sightseeing this weekend. The Tate Britain tomorrow, and if I've got time, I'll take the riverboat to the Tate Modern. I've reserved Sunday for Kensington Palace, with a walk around Hyde Park afterward."

"They've got a gorgeous tearoom there, in the Orangery. You should treat yourself."

"Good idea—why don't you join me?" I say, because I'm not going to be seeing her for much longer. "My treat for being such a lovely neighbor." I don't want to tell her that I'm leaving The Circle, because she would ask why and I haven't worked out what I'm going to say yet.

"I'd love that, especially as Will has rehearsals all weekend," she says.

"Great! Shall we meet there at 3 p.m.?"

"I think we might need to reserve. Would you like me to do it?"

"Yes, please."

The next evening, Thomas calls.

"I hope you don't mind me disturbing you at the weekend; I wanted to see how you are."

"I'm fine, thank you," I say, touched that he's called. "Well, not fine exactly because I'm still coming to terms with Leo not being the person he said he was. I'm trying to take my mind off it by exploring London."

"That sounds like a great idea. Where have you been?"

I tell him about my trips to the Victoria and Albert and the two Tate museums. "Tomorrow I'm going to Kensington Palace and for a walk in Hyde Park. What about you? Have you had a good weekend so far?"

"Yes, I have my son here. My ex-wife and I have Louis alternate weekends. I took him to Harry Potter World today, which exhausted me far more than it exhausted him."

I laugh. "Hopefully you'll have a quieter day tomorrow."

"I hope so. We'll probably end up going to kick a ball in the park."

"That still sounds energetic. Actually, I'm glad you called because there's something I've been meaning to ask. When you turned up on the doorstep the other day, was it only to ask if I'd received a letter from Helen? I mean, you could just have called."

"You're right, I could have. But when we spoke the week before, you hung up rather abruptly and I didn't know if I'd upset you in some way, or if what we'd been talking about had upset you. It played on my mind, so when Helen told me she'd written to you, I felt I had an excuse to call round and check that everything was all right."

"It wasn't you," I say. "I can't remember what we were talking about but it definitely wasn't anything you said that upset me."

"We were talking about your neighbor and wondering if there was someone who hadn't liked you asking her about Nina."

"Oh, yes." I pause, remembering it was the thought that Tamsin might have been listening at Lorna's that day. "I still don't know what to think. I can't believe she was worried about Edward hearing what she was saying, and the other suspect I had—well, I've dismissed her now. But I'm certain there are secrets here in The Circle."

"I'm sure there are."

Thinking of Tamsin has made me remember something that I've been meaning to ask Thomas. "Tamsin mentioned something the other day. Apparently, after Nina was killed, she cut her hair and she wondered if subconsciously, she was worried that if the killer had a fetish about long hair, he might come after her next. Do you think he did? Have a fetish, I mean?"

"It could be that. Or it could be symbolic. Throughout history, cutting off a woman's hair was often used as punishment for those thought to be immoral, as a shaming tactic. During World War Two, in France, it was the fate of many of the women who slept with Germans. They were seen as collaborators."

"So, if Nina's murderer thought she was immoral because she was having an affair, surely that points the finger at Oliver?"

"Or someone who wanted to have an affair with her and was jealous that she was having an affair with someone else. Or someone who was judging her for having an affair." There's a pause. "Sorry, Alice, Louis is waiting for me to read him a bedtime story. I'd better go."

"Of course."

I hang up, smiling at an image of him reading a story to his son. Louis. It's a nice name.

THIRTY-FOUR

It's raining the next day, so instead of going for a walk in Hyde Park, I head to the British Library, where I wander around in awe at the magnitude of the place. When I come across a bank of computers, I remember my conversation with Thomas the previous day and type in "hair fetishism." I read a few articles and then, on impulse, type in "hair fetishism in murders." Several links come up, to articles that appeared in a variety of French newspapers and as I scan them quickly, I realize that they all are about the same murder, which took place in Paris. My French is quite good and, as I read the first article, my blood begins to run cold. The victim, a thirty-one-year-old woman called Marion Cartaux, had had her hair cut off before she was strangled.

I study the photos of her. Like Nina, she had long blond hair. I look at the date of the murder—11th December 2017, approximately fifteen months before Nina was murdered.

It doesn't take me long to read everything I can find.

I want to dig deeper but when I check the time, I'm already late for my appointment with Eve.

I hurry to the Orangery.

"Sorry I'm late," I apologize, tucking my wet umbrella under the table and giving her a hug. "I went to the British Library and got carried away looking at all the beautiful first editions."

"When I saw the rain, I thought you might change your plans."

"This is lovely," I say, looking around. "I'm glad you managed to get a table by the window."

"I nearly didn't get a table at all. Apparently, you have to book ages in advance. They'd just had a cancelation, so I was lucky."

We order tea and while we're waiting for it to arrive, Eve tells me that she couldn't sleep last night and almost called me for a chat, because she saw my lights on.

"I actually slept well last night," I say. "But there've been a few times when I thought there was someone in the house, and even though I know it's just my imagination," I add, because I'm not about to tell her that I believe in spirits, "I always leave the light on in the stairwell now." She frowns, so I carry on guiltily, "I know I shouldn't waste electricity but it makes me feel safer."

She shakes her head. "That's not why I'm frowning. It's just that there were a couple of times when Nina thought there was someone in the house. But as it was always when Oliver was away, like you, she put it down to her imagination. It used to freak her out, though."

My heart thumps. "When was this?"

"A few months before she died."

"Did you tell the police?"

"No, because it was only you saying the same thing that made me remember. As it happened when Oliver wasn't there, I thought the same as she did, that she was feeling vulnerable because she was alone in the house. I know if Will is away, I'm much more aware of noises in the house. Every creak could be a footstep on the stairs, that sort of thing."

I sit back to let the waiter place a stand of sandwiches, scones and cakes on the table, followed by two pots of tea. "What did Nina say, exactly?"

"Just that she would wake suddenly and think there was someone in the room. Then the feeling would disappear."

I reach for one of the teapots and fill her cup, not wanting her to see how much her words have affected me. If Nina experienced the same thing as me, maybe it's time to stop trying to convince myself that it's her spirit I've been sensing—and face up to the horrible reality that someone really has been coming into the house at night.

I don't say anything to Eve, but when I get home, I open my laptop and find a small boutique hotel not far from The Circle. I book myself in for four nights, then go upstairs to the bedroom where Leo and I used to sleep and begin filling a large canvas bag with a few basic necessities—pajamas, underwear, toiletries. I don't like giving up but I can't sleep in the house, not since my conversation with Eve. But if someone has been getting into the house, how have they been doing it? And why would they come back time and again and risk being seen? How do they manage to slip away undetected, without leaving the slightest trace of themselves? Whoever it is must have keys. As far as I know, only Leo and I have keys.

I open the wardrobe to get some jeans and T-shirts and give a sigh of exasperation. Once again, some of my shoes have been pushed to one side and I'm suddenly overwhelmed by memories of me and Nina playing hide and seek in the cottage in Harlestone. There were plenty of places to hide but Nina would always choose one of the wardrobes, knowing I'd be too scared to open the door in case she jumped out at me. Sometimes I'd get Dad to help and we'd creep quietly to the wardrobe where I thought Nina was hiding and, when I opened the door, he would roar and scrabble among the clothes like a tiger, giving her an even bigger fright than she would have given me. Sometimes we chose the wrong wardrobe and we'd all end up in fits of giggles.

I blink away the tears that happy memories of my family always bring. I miss Nina, I miss my parents, I miss all the things we were never able to do together. And then, as I stand there in front of the wardrobe, it hits me. Someone, at some point, has hidden inside it.

Stunned, I sink onto the bed. It has to be Leo. The day I thought I saw him at the study window, I had smelled his aftershave in this bedroom. I'd thought he was hiding behind the bathroom door but he must have been in the wardrobe. He told me he wasn't here, and Ginny had confirmed he was upstairs in the bedroom at hers when he called. Ginny wouldn't lie to me, so he must have sneaked out when she wasn't looking, while Mark was playing golf with Ben. Why didn't he want me to know he'd been here? I can't get my head around it. It's such a bizarre thing for a grown man to do, hide in a wardrobe. Would he even fit? It's extra deep, with a good space between the door and the rail, so maybe he would.

I go over and step inside, then turn myself around so that I'm facing the bedroom, and close the doors. There's plenty of room for me, plenty of room for Leo once he'd made enough room for his feet. And more importantly, if someone were to come into the bedroom now, I'd be able to see them through the slats in the doors. But they wouldn't be able to see me.

I push open the doors and step back into the room, freaked out at the thought of Leo hiding in the wardrobe. All I want is to get out of the bedroom, out of the house. I reach up to the shelf above the rail where my jumpers are folded in a neat pile. The one that I want— navy, to match my jeans—is at the bottom of the pile. I put my hand under it to ease it from the shelf without disturbing the rest of the jumpers and my fingers brush against something soft, like fur. I cry out and instinctively pull my hand back, shuddering at the thought of what I might have touched, thinking a dead mouse or a giant spider. I wait for my heartrate to slow; I want to be able to lift the pile of jumpers so that I can see what's lurking underneath, rather than pull the whole lot out, bringing whatever it is with them. The shelf is too high, so I fetch the chair from the corner of the room and place it in front of the wardrobe. I climb onto the chair and, steeling myself, carefully lift the jumpers.

A scream bursts from me and, losing my balance, I topple over the back of the chair, the jumpers flying from my hands as I crash to the floor. Horribly winded, I struggle to catch my breath, assessing myself for damage. My elbow and left leg are throbbing painfully and the back of my head doesn't feel good either. I take a moment, then force myself to my feet, using the fallen chair to lever myself upright, ignoring the needles of pain shooting through my arm. Tears of fright spring to my eyes. I want to believe that I imagined the swathe of long blond hair that was hidden under the jumpers but I know that I didn't. My mind spins with jumbled denials—*it can't be Nina's hair, it can't be, Leo didn't know her, he didn't kill her, he can't have, he wouldn't have*—which collide with the facts—*he wanted this house, this particular house*—and reach a terrifying conclusion—*he knew Nina, he killed her here in this house, he cut off her hair and kept some as a trophy. And now, he's returned to the scene of the crime.*

My fear that the hair is Nina's is greater than any pain I'm experiencing. I reach for my cell phone to call the police, aware that I'm going to sound crazy. Maybe I am crazy, maybe it was my imagination, maybe it was something else I saw. Shaking, I inch nearer to the wardrobe, craning my neck toward the shelf. It's still there, an amputated ponytail of long blond hair, tied top and bottom with red ribbon.

Except that Leo can't have killed Nina. And while I'm going through all the reasons why Leo can't be

Nina's murderer, my eyes still fixed on the hair, my mind is registering that there's something not quite right about it. I move nearer for a closer look; the texture—unnaturally glossy—looks too perfect. I don't want to touch it—but I need to know, so I reach out and run a tentative finger along it. And breathe a sigh of relief. The hair isn't real, it's synthetic.

I slump onto the bed. Why has Leo hidden a pony-tail of synthetic hair in the wardrobe, which anyone seeing it—anyone who knows what happened to Nina here in this house—might mistake for her hair? Did he put it there to frighten me? Did he see me take the key from his wallet that day and decide to play a little game with me in retaliation?

A cold anger takes hold. I'm tempted to call the police and tell them I've found a ponytail of Nina's in my wardrobe, tell them they should arrest my partner. But they'd come here first to check, and would see that it's synthetic. Maybe I should call Leo and pretend that I've called the police, frighten him a little. But he would laugh at my naïvety, tell me it was just his little joke. I'm dismayed at how little I know him, dismayed that he could stoop so low. Furious, I send him a message. **FYI, the hair is pathetic!** He replies almost at once. **I didn't do it for you to like it.**

I pick up my navy jumper from the floor but leave the others where they are, wanting to get out of the house as quickly as possible. My arm is still throbbing so I go to my study and peel off my T-shirt to check for damage. There's a huge lump below my elbow, where I whacked it against the chair as I fell, and I'm betting on a massive bruise appearing on my leg in the next few days. There's also a bump on the back of my head.

Needing some water, I head to the kitchen. There are more strands of my hair on the worktop and it seems like the last straw in an already lousy day. I go to brush them into the bin, and stop. Caught in the light coming from the fluorescent bulb fixed to the underside of a shelf, they are a pale blond, a shade paler than my hair. I pick one up carefully and roll it between my fingers. It isn't real.

Dropping it into the palm of my hand, I run back upstairs to the bedroom and take the ponytail from the shelf. It confirms what I expected; the hair I found on the worktop comes from the ponytail.

It's hard to get my head around this new twist in Leo's game; I never told him about losing my hair after my parents and sister died, so he wouldn't have known how much it would upset me to find strands of it all over the place. He must have had some other motive. Was I meant to think that it was Nina's hair? Has it been him creeping around the house at night, leaving hair for me to find? It can't have been, because that very first time, on the Sunday after our drinks evening, he was the one who heard someone in the house, not me. Unless he only pretended to have heard someone, so that in the future, I would blame the prowler for any nocturnal creeping I heard.

But why would he have done that? The answer comes to me almost immediately—so that, when I found out about Nina, if I didn't want to be with him because of his lie, I'd be too anxious to stay by myself. And he'd get to stay in the house while I moved out.

Except that it hadn't worked out like that. He had moved out and I had stayed. So he had upped his game and prowled the house at night, hoping to terrorize me into leaving. I remind myself that he's been in Birmingham most of the time, not in London. But I don't know that he actually stayed there. He could have been here, staying in a hotel at night and commuting to Birmingham each morning, just like he had before. I try and reconcile the Leo I know with a person who would creep around a house where his ex-partner is sleeping, to scare her into leaving, and can't. I'm being ridiculous. If Leo had wanted me to leave before now, he would have told me. After all, the house is his.

THIRTY-FIVE

The hotel is lovely, the room beautifully decorated in subtle shades of gray, with a gray marble bathroom and white fluffy towels. Relief washes through me. For the first time in weeks, I feel safe.

So that Ginny and Eve won't worry, I message them to say I'm going away for a few days and that I'll be back at the house on Thursday. I ask Ginny not to tell Leo and she promises she won't. If Leo knows I'm not there, he might move back in.

I toss and turn all night, and in the morning, I feel so empty that all I want to do is hibernate until I check out on Thursday morning. I'd intended to carry on working from the hotel but I don't want to think about anything, not my translation, not my parents or my sister, not Leo and his lies, not Nina's murder. All I want is to lie in the dark, with the curtains drawn, and switch off from everything.

For the next two days, I sleep, listen to podcasts, take long baths and order food from room service, telling the lovely girl who brings it that I'm feeling under the weather. At one point I find myself thinking about Thomas, and remembering that I haven't told him about the murder in France, I call him.

"Both women had their hair cut off," I say once I've told him about Marion Cartaux. "Do you think the two murders could be linked?"

"They could be," he says. "But it's more likely to be two murders committed by two different people with the same fetish. It's infuriating to think that nobody on my team—or me, for that matter—thought to look abroad. You'd make a very good investigator, Alice."

"Thank you," I say, pleased.

"I'll get my people to do a bit of digging and get back to you." I sense him hesitate. "Maybe I could come by tomorrow afternoon and let you know what I find? Or Friday, if you prefer."

"Tomorrow is better for me."

"Two o'clock?"

"Perfect."

I hang up. I could have chosen to see him Friday, because I'll be back at the house by then. But it seemed too long to wait.

The next day, I walk back to the house at the end of the morning, feeling bad that I'm looking forward to seeing Thomas when Leo and I have only just split up. But at this moment in time, he's one of the few people I can trust.

It's a crisp October day and apart from a handful of parents and children in the play area, the square is almost deserted. I glance over at Tamsin's house, wondering what her plans are for the morning, and see someone standing at one of the upstairs windows. I'm unable to make out if it's her or Connor but I lift my hand in a wave, knowing that whoever it is can see me.

"Alice!"

Turning, I see Will running to catch up with me, a brightly colored scarf around his neck.

"Hi, Will," I say cheerfully, hoping he didn't see me coming out of the hotel. If I didn't want anyone to know I was staying there, I should have chosen one further away from The Circle. "Have you been shopping?"

"No, just for a walk. I'm reading through a new script and I needed a break. Are you back already? Eve said you'd gone away."

Too late, I remember that I was meant to be away until tomorrow. "Yes, I just got back," I tell him.

He nods distractedly. "Eve really enjoyed the Orangery the other day."

"Me too. I don't know about Eve, but I ate far too much."

"I just wanted to say—Eve told me that there's been a couple of occasions when you've thought there was someone in the house at night?"

"It was probably my imagination," I say, wondering why he's mentioning it.

He gives me a quick look. "I don't want to worry you but I think Eve told you that Nina thought the same thing."

"Yes, she did."

"Then—are you sure you're happy staying there on

your own? If Leo isn't coming back yet, you're welcome to stay with us."

"That's lovely of you but honestly, I'm fine."

He turns his blue eyes on me. "I'm sorry, Alice, I don't understand why you're willing to risk it, especially after what happened to Nina."

"But if Oliver killed Nina, how can I be at risk?"

"What if he didn't?"

I stop walking. "What are you saying, Will?"

He shoves his hands in his pockets. "Just that I've never been entirely happy with the theory that he killed her. I didn't know Oliver well, we'd only been neighbors for five months, but I knew him well enough to be as shocked as everyone else when he was accused of murdering Nina. But when they said his suicide proved his guilt—that I couldn't believe. I didn't say anything because as I said, everyone knew him better than me, so I thought there was something about him that I'd missed. Then you arrived and began questioning things, and now, I don't know. What if the real killer is still living among us, hiding in plain sight?"

He seems so genuine, so completely genuine. But at the back of my mind, there's a voice telling me that he's an actor, an incredibly good actor. If Eve told him of the conversation we had in the Orangery, did she also tell him what I said last week, that I no longer think there's a mystery to solve? Has Will just laid a trap for me?

"I'm really sorry if I've made you question what happened," I say, walking on, because I want this conversation to end as quickly as possible. "I didn't have all the facts at the beginning but now that I do, I honestly believe that Oliver killed Nina over the affair she was having. And if the police didn't think there was anything further to investigate, I'm not quite sure why I did." I give a self-conscious laugh, because I can act too. "Sometimes I wonder if it was just to make myself more interesting than I actually am—you know, to try and make my mark here in The Circle."

"Oh. Well, in that case, I guess I'll have to accept it too," he says, and I can't work out if he's disappointed or relieved.

We reach the gate opposite our houses.

"Good luck with the script," I say, heading toward my drive.

"Thanks, Alice. And remember, if you need anything, I'm just next door."

I give an involuntary shiver. It should have sounded comforting. But somehow it had felt like a threat.

THIRTY-SIX

Thomas turns up at two-thirty, wearing a dark blue suit and light blue shirt, and looking paler than usual.

"I've just come from Helen's," he says.

"How is she?"

"Not good. It's hard sometimes, remembering how she was."

"I'm sorry," I say, wondering again if he and Helen were more than friends.

We go to sit in the kitchen.

"We went out together once or twice when we were at university," he says, uncannily reading my mind. "But we realized we were better friends than girlfriend and boyfriend." He dips his hand into the inside pocket of his jacket and draws out his wallet. "This is us in better days," he says, taking out a photo. "I took it with me this morning, to show Helen."

I study it a moment. The younger version of him has longer hair, and his arm is around the shoulders of a girl with a pretty face and laughing blue eyes. They look so carefree that I wonder how hard it was for Helen to see the photo.

"She said she was glad she didn't know then that her life would be cut short at the age of forty-three," Thomas says. "Sometimes I wonder if Nina had the same thought, when she knew she was about to die."

I hand the photo back to him. "Don't."

"Sorry," he says, chastened. "I always feel down after I've visited Helen, but it's unprofessional to bring my low mood to work with me." I feel a momentary disappointment that he thinks of me as work. "Also, I didn't have time for lunch so I probably need sugar. I'm diabetic."

I jump to my feet. "You should have said, I thought you looked pale. Let me give you something to eat— what can I get you?"

"A biscuit or banana will be fine, if you have either of those."

"I do, but I haven't had lunch yet and I was going to make myself an omelette. Cheese and mushroom— will that do?"

"It sounds amazing, but I don't want to put you to any trouble."

"It's not a problem."

He takes out his phone and lays it on the table. "I'm afraid I don't have any news about the murder in France. I should hear back before the end of the week, though."

"I couldn't find anything about anyone being arrested for it," I say.

"I couldn't either. Which makes me think it's an ongoing case. That said, I still think it's a long shot that the two murders are connected, given that they occurred in different countries."

While I peel the mushrooms, I tell him about the conversation I overheard between Eve and Tamsin when I went to Tamsin's for coffee. I feel bad for telling him, but I want his take on it.

"Does Leo know about the gaps in the fence between your house and your neighbors?" he asks.

"Yes, I told him. He thought it was a good idea."

"I hope you don't mind me asking, but how are things between you?"

"He isn't living here at the moment."

"I'm sorry."

I turn away, not wanting to think about Leo. I tip the whisked eggs into two frying pans and begin cooking them slowly. The simple act of pulling the cooked edges into the center and letting raw egg run into the space left behind is strangely soothing.

"Have you met Tamsin's husband?" Thomas asks.

"Yes."

"What do you think of him?"

"I don't think he's a murderer, if that's what you mean."

"I know I'm not telling you anything that you don't already know, but appearances can be deceptive."

"You're right, I do already know that," I say feelingly, adding the mushrooms and a sprinkling of cheese to the eggs.

He gives a sympathetic smile. "But if Tamsin thinks he had an affair with Nina," he begins.

"He didn't," I say quickly, and launch into an

account of my conversation with Tamsin in the café. "The thing is," I say when I finish, "I'm not sure how much of it was genuine."

"Oh?"

I fold the omelettes in half, pressing down on them lightly with the spatula to melt the cheese inside. "Just that a part of me wonders if I'm not being set up by Tamsin. When people asked how I found out about the murder, I told them that a reporter called me. And ever since, Tamsin has been worried that the reason the reporter contacted me is because the police are actively looking into the murder again. Even though I've denied it, I'm sure she thinks that I'm still in contact with the reporter. What if she's feeding me misinformation on purpose? Those two back-to-back conversations—the one I overheard, and the one I had the next day with her in the café—there's something off about them."

"It does sound as if Tamsin is doing everything to let you know that her husband didn't kill Nina. On the other hand, she also told you that he didn't take rejection easily."

"I know exactly how Eve and Tamsin must have felt when they heard that Nina had had an affair," I say, sliding the omelettes onto plates and carrying them over to the table. "Those few seconds last week, when there was the possibility of Leo having known Nina, were hard. Even Maria must have wondered about Tim, if only for a few seconds. And he's the least likely candidate."

Thomas looks appreciatively at the omelette. "This looks wonderful, thank you." He picks up his knife and fork. "I'm curious as to why you think Tim is the least likely candidate. He and Nina could very easily have bonded over their interest in psychology."

"Maybe, but he and Maria are a really solid couple. So are Eve and Will, which is why my money would have been on Connor."

I sit down opposite him and watch him surreptitiously from under my eyelashes while we eat. It feels right, him sitting here at the table with me.

"You know when you said that Nina having her hair cut off could have been some sort of judgment?" I say. "If someone *was* judging her, isn't it more likely to have been a woman?"

I regret my words immediately.

"Are you thinking what I'm thinking?" Thomas asks, reading my face.

"I don't know." But I am, it's just that I feel terrible for thinking it.

"Tamsin definitely had a motive," he says. "Not only had Nina turned her back on her, she also suspected that her husband was having an affair with her—"

"But she's always believed that Oliver didn't murder Nina," I interrupt. "She's thought all along that he's innocent. Why draw attention to the fact that someone else killed her, if she was the one who did it?"

"Because, as we've already worked out, she could be playing a very clever game. And didn't you overhear her say that everyone is capable of murder?"

Suddenly, it becomes too much. "No. No. I'm a hundred percent sure it wasn't Tamsin. I can't believe the thought even crossed my mind." I sit back in my chair, needing to physically distance myself from him, from everything that we're doing. But it's not far enough, so I stand and start gathering up our plates. "I'm sorry, but this isn't right. Can't we just accept that Oliver murdered Nina?"

"Like everyone here was happy to do," he says softly.

"Maybe it was him," I say.

He stands and takes the plates from me. "Maybe it was," he says. "But until I know for sure, I can't rest, for Helen's sake and for Oliver's sake. Believe me, if I thought he was guilty, I wouldn't be investigating the murder. But there's too much that doesn't add up. Also, Oliver swore to Helen that it wasn't him. She says he wouldn't have lied to her and I believe her." He carries the plates over to the sink, then turns to face me. "I'm feeling more and more uncomfortable about having dragged you into this. I'm not sure—maybe it would be better if I leave?"

"No, please don't. But perhaps we could talk about something else."

"Yes," he says, relieved. "Good idea."

I don't know if it was the simple act of cooking for him that allows us to move to the point where we feel comfortable sharing information about ourselves. Thomas tells me he and his wife divorced three years ago and that he now lives in South London. I feel for him when he explains that he and his wife wanted to share childcare for their six-year-old son but because they didn't want to disrupt his daily routine, they agreed that his wife would be the main carer for the moment.

"All that will change when he moves school next September," Thomas explains. I've made coffee and we're back at the table. "His new school is nearer to where I live, so he'll be staying at mine every second week. I can't wait. I miss him so much."

He also tells me that he grew up reading Sherlock Holmes and, after studying Psychology and Criminology at university, he decided to become a private investigator instead of joining the police force, as he'd intended to do. In return, I tell him about me and Leo, how the move to London was meant to be our new start, how I feel guilty that I can't forgive him for lying to me and how bemused I feel for not realizing that he could.

"When you think about it, it's not surprising you found living together hard if you only used to see each other at weekends," Thomas remarks. "Two days a week over what—twenty months?—only amounts to around three to four months in real time."

"I never thought of that," I say, feeling slightly less guilty.

I also tell him about losing my parents and sister and admit that I'm worried my sister is the reason I've become invested in Nina's murder.

"I think, if it wasn't for Nina—my sister Nina—I wouldn't be here, talking to you, trying to help you get to the truth. I'm confused about my motives, I'm worried they're not pure. I didn't know Nina, I shouldn't be this involved. But sometimes, when I think about my sister, or about Nina, they become intertwined. It's like they're the same person."

His eyes are full of compassion. "Do you think you and Leo are going to be able to work things out?"

"No, because there isn't any me and Leo, not anymore. Hiding his past from me is a lie too far. I can't be with him."

He nods slowly. "What are you going to do?"

"This is his house, not mine, so I'll be going back to Harlestone. He's agreed that I can stay here until next weekend. I think he felt it was the least he could do."

"Then—Helen was asking if she could meet you. I wasn't going to mention it yet because I didn't know if it was something you'd feel comfortable doing. But if you're only here for another week or so—" His voice tails off.

"I'd love to meet her," I say.

"Are you sure?"

"Yes."

For the first time since I've known him, he looks slightly awkward. "What about next Wednesday? Perhaps I could take you to lunch, and then we could go to Helen's together?"

I feel a rush of pleasure. "That would be lovely."

"And while we're having lunch, maybe you could explain to me how to get to Harlestone. Just so that I can let you know if there are any developments," he adds with a smile.

"I'm sure I could," I say, smiling back at him.

"Good." He looks curiously at me. "How did Leo take it when you told him it was over?"

"Resigned, I think. It's not just his lies, it's also the stupid thing with the hair."

"What stupid thing?"

"It's actually really embarrassing, which is why I didn't mention it before."

"What happened?"

Reluctantly, because it shows Leo in such a bad light, I tell him about the hair scattered around the house and how I found a blond ponytail in the wardrobe.

"The funny thing is, he was probably trying to scare me into thinking it was Nina's hair that I kept finding," I say. "Except that it didn't occur to me that it was. I presumed it was mine, because I lost a lot of it after my parents and sister died and I thought it was happening again, because of the stress of the murder."

"Is that why you always wear it up?"

I raise my hand and touch my hair self-consciously. "Yes, it's become a habit now. I also think Leo has been prowling around the house at night, another tactic to scare me. I can't be with a man who thinks it's all right to psychologically manipulate someone."

Thomas frowns. "What do you mean, prowling around the house? I thought you said he wasn't living here."

I give a dry laugh. "Exactly."

"I'm not sure I understand."

"Just that there have been a few nights when I've thought there was someone in the room, watching me. It was pretty terrifying the first couple of times, but as nothing ever happened, I managed to convince myself that there wasn't anyone there, that it was Nina's spirit I could sense." My cheeks grow hot. "I know that sounds stupid, but after my sister died, I used to sense her presence, especially at night, so it was easy to convince myself I was experiencing the same sort of thing. As I said, nothing ever happened and there was never any trace of anyone having been here, so I was fine with it. But then, the other day, Eve told me that before Nina died, there were a couple of occasions when she'd also thought there was someone in the house. Which kind of smashes my spirit theory."

"But why would Leo do that?"

"To scare me into leaving the house."

"But, as it's his house, he would have been entitled to ask you to leave."

"Yes—but maybe he wanted it to come from me, so that people in The Circle would think I was leaving because I was too scared to stay in the house, not because he was kicking me out. Everyone knows he didn't tell me about Nina. He needs to redeem himself if he's going to carry on living here."

"But if Nina experienced the same thing, it must be someone else doing the prowling." Thomas sounds perplexed. "Who else has keys to your house?"

"No one, as far as I know."

"Are you sure about that? It's quite usual to give keys to neighbors, in case of emergencies. My neighbor has a set."

"Leo never said that he'd given anyone keys but I can always ask him."

"Did you ask him about the prowling?"

"No, I forgot, probably because it didn't seem important compared to his other lie. But I asked him about the hair. I told him it was pathetic and he said he didn't do it so that I would like it. It makes me wonder if I ever really knew him." I give him a rueful smile. "Can we change the subject?"

By the time he leaves an hour later, I feel we're finally friends. I know he feels it too. As we stand at the door, saying goodbye, I don't think either of us wants the afternoon to end.

"Are you sure you still want to be involved in all this?" he asks, locking me with his eyes so that I can't look away.

"If Oliver didn't kill Nina, I want her killer brought to justice."

"No matter who it is?" he says softly.

I think of the people here in The Circle, some of who I consider friends. But then I think of Nina, of how she died and how she must have suffered. And of my sister, who didn't get justice for her death.

"No matter who it is," I reply firmly.

THIRTY-SEVEN

Before going back to the hotel, I call Leo. He's still at work but I'm no longer worried about disturbing him.

"Apart from you and me," I ask, plunging straight in, "does anyone have keys to our house?"

"Why—is there a problem? Have you locked yourself out? I can come over."

"No, it's not that." I take a steadying breath. "I'm going to ask you something and I'd like an honest answer. Have you been letting yourself into the house at night?"

"Sorry?"

"It's a simple question, Leo. Have you been letting yourself into the house at night and creeping around, trying to scare me?"

"It's also a bizarre one. Why would I do that?"

"To get me to leave the house."

"You really think that's something I'd do?" His voice is low and I remember that he's at work. "Anyway, I'm in Birmingham most of the time, remember?"

"But not all of the time."

"Can you hold on a moment?" I hear him say something to someone about needing to take a couple of minutes and then he's back. "Look, I might be dishonest but I'm not a psychopath."

"Really? What about the hair?"

"What hair?"

"The ponytail in the wardrobe."

"I have no idea what you're talking about."

"Come on, Leo, you admitted it!"

"Admitted what?"

I can't keep hold of my anger. I'm tired, so tired of his lies.

"Hiding hair in the wardrobe and spreading it around the house to make me think that it's Nina's!"

There's a long pause. "Alice. You're beginning to worry me. I honestly have no idea what you're talking about."

The calmness of his voice infuriates me further. "I messaged you! I told you the hair was pathetic and you said you didn't do it so that I would like it!"

"Yes, the shorter hair, my beard. It wasn't for you, I wasn't trying to impress you or anything. I just didn't shave for a few days and liked it, so thought I'd carry on letting it grow." There's a pause. "Can we rewind? To the part where you accused me of creeping around the house?"

My mind is still trying to catch up with what he said about the hair. "I'm not imagining it, Leo."

"I didn't say you were. I thought there was someone in the house after our drinks evening, remember?"

"After the first couple of times, I did think I was

imagining it," I say. "Because nothing ever happened. But Eve told me that before Nina died, she used to think there was someone in the house."

"The first couple of times?" His voice rises in alarm. "How many times has this happened?"

"I don't know—four or five, maybe."

"And you've carried on staying there?"

"Yes, because nothing ever happened. As I said, I thought I was imagining it. But to get back to my original question, does anyone else have keys to the house?"

"Yes, Will and Eve. I gave Will a set after we moved in."

My heart plummets. "Right."

"You don't seriously think either of them have been letting themselves into the house to try and scare you?"

"No," I say, although my mind is screaming Will's name.

"What was all that about hair in the wardrobe?"

I cringe internally at the mix-up. "Sorry, I've got a call coming through. It's Debbie. Can I call you back later?"

"Sure."

I hang up. Debbie isn't calling but I need to think. I really need to think.

Ten minutes later, I'm on Eve's doorstep waiting for her to answer the door.

She flings it open. "Perfect timing!" I can hear voices coming from the kitchen. She opens the door wider. "Come in."

"No, it's fine, I don't want to disturb you, I just—"

She reaches for my arm. "Don't be silly, the others are here. It's a bit noisy with the children but I thought it was about time we had tea at mine."

"Great," I say, remembering that after their yoga session on Wednesdays, Eve goes with Tamsin and Maria to collect the children from school, and then they have tea together.

I follow her to the kitchen, which is full of people. Despite the cooler weather, the French doors to the garden are open and Maria's three boys and Tamsin's two little daughters run backward and forward, taking cake from the table and carrying it outside to eat. Tamsin and Maria are sitting at the table and Will and Tim are leaning against the worktop, mugs of tea in their hands.

"Hi, Alice," they chorus.

I give a little wave. "Hi, everyone." I look over at Will and Tim. "I didn't realize you were part of the Wednesday afternoon gatherings too."

"We're only honorary members this afternoon, because we both happened to be at home," Tim explains.

"And because I overheard Maria offering to bring one of her chocolate cakes," Will says. "You need to try some, Alice, it's the best."

"Sit down." Eve hoists herself onto the worktop next to the table. "Will, pass Tamsin a mug for Alice."

I pull out the chair next to Maria and she cuts me a slice of cake while Tamsin fills my mug with tea.

"Thanks," I say, trying not to think that at one time or another, I've suspected three of the people in the room of having murdered Nina.

"Did you have a nice time away?" Eve asks.

"Yes, thanks. Actually, that's why I came over—Debbie, the friend I was staying with, is coming to spend a few days with me and I'd like to give her keys so that she can come and go as she pleases. Leo said that you have a set?"

"Yes, hang on a second." Will goes over to the wall next to the fridge. "How is he, by the way?"

"Fine, thank you. Working hard as usual." I still don't feel ready to tell them that it's over between me and Leo.

"They're here somewhere," Will says, running his eye over a row of keys. He chooses a keyring and holds it up. "It's not this one, is it?"

"Those are mine," Tamsin says.

"I thought they were." Will frowns and turns to Eve. "Apart from your mum's spare set, Tamsin's seem to be the only ones here that aren't ours. Have you got Alice's?"

"No, I didn't even know we had a set."

"Leo gave them to me after they moved in. I put them here with the others." He turns back to the hooks. "Come and have a look, Alice, you'll recognize them better than me."

I leave my cake and walk over to where he's standing.

"Can you see them?" he asks.

"No."

"We did have them, because I remember seeing a label with number 6 on it. I don't remember Leo taking them back but maybe you could ask him."

"I just spoke to him, he was the one who told me you had a set."

Will scratches his head. "I don't know where they could be. Eve, did you move them, put them somewhere else?"

"How could I, when I didn't know we had any?" she says archly. She jumps down from the worktop. "Maybe they're in the study."

"Why would they be there?"

"I don't know but it's the only other place I can think of to look. Come with me, Alice."

I follow Eve to the study, and we search the desk and its drawers. But there's no sign of the keys.

"Weird," Eve says. "I'm sorry, Alice, I'll carry on looking once everyone has gone."

She doesn't sound too worried and another possibility adds itself to the ones already crowding my mind, none that I like very much. Could Will be lying? Maybe he's put the keys somewhere else, or they're in the pocket of the jeans he was wearing last time he went on a night prowl. But maybe it's not him, maybe someone saw our keys on the wall by the fridge and took them. I look over at Tamsin, then at Tim and Maria. They are all frequent visitors here.

"No problem," I say, except that it is a problem, because now I know that Leo isn't my prowler, I won't be able to sleep in the house when I leave the hotel tomorrow, not when a set of keys has gone missing.

I finish my cake, make my excuses and leave.

"When is your friend arriving?" Will asks, coming to the front door with me.

"Friday," I say.

"Well, let's hope we can find the keys before then."

Back at the hotel, my phone rings. It's Ginny.

"How are you?" she asks.

"I'm fine."

"Are you sure?"

"Yes, why?"

"I had a call from Leo. He's worried about you, Alice. He said you were accusing him of prowling around the house at night, and something he didn't understand about him spreading hair everywhere."

"It was a misunderstanding," I say. "And anyway, he's exaggerating."

"Hm." She doesn't seem convinced. "Are you still away?"

"Yes."

"I'm sorry, Alice, that's what I don't understand. You ask Leo if you can have the house for two weeks and then you go away."

"I'll be back tomorrow."

She sighs. "Are you going to tell me what's going on?"

"There's nothing going on. Sorry, but I really need to go. Can I call you in the morning?"

"All right, but—"

"Thanks, Ginny, I'll speak to you then."

PAST

I like my new client. I can already tell she's going to be more of a challenge but that's OK. She sits opposite me, her slim legs crossed, oozing confidence. She is a woman at peace with herself. But we all have darkness within us and the deeper it's buried, the more interesting it is.

I take my pad from the table and my pen from my pocket. I could use a laptop for my notes but clients still like to see a good old-fashioned notepad. The problem with using a screen, I guess, is that the client never really knows what we're doing behind it, whether we're taking notes or watching something on Netflix.

I begin asking her the standard questions and she raises an amused eyebrow.

"Really?" she says.

I frown and, chastened, she sits upright, uncrosses her legs, straightens her skirt, and turns her attention to giving me her answers.

"Why are you here?" I ask, when we get to the end.

And then I give her the usual spiel about how anything she says won't go further than this room.

This room. I look around it, at the pale pink walls, at the window that looks onto the road outside. There are no blinds on the window shielding us from prying eyes, just curtains which I can't close, not at this time of the day. It's why I've made sure we're sitting toward the back of the room. Discretion, as always, is everything.

"I don't have any major problem," she says. "I just think that it would be good for me to be in therapy, to experience what it's like. And to talk. It's always good to talk, isn't it?"

"It certainly is," I agree.

So we talk, about her childhood—happy; her teenage years—no real problems; her career—she loves it. The one thing she doesn't talk about is her husband. I know she's married so that in itself is telling.

I put down my pad. "How long have you been married?" I ask.

She looks surprised, so I look pointedly at her left hand, at the thin gold band on her ring finger.

"I might be widowed," she says.

"Are you?" I ask.

"No." I wait. "Seven years," she says. "I've been married seven years."

"Seven happy years?" I ask.

"Seven ecstatic years. Not an itch in sight."

I suppress a sigh. She's disappointed me.

I lean toward her and fix her with my eyes. "Do you

know what Henry David Thoreau said about happiness?"

Now she looks disappointed. She leans forward too, stares right back at me. "Yes," she says. "I know exactly what Thoreau said about happiness. And it's a load of bollocks."

THIRTY-EIGHT

The next morning, I check out of the hotel and cross the square to the house, my feet rustling crisp fallen leaves as I walk. I could have booked myself in for another couple of days but I don't like being bullied, and making me afraid to stay in the house is a form of bullying. So, I'm going to do what I did before, and stay awake during the night. If I hear anything, anything at all, I'll call the police.

It's cold, and there's no one sitting on the benches in the square, no one even walking across it on their way to work, which isn't surprising, given that it's half-past ten. It's amazing how conspicuous it makes me feel. For all I know, any number of people could be watching me from their upstairs windows. I raise my eyes and turn my head, scanning the houses as I walk, starting on the left-hand side with number 1 and carrying on to numbers 2, 3 and 4, then to Eve and Will's, past theirs to ours, onto Lorna and Edward's, then Geoff's, then Maria and Tim's. And stop. Because Tim is there, in one of the upstairs bedrooms, watching me watching him. I raise my hand in a wave, glad he can't see the shiver that runs down my spine, and he waves back. I pick up my pace, eager to be inside but as I go through the gate, Edward comes out of his house, his gardening shears in his hand.

"Good morning, Alice," he calls. "Been for a walk?"

"Yes, it's always lovely at this time of the year. How are you and Lorna?"

"We're fine, doing well."

"Actually, I wanted to tell you that I'm going to be leaving The Circle. But not Leo. He'll be staying."

"Oh dear, I am sorry," he says. "When will you be leaving?"

"I was going to leave next weekend but I might go earlier."

"Really? Right. Well, we'll be very sorry to see you go."

"Would you tell Lorna?" I ask.

"Yes, of course."

"I'll come and say goodbye," I promise.

"You do that. Lorna will be pleased to see you."

I flick my eyes toward Maria and Tim's house. Tim is still at the window. Edward follows my gaze and gives Tim a wave.

"Bye, Edward," I say distractedly. I start to move off but he shuffles closer.

"Don't tell anyone when you're leaving," he whispers. He pitches his voice back to his normal level. "Bye, Alice."

* * *

I let myself into the house, my heart thumping. First Lorna, now Edward. Two warnings, don't trust anyone and don't tell anyone. Who are they warning me against? Edward had seen Tim watching us. Is that why he said it?

I pace my study, thinking about Tim. There's nothing physically creepy about him and when they all came for dinner, he was perfectly lovely, helping me in the kitchen. But there's something slightly creepy about the way he always seems to be watching from the window. It could be perfectly innocent. He's studied psychology, and isn't psychology the study of people, how they act, react, interact? And if he's training to be a psychotherapist, it's normal that he finds people fascinating. Anyway, psychologists and psychotherapists help people, they don't kill them.

No sooner has that thought entered my head, something shoots forward from the recesses of my mind, a news story from a few years back about a woman and her therapist, who ran off together. It had made the headlines, because at first, the woman had been reported missing and when she hadn't been found after a few days, the media focus was that she had possibly been murdered. I can't remember why that changed, if she herself had come forward to say she had run off with her therapist or if someone had seen them together.

I find my laptop, open my search engine and type in "woman and therapist." There are several links to news articles, from June 2016. I click on one; it's more or less as I remembered—a thirty-year-old solicitor, Justine Bartley, left her office one lunchtime to go for an appointment with her therapist and never returned to work. She was reported missing the next day by her husband, after she failed to return home the previous evening. I trawl through other articles about the same story and discover why it had no longer become newsworthy. Justine's best friend told the police that Justine had fallen in love with her therapist and in the weeks leading up to her disappearance had become both excited and secretive. The friend also told the police that Justine had been experiencing problems in her marriage, hence the therapy sessions. Because no trace was found of her therapist—a Dr. Smith—her friend believed he and Justine had run off together, and the police seemed to agree that it was the likeliest possibility. I search for further news stories about the case, but like Justine Bartley, it never re-surfaced.

June 2016. Eighteen months before Marion Cartaux's murder in France. I don't get too excited. Apart from Justine Bartley having long blond hair, there is nothing to link her disappearance to the murders of Marion Cartaux and Nina, especially as nobody seems to think there was anything sinister in her having gone missing.

I carry on looking into Justine Bartley's disappearance anyway, watching videos of news bulletins and interviews. She was last seen turning into a street in Hampstead. Her phone had been turned off not long after.

I call Thomas.

"Did you know that Nina saw a therapist?" I ask.

"No, but I think it's quite usual for therapists to be in therapy."

"It's just that when Tamsin told me that Nina saw a therapist, I presumed the therapist was a woman. But what if it was a man?"

"Um—what if it was?" Thomas sounds puzzled.

"Do you remember the case about three years ago, the solicitor who went missing, Justine Bartley?"

"Yes, I think so. Didn't she disappear after going for an appointment during her lunch hour? Ah, I see where you're going with this—her appointment was with her therapist. I'm not sure that there's a connection with Nina, though, because didn't the police come to the conclusion that they had run off together?"

"Yes, but what if they didn't? I've just read up on the case and apparently, the police couldn't find any trace of a therapist called Dr. Smith. What if that wasn't his real name? Maybe they didn't run off together, maybe he murdered her."

There's a pause, as if he's wondering how to tell me that I'm being ridiculous.

"If you're thinking that Dr. Smith might have been Nina's therapist, I think—again—that it's a long shot," he says diplomatically. "But you could always check with Tamsin, see if Nina ever mentioned the name of her therapist, that sort of thing."

"I'll try, but Tamsin isn't always very forthcoming about Nina. I don't know if it's relevant or not but Tamsin asked Nina to refer her to her therapist, and Nina never came back with a name."

"Maybe she didn't get around to it or maybe she felt uneasy about Tamsin seeing the same person as her. But it's good to keep it in mind. I'll call Helen and ask her if she knows anything about Nina seeing a therapist. If we don't come up with a name, I'll speak to my police contact."

"Great."

"Thanks, Alice, let's speak soon."

I hang up, realizing I've already hit a problem. I can't call Tamsin and start asking her about Nina's therapist. I need to be subtler than that, see her face to face, chat about other things first. It would also be easier if Eve were there. Except that it's Thursday, and Eve spends Thursdays with her mum. The thought of not being able to speak to Tamsin until tomorrow is frustrating—and that's presuming that both she and Eve are free to meet up.

I think for a moment, then message Eve, asking if she's free for lunch the next day as I feel like getting out and there's a brasserie I want to try near Finsbury Park. I've eaten there before, with Leo, but she doesn't have to know that. I also suggest that we ask Tamsin and Maria to join us, if they're free.

Her reply comes in ten minutes later—it's a brilliant idea, she's already checked with Tamsin and Maria, they can both come if we meet at one o'clock, as that's the time Maria has her lunch break. Relieved that they can make it, I message her back with details of the brasserie and tell her I'll make a reservation.

In the middle of the afternoon, there's a ring on the doorbell and I run down to answer it, thinking it's Thomas, because it's about the time he usually calls. Maybe he's had news about the murder in France. I check my hair quickly in the mirror and open the door.

But it isn't Thomas, it's a young man with sandy hair and a confident smile.

"Ms. Dawson?" he asks.

I look at him warily. "Yes."

"We haven't met before." He holds out his hand. "Ben, Ben Forbes. From Redwoods, the estate agents."

THIRTY-NINE

It takes me a moment to swallow the disappointment of him not being Thomas.

"Oh, hello," I say, shaking his hand. He's younger than I expected, early thirties, I'm guessing, and very good-looking. "Well, it's lovely to meet you, Ben."

"I was at a property here in The Circle, discussing a possible sale, and I thought I'd come by and introduce myself seeing as we only met over the phone."

"I should have called you back to apologize," I say, embarrassed that I hadn't. "It never occurred to me that Leo already knew about the murder."

"Please don't worry. I'm just glad it didn't put you off living here."

"It hasn't been easy," I admit. "And I won't be here much longer. Another week and I'll be going back to Harlestone. Leo is staying," I add, in case he thinks that the house is going to be back on the market.

"Right." He doesn't seem surprised and I wonder if he already knows from Mark that Leo and I are splitting up. He peers behind me into the hall. "Ginny told me you knocked two of the upstairs bedrooms into one. It must be amazing."

It's on the tip of my tongue to invite him in to see it. But something holds me back.

"Why don't you drop in next time you're in the area? I'm sure Leo will be happy to show you around."

"I'll do that, thanks. I'm sorry it didn't work out."

"Me too." I give him a smile. "How's the golf going? You can't believe how grateful Ginny is that you're getting Mark out of the house at weekends."

He laughs. "He's becoming very good. Well, I'd better get on. Perhaps I'll see you again, if ever you're at Ginny's."

"I'm sure I will be. Thank you for coming by. It was nice to meet you."

"Likewise."

He leaves with a wave and I watch as he crosses over the road and disappears into the square.

I take out my cell phone and text Ginny—**I just had a visit from Ben.**

She texts back—**Lucky you! How come?**

He was in the area and wanted to introduce himself.

That was nice of him. He's lovely, isn't he?

I want to tell her that he is, but not as nice as Thomas, and I feel guilty that I can't, guilty that I've never told her about him, because I usually tell her most things.

I go back to my study but I can't concentrate on work because Ben's visit is on my mind. Is it weird that he turned up? Ginny didn't think it was, she said it was nice of him to call. I need to stop being suspicious of everyone.

Even of Will, it seems, because at eight o'clock, he comes to the door with a set of keys dangling from his finger.

"Found them," he says, smiling happily.

"Great!" I say. "Where were they?"

"On the side, among Eve's clutter. They must have fallen off the hook and got buried before anyone noticed."

"It happens," I say, because it does. "Thanks, Will."

When evening comes, even though I no longer have to worry about a set of keys being in the wild, I move to the sitting room. I plan to spend the night watching television. If I feel tired, I can doze on the sofa.

I don't have the volume on the TV turned up loud but at around three in the morning, I find myself muting it. There was a noise, from the kitchen, I'm sure of it. My heart in my mouth, I get up from the sofa and look around the room. If someone has got into the house, I need to stop them getting in here. They'll have heard the television, they'll know where I am.

Moving quietly, I take a low table and put it tight up against the door, then fetch a couple of lamps and put them on top of the table. If someone opens the door, the table and lamps will go flying, buying me enough time to dial 999.

I wait five minutes, my body tense with nerves, my phone ready in my hand, then wait five minutes more and when I don't hear anything else, I try and relax. But I can't bring myself to go and check if there was anyone there. I don't feel like going back to the film I was watching so I curl up on the sofa and wonder if it really is worth staying another week. The reason I asked for two weeks was because I hoped Thomas would have made some progress by then. And because, if I'm honest, I didn't want to never see him again. But now that he's said he'll come and see me in Harlestone, I no longer have to worry. It's probably better that I go. I told Thomas that I want Nina's killer brought to justice, no matter who it is. But what if it does turn out to be someone from here, how will I feel then?

At six o'clock, I open the curtains and look outside. It's still dark but there are lights on in some of the houses, people getting ready to go about their everyday lives. That's what I want, I realize, an everyday life, not one with secrets and lies, fear and mistrust. I'm going back to Harlestone today.

The feeling of a huge weight being lifted off my shoulders is incredible. I go back to the sofa and sleep until my alarm rings at ten. The table and lamps are still in front of the door so I put them back where they're meant to be and head to the kitchen for coffee. Now that I've decided to leave, I need to pack, call Debbie, Leo, Ginny, and Thomas. I can tell Eve that I'm leaving when I see her at lunch. For the first time in a long time, I feel happy. I don't belong here.

As soon as I walk into the kitchen, I know that something has changed. I come to a stop, the weirdest of sensations coursing through my body. I was right, someone has been here, I can feel it on my skin, taste it on my tongue. I walk further in and take a careful look around. I can't see anything but something is definitely different.

My eyes fall on the French windows that give onto the terrace. I go over and try the handle—they're still locked. I stoop to examine the lock; it doesn't look as if it's been tampered with, but when I think about it, it's logical that whoever is getting in is getting in this way, because of the mortice lock on the inside of the front door. Even with keys, nobody can get in if I've locked it from the inside. There have been times when I've forgotten to lock it. But not recently. Since Leo left, I've been obsessive about it.

I go to my study and find the keys that Will gave me last night. There are only the two keys for the front door. The smaller one that would open the French windows isn't there. Did Will remove it before he gave the keys back to me? Or was it never there?

I call Leo.

"Is everything all right?" he asks, as if he knows that it isn't. It puts me on my guard. Everything puts me on my guard. I'm suspicious of everyone and everything.

"Why shouldn't it be?"

"It's just that you seem a bit all over the place at the moment."

I bite back an angry retort. He's right, I am.

"The keys you gave Will—were they only for the front door or was there one for the French windows?" I ask.

"Um—only for the front door. There are only two

keys for the French windows, the one we keep in the drawer in the kitchen and the spare in my study."

"Where in your study?" I ask, already checking the kitchen drawer to see if the key is there. It is.

"In my desk, top drawer on the right. Is there a problem?"

"If someone *is* getting into the house," I say, running up the stairs, "the only way they could get in would be through the French windows, as long as I've locked the front door from the inside." I get to his study and open the right-hand drawer. The spare key is there.

"Or through a window," he says.

"They'd make too much noise. Are you sure there aren't any more keys for the French windows?"

"Quite sure. Ben gave me all the keys he had."

"Ben?"

"From Redwoods."

"But you changed all the locks, so the keys he gave you wouldn't work anyway."

"I changed the locks on the front door, but not on the French windows. It didn't seem worth it."

Alarm bells clang in my head. "So," I say slowly. "How do you know that Ben didn't keep back a key for the French windows?"

"Why would he do that?"

"If the only logical way someone could get into the house is through the French windows, someone else must have a key, because the two that we know about are both here, I just checked."

"Don't tell me—you think Ben kept one back and

has been breaking into the house." I can hear the resignation in his voice.

"Don't sound so skeptical. I'm only thinking that because he came here yesterday."

"What—Ben did?"

"Yes."

"Why?"

"He said he was in the area and wanted to introduce himself."

"Maybe he was just being nice."

"Or maybe he had an ulterior motive. He sort of hinted that he wanted to come in and see the work we had done upstairs."

"You didn't let him in, did you?"

"No, I told him to come back when you were here. It seemed a bit strange and then, last night, I was in the sitting room and I heard a noise in the kitchen. There's no sign of a break-in or anything and nothing is missing. But now I'm wondering—what if it was Ben?"

"That's a huge jump to make. I mean—what would his motive be, if nothing is missing?"

"Maybe he knew Nina—"

"No." Leo's voice is firm and for a moment I think he's telling me that he knows Ben didn't know Nina.

"But what if he sold Nina and Oliver the house?"

"Alice. This has got to stop."

"What?"

"Your obsession with this murder. It's bad enough that you've suspected me and almost every one of our neighbors of having been involved. But when you start accusing our estate agent, when you don't even know if he knew Nina—it can't go on."

"I'm not going to stop until I know who's been creeping around the house at night," I say fiercely. "Because somebody has."

"Then find proof. If you have proof, we can call the police. But we need proof. We can't just tell them that we *think* somebody has broken in, they'll laugh at us. So, until you find something missing, or something that isn't as it should be, we can't do anything." He pauses. "I'm going to come back, Alice. You shouldn't be there on your own."

"It's all right, I'm leaving. I'm going back to Harlestone."

"When?" His relief is evident.

"Today, at the end of the afternoon. I've got lunch with Eve, so I'll leave after. You can move back in tomorrow."

"I'm really sorry it's come to this," he says quietly.

My eyes fill with tears. "So am I."

FORTY

I find two suitcases in the garage and start filling them with the clothes I have in the study, then head upstairs, because I need some jeans and jumpers to get me through the next few weeks. My jumpers are still scattered on the floor from when I fell off the chair. It's bad enough that I accused Leo of leaving a ponytail of blond hair in the wardrobe, thank goodness I didn't accuse him of hiding inside it. But somebody did and they were here the day I saw the face at the window, I smelled their aftershave. I thought it was Leo's, because he has several different ones and I don't always recognize them.

The thought of someone being in the wardrobe, watching me, when I was looking for Leo behind the bathroom door, makes me feel sick with retrospective fright. And what about the day after our party, when Leo had thought there was someone in the bedroom? The next morning, I had found my shoes pushed to one side so had there been someone hiding in the wardrobe that night too?

"For God's sake, Alice, get a grip!" I say the words aloud, trying to make myself see sense. Nobody in their right mind would hide in a wardrobe if people are sleeping close by. The only thing I'm sure of is that someone has been coming to the house. What does he do when he's here, other than drape strands of hair for me to find? Are there other signs I've missed?

I sit down on the bed, remembering the things that have never quite added up, like the time I couldn't find my white sundress before it suddenly turned up, a couple of days later, smelling fresh and clean. But no one would sneak into a house, take a dress, wash it, and put it back in the wardrobe. Not unless they wanted to see how much they could get away with before anyone really noticed.

My mind continues its processing. I take out my phone, call Leo again. He'll be at work now but this is urgent.

"I know this is a really stupid question but after the party, did you wash my white sundress for me?"

"Er—no."

"And the cards we got from everyone, that I put on the mantelpiece in the sitting room. Did you put them lying flat, for a joke?"

"No."

"OK. So did you leave a white rose for me on the window sill by the front door?"

"When?"

"It doesn't matter when, I only want to know if it's something you've ever done."

"No."

"You've never left me a rose?"

"No."

"Great, thanks."

I hang up, think for a moment, then call him a third time.

"Sorry," I say, "I won't call you again, I promise."

"It's OK." He pauses. "Was I meant to have left you a rose?"

"No. I just wanted to thank you for the champagne you left for me in the fridge. I forgot at the time."

"What champagne?"

"The Dom Pérignon."

"Dom Pérignon?"

"So it wasn't you?"

"No. Are you saying someone put a bottle of Dom Pérignon in our fridge?"

"It was probably there from when we had drinks," I say hurriedly. "Somebody must have brought it along and stuck it in the fridge."

"A bottle like that would have jumped out at me," he says. "Alice, what's going on?"

"Just trying to work things out."

I hang up before he can ask any more questions.

I leave my clothes and run downstairs, wondering how many other calling cards I missed. I'm sure he left one for me last night in the kitchen. I stand in the middle of the floor and turn slowly on the spot, scanning the room, looking for something that shouldn't be there.

"Where are you?" I cry in frustration. I go back to where I was standing this morning, when I first sensed that something was different, just inside the door. This time, I keep perfectly still. Only my eyes are moving as I make a detailed, inch-by-inch search, letting them travel slowly over each of the worktops, then up and down the cupboards, back and forth along the shelves, along the rack where the saucepans hang, over the cooker, the ovens, the fridge. But I can't see anything out of place.

I send a text to Debbie to tell her I'll be arriving this evening. For a moment, I wonder whether to cancel lunch with Eve and the others and leave straightaway, but while half of my brain is telling me that I'm in danger, the other half is telling me that everything I'm imagining can't be true. Anyway, I don't want to leave without seeing Eve. I might not have known her for very long but I feel close to her in a way that I can't explain.

Debbie replies that she'll have a bottle of wine ready. I message Ginny and tell her that I've decided to go back to Harlestone today, and that we'll speak over the weekend. And then I call Thomas.

"Am I disturbing you?" I ask.

"It's fine, I can take a few minutes. Have you managed to find the name of Nina's therapist from Tamsin?"

"No, and I'm not sure it's even relevant. Sometimes I wonder if I haven't gone a bit mad. I mean, isn't it a little crazy to link a disappearance three years ago with

Nina's murder, just because the word 'therapist' came into it? Even the murder in France—it's ridiculous to think it's connected to Nina's, just because both women had their hair cut off. Leo told me I need to let go of my obsession with Nina's murder and I couldn't be angry with him because he's right, I am obsessed. I'm so obsessed that I've suspected everyone that I know of being involved, even though everyone tells me that Oliver killed her."

"I'm sorry," he says quietly. "You don't know how much I regret dragging you into my investigation— which, to be honest, I probably would have closed by now, despite Helen." He sighs. "You're not the only one questioning your motives."

"What do you mean?"

"Just that sometimes, I wonder if I've only been keeping it open so that I can carry on seeing you."

I feel a surge of happiness. "You can carry on seeing me anyway."

"But only because you're no longer with Leo. Until you made that decision, I only had the investigation as a reason to see you."

"Are you saying that you think Oliver murdered Nina?"

"No, I don't think he did. I think her killer is out there. But I don't think I'm ever going to find him. Too many people are lying, and untangling that web of lies is proving impossible. And if they're not lying, they're covering something up."

"Like a conspiracy, you mean?"

"Yes. And if several people in The Circle are all

covering up for each other, the only way we'll ever be able to get to the truth is if someone breaks rank."

"It's just as well I didn't tell you my other theory," I say.

"Which is?"

"Do you really want to hear it?"

"I haven't given up totally yet."

"OK. It's that Ben is somehow involved."

"Ben? I haven't heard of a Ben. What number does he live at?"

"No, Ben from Redwoods. The estate agent who sold us the house."

"Wow," he says. "OK." There's a pause. "I'm not saying you're wrong," he adds hastily, "I'm just wondering how you got there."

"You know I think that someone has been getting into the house at night? Well, I think they've been getting in through the French windows at the back. Leo told me Will had keys to the house so I got them back from him and there were only two keys on the ring, both for the front door. I checked with Leo and he said Will never had a key to the French windows, that there were only two, and both were in the house. And both are in the house, I checked. It means that if someone is getting in through the French windows, there must be another key."

"And you think Ben has it?"

"Only because he would have had keys to the house so that he could show people round and the only lock we haven't changed is the one on the French windows. And because yesterday, he turned up here."

"What—he came to the house?"

"Yes."

"Did he say why?"

"He said he'd been at a property here in The Circle, discussing a possible sale, and wanted to introduce himself. But he also hinted that he was interested in seeing the work we had done upstairs."

"Did you let him in?" He can't quite hide the worry in his voice.

"No."

"Thank God. Do you know his surname?"

"No, he mentioned it but I can't remember."

"It doesn't matter, I can look it up on the website. Redwoods, you said? Hold on a sec—here he is, Ben Forbes. Do you know when Nina and Oliver moved into the house?"

"No, why?"

"Because maybe it was Ben Forbes who sold it to them."

My heart starts beating faster; he's had the same thought as me. "Do you think there could be a connection?"

"That's what I'm going to find out. I'm willing to look into anything just to be able to tell Helen I've left no stone unturned. I want this over and done with, Alice."

"Me too," I say. "Which is why I'm going back to Harlestone today. I'm too worried to stay in the house now, anyway. But don't worry, I'll come back next Wednesday to meet Helen."

"And to have lunch with me," he says.

"That too," I say, smiling. "I need to go, Thomas, I'm having lunch with Eve, Tamsin and Maria, although I'm not sure there's any point trying to find out who Nina's therapist was."

"See how you feel. What time do you think you'll be back?"

"By four, I should think."

"Then maybe I could come and say goodbye. Next Wednesday seems a long way off."

"I'd like that," I tell him.

"Good." His voice is warm. "I'll see you about four, then."

FORTY-ONE

On the way to the brasserie, my cell phone rings. It's Ginny.

"What did you say to Leo?"

"About what?"

"The murder."

"Um—" I don't know what to say in case Leo told her what I said about Ben. And she and Mark both really like Ben.

"I'm only asking because he's spent the whole morning reading articles about it online."

"Didn't he go to work?"

"No. He said you were still convinced there'd been a miscarriage of justice and that it wasn't like you to take on a cause for no reason at all. He was trying to find the article you read that made you decide the husband wasn't guilty. And now he's trying to speak to Ben, I'm not quite sure why. Something about wanting to know if he sold the Maxwells the house."

I feel a twinge of alarm. I'm touched that Leo wants to help but I feel bad that he's wasting his time looking for an article that doesn't exist. And what if Ben is involved in Nina's murder, and Leo's questioning spooks him?

"I think he just wants to know when the Maxwells moved to The Circle," I tell Ginny.

"That's all right, then."

"I'm sorry, I have to go. Lunch date with Eve, Tamsin and Maria."

"Good luck," she says.

"I need to tell them I'm leaving. I'm sure Tamsin will be relieved."

She laughs and hangs up.

They're waiting for me when I arrive at the brasserie, seated at a round table. They've left me the place opposite Tamsin, so I give each of them a quick hug and sit down between Eve and Maria.

"Sorry I'm late," I say, while Maria pours me a glass of wine. "I was busy packing."

"I thought your friend was coming to stay?"

"No, I've decided to go to hers instead. But not just for the weekend. I've decided to go back to Harlestone for good."

Eve pauses, her glass halfway to her lips. "Really?"

"Yes."

She puts her glass back on the table. "Oh."

"What about Leo?" Maria asks.

"He's staying here."

She puts her hand on mine. "I'm so sorry, Alice."

"Me too." Eve looks as if she's about to cry.

"Don't worry," I say, leaning into her. "I'll come back and see you."

"But you won't be next door," she says mournfully.

"I'm going to miss you all. You've been so welcoming." I pick up my glass. "Come on, let's drink to our continuing friendship."

Maria passes me a menu and we choose our meals. Eve asks me if I'm going to be able to get my house back in Harlestone and I tell her that I'll be staying with Debbie until I can sort something out.

"Is there any chance of you and Leo getting back together?" Tamsin asks.

"No," I say, reaching for my glass. "I don't think so."

"Because he didn't tell you about the murder?"

"It's not always black and white," I tell her. "Just like the murder."

She groans. "You're not going to start going on about that again, are you?"

"I just want to know one thing," I say quickly, "and then I won't ask you anything else."

"What?" she asks warily.

"You said Nina saw a therapist. Male or female?"

"Male."

"Did she ever mention his name?"

She arches an eyebrow. "That's two questions. No, I did ask her for it, but as I told you, she didn't give it to me."

"Do you know where his practice was? Was it local?"

"It doesn't matter where it was because he came to her," Eve intervenes before Tamsin can tell me I've run out of questions. "That's why she stopped coming to yoga with us. It clashed with her therapy sessions."

"Yes, but she only arranged to have her sessions on a Wednesday afternoon so that she would have an excuse not to see me," Tamsin points out.

I frown, remembering that Nina had started avoiding her about four months before she died.

"So the therapy sessions were a new thing?"

"Yes."

"And he came to see her at the house? Is that usual?"

"I know it's not the same, because I'm a speech therapist," Maria says. "But I wouldn't normally go to a client's house unless they can't get to me for some medical reason."

"I don't suppose Tim would know the name of Nina's therapist," I say, turning to her. "I know he decided to specialize in psychotherapy largely because of Nina. Maybe she mentioned a name to him?"

"I can certainly ask him. But why do you want to know? If you're leaving, wouldn't you rather see a therapist nearer to where you'll be living?"

"It's not for me," I say. And then I stop, because I don't know what reason I can give for wanting to know the name of Nina's therapist.

But it's too late. "Don't tell me—you think her therapist murdered her," Tamsin drawls, an amused look on her face.

"No, but I don't believe Oliver did. And neither do you," I add, infuriated that she's laughing at me.

"I've never said that."

"Yes, you did! The day you invited me for coffee, I

overheard you talking to Eve and you said that you had never believed that Oliver killed Nina."

Her green eyes flash with annoyance. "I guessed you were there, listening in the porch, but it's good to have it confirmed that as well as everything else, you're also an eavesdropper." She glares at me across the table. "I'm glad you're going. We'll be able to get on with our lives now."

"Tam." Maria puts a hand on her arm.

"So you don't mind that Nina's killer hasn't been caught?" I say angrily. "You know it wasn't Oliver but you prefer to sit there and do nothing, say nothing?"

Tamsin flushes. "Well, you've certainly done plenty. We were all happy before you came along and decided to stick your nose into something that had absolutely nothing to do with you. You didn't even know Nina, or Oliver, so why the hell did you get involved?" She looks appraisingly at me. "Shall I tell you what we all think?"

"No, Tam," Eve pleads. But Tamsin is too far gone to listen.

"You're a fantasist, Alice. You invent a whole load of crap and then you start to believe it. We knew it the moment you pretended that a man had turned up at your drinks evening, a man that nobody saw except you, a man that nobody spoke to except you. That's why we didn't care whether or not you found out who he was. We knew he was just something you made up to make you appear more interesting than you actually are." She gives a snort of disgust. "You even admitted to Will that that's what you do."

"I didn't make him up!" I say furiously.

She looks at me pityingly. "We know, Alice. We know that at one time or another you've suspected us or our husbands of killing Nina, we can see right through your invitations to lunch and dinner, right through the questions you ask, right through the lies you tell. You're dangerous. You need to get a life, before you destroy everyone else's."

I wait for Eve or Maria to come to my rescue. But Eve, who would normally do her best to smooth things over, doesn't say anything.

The silence becomes unbearable. Tamsin pushes her chair back. "I've just remembered I need to be somewhere," she says, her voice tight.

I push my chair back too. "No, you can stay, I'm going." I grab my bag from under the table. "If you must know, the reason I got involved was for Oliver's sister. I was doing it for her. But as nobody else seems to care—not even you, Nina's best friends—well, why should I?" I start to move away and then stop. "And by the way, I didn't make the man up, the one who came to the party. Lorna admitted to letting him in, remember?"

I manage to hold on to my tears until I get to the street outside. Then I dissolve. I walk quickly to Finsbury Park, my head down, my scarf pulled up around my ears, and crumple onto the first bench I find. Is that what I am, a fantasist? When I look at all the things I've allowed myself to believe over the last few weeks, I'm

ashamed. Tamsin's right, at one time or another I've suspected all of them of being involved in Nina's murder.

My cheeks burn when I think of them laughing at
me behind my back. What Tamsin said about me getting a life—it hurt more than anything because she was
right about that too. I haven't really had a life since my
parents and sister died. It's why I launched myself so
fervently into helping Thomas and Helen. I needed
something in my life, something to make me feel alive,
make me feel that I was doing some good because most
of the time, I just exist. But I've taken it too far. When I
think of Leo and Thomas, both of whom are trying, at
this very moment, to find out if Ben had something to
do with Nina's murder, I'm scared. I need to tell them
to stop.

I get a grip by thinking about Nina—my sister, not
Nina Maxwell. I can almost hear her telling me to stop
feeling sorry for myself, to accept that I had a kind of
brain-storm, and move on. She's right, I need to move
on. By the time I get home, it will be almost three
o'clock. I'll just have time to throw the rest of my stuff
into a case before Thomas arrives. In a couple of hours,
I'll be on my way to Harlestone, and Nina Maxwell and
my time in The Circle will just be a memory.

FORTY-TWO

I start walking back to the house, part of me wanting to blame Leo for what happened at the brasserie. If he had been upfront with me about the murder, I would never have come here. The only good thing to have come out of my time in The Circle is Thomas—if our friendship manages to survive when there isn't the investigation to bind us together. It worries me that it might not.

My phone rings. I take it from my bag, hoping it will be Thomas. It is. I stop walking and move to the side.

"Alice. Am I disturbing your lunch?"

"No, I'm on my way back to the house." I press a finger to my other ear, shutting out the noise so that I can hear him better.

"Good. Would you believe that one of your neighbors was in Paris at the time of Marion Cartaux's murder?"

My heart plummets. "I'm not sure I want to know who."

"Don't worry too much, because her murderer is

behind bars, awaiting trial. He gave himself up a few months ago."

"Oh. Well, that's good, isn't it?"

"Normally, I'd say yes. But not everyone thinks that he did it. He's an SDF—a homeless person—who had been out of prison for a year at the time of the murder. Unfortunately, there are more cases than the judiciary would like of homeless people pleading guilty to just about anything so that they can get back inside. Being on the streets is far more frightening to them than being in prison."

"But he might have done it."

"We'll only be sure after his trial, once his account of events has been verified."

"So, which of my neighbors was in Paris at the time of the murder?" I ask.

"William Jackman."

I close my eyes. "I wish I hadn't discovered that gap in the fence between our gardens."

"It doesn't mean anything yet. I thought I'd let you know, that's all. Did you manage to get the name of Nina's therapist?"

"No, but it was a man. And she didn't go to him, he came to see her. That's not very usual, is it?"

"No, it isn't. But without a name, there's not much we can do." There's a pause. "Are you all right? You sound a bit down."

"Let's just say lunch didn't go according to plan. I'm glad I'm leaving today. It's the right decision."

"Would you rather I didn't come over? You must have a lot to do before you leave."

"I just need to throw some clothes into a case. I'll come and get the rest of my stuff another time. So please do come over. It will be nice to see you."

"If you're sure."

"I am."

"I'll see you in around an hour, then."

I've barely hung up when my phone starts ringing again. It's Tamsin. I give an angry laugh and let it ring out. It's taken Eve and Maria thirty minutes to persuade her to call and apologize, because I'm sure that's why she called. The phone starts ringing again, another call from Tamsin. I let it ring out again and a minute or so later, I get a message telling me I have a voicemail. I'm in no mood to listen to it, nor to the next voicemail she leaves me.

Five minutes later, it's Eve who calls. I'm still sore that she didn't say a word to defend me so I don't answer her either. I know I'm being unfair; she and Tamsin have been friends for years, it's normal she would take Tamsin's side. But I don't want to speak to her, especially now that I know Will was in Paris at the time of Marion Cartaux's murder. Thomas said it probably doesn't mean anything. But still.

I reach The Circle and trudge across the square to the house. School has finished for the day, so there are quite a few people heading toward the play area. Although there's a chill in the air, the sun is out and despite everything, I smile to see children clambering over the wooden climbing frames. The rest of the square is deserted. As I go through the gate opposite the house, I see Edward going into his garage and give him a wave. My eyes are drawn involuntarily to Maria and Tim's house; once again, Tim is standing at the upstairs window. He gives me a wave and I wave back. It's funny that he doesn't try and hide the fact that he's watching the square. Most people, even though they're doing nothing wrong, would jump back guiltily, or at least turn away once they've waved. But he just carries on watching.

I gather my things together and put my case and handbag by the front door, ready to leave once I've seen Thomas. There's a ring on the doorbell. I look up sharply; it's too early for it to be him. What if it's Eve? If it is, I won't let her in. I can't, not with Thomas due to arrive.

I latch the chain before opening the door.

"Oh, hi," I say, unsettled to see Tim standing there. He's dressed in his usual jeans and rugby shirt and I find myself wondering if he's ever played rugby.

"Hi, Alice, I thought I'd come over and see you myself," he says, giving me a smile. "Maria called to ask if I knew the name of Nina's therapist, she said you were asking about him?"

"Yes, but it doesn't really matter."

He looks relieved. "Oh good, because Nina never mentioned it to me." He pauses. "Maria said you're leaving?"

"That's right, I am. Which is why I don't have time to invite you in," I add, in case he's wondering why I'm speaking to him through the chain on the door. "I need to finish packing."

He takes a step away from the door. "No worries,

I need to get on myself. I'm sorry it didn't work out, Alice. Hopefully we'll see each other again."

"Thanks, Tim," I say. "I'm sure we will."

I close the door behind him and go to the kitchen. I lean against the worktop, thinking about Nina helping Tim with his psychotherapy studies. I had presumed she helped him study for exams, looked over his essays, that sort of thing. But what if it was more hands-on? What if the help she gave him was based on role-play, where she took the role of a client and Tim took the role of the therapist?

I push away from the worktop, feeling as if I'm on the brink of something. Could it be Tim who Nina saw on Wednesday afternoons, when Maria went to yoga with Eve and Tamsin, then on to pick up the children up from school? It would explain why she wouldn't give Tamsin the name of her therapist, if it was Tim she was seeing.

I stop, disgusted with myself. Tamsin is right, I am a fantasist. But not a total one. I know, one hundred percent, that someone has been getting into the house.

I go to the fridge to get some juice. As I close the door, my eyes, already looking toward my glass, swivel back to the fridge, caught by something that shouldn't be there. They come to rest on a small, passport-sized photo stuck in the middle of all the other photos, and my heart doesn't just miss a beat, it stops. For a moment, I can't breathe. I know who it is in the photo, I just don't want to believe it.

I run into the hall and take my cell phone from my bag.

"Thomas, are you on your way?" I try to keep my voice calm but I can't.

"Yes, I'm not far. Why, what's happened?"

"I just found a photo of Nina on the fridge."

"Nina?"

"Yes, Nina Maxwell. I knew this morning that someone had been in the kitchen but I couldn't see anything different, I could sense it but I couldn't see it, I was too far away," I say, my voice high with panic. "But just now, I was right up close to the fridge and there it was, stuck among the other photos. I don't know what to do," I add breathlessly.

"Have you touched it?"

"No."

"Then don't. I was just speaking to my contact in the police about Ben Forbes. You're not going to believe what we discovered. We were right, there is a conspiracy."

"What do you mean?"

"It seems that not only did Ben Forbes sell the Maxwells their house, he's also a friend of Tim Conway."

I freeze. "He just came here," I say.

"What? Tim Conway did? Why?"

"Because I asked Maria to ask Tim if he knew the name of Nina's therapist and he came to tell me that he didn't. But I've been thinking—what if he was the therapist that she was seeing? Her sessions were on Wednesday afternoons, Maria is at yoga on Wednesday afternoons. And Nina used to go to yoga, but she stopped four months before she died." I can hardly catch my breath.

Thomas's voice is calm but urgent. "Alice, I'm going to hang up now. The police might arrive before me but I'll be there as soon as I can. Until then, if anyone comes to the door, don't let them in."

FORTY-THREE

My mind spinning, I lock the front door from the inside, check that the chain is in place and hurry upstairs to Leo's study to wait for Thomas. I'm trembling, shaken by the knowledge that Tim has been the one coming to the house at night. Everything points to it, including the way he was so at home in my kitchen the day he came to supper. He must have got a key to the French windows from Ben, then used the gap in the fence between ours and Edward's to get into our garden— maybe there's even a gap in the fence between his garden and Geoff's to make things even easier.

The questions keep coming. Was Ben also involved? If Tim murdered Nina, was Ben his accomplice? And how much does Maria know? Is she completely innocent, or is she part of a conspiracy that includes Eve and Tamsin, even Will and Connor? Unless Ben murdered Nina. Maybe he became obsessed with her when he sold her and Oliver the house, and they had an affair. Did he kill Nina and then tell Tim what he had done? Is that when the cover-up started? Or has everyone been in it together from the start, wanting Nina killed for reasons of their own and setting up Oliver to take the blame?

The thought that I might have been manipulated left, right and center by the people I thought were my friends is overwhelming. Lorna tried to warn me, she had told me not to trust anyone. But I had plowed ahead, unwilling to believe that people would lie to me. I should have listened to Edward too; instead of telling nobody I was leaving, I ended up telling everyone.

The sense of impending danger is incredible. I keep my eyes on the gate at the other end of the square, knowing I'll only be able to relax when I can actually see Thomas. I feel a momentary anxiety. Maria will have gone back to work but what if Eve and Tamsin see Thomas as they walk back across the square from the restaurant? I imagine the two of them nudging each other when they see the tall, good-looking stranger striding along. Will they watch to see where he goes? What if they see him come to the house?

It doesn't matter if they do, I realize. I don't have to explain anything to them, I'm not even going to be here. I won't have to admit that he's the man who turned up at the party, I won't have to tell them that I kept him a secret because I've been helping him investigate Nina's murder—a murder which has now been solved. I think of Helen, how thrilled she's going to be that at last, she'll have justice for her brother.

And then I see them, Eve and Tamsin, coming into the square. I wait for them to turn toward Tamsin's house but they stop in the middle of the path. *Move!* I urge them. *Go!* They're huddled together, deep in conversation but that won't stop them seeing Thomas. He's not the sort of man to go unnoticed.

Except—he has. Not just at the party but also all the other times he's visited me. There must have been people around as he walked across the square on his way over, or on his way back, but no one ever mentioned seeing a tall, dark-haired stranger, despite everyone knowing that I was trying to trace a man who fitted that description. Because nobody really believed he existed.

Tamsin rummages in her bag for something. She begins to move toward her house, Eve following behind. I breathe a sigh of relief but at that moment, Tamsin turns and looks toward the house, her cell phone clamped to her ear. I move from the window, hoping she hasn't seen me. My cell phone, which I've got in my hand, starts ringing, making me jump. It's her.

A ring on the doorbell sets my heart racing. Thomas told me not to open the door to anyone. It might be the police; he said he was going to call them. Maybe they've come in an unmarked car. I push my cell phone into my pocket and run downstairs.

"Alice, it's me." Thomas's voice comes through the door.

I open it quickly, blinking back the tears that have sprung to my eyes.

"It's all right," he says, catching sight of my face. He lays a steadying hand on my arm. "I'm here now."

"I watched for you coming across the square but I didn't see you."

"I walked around the outside, I always do. I don't like to draw attention to myself. Is that your phone ringing?"

"Yes, but it's only Tamsin."

"Are you sure? It might be the police. I gave them your number."

"Yes, look." I show him my phone.

"Don't you want to answer it?"

"No, it's fine." We move to the kitchen. "We had a row over lunch. I told you, she hates me asking questions about Nina." I point to the fridge. "There's the photo."

He peers at it. "I wonder why he put it here?"

"It's a calling card," I explain. "I realized this morning that there were other things I missed, things that I put down to Leo, like a rose on the window sill, a bottle of champagne in the fridge, a photo turned upside down. Each time, he does something—there must be other things I missed. It's like a game. He's been playing with me." I look up at him. "What did the police say when you told them about the photo and Tim's connection to Nina?"

"I left everything with my contact there and he went to speak to his superiors. I'm surprised they're not already here."

"Let's have coffee while we're waiting." My phone starts ringing again and I groan. "Tamsin again. Maybe I should just answer it, get it over and done with?"

"You may as well. But don't take any stick from her. I'll make the coffee."

"Thanks." I take the call, loving that he feels comfortable enough to take over.

"Alice, don't hang up!" Tamsin's voice comes urgently down the line. I don't say anything, just wait for her to continue. "You said you were doing this for Oliver's sister."

"That's right," I say, hoping she feels guilty.

"Oliver didn't have a sister."

I laugh. "Nice try." Thomas turns from the sink and gives me a smile, pleased to hear me stand up for myself.

"Look, I knew Nina and Oliver really well and he told me he was an only child," Tamsin says. "Nina also mentioned it, his lack of a family, because his mother died when he was young and his father lived abroad."

"Don't call me again, Tamsin."

"Wait, there's something else! The man that you said turned up at your party?" My heart sinks. She and Eve must have seen Thomas walking around the outside of the square. "If it's true that Lorna let him in," Tamsin goes on, "if he did exist, why did you never think that he might be Nina's killer? Shouldn't he have been the first person you thought of, instead of suspecting us? Because why would he have turned up at your housewarming, otherwise?"

For one terrible moment, the world stops moving.

"Alice?" Tamsin's voice comes down the line. "Are you there?"

Thomas looks over at me, gives me a smile. It jolts me back to reality.

"As I said, don't call me again," I say, cutting the call.

I put my phone in my pocket, wishing I could have told her that Thomas is a private investigator looking into Nina's murder and that he's found her killer.

"I take it her apology wasn't good enough?" Thomas says.

I shake my head. "No, it wasn't."

"I don't suppose you managed to find out anything about her therapist?"

"Only what I told you. But he's hardly relevant now, as Tim is the culprit." I smile at him and he smiles back but Tamsin's words won't stop crashing through my brain. *Oliver didn't have a sister.*

I take out my phone. "I need to tell Leo what time I'm leaving so that he can move back in; he's been hassling me to let him know. I was going to leave in about an hour but maybe I should wait, in case the police come."

"Why don't you tell him you can't give him a time, so he'll have to wait until tomorrow?"

"Good idea," I say, already texting Leo.

Can you find out if Oliver had a sister? It's urgent, really urgent.

He texts back almost immediately. **You told me he did. And how am I meant to find out?**

"I knew he'd moan," I say with a rueful smile. "He's not happy about having to wait until tomorrow."

"Tell him he doesn't have a choice."

"All right."

I don't know! I text back. **Just find out. Please!**

I'll do my best. Btw, I spoke to Ben. He didn't

know the Maxwells. He's only been with Redwoods two years. Ours was the first house he sold in The Circle.

My heart begins a slow, dull thud in my chest. I look over at Thomas, Tamsin's voice echoing through my brain.

Why did you never think that he might be Nina's killer?

"What did Leo say?" Thomas asks.

"That I win," I say, putting my phone face down on the table so that he won't be able to see what Leo says when he texts me back about Oliver having a sister. "He'll wait until tomorrow."

"Good."

He finishes making the coffee and brings it over to where I'm sitting.

"Did you tell Helen that I'm looking forward to meeting her on Wednesday?" I ask.

"I did, and she said to tell you that she's looking forward to it too." He pulls out the chair opposite me. "I've been thinking—I know it might seem a bit—well, early—but I'd love you to meet my parents at some point. And Louis."

"I'd like that," I say, lifting my cup to my lips. I try and sort through the thoughts careering through my mind, colliding with each other, canceling each other out. Thomas had shown me a photo of him and Helen at university together. No, he had shown me a photo of him with a young woman.

"It will be great if you can tell Helen you've found

the person responsible for Nina's murder. If it does turn out to be Tim," I say.

"I'm a hundred percent sure that it's him."

"What would his motive have been?" I raise my eyes to his face, a face I've come to know well, the green specks in his eyes, the way his hair falls onto his forehead. He looks too kind, he has a son, he has parents, he wants me to meet them. He can't have murdered Nina, it's not possible, how would he have even known her? Unless she hired him to investigate Oliver. Or Oliver hired him to investigate Nina, because he suspected her of having an affair. The one thing I do know is that Thomas Grainger is a private investigator, because I checked out the address he gave me. Unless he lied, like Leo did. Maybe his name isn't Thomas Grainger. Maybe he's not a private investigator. Maybe he doesn't have a son, or parents.

"Who knows?" he says. "Maybe he fell in love with Nina when she and Oliver moved in here. Maybe they had an affair, and when she tried to end it, he killed her."

Is that what happened, I wonder? Is that his story? Did Thomas, if that is his name, have an affair with Nina? If he did, when and how? How come nobody saw a stranger, coming regularly to the house? But then, Thomas has been visiting me once a week for the last five weeks and nobody saw him coming to the house on any of those occasions, not even Eve, and she lives next door. And I realize—she wouldn't have seen him because, apart from today, Thomas always comes to see me on Wednesday afternoons, when Eve goes to yoga with Tamsin and Maria. Nina used to go with them but she stopped, because on Wednesdays, she saw her therapist.

And that's when I know.

He is the therapist.

PAST

I know as soon as I arrive that something has changed. The smile she gives me isn't as wide as it usually is, and doesn't quite reach her eyes.

"Is everything all right?" I ask, once we're both sitting down.

"Not really."

"Oh?"

"Much as I've enjoyed our sessions, I'm afraid I'm not going to be able to continue with them," she says.

I can't believe it's happening again. Just when I think I've got them, they slip away. I don't understand; I've always taken such care in choosing my victims, watching them for months, waiting for the right moment to insinuate myself into their lives. Because of the circumstances I found myself in, this one was always going to be more problematic. But I can't believe I've got her wrong too.

"May I ask why?"

"Because you're not a therapist," she says. "You

may have studied psychology, but you're not a psycho-therapist."

I sit back in my chair. "What makes you say that?"

"You ask too many questions."

"If I've asked questions, it's because I'm trying to get to the bottom of your dissatisfaction with life."

"That's the other thing that gave you away—your insistence that I'm unhappy. At first, I thought it was part of our therapist-client training, but I've come to re-alize that you're working to your own agenda. Which is dangerous." She leans forward, fixing me with her eyes. "It's also intriguing. In fact, I think what we should be exploring is why you want me to think I'm unhappily married."

"I've observed you, Nina. For months."

"I think, if you look back on our sessions, I've never given the slightest indication that I have anything but a happy life."

"Before that," I say. "Before our sessions even started, I observed you."

She frowns. "What do you mean, observed me? When?"

"If you're so happy with your life and your hus-band," I say, ignoring her question. "How do you ex-plain the string of men that come to your house when he's away?"

She bursts out laughing. "I hope you also observed the string of women who come to the house. Really, is that the best you can do?" She gives me an amused smile. "Shall I let you into a secret? I've known from our third session that you're not what you say you are and the only reason I continued to see you is because you make a great case-study. If I'm stopping these sessions now, it's because I've come to the conclusion that you have a personality disorder that I don't have the expertise, or the wish, to explore any further. At best, you're manipulative, at worst—well, I'd say you have psychopathic tendencies. It's why I never gave Tamsin your number, because you could have done her untold damage and she has enough problems as it is." She stands up. "I'd like you to leave. But you should know I'll be reporting you to the relevant bodies so that you'll be banned from working as a therapist, if you ever decide to set up a practice somewhere."

Another one who thinks she can reject me, who wastes my time, who leads me on, fiddling with her hair during our sessions, teasing me.

I get to my feet and leave without a fuss.

"Don't come back," she says.

"I won't."

But, of course, I do go back. I go back that evening and ask her for the book that I lent her, which I know she keeps in the bedroom, because I've seen it there during my night-time visits.

She goes to get it and I follow her silently up the stairs.

The book is **Walden,** *the author Henry David Thoreau.*

One way or another, Thoreau always works.

FORTY-FOUR

Thomas smiles at me. I put my cup down, smile back at him.

"I'm just going to get a sweater," I say, pushing my chair back. "It's turned a bit chilly."

"Can I get it for you?"

"No, it's fine, there's one in my case. It's in the hall."

I go out to the hall and open my case, tugging the zips hard so he'll be able to hear. Then I crouch down, find my house keys in my bag and slip them into my pocket.

"Do you need help?"

I look up and see him filling the doorway.

"No, thank you." I put my hand into the case and tug out a pale blue sweater. "This will do."

My heart is thumping as I stand up. I shouldn't have bothered taking my keys, I should have got out of the house while I could. But I had wanted to lock the door behind me, lock him in so that he couldn't come after me. With him standing there, it's too late. If I make for the front door, he'll know that I've guessed and will be on me before I've even opened it. I have no choice but to go back to the kitchen.

He sits down but I stay standing. I want to take my phone from where I left it on the table but it's too far away for me to reach. I pull the jumper over my head but it snags on the clip holding my hair up. I undo the clip and tug the jumper down. My hair gets stuck so I reach up and pull it free. Something flickers in his eyes.

"You have beautiful hair," he murmurs.

I force the words out. "Thank you."

"By the way, you got a message from Leo."

I freeze. How does he know it's from Leo?

"It's all right," I say. "I'll look at it later."

"Aren't you going to sit down?"

"Yes, of course." I pull my chair further out.

"I can tell you what it says, if you like." The hairs on the back of my neck, and then on my arms, prickle with fear. I stay as I am, halfway between sitting and standing.

"It says," he goes on, looking me straight in the eyes. *"Oliver didn't have a sister."*

It happens so fast. He lunges toward me but I get there first, picking up my chair and hurling it across the table at him. Caught by surprise, he cries out. But I'm already gone. I get to the front door and as I open it, I hear him come into the hall. Slamming the door shut behind me, I take the keys from my pocket, almost dropping them in my panic, and lock him in. I expect him to start hammering on the door, and when he doesn't I realize he's gone to look for another way out.

The key to the French windows is in the kitchen drawer, it'll take him a while to find it.

I start running down the drive then stop, my eyes darting. I don't know where to go. I was going to go into the square, get help from someone there but there's no one around. I don't have long. I need to find somewhere with a phone so that I can call the police. I look toward Eve's house then remember she's at Tamsin's. I run up the drive to Edward and Lorna's.

I press on the bell, over and over again.

"Lorna, Edward!" I call, hammering on the door. "It's Alice! Can you let me in? It's urgent!"

I hear them shuffling as they come into the hall. "Please hurry!" I urge. I don't want to alarm them but I need to get inside.

There's the sound of bolts being drawn back. The door swings open and I burst into the house, smashing it back against Edward. I barely give him a second glance, my eyes caught by Lorna standing further down the hallway, her face white with fright.

"Sorry, Lorna," I say. "It's urgent." I turn to Edward hurriedly. "Can I use—" The words die on my lips. Standing behind Edward, his hand gripping the back of Edward's neck, is Thomas.

The blood drains from my face as he pushes the door shut with his free hand. "How did you—?"

"Get here?" He sounds amused. "Out through your French windows and in through ours."

I stare at him in confusion. "Yours?"

"Yes." Now he laughs. "I did say I wanted you to meet my parents."

His *parents*. I look in shock at Edward, and my shock quickly turns to fright. His face is dangerously red and his eyes are slipping out of focus. Adrenaline surges; I need to get help. I take a step back, look toward the door. But I'm too late. Still holding Edward, Thomas reaches out with his other hand and grabs me by the throat.

He waits until fear registers in my eyes, then tightens his grip.

"You're hurting me," I gasp.

The last thing I hear is his laugh.

When I come back to consciousness, I find myself tied to a chair. My instinct is to struggle free but I sense someone behind me and everything comes rushing back. Survival mode kicks in. *Don't let him know you're awake.* My mouth is dry; I swallow carefully, quietly, and have to stop myself crying out from the pain in my throat.

I try and regroup my thoughts but it's difficult when battling fear is my primary concern. Fear for Lorna and Edward—where are they? Fear that I might not get out of this alive.

Did he say Lorna and Edward were his parents? In a way, it makes sense. He must be the son they said died four years ago, in Iraq. What had he done to make them deny the existence of their only child? Justine Bartley had disappeared three years ago after going to meet her therapist. If Thomas was Nina's therapist, was he also Justine Bartley's therapist?

I inadvertently swallow and, unprepared for the pain, a groan escapes my lips. A hand winds itself in my hair and my head is pulled back, stretching my neck, making the fire in my throat worse. I close my eyes. I don't want to see his face.

"Awake, are we? Good!"

"Stop, John, please!" I recognize Lorna's voice and open my eyes, moving them in her direction. I can just about see her, crouching down beside Edward, slumped against the wall. "Your father needs an ambulance. It's his heart."

"Be quiet!" Thomas snaps. I'd thought at first that Lorna was speaking to someone else. But of course, Thomas isn't his real name.

He tugs my head back further, causing my swollen throat more injury. The pain is excruciating but I refuse to let him see how much it hurts.

He bends over me, bringing his face close, so that I'm looking right into his eyes, upside down.

"Guess what's going to happen now?" he says.

You're going to kill me.

I hear a noise, a noise I recognize as a pair of scissors being sliced open and closed. Lifting his arm, he brings them into view and I remember what happened to Nina.

"You're going to cut my hair." It comes out in a hoarse whisper.

"That's right." He moves his hands to either side of my head and pushes it forward, so that I'm looking straight ahead. At first, I think there's another woman in the room with us, until I realize it's my own reflection staring back at me from a gold-framed mirror, speckled with age, set up on a table in front of me.

I quickly work out that the room I'm in corresponds to my study in our house next door. The two windows have been boarded up; the only light comes from two ornate lamps, placed on either side of the mirror. As I watch, he takes hold of my hair, lifts it high above my head and slowly, gradually, lets it fall around my shoulders. I watch him in the mirror and shudder at what I see. He looks so different to the man I knew—or thought I knew—that it's like looking at someone else. Somehow, it makes it easier.

He separates a length of my hair, about an inch thick, from the rest and, like before, holds it high above my head. Opening the blades of the scissors around it, he moves them downward, stopping now and then as if deciding where to cut it.

"Here, or here?" he muses. Our eyes meet in the mirror. He waits for a reaction so I stare back, not giving him one. With a sudden movement, he moves the scissors down to within an inch of my skull and saws through the length of hair. I don't move, I don't flinch, not even when he drops it onto my lap. I'm too worried about Edward to think about what Thomas is doing. I can't see him at all now, I can only see the top of Lorna's head as she crouches beside him. It comes back to me then, how Lorna and Edward had wanted to move away after Nina's murder but Edward had had a heart attack. Was it from the shock of knowing that his son was a murderer? Had Thomas been staying here at the time? Or maybe all the time. Maybe he has been living here, in this house, in secret. It would explain why I hadn't seen him walking across the square earlier, why nobody has ever seen him walking across the square, not even on his visits to Nina. Because all that time, he had been living right next door.

"Why did you kill Nina?" I ask.

"Why don't you tell me what you think?" he says. "I'd love to hear another of your theories."

"You killed her because you were having an affair with her and she wanted to break it off." He doesn't say anything. "What about Justine and Marion? Did you have an affair with them too?"

He grins. "I saw what you did there. But you're wrong. I didn't have an affair with them. Or with Nina."

"But you killed them."

"Correct."

"Why?"

"Because they didn't know their own minds. Not like you, Alice."

"What do you mean?"

He smiles, lifts another length of hair. "Where shall I cut this one?"

"Wherever you like." Again, he snips it near my skull and drops it onto my lap. I can't pretend I'm not distraught at the sight of uneven clumps of hair sprouting from my scalp, but I keep it to myself. "Are you really a therapist?"

"How can I be a therapist if I'm a private investigator? Oh, wait—maybe I'm not a private investigator." He waves the scissors around. "The trick is to be who people want me to be. A therapist worked well for the others. For you, I had to think of something else. You needed a savior, a redeemer. Someone you could help, so that you could atone for your sins." He looks triumphantly at my reflection in the mirror. "I'm right, aren't I, Alice? You were the one driving the car the night your parents and sister died."

I stare at him, not letting my gaze waver, not letting him know that he's right. He lifts another length of hair and I focus on the sound of the scissors sawing through it to stop the sounds that have haunted me for almost twenty years, that will haunt me for the rest of my life, the screech of brakes, the tearing of metal, the screams of pain and fear.

"It's a shame you decided to leave The Circle so abruptly," he continues. "It was fun listening to all your different theories about who killed Nina. I could barely keep up with your suspicions. A headless chicken came to mind. You suspected your friends, their husbands, the man you were meant to love, even the estate agent." The scissors slice through my hair again. "You're not a very nice person, Alice. You do realize that, don't you?"

"Compared to you, I'm an angel," I say scathingly, to hide the shame I feel at his words. "You used your knowledge to manipulate me into thinking everyone had something to hide. I suppose it was you who told Lorna to tell me not to trust anyone."

"No, foolishly, she did that of her own accord. But I overheard her and made sure she paid for it."

I give him a look of pure disgust. "Were you born evil or did you become evil?"

"Why don't you tell me what you think?"

I swivel my eyes to where Lorna is crouching. She looks terrified.

"I'm guessing a normal family background so it must be rejection by a woman, or women, that made you hate us so much." I pause. "It was the woman in the photograph you showed me, wasn't it, the one you told me was Helen? She had long hair—and I think she was blond." I curl my lips in a pitying smile. "Is that what happened—she rejected you and you couldn't cope? Are you really that pathetic?"

He laughs, a harsh, detached laugh. Why had I never heard him laugh like that?

I've needled him. Ramming the scissors into my hair, he begins making furious cuts close to my scalp, nicking my skin so that I can't help but flinch.

"Where did you get the key to our French windows?" I ask.

"It was on the set of keys that Nina and Oliver gave to my parents. I kept them, hoping they would come in useful." He sighs in pretend despair. "Leo really should have changed all the locks, not just those on the front door." Then he grins. "I love that you thought I was Nina when I visited you at night."

I hate that he heard me talking to her, hate that he has seen me in all my weaknesses.

"How pathetic of you to hide in the wardrobe," I sneer.

"John, I think he's dead." Lorna's trembling voice breaks through Thomas's amusement. The scissors stop moving. "I think your father's dead."

I watch in the mirror as he walks over to where Lorna is standing. He bends down, then straightens up, a look of confusion on his face, which he quickly hides.

"I think you might be right," he says, feigning nonchalance.

Lorna bursts into tears. "We need an ambulance," she sobs. "Please, John."

"Why, if he's dead?" His voice is harsh.

He comes back to where I'm sitting, powerless in the face of his suppressed anger at his father's death. I want to comfort Lorna, get her away from Thomas. But tied to a chair, I can't do either of those things. I can't do anything. For the first time, it hits me. I am going to die.

"They moved here to get away from me." He starts to chop at my hair again but his heart has gone out of it. He might have been prepared for my death, but not his father's. "They didn't tell me they were leaving Bournemouth. When I came back from Paris, after I killed Marion, I had to hire a private investigator to track them down—which is where I got my idea for you." He pauses, drops another length of hair onto my lap. "You came along at just the right time. My sights were set on Tamsin, I had her lined up, ready to go. I knew from Nina that she was looking for a therapist but she didn't want to share me with anyone." He laughs again. "I was her little secret, just like I was yours. I knew Tamsin would need a therapist even more once Nina had died, so it was perfect. But then she cut her hair."

"You came here, to The Circle, after killing Marion?" I say, backtracking, needing to keep the conversation going, because as long as we're talking, I'm alive.

"Yes. It was ironic, really. My parents chose London, thinking it would reduce them to needles in a haystack, plus a gated community, thinking they'd be able to keep me out. But it proved the perfect hiding place for me."

"He wouldn't let us go anywhere, he kept us prisoner," Lorna says, her voice stronger now. She moves nearer, coming into my vision. "He locked us in here during the day, in our bedroom at night. There wasn't anything we could do, he was too strong for us. We were only allowed to put the bins out, or do a bit of gardening at the front of the house, so that people would see us from time to time and not worry about us. But never together, he always kept one of us hostage. When Edward went to hospital with his heart attack, John told him he would kill me if he said anything to the doctors. He wouldn't let me visit Edward, I had to pretend to the hospital that I was too frail to make the journey."

"But you're not frail, are you, Lorna?" I say, trying to catch her eye in the mirror, needing her to understand that if we're going to get out of this, she has to be strong. But she's too deep in her own story.

"He made me lie to the police. I had to pretend I'd heard Oliver and Nina arguing, pretend that she'd admitted to me that she was having an affair. I had to say that I'd seen Oliver go straight into the house the night she was murdered." She clutches her pearls, a lifebuoy in the tumult of her emotions. "He must have seen Oliver go into the square and took his chance to go and kill Nina. I didn't know, I didn't know what he'd done, not until he came back and told me exactly what I had to say to the police if they came knocking. He threatened to kill Edward if I didn't, he was always threatening to kill us." The tears come back. "Oliver and Nina never argued. They loved each other."

Thomas shakes his head angrily. "No. Nina did not love him, she loved me. She couldn't see it, that's all. Just like those other two bitches. But you were different, Alice. If only you'd given me a little more time. We were so close."

"What do you mean?"

He stoops, bringing his face up against mine. "Admit it, Alice," he says softly. "You were beginning to fall in love with me."

I look at our reflections in the mirror, captured within its ornate frame. We could be a photograph.

"Lorna," I say, my voice firm.

Her eyes lock with mine and I look toward the scissors, still in Thomas's hand but within her grasp, hoping she'll get the message. But Thomas sees and with an almost childish laugh, raises them high above his head.

"She's not going to help you, Alice. I'm her son."

He's right, I know that. Lorna is no match for his strength anyway. She wouldn't be able to wrestle the scissors out of his hand, let alone use them against him.

"Did she turn me in to the police after I killed Justine, after I killed Marion?" Thomas goes on. "No, she didn't. Did she cover up for me after I killed Nina? Yes, she did. Blood is thicker than water, Alice. Justine, Marion, and Nina were just that—water."

"But Edward wasn't," I say. "Edward was blood. And you killed him."

I've struck a chord. "I didn't kill him!" he shouts.

"Well, technically, you did."

Lorna screams then, not a scream of fear, or of suffering, but a scream of white-hot anger that goes on and on and on. It comes from deep inside her, canceling out a mother's innate desire to protect her child, no matter what they do. And Thomas, sensing that something has changed, freezes for a few precious seconds, just enough time for me, still tied to the chair, to spring up and back, smashing into him. He crashes to the floor and I land heavily on top of him. Caught unawares, the scissors fly from his hand.

"Lorna!" I cry. She stops in mid-scream and stares, seemingly paralyzed, at Thomas and me on the floor. He grapples with the chair, trying to throw the weight of it off him. But I force my body downward, pinning him underneath me.

"Lorna!" I call again. "Get help!"

With a roar of anger, Thomas gets his arms around the chair and throws it off him, slamming me to the floor. The air is expelled from my lungs and as I lie helpless, he throws himself across my chest, compressing it. His hands move to my neck, his face contorted with fury. As the pressure builds in my throat, I realize that even if Lorna does get help, it will be too late for me.

I hear him grunt and the weight of him on my chest increases. But his hands lose some of their grip and I twist my head to the side, gasping desperately for air.

His hands slacken more, then fall from my neck and, at the same time as his head crashes onto mine, I become aware of a dull rhythmic thud, repeating itself over and over again.

SIX MONTHS LATER

There's a knock at the door, so timid that it barely registers.

I place my book on the scrubbed pine table, and wipe suddenly clammy hands on my jeans. Even though I've been expecting Eve, I'm still horribly nervous about seeing her. What if she knows?

It's all right, I remind myself, as I walk to the door. *She doesn't know. Thanks to Lorna, nobody will ever know.*

I thought I would die that day, crushed by the weight of Thomas's body across my chest. Although I'd managed to twist my head to the side, I couldn't get air into my lungs. Lorna had gone into shock, paralyzed by what she had done. My strangled gasp pulled her back. She tried to lift Thomas off me but he was too heavy for her.

"Pull me out!"

Understanding, she got her hands under my arms and freed me just enough to release the pressure on my chest. The rest is a blur; the police arriving, the gentle questions, the walk to the ambulance, the shocked faces of the people huddled outside, brought by the sight of an ambulance and a police car screeching into The Circle. And Eve and Tamsin, staring at me in stunned disbelief as I followed Lorna to the ambulance, realizing there was more to what they were witnessing than Edward having died.

It dawned on me then, how everyone—not only the police but also Leo, Ginny, Debbie and all who lived in The Circle—would know how I'd been taken in by the stranger who had come to our house six weeks before.

"They'll all know," I wept in anguish to Lorna as we sat in the ambulance, waiting for it to leave. "They will know how stupid I've been. I can't bear it."

And Lorna had reached for my hand under the blankets that had been wrapped tight around us. "All anyone needs to know is that you came to see me and Edward to say goodbye, and were taken captive by a man, who you recognized as the man who turned up at your drinks evening," she whispered. "When the police ask, that's what you tell them. They don't need to know anything else, nobody does." I stared at her, not daring to believe it could be so simple. "It will be all right," she promised, giving my hand a squeeze.

I took it, this lifeline she had thrown me, and clung on to it. I made the end of my story the beginning, and never mentioned the name Thomas Grainger. He had existed only for me; nobody needed to know how stupidly gullible I'd been. As far as the police and everyone else was concerned, it was as Lorna had said; I had gone round to say goodbye to her and Edward, and had found a man there, who I recognized as the man who had gate-crashed our drinks evening. He had Edward by the throat and before I could react, he attacked me. When I regained consciousness, I found myself tied to a chair and while he hacked at my hair, he told me that he was Edward and Lorna's son, that he had killed Nina Maxwell and that I would suffer the same fate. And I'd thought I would die, until Lorna saved me.

This small part of the truth is all anyone knows.

Eve looks different. The pink tips have gone from her hair and her face is fuller.

"Thank you for agreeing to see me," she says awkwardly.

We stare at each other for a moment. Then my emotions take over and I pull her into a hug.

"It's so good to see you," I say, and she sinks against me.

"Really?" There's a catch in her voice.

"Yes," I say. "I've missed you."

"I've missed you too." She moves back, searches my face. "How are you?"

"I'm good," I say. "Getting there."

She nods, then grasps my hand. "I need so much to apologize," she says, her voice anguished.

I frown. "Apologize?"

"Yes. I feel awful about everything. We all do." She gives an awkward smile. "I don't suppose I could sit down, could I? I'm pregnant and it's been a long drive."

"Oh, Eve, that's wonderful, congratulations!" Spurred into action by her lovely news, I lead her to the kitchen and pull out a chair. "Here, have a rest while I make some tea."

She looks around, captivated.

"This is lovely, Alice. I love that plate rack, and your amazing AGA—and is that a bread oven?"

I can't help laughing at her enthusiasm. "Yes," I say, turning to fill the kettle.

"Your cottage is gorgeous, I'm not surprised you found leaving it hard. When did you move back in?"

"Two months ago. I stayed with Debbie at first."

"You must be happy to be back."

"I am. I feel safe here."

She tips her head to one side, observing me. "Your hair. It suits you."

"Thanks." I raise my hand to my head. "I always wanted to know what it would be like to have short hair and now I know." I don't tell her that I hate it, that every time I look in the mirror, I see Thomas Grainger standing behind me, his face contorted with malice. But I'm getting good at blinking the image away; I refuse to let him carry on impacting on my life.

I glance at her neat little bump.

"When is your baby due?"

"At the beginning of August."

"Wow. In four months. I'm so pleased for you, Eve. Will must be delighted."

She laughs. "He is. You'd think he was the first man to become a father."

I take mugs from the cupboard and milk from the fridge. "So, how is everyone?"

"Struggling," she says and I nod, because I know this from Leo. "Maria and Tim have already left; they put their house on the market almost at once, for less than it was worth, and managed to sell it relatively quickly. Tamsin and Connor will be the next to leave. Then Will and me. We're trying to stagger it so that the price of the houses isn't affected too much. But we'll still be selling at a loss."

"I'm sorry," I say.

She gives me a little smile. "It's not your fault." But she's wrong, it is my fault. If I hadn't been so gullible, it wouldn't have come to this. Shame heats my cheeks, and I busy myself making the tea so that she won't see.

"We feel so bad, Alice, and not just because we didn't really believe that a strange man had turned up at your party. We feel terrible about Oliver. We accepted too easily that he was guilty. We needed so much to believe that her killer had been caught so that we could carry on with our lives. We took the easy way out and that's hard to live with."

I carry the mugs over to the table and sit down opposite her. I want to say something to comfort her, but I can't find anything.

"Leo said that you saw Lorna," Eve says, breaking the silence that has grown between us.

"Yes, a few months ago."

"How is she?"

I give a slight smile. "Struggling. She's living with her sister in Dorset while she's awaiting trial."

"They'll be lenient with her, won't they?"

"I hope so."

While Eve sips her tea, my mind goes back to the day when Lorna and I were in the ambulance together. She had been so strong. A sort of euphoria had set in; she had managed to free herself, she had managed to save me. It hadn't yet hit her that Edward was gone forever, and that she had killed her son. That although one nightmare was over, another was about to begin.

When I'd next seen her, two months later in Dorset, it was very different. She was huddled in a chair, her sister hovering behind her. She seemed to have shrunk to half her size, and aged by ten years. It was hard to see her so diminished.

"Oliver killed himself because I betrayed him," she whispered, her eyes blurred by tears. "He said I was the mother he never had and I betrayed him. I betrayed you too. John made me write that letter."

It took me a while to remember the letter I received, supposedly from Helen, the letter that had given me new resolve just when I was beginning to have doubts about helping solve Nina's murder.

I took her hand. "It doesn't matter."

She told me then, how it had all started, how even as a child John would quickly become obsessed by a particular person; first, the little girl who lived next door, then classmates at school, to the point where the mothers and teachers had worried words with Lorna before putting a distance between her child and the others. As a teenager, he developed a dangerous obsession with one of his teachers, and it had come out during his police interview—when, at fifteen years old, he'd been cautioned for stalking her—that he had interpreted innocent actions on her part as a sign that his love for her was reciprocated. One example he gave was that she would sometimes release her hair from its ponytail and let it swing around her shoulders for a moment before attaching it again, in what he believed was a secret and intimate message to him. Lorna and Edward sought help from doctors and therapists and John was diagnosed with Obsessive Love Disorder. He cleverly played along, leading everyone to believe that his obsessive personality was under control.

During his university years, Lorna and Edward rarely saw their son and after graduating in 2003, he disappeared from their lives completely. It was the start of the Gulf War, and without news, Lorna and Edward convinced themselves that he had joined the army. One night, thirteen years later, he turned up at their Bournemouth home. He told them that he had come to stay for a couple of weeks and when they asked him if he was in the army, he told them that yes, he'd been fighting in Iraq. He was charming to the neighbors, telling them that he was home on leave, and was going to build his parents the terrace they had always wanted. For three weeks, he worked long into the evenings until he left as suddenly as he came, taking their car with him and leaving his behind.

"Did you have any idea why Thom—" I caught

myself, "John, was building the terrace?" I asked Lorna, because after her interviews with the police, the terrace at their former home had been dug up. Human remains had been found, later identified as Justine Bartley.

She shook her head violently. "We knew there was something not right but not that, never that. All the time he was with us, we hadn't felt safe. He was aggressive, threatening, and we were frightened of him. We told ourselves it was because of his experiences in Iraq but deep down, we knew that he had never been in the army and that the darkness in him came from something else. It was a relief when he left and we were scared that he would come back, so we decided to move somewhere he wouldn't find us." She touched her hand to her pearls and I was glad to see this old gesture of hers, glad that there was still something left of her previous self. "We told our neighbors we were moving to Devon and moved instead to London. And when we arrived, we told everyone our son had been killed in Iraq. I know it sounds terrible, disowning our son like that but—" Her voice trailed off. "And then, one day, we woke up and found him waiting in the back garden."

"Is that when he began keeping you prisoner?"

She nodded and repeated what she had already told me while I'd sat tied to the chair. "He kept to the bedrooms at the back of the house and at night, we could hear him moving around. He never seemed to sleep. But often, at six in the morning, he would wake us and lock us in the downstairs room and only let us out at lunchtime, so we thought that was when he probably slept." She paused to gather her thoughts. "I wasn't allowed out of the house, only Edward was, to put the bins out and do some gardening at the front, to keep up appearances. He would put his hands around my neck and squeeze until I could barely breathe and tell Edward he would strangle me properly if he tried to alert anyone to what was going on. We were allowed to answer the door but he would stand behind us, listening to everything we said." Her hands moved to the pink patchwork blanket covering her knees and began plucking at it. "The day that you came over, asking about Nina, he was listening to everything. I tried to warn you, I tried to tell you not to trust him, I couldn't give you a name because I knew he wouldn't be using John. I knew he'd gone to your drinks evening, he'd seen the invitation on the WhatsApp group and after what he did to poor Nina, I was scared for you." Tears rolled down her cheeks as she quickly dug a tissue from her sleeve.

"I thought you said that I wasn't to trust anyone," I told her.

She dabbed at her eyes. "No, I said 'Don't trust him.' But he knew I had whispered something to you and he was so angry. I swore that I hadn't but then he found out that I had and he hit me."

"It was me," I said, appalled that I had been the cause of such violence. "I told him you'd told me not to trust anyone. But Lorna, there's something I don't understand." I moved closer. "When I told you and Edward that a man had turned up at our drinks evening, why did you say that you had let him in to The Circle?

Wouldn't it have been better to deny all knowledge of him?"

"I was going to, but then you said that Leo wanted to go to the police and I panicked. John was there, listening, and I was scared that if he thought the police might turn up, asking questions, he would kill us in case we gave him away."

There was something else that had been puzzling me but I wasn't sure she could give me an answer. "I don't understand why he pretended to be a private investigator looking into a murder that he himself had committed. It seems such a risky thing to do."

"I suppose it was the only way he could think of to hook you in, tell you that he was looking into a miscarriage of justice and ask you to help him. He would never have expected you to get to the truth. It was why he was willing to take the risk."

"But if I had told everyone about him?"

"He must have known that you wouldn't," she said and I blushed, realizing how well he had read me. "And even if you had, it wouldn't have mattered. The private detective would have disappeared into the night. But he would have found some other way to get to you," she added, and I wondered how he had got to Nina, if it had been a card through the door advertising his services as a therapist to therapists. "It was a game to him, everything was about manipulating people into thinking he was something he wasn't, like pretending to our neighbors in Bournemouth that he was the perfect son, and that the reason he hadn't been home for years was because he used his leave to help war orphans. He was so charming that everybody believed him. Even Edward and I believed him at first." She paused. "Perhaps that was because we wanted to believe there was good in our son, even though he scared us. But we never imagined he was capable of evil, not until he told us he'd killed Nina. I hate myself for lying for him, for telling the police that I had heard Nina and Oliver arguing, that Nina had told me she'd been having an affair. But he threatened to kill Edward if I didn't and somewhere underneath it all, he was still my son." Her hands began to shake. "I can't believe what I did, I can't believe I killed him."

I held her hands between mine, stilled the shaking. "You saved my life," I told her. "That's what you did. You saved my life." I leaned to kiss her. "Thank you."

It didn't seem enough. But what do you say to a mother who killed her son, who severed, so violently and with such finality, the umbilical cord that bound them together, to save the life of an almost-stranger?

She rallied then, became suddenly stronger. "Then if I saved your life, will you do something for me?" she asked. "And for Edward, because he would have wanted it too."

"Of course," I said. "Anything."

"Live it." I looked at her uncomprehendingly. "Live the life you have. You've spent the last twenty years living in the past. Now you have a whole life ahead of you. Don't let guilt consume you. We all make mistakes."

Some more than others. I can make any number of excuses for myself. Despite therapy, I have never recovered from killing my parents and sister. The judge's refusal to send me to jail, even though I begged him to, robbed me of my need to be punished and I've been punishing myself ever since. Leaving Harlestone, where everyone knew my story and came together to stop me from sinking into despair, meant that I was left without my support group. But I had Leo, the only other person I had confided in, because there were meant to be no secrets between us. He knew everything, including my anguish at not being properly punished. It's why, when I discovered that he had served a prison sentence, it wasn't his criminal record that made me unable to forgive him, but jealousy. I was jealous that he had been able to atone for what he did and move on with his life, while I was stuck in the past. Already floundering because he hadn't told me about Nina, I became even more disorientated and turned to the one person I felt I could trust, the one person who represented stability when distrust and suspicion, created unwittingly by Lorna's whispered warning, began to color my friendships with those around me. But the only thing I can really blame Thomas Grainger for is instilling fear into me with his night-time prowling. For the rest, I played right into his hands.

Eve and I talk a while longer. It's almost the same as before, but not quite. And that's OK, because I know it can never be the same, not when I haven't told her the whole truth. It's the same with Leo; I still see him, we are still friends and he's made it clear that he'd like us to be together again. But how can I if I'm keeping secrets from him, when I couldn't forgive him for keeping secrets from me?

Sometimes, I think he knows there's more to what happened than the version I gave him. The last time he was here, he caught hold of my hands and pulled me to him.

"I would never judge you," he said softly. "How could I, after the things I kept from you?"

Eve leaves me with a hug, promising to let me know when the baby arrives.

"Tamsin would love to see you," she says and I wish I could tell her that I owe Tamsin a huge debt, because if she hadn't told me about Oliver not having a sister, I doubt I'd be here. I'm sure Thomas intended to kill me that day to stop me from leaving The Circle, that he would have led me upstairs on some pretense, and I would have suffered the same fate as Nina, Marion and Justine.

"I'd like that," I say truthfully, although I'm not sure it will ever happen. "Give her my love."

I walk slowly back to the kitchen. It's not always easy doing as Lorna asked, but I'm glad I agreed to see Eve. I sit down at the table, happy to get back to the book I was reading, then pause. Leo will be calling later to see how it went. I've already taken one huge step today; maybe it's time to take another and finally tell him the truth about the man who turned up at our drinks evening.

The truth, and nothing but the truth.

ACKNOWLEDGMENTS

First and foremost, thank you to my amazing agent, Camilla Bolton. After five books together, you are so much more than my agent. I'm proud and honored to call you my friend.

Thank you to Kate Mills at HQ and Catherine Richards at St. Martin's Press for your precious input and unwavering support. And to all my other editors abroad, more than forty of you now! Your continued faith in my books is humbling.

Huge thanks also to the following:

The teams who work with my editors to proofread, design, promote, and market my books. I wish I could mention each of you by name. But you know who you are, and I also hope you know how grateful I am for your hard work and enthusiasm.

My fellow authors, who kindly take time out from their busy lives to read my books. In particular, I would like to thank Louise Candlish, Jane Corry and

Tim Logan for their generous quotes in relation to *The Therapist*.

The bloggers and readers, who give up their precious time to read and review my books.

My friends, both in France and in the UK, for always being interested in what I am writing, and for buying my books when they are eventually published.

And, of course, my thanks to the wonderful members of the Curran and MacDougall families, most of all my husband, Calum, and my daughters, Sophie, Chloë, Céline, Eloïse and Margaux. You hold me up.

Turn the page for a sneak peek at
B. A. Paris's new novel

Available now

ONE

PRESENT

I sense the shift of air beneath my nose a millisecond before something—thick, sticky tape—is clamped over my mouth, silencing the scream that would have ripped from me. My eyes snap open. A dark silhouette is bending over my bed.

Adrenaline surges. *Move! Grab the knife!* I twist my arm toward my pillow, but a hand slams onto my wrist, holding it still. Pulled from the bed, I kick out. But my feet flail uselessly, find only air. I try to focus but my mind is spinning. Why did I fall asleep? I should have been expecting this.

My arms are pulled behind my back, my wrists bound together. I try to twist away but something is pulled over my head, material, rough and tight, a hood of some kind. Panic spreads through me like wildfire. *Don't. Keep calm, Amelie. You know what this is.*

He pushes me from the room, my feet tangle, I stumble, he jerks me upright. Under the hood, my head is filled with the frantic pulse of my heartbeat. I fight back the fear. *I can outwit him; I've done it before.*

The soft carpet beneath my feet gives way to the cold polished floor of the landing. My toes bump the edge of the carpeted runner; in my mind I see its intricate green and red pattern of leaves and animals. I inhale the chemical smell of glue from the tape and a mix of a cough and a choke burns my throat. I draw a breath, and the material from the hood sucks into my nostrils. *Where is he taking me?*

The grip on my shoulders tightens a little; there's a slight pulling back. Instinct tells me we are at the top of the stairs and I hesitate, afraid to fall. Pushed forward, I find the first step, then move downward until the soles of my feet touch the cold checkered tiles of the hall. We move down the hallway to the left, my ragged breathing amplified in the eerie silence. I know where we're going. He's taking me to the basement, where the garage is.

I turn, wrenching my body away from him, and for a precious moment, his grasp on me weakens. But it's not enough; I'm hauled back into place, and pain flashes up my arms. Angled to the right, more steps down, the space narrows, the air shifts, becomes cooler.

And then, an influx of sounds, stifled by the hood but recognizable still—scuffling feet, a muffled whine, a sense of others there waiting. I push back, then stop. The scuffling, the whine—they didn't come from me. My mind reels. *It can't be, it's not possible.*

But I know the voice behind the smothered protests—Ned.

This is not what I thought it was.

TWO

PRESENT

Under my hood, my eyes dart, looking for a way out of this nightmare. *Think, Amelie, think!* But my mind is paralyzed. *What is this? Who are they?*

I hear the clunk of a car trunk opening. There's more scuffling; Ned's muted protests become louder. A grunt and a thud; have they put him in the trunk? My body tenses; I can't be put in there with him. Then, without warning, I'm pushed into the interior of the car, face-down in the space between the seats, my knees forced up against the thin material of my pajamas. Heavy shoes push against my back, holding me down when I try to get up.

At first, I attempt to keep track of where we're going. But I quickly become disoriented. I concentrate instead on drawing small sucks of air into my lungs. My stomach heaves; I'm breathing too fast. I close my eyes, imagine I'm outside in the cool night air, looking up at the sky, the stars, the infinite space. Gradually, my breathing calms.

Later, hours it seems, the car slows, the road becomes rougher. My mind has wandered. I force myself to focus; I know that for survival, every second counts. The car rocks; I picture a dirt track under the wheels, a forest around us. I should be more afraid. But I'm not scared of dying, not anymore. Not after everything.

There are sudden thuds from the trunk and cries of pain from Ned. He must be terrified—but shouldn't he have been expecting this? Hunter, his security guard, brutally murdered three days ago, replaced by Carl, an unknown quantity. Where was Carl while we were being abducted? For this to have happened, there has to have been a massive breach of security. *All eyes on Carl.*

The car comes to a halt. Doors click open, the shoes are removed from my back. I'm pulled from the footwell, made to stand. The cool August night air wraps itself around my legs; goose bumps rise on my arms. There's the smell of dirt, foliage, tree sap.

I hear Ned being dragged from the trunk. We're pushed forward, Ned in front; I can hear him mumbling. The ground is sharp under my bare feet, stones digging into soft flesh, like shingle on a beach. I wait for the softer undergrowth of bracken, the crisp snapping of twigs. But the stones become smooth slabs, a path of some kind. *Not an execution then. At least, not in a forest.*

We stop. I hear the creak of a door pulled open, the scrape of wood along the ground, not a door to a house, an outbuilding perhaps. Propelled forward into a blast of cold air, I tremble. It's not a shed; it's a dungeon or basement, its thick walls untouched by the warmth of the sun.

I'm shivering now despite the crush of bodies around me. A door opens somewhere in front, another scuffle, Ned frantic, my foot trampled as they move to contain him. I hold my breath, wait it out. A door slams, followed by thuds as Ned throws his body against it, raging from behind his gag. *Be quiet. It's not going to help.*

We move on, climb stone steps; I count them, twelve in all. Then, at the top, the worn stone under my feet becomes warm wood, softer against my skin. A door is opened; I'm moved forward.

There's a movement behind me and I steel myself for a blow. Instead, the hood is pulled up and off my head. My hair crackling with static, I draw a deep breath in through my nose, then blink and blink again, waiting for my eyes to adjust to the darkness. But there's nothing. No flicker of light, no paler shade of black.

Without warning, there's a tug on my hand, strong fingers on my wrists. A cry of alarm builds, pushing against my throat. *Not this.* I kick back and my feet connect with flesh and muscle, but whoever is behind me holds me tighter. Then, a sawing sound and the rough scratch of a knife echo around the room until suddenly, there's an audible snap. The pressure on my wrists releases and the momentum trips me forward.

Before I can turn, there's the slam of a door, the click of a lock.

That's when I realize: From the moment the man came into my bedroom, our abductors haven't said a word.

"Years ago my daughters and wife were inhaling Robin Gunn's stories and loving them, so I had to take a peek myself to find out why. I did. Robin's characters are believable, and her stories have just the right blend of hope, broken hearts, disappointments, lighthearted fun, joy, and an eternal perspective. The Lord Jesus always plays a role, whether behind the scenes or in the thick of things. Robin lives the faith that's so evident in her books. She knows how to tell a story—and the stories she tells make an eternal difference."

RANDY ALCORN, AUTHOR OF *DEADLINE*

"When you read a Robin Gunn book, you know you're going to receive a tender lesson in what it means to belong to Christ—and you will be blessed for it."

FRANCINE RIVERS, AUTHOR OF *REDEEMING LOVE* AND
THE MARK OF THE LION SERIES

"Gratefully Robin's warmth, insight, and humor spill over from her heart onto the written page. She delights us with the well-woven fabric of a well-told tale and I'm certain Robin delights the Lord with her obvious passion for him."

PATSY CLAIRMONT, AUTHOR OF *GOD USES CRACKED POTS* AND
SPORTIN' A 'TUDE

"Robin Jones Gunn cares. She cares about her characters, she cares about her readers, and most of all, she cares about their mutual search for a life that pleases the Lord. Her novels are a delight to read—perfectly crafted, heartwarming, and fun. I'm always thrilled when one of Robin's books appears on the top of my to-be-read stack!"

LIZ CURTIS HIGGS, AUTHOR OF *MIXED SIGNALS, BOOKENDS,* AND *BAD GIRLS OF THE BIBLE*

"Robin Jones Gunn is one of those rare and wonderful writers who infuses her stories with bountiful doses of humor, wisdom, and warmth. Her books have touched and changed countless hearts and given a whole generation of readers a host of fictional characters who feel like dear friends!"

CAROLE GIFT PAGE, AUTHOR OF *HEARTLAND MEMORIES SERIES*

"Whenever I think of stories that touch the heart, I think of Robin Jones Gunn. They touch my heart and leave me wanting more. Reading a novel by Robin Jones Gunn is like spending time with a good friend…troubles are lighter and joys are deeper."

ALICE GRAY, AUTHOR OF *STORIES FOR THE HEART* BOOK COLLECTION

"Robin Jones Gunn writes from a heart of love. Her tender stories honor the Savior and speak truth to a world desperately eager to hear it."

ANGELA ELWELL HUNT, AUTHOR OF *THE TRUTH TELLER*

"Robin Gunn is a gifted and sincere storyteller who gets right to the heart of matters with her readers."

MELODY CARLSON, AUTHOR OF *HOMEWARD*

THE GLENBROOKE SERIES

Woodlands

ROBIN JONES GUNN

Multnomah®Publishers *Sisters, Oregon*

WOODLANDS
published by Multnomah Publishers, Inc.
© 2000 by Robin Jones Gunn

International Standard Book Number: 1-57673-503-6

Cover image by Digital Stock
Cover designed by David Uttley Design

Scripture quotations are from *The Holy Bible,* King James Version
New American Standard Bible (NASB) © 1960, 1977 by the Lockman Foundation

The Holy Bible, New International Version (NIV) © 1973, 1984 by International
Bible Society, used by permission of Zondervan Publishing House.

Printed in the United States of America

For information:
MULTNOMAH PUBLISHERS, INC.
P. O. BOX 1720
SISTERS, OR 97759

Library of Congress Cataloging-in-Publication Data
Gunn, Robin Jones, 1955–
   Woodlands/by Robin Jones Gunn. p.cm.–(The Glenbrooke series; bk. 7)
   ISBN 1-57673-503-6 (alk. paper) I. Title.
   PS3557.U4866 W66 2000
   813'.54–dc21   99-051803

00 01 02 03 04 05 06 07 — 10 9 8 7 6 5 4 3 2 1 0

To my exceptional friend, Anne de Graaf, who prayed.
And to Liz Curtis Higgs,
with whom Anne and I shared cheesecake
at 2 A.M. in a Toronto hotel room
when heaven broke through.

"The LORD thy God in the midst of thee is mighty, he will save, he will rejoice over thee with joy, he will rest in his love, he will joy over thee with singing."

ZEPHANIAH 3:17

Chapter One

*H*ey batter, batter, batter—swing!" Leah Hudson leaned over the counter of the Snack Shack at the Glenbrooke Little League ball field and yelled. "Swing, batter, swing!"

The young batter swung and missed.

"Stree-ike three!" the umpire called.

Leah checked the scoreboard. Bottom of the ninth. Score tied 7 to 7. The Edgefield Pirates took the outfield as her beloved Glenbrooke Rangers hustled up to bat.

Leah smiled. She took a sip from her can of Dr Pepper and flipped her feathery blond hair behind her ears. "It doesn't get any better than this," she murmured to herself, gazing at the lavender sky. The retiring sun had left a dozen pale pink streak marks on its way home. A flock of chattering wrens flitted overhead.

Little blond-haired Travis ran over to the Snack Shack with a golden retriever bounding behind him. Chinning himself up on the counter, the almost five-year-old asked, "Can I have a Sno-Kone, Auntie Leah?"

Leah was "auntie" to lots of children in Glenbrooke. She had lived there all of her twenty-seven years. Twenty-seven single years. Twenty-seven years of helping everyone else raise their children.

"Here you go, Travis," Leah said, handing him the rainbow Sno-Kone. He smiled and produced a fistful of money.

"Tell your mom I'm coming over early on Saturday to help with the Easter egg hunt, okay?"

"Okay," Travis said. Without looking back, he trotted to the bleachers with the retriever beside him.

That's when Leah noticed the guy in shorts. He leaned against the side of the bleachers with a large Dairy Queen shake in his hand. His black shorts and forest green knit shirt were the uniform of the Parker Delivery Service, which made almost daily deliveries to the admitting desk of Glenbrooke General Hospital where Leah worked. She knew all the delivery guys. This one had to be new. She would have remembered those legs. No one in Oregon had legs that tan this early in spring.

A cheer rose from the home crowd, and Leah realized she had missed a hit. The tallest of the Glenbrooke Rangers dashed to first base while the Pirates fumbled with the ball in the out-field. The runner made it to third base before the ball was back in the pitcher's mitt.

"Come on, Rangers!" Leah yelled, as the next batter stepped up to the plate. "You can do it! Bring him home!"

Her voice must have really traveled because the delivery guy with the bronzed legs turned halfway around and watched her instead of the game. Leah allowed her gaze to linger in his direction a little longer. She strained to make out any distinct facial features, but his baseball cap cast too much shadow for her to come to any real conclusions. She was pretty sure she had never seen him before.

Leah turned away when another young customer came up and asked for a candy bar. Just then, a cheer rose from the bleachers.

"What happened?" She didn't have to wait for an answer. The whoops and hollers from the bleachers indicated that the Rangers had just scored a run. Dozens of parents stood and cheered for their kids. Leah knew almost everyone.

She felt a familiar twinge of pain as she watched the parents' joyous outburst. It was the same ache she felt whenever she realized she was on the sidelines while all the women her age were holding babies or hugging their husbands or both.

Leah glanced again at the uniformed delivery guy. He had squatted down and was using both hands to rough up the golden retriever behind the ears.

Look away, Leah, look away! Don't do this to yourself.

A well-used recording played in her psyche right on cue. The voice was that of her oldest and least favorite sister. The words had been spoken a long time ago, yet Leah never had forgotten them: "You have neither the frame nor the frame of mind to ever attract someone stable."

Leah's three oldest sisters were willowy blonds, like their mother. They all married before they turned twenty-two. The next two sisters had inherited their father's height as well as his thick, brunette hair and milk-chocolate brown eyes. Both of them had married intelligent men and had moved to the East Coast.

Somehow Leah managed to be the only daughter who inherited what she considered the lesser qualities of both parents. She had her father's round face and candy apple cheeks and her mother's long neck. Her eyes were a cloudy gray, and she had worn glasses starting in the second grade and contacts since ninth grade. Her blond hair, which she had inherited from her mother, was the only attribute she liked. She had her mother's short stature but her father's strong, muscular frame. The years she had spent transferring her heavy father from his sickbed to his wheelchair had done her figure a favor by giving her great muscle tone. Perhaps that would be her only reward for being the daughter who stayed in Glenbrooke to care for her elderly parents, which she did faithfully until they both passed away a year ago.

Leah's Glenbrooke friends were her family now. She knew better than to be deluded about the possibility of marriage and family over some guy with tan legs. A guy who obviously loved dogs. And Dairy Queen shakes. And Little League games and gorgeous spring evenings.

Oh, stop it, will you! Leah chided, forcing herself to turn away from the delivery guy by the bleachers. She tried to focus on the price list sign behind her. One of the *r*s in "burrito" was crooked. She fixed it and brushed a spider web from the top right-hand corner of the sign.

Another blast of hurrahs echoed from the bleachers. Leah turned to see the Rangers galloping out to the field, tossing their caps and mitts into the air.

She let out a loud cheer. "Way to go, Rangers!"

The exuberant crowd came rushing in her direction, looking for post-game refreshments. Leah snapped into action, reaching for canned drinks in the ice chest and counting out Pixie Stix. The faster she worked, the louder the crowd grew—and the larger. Just when she had appeased nearly all the parents from the bleachers with their toddlers, the players on both teams joined in the mob, waving tickets from their coaches for free treats.

The side door of the Snack Shack trailer opened, and without looking to see who it was, Leah said, "Hey, we have to keep that door shut, you guys."

"I thought you could use some help," a deep voice said.

Leah looked up at the delivery guy, who was now standing beside her. She realized again the disadvantage of being only 5'4". It meant she constantly had to look up to men. That had been a problem for her more than once and in more ways than one.

"Ah, well, okay," she stammered, feeling her apple-round cheeks begin to blush. "I guess."

He had the gentlest, deep blue eyes she had ever seen. And the whitest smile. Or was it just his rich tan that made his eyes and smile stand out?

"Who's next?" he asked.

A chorus of eager sugar hounds responded with one, high-pitched note of "Me!"

"Point to them one at a time," Leah suggested. "The yellow tickets are worth a dollar each. The blue ones are fifty cents. And if you can get them to form a line, you'll do better than I have."

A shrill whistle pierced the air. Leah nearly dropped the Sno-Kone she had just finished making for her customer.

"Line up! Single file. Let me see two lines here. That's it. You guys are awesome. Now what can I get for you?" he asked, pointing to the first sweaty face in the line.

Leah looked on in amazement. "How did you do that?"

"Years of practice," he said. "Where are the drinks?"

"In the ice chest. I only have cans. The ice over there is for the Sno-Kones."

"Do you have frozen Snickers bars?" Leah's next customer asked.

"No, sorry. I'll be sure to freeze some before the next game. Do you want an unfrozen Snickers instead?"

He nodded, and she handed him the last one.

"Nope," Leah heard her partner say to his next customer above the rising noise level. "Looks like that was the last one. How about a Hershey's bar? Or what else do we have here? A Milky Way?"

Leah had orders for five Sno-Kones in a row, followed by a burrito, which she tossed in the microwave while scooping up two popcorns and passing out a few candy bars. And then the customers were all gone. In record time.

"How do these tickets work?" the guy asked, examining one of the yellow slips of paper.

"They're marked with the player's name and the coach's name. The players can pay into a snack fund when they sign up for Little League so their coins don't fall out of their pockets while they run around the field. All I have to do is sort them and give them to the coaches, who pay me back."

"'Buchanan,'" he read on one of the slips. "Would that be the same Buchanan with the golden retriever?"

"Yes, Kyle." Leah scanned the nearly empty field and spotted Kyle in the twilight. "Do you see him over there by home plate? He's the coach. How did you know?"

"I read the dog tag." He graced Leah with a gentle smile and then turned to go. "Maybe I can still catch him."

Leah felt the need to say something more. Her handsome prince was leaving, and she didn't have a clue as to his identity. His work boots definitely weren't glass slippers, and neither of them looked as if it was about to fall off.

"Hey, thanks!" she called out, as he opened the door to exit. "Sure you don't want a free Sno-Kone for your trouble?"

"No," he said with a wave over his shoulder. "Thanks!"

"Thank *you*," Leah called out. And then he was gone.

"'Sure you don't want a free Sno-Kone for your trouble?'" Leah repeated under her breath. "Oh brother, what kind of line was that?"

Leah pulled herself back into reality by sorting out blue and yellow slips and beginning her routine to close down the Snack Shack. Her gaze wandered out to the ball field twice as she cleaned up. The first time she saw her mysterious stranger talking to Kyle, but on the second glance they were both gone. She turned the crank that rolled down the front window of the Snack Shack and unplugged all the electrical appliances. Balancing her keys and the cash box on top of an ice chest containing the leftover frozen burritos, Leah locked the outside door of the Snack Shack and headed for her car.

The field appeared empty now. Only three cars remained in the dirt parking lot. A cool breeze came sweeping through as soon as the sun set, a reminder that spring wasn't here yet. Leah climbed into her Blazer but before turning the key in the ignition she looped her arms over the steering wheel and stared at the first star that had risen in the clear night sky. She knew it was probably a planet since it was so bright. Venus, most likely.

Venus. Isn't that supposed to be the planet of love? What if I make a wish upon a planet—the love planet—instead of a star? Will I have a greater chance of my wish coming true?

Leah thought of the promises she had made to herself since her parents had passed away. She had been so determined to start fresh and to build a new identity for herself. Unfortunately, all her Glenbrooke friends seemed to have a set image of her. And their expectations had remained the same making it difficult for her to change.

However, this tan-legged delivery guy with the deep blue eyes didn't know who she was. He didn't have any expectations. He didn't know she had been her fataher's last hope for a son.

Most of Glenbrooke had heard her father tell the story of how he chose the name Leah for his sixth daughter. The book of Genesis contained the account of Jacob's first wife, Leah. Jacob had worked seven years to earn adorable Rachel's hand in marriage, but he was tricked into marrying Rachel's less desirable sister, Leah. When Jacob woke the morning after his wedding, he turned to see that "behold, it was Leah" next to him and not his long anticipated Rachel.

Leah could hear her father's voice echoing in her imagination. *"Saddest verse in the Bible, Genesis 29:25. 'Behold, it was Leah.' Yup, after five daughters, when I saw her I felt just like Jacob, and I said, 'We'll call her Leah.'"*

Early on Leah learned that if she worked hard—as hard as a son would have worked—she could please her father. So she became his tomboy and was one of the first girls in Glenbrooke to play Little League baseball on this very field.

Leah wondered if that bit of news would impress the mysterious newcomer. Or did he prefer soft-spoken women with manicured nails? He had said he had experience getting kids to line up. Did he work with kids? He definitely appeared to like dogs. That was a good sign.

Gazing up at the bright planet, Leah whispered, "I wish…I wish…."

It was no use. She had stopped wishing a long time ago. She didn't dare permit herself to speak aloud the silent wish that had long lay nestled in her heart. The dream, the wish, for someone to love and for that someone to love her back. The unattainable dream of one day handing a Sno-Kone to her own son and at long last being the mother in the bleachers who yelled the loudest when her boy was at bat.

Leah blinked and swallowed quickly. Bright Venus was still shining down on her.

Yeah, well, for all I know, I'm looking at Pluto, not Venus. What happens if I wish on Pluto? Does a floppy-eared dog with big feet show up on my doorstep?

Leah glanced at her watch. "Yikes! What am I doing sitting here talking to myself?" She started her car and headed for home. But first she had an important stop to make at the grocery store.

Chapter Two

$\mathcal{D}$ashing to the checkout stand with a cartful of groceries, Leah greeted the clerk with, "I know, I know, I'm the last one in the store, right?"

"That's okay," he said. "Looks like you were a little low on the essentials." He rang up the four cartons of a dozen eggs and looked at her over the top of his glasses.

"It's Easter," Leah said merrily. "They're for the big egg hunt at Kyle and Jessica's."

"Of course. I should have guessed. My kids are going."

"It's going to be fun," Leah said. "I hope the weather stays clear. It was beautiful today."

The clerk rang up an economy-size package of newborn diapers. "Looks like you're going to be ready for just about everything."

Leah only nodded. *Do you have to comment on everything I'm buying?*

Apparently he did because he kept going. "Great price on

the roast beef this week, isn't it?"

Leah nodded again.

"My wife likes these crackers. Are they any good?"

Leah didn't know. She had never tried them. In an effort to speed up the process and avoid further questions, she stepped to the end of the checkout stand and assisted in bagging her own groceries. She wanted to get as much as she could into two bags and keep the eggs separate in a third bag. The clerk chose to comment on that as well.

"You know what they say about putting all your eggs in one basket? You should put only two cartons in a bag. Eggs can be heavy, you know."

Leah didn't know. But she followed his instructions and left the store as quickly as she could. One of the disadvantages of living in a small town was that everybody could figure out what everyone else was doing, which made it difficult for Leah to cover her tracks. She had come to the grocery store late so she would be the only shopper. People who knew her well would have realized she would never buy a roast for herself since she rarely ate red meat.

Stashing the groceries in the back of her Blazer, Leah took off for the address she had scribbled on a sticky memo pad at work that afternoon. The dashboard of her car was freckled with notes she was forever writing to herself. Reminders of things to do, places to go, people to see.

She had a pretty good idea of where this house was located. It was one of the many homes on Glenbrooke's outskirts, tucked behind a forest of evergreens and then down a poorly marked dirt and gravel road.

Leah found it on her first try. She turned off the engine as soon as the porch light came into view. The Blazer rolled to a stop. As quietly as she could, Leah collected the two bulging bags of groceries and stepped lightly, heading for the front door.

From inside the house came the sound of a newborn's cries. As soon as Leah heard them she walked faster, feeling sure that the baby's cries would cover up any noise she made. It had only been a week since Leah had filed the papers at her hospital desk to send this newborn baby home. Four days later, the father had shown up in admitting with a mandatory hernia operation. He was teased plenty about overdoing it with the sympathy pains for his wife's recent delivery.

Leah had read the concern in the faces of the young couple. This was their first child. The husband worked construction and would now lose income during his recovery time. Their insurance had a $500 deductible.

That afternoon the hernia patient had been sent home, and Leah hoped the groceries would save the new mom from having to make a trip into town for a few days.

Leah carefully balanced the two heavy bags on the front door mat and gingerly made her way back to the car. When she was sure she was out of sight from the front door and that her car was sufficiently camouflaged down the road, she reached into the glove compartment for her cell phone. Holding a penlight between her teeth, she read the number off her sticky note and dialed the phone.

A woman's voice answered. The sound of the wailing baby came through the receiver so loud Leah had to pull the phone away from her ear.

"Hello?" the woman said a second time.

Leah lowered her voice to the basement of her range and said, "Yes, hello. I'm calling to let you know a gift is waiting on your doorstep. God bless you. Good night."

She hung up and waited. From her hiding place, she could

see the door slowly open. Her heart started to race. It always did when she thought of what her gift receivers must be thinking and feeling in that first moment of realization.

The woman stood a moment in stunned silence, holding the crying baby in her arms. She looked left and right and then tried to pick up one of the bags with her free hand. It was too heavy.

I should have put the groceries in more bags so they wouldn't be so heavy. What was I thinking? She just had a baby, and he just had hernia surgery.

It was all Leah could do to stay in the car and not hurry to the front door to help carry the groceries inside. But whenever Leah made her secret deliveries, it was incognito. That's the way she wanted it to stay. Her joy was in the giving, not in being discovered.

The woman went inside and came back with her arms free. Slowly she lifted the bags one at a time. When the front door closed, Leah waited a few minutes before starting the engine and backing down the road. It was difficult to maneuver in the dark so she went slowly. She kept thinking about the fifty eggs that were bouncing around like crazy in the back of the Blazer.

Just as her tires hit the paved street, her cell phone rang. Leah jumped. She stopped the car to answer the phone.

"Who is this?" the male voice asked.

"Who is this?" Leah retorted.

After a pause, the man said, "I got your number off my caller ID so I know that you, or someone at this number, just called us and said a gift was on our doorstep."

Leah's heart began to pound. She had never been traced this way before. She felt a rush of disappointment mixed with fear at the thought of being found out. No one had come this close to catching her after almost eight years of clandestine drop-offs.

"I just want to say thanks," the man said. "You don't know how badly we needed some of this stuff. Especially the diapers."

Leah smiled but didn't say anything. She had answered the phone in her natural voice but made the original call in a deep voice. She wasn't sure now which voice to use.

"You don't have to say anything," the man said after another pause. "We just wanted to say thank you. And God bless you, too." He hung up.

Leah drove home quickly. A sense of joy overpowered the rush of fear she had felt when she was nearly found out.

The next day at work Leah was all set to carry out another undercover mission. This time to find out the identity of the tan-legged PDS delivery guy by asking Harry, their usual PDS man.

However, by lunchtime not a single delivery had been made to the hospital. Leah had planned to run errands during her lunch break, but now she didn't want to leave the hospital in case Harry came while she was gone. She ate in the lunchroom, facing the door so she could see the admitting desk.

Harry never arrived. Leah found it hard to believe the hospital had no deliveries all day. When she left at four-thirty, still no deliveries had arrived.

Leah closed her car door and checked the sticky notes on the dashboard for her list of errands. The first note reminded her to drop off three muffin tins at Ida Dane's home on Fourth Avenue. Ida was making cupcakes for the Easter Saturday event and had left a message on Leah's phone the night before asking if she had extra tins.

Leah parked in front of the blue house and paused a moment to take in the carousel of color that surrounded the fifty-year-old A-frame home. Ida's flowers were her joy. Bright red tulips, nodding yellow daffodils, and deep purple pansies lined the steps to her front door where a clump of tall iris stalks looked as if they were getting ready to open in time for Easter Sunday. Ida's dogwood tree on the side of the house had burst into a canopy of bright pink blossoms.

Heading for the front door, Leah noticed the dainty white alyssum and abundant grape hyacinth that ran the length of the border along the front of the house. She knocked on the front door and watched as the afternoon breeze danced through the dogwood tree, causing the blossoms to flutter to the ground like confetti.

"Ida?" Leah called out, knocking again. "It's Leah."

The front door was closed. Leah guessed Ida was running errands. She was one of Glenbrooke's most active senior citizens, although in the past few years Leah had noticed Ida becoming more easily confused and keeping more to home than she used to. Leah left the muffin tins propped against the side of the screen door and told herself to call Ida later to make sure she had found them.

Leah was down the front walk and opening the door to her Blazer when she heard the deep rumbling sound of a delivery van rounding the corner onto Fourth. Something prompted her to duck inside her car and watch to see who was driving the van. It might be "him."

The brakes squealed as the van came to a stop in front of her car. She peered expectantly, waiting until the driver hopped out and headed up Ida's walkway with a clipboard and a small package.

Leah smiled. There he was, tanned legs and all. With her window rolled down, she sat back and decided to watch and listen. He obviously hadn't noticed her when he rushed up to Ida's door to make the delivery.

He was knocking on the door when thin, little Ida came

bustling around the far side of her house wearing garden gloves and waving a pair of clippers in her hand. "Yoo-hoo! I heard your truck pull up. I was hoping my package would arrive today. Oh, why, you're new, aren't you?"

He handed her the clipboard. "Yes, I am. Could you sign for me, please? Line 19."

Leah watched as Ida signed the paper and then looked him over. "Do you have time for a glass of lemonade?"

Leah thought this was the perfect setup. If he went inside for lemonade, she could go back to the front door saying she wanted to make sure Ida had found the muffin tins. Ida would invite Leah inside for lemonade, too, and voilà, Leah could meet Mr. PDS.

"No, I have a few more deliveries to make," he said. "Thank you, though."

"Oh!" Ida said, reaching over and picking up the muffin tins. "Did you leave these also?"

"No, they were there when I came up."

"Really?" Now Ida seemed intrigued. She looked around but didn't notice Leah in the car. Leah didn't know if she should wave and call out or start the car and dash away. Either choice seemed awkward so she stayed where she was, feeling relieved that neither of them seemed to have noticed her sitting there, spying on them. The lilac bushes must have hidden her from easy view.

Ida held up the muffin tins and triumphantly announced to the delivery guy, "I bet the Glenbrooke Zorro left these for me. He must have known I do lots of baking for Easter. I've always hoped I'd be visited by the Glenbrooke Zorro, and it looks like today was my day!"

Leah sank down in her seat. She couldn't drive away now. How could Ida have forgotten that she had called Leah to bring over the muffin tins?

"Well, have a nice afternoon," the delivery guy said before turning to go.

"Wait!" Ida called out. "I don't know your name, young man."

Leah thought that was a much better departing line than "Care for a Sno-Kone."

"Seth," he called to Ida from the middle of her garden walk. "Seth Edwards."

"Next time you come to my door, Seth Edwards, you make sure you have time for a nice glass of lemonade."

"I will. Thanks." He waved and hustled back to the delivery van.

Leah stayed slumped in her seat, watching and waiting for him to leave. Seth. Seth Edwards. It had a nice, stable sound to it.

Seth settled into the front seat of his van and appeared to be checking a map before pulling out. Leah waited. Seth put down the map and glanced in the rearview mirror. He was at just the right angle to look into the cab of Leah's Blazer, and when he did, their eyes met. Leah sheepishly waved. Seth smiled and waved back. He looked to the front door of Ida's house. Ida had gone in and taken the package and muffin tins with her. Seth looked back at Leah and smiled again.

Did he just deduce that I was the one who left the muffin tins? He's new in town. He can't know anything about the Glenbrooke Zorro. I hope he ignores that comment as the prattling of an old lady.

Leah expected him to start up his van and be on his way. After all, he had said he had several more deliveries to make. But to her surprise, he grabbed his map and exited the van. Before Leah knew what was happening, the bronzed, bare legs of Seth Edwards were striding toward her.

Chapter Three

$\mathcal{R}$esting his arm on the open window of Leah's Blazer, Seth leaned in and said, "Hi there."

"Hi." Leah felt certain her round cheeks were a bright shade of tulip red.

"I wonder if you could do me a favor."

"Sure," Leah said quickly. Too quickly, she thought, so she added, "I owe you a favor after the way you helped me out last night. You really saved the day for me."

"Good. Now maybe you can save the day for me. Can you tell me how to get to Medford Court? The map shows it as being off Nineteenth, but I was just there, and Nineteenth doesn't go through."

"What's the name on the package?" Leah asked.

"I think its Jamison or Jameson."

"Oh, sure, the Jamelsons'. I know right where that is. It would be easier for me to show you than to tell you. Why don't you follow me?" Leah volunteered.

"You sure it wouldn't be too much trouble?" Seth's deep blue eyes expressed his appreciation.

"No trouble at all." Leah turned the key in the ignition, but nothing happened. She checked to make sure the key was in all the way and tried again. Still no spark. "That's odd."

"Want me to look under the hood?" Seth asked.

"Sure." Leah popped the catch on the hood. She got out, and the two of them stood next to each other, both checking the engine. Leah was aware again of how small she felt next to this man. She concentrated on the equipment under the hood, her eyes running through all the familiar connections in the engine.

"Looks okay from what I can see," he said. "Do you think it might be the battery?"

"Not likely," Leah said. "I replaced it two months ago." She decided not to mention that she had literally been the one to replace it with only the aid of the car manual.

Would he be put off if he knew I'm mechanically inclined?

"We could try to jump-start it," Seth suggested. "I might have cables in the truck."

"I have some," Leah said, going to the back of her car and reaching for the cables, which were next to her tool chest. She returned and connected them quickly and easily.

"I'll pull the van closer," Seth offered. When he did, he popped open the hood and Leah connected the cables to the battery, then she returned to her car and tried to start it up.

Nothing happened. The key turned, but the engine didn't respond. Seth got out of the delivery van and disengaged the cables.

"Could be the starter," they said in unison when Leah climbed out of her car. They both laughed.

"Can I give you a ride somewhere?" Seth offered.

"Why don't I go with you to show you how to get to the Jamelsons'. Then, if you don't mind bringing me back here, I can call for a tow truck."

"That would be great," Seth said, checking his watch. "I'm supposed to have these next two deliveries made before five o'clock, but I don't think I'm going to make it."

Leah grabbed her cell phone and her backpack. "Let's go," she said. As a last attempt to figure out what was wrong with the car, Leah tried her keypad to see if the automatic lock would respond. It didn't.

"This is really strange," she muttered, jogging to the passenger side of the delivery truck. She hopped up into the seat and moved a portable CD player. She wondered what kind of music he listened to. Settling the CD player onto the floor, she allowed herself to feel a fresh sense of delight at the adventure of all this. Maybe she was glad her car didn't start.

"Which way do I go?" Seth asked, maneuvering around Leah's stalled vehicle and rolling down Fourth Street.

"Turn right at the corner, then right again on Madison," she said.

"Have you lived here long?" Seth asked.

"All my life," Leah said.

He glanced over at her and smiled. She couldn't help but smile back.

"I'm Seth Edwards, by the way," he said.

"I'm—"

Before she could answer, he finished for her. "Leah. Leah Hudson. Right?"

Leah looked at him more carefully. "How did you know that?"

"I asked Kyle last night."

She nodded slowly, squinting her gray eyes when he

glanced at her again. "And what else did Kyle tell you about me?"

"Enough," Seth said with a tease in his voice. He came to a four-way stop and said, "This is where I turned left last time."

"You need to keep going straight," Leah told him. "We'll go about four more blocks. You're going to take a left and then another left. It's a new housing development, and I don't think it's on the maps yet."

"That would explain it," Seth said.

"How long have you been in Glenbrooke?" Leah asked. She had no way of knowing how many details of her life Kyle had divulged to Seth. It seemed only fair that Seth volunteer some information about himself.

"This is my fourth day in Glenbrooke," he said. "I started working for PDS on Monday. You can see why I still can't find my way around town."

"Don't worry," Leah said. "It's pretty small; you'll have it figured out in no time. This is where you want to turn. Right here."

He rounded the corner and then turned right again when they came to Medford Court.

"It's the beige house at the end of the court," Leah said.

"You can sure tell this is a new neighborhood," Seth said. "It seems bare without all the trees and flowers the last street we were on had."

"I don't care for the way all these houses look alike," Leah said. "On the street where I live every house is different. Some are big with gorgeous landscaping. Then there's my little cottage. I think the maple tree in the front yard is bigger than my house."

"I'd like to see it sometime," Seth said before parking the van and jumping out. He went around to the back. A moment later he wheeled a large box up the Jamelsons' driveway on a dolly.

Leah leaned back in the seat and crossed her arms, watching Seth carry the large box up to the front door. *What's going on here? Why is this guy so attentive to me? He asked Kyle about me. Why? What did he mean when he said he'd like to see "it" sometime? Did he mean the maple tree or my house? Why would he want to see either of them? Who is this guy?*

Seth returned and showed Leah the next address on his clipboard. "This is the last one. The *Glenbrooke Gazette* on Main. I know how to get there. Would you like me to drop you off first, or do you have enough time to drive around with me?"

Leah was loving this. Of course she wanted to ride around with him some more. But all her suspicions had risen to the surface, and first she felt compelled to explore them. "I have the time," Leah said slowly.

"Good," Seth said.

"But I have to ask," Leah added. "Why are you doing this? I mean, first helping me at the Snack Shack last night and now this."

Seth smiled and reached for his sunglasses as they turned left and headed into the early evening sun. "I guess this isn't exactly fair to you. You see, I'm related to one of your biggest fans."

"My biggest fan? I didn't know I had any fans."

"How about Franklin Madison?" Seth flashed her a grin.

Franklin Madison and his late wife had been close friends of Leah's grandparents and lived three doors down from them. As a child, Leah took bouquets of tulips to the Madisons' every year on May Day. She used to leave the flowers in a water-filled mayonnaise jar on their front doorstep, ring the doorbell, and run and hide behind the neighbor's lilac bush.

At ninety-two, Franklin was the last living relative of Cameron Madison, who had founded Glenbrooke in the 1870s.

"You're related to Franklin Madison?" Leah scanned Seth's profile for a resemblance. He certainly didn't have Franklin's long nose and narrow chin. Seth's chin was rounded and more masculine than Franklin's was. Seth's nose was broad, but not too broad. It fit his face and was a good balance to his deep-set, dark blue eyes, which were hidden behind his sunglasses.

"Franklin is my great-uncle." Seth grinned. "Last week was the first time I've seen him in ten years. Maybe even longer. Twenty years, maybe." Seth stopped at a red light and put on his turn signal, prepared to turn onto Main Street without any direction from Leah.

"You know what?" Leah said, studying Seth's profile another moment. "I've seen your picture. Franklin has your high school graduation picture on his mantle."

"Yes, he does. I saw it there the other day," Seth said.

"And I remember Franklin talking about you, too. You're the one who went to Europe instead of going to college, aren't you?"

"I went to college," Seth said defensively. "True, I took some time off and traveled through Europe, but I returned home to Boulder; that's where I grew up. I went to the University of Colorado there. Took me five years, but I graduated."

Leah had heard so many stories about Franklin's twenty-four grandchildren and great-nephews and -nieces that she wasn't sure which of the stories were about Seth. "He may have told me that. I don't remember."

"Did he tell you I've been in Costa Rica for the past four years?"

Leah laughed aloud as she made the connection. "So you're the one! Yes, he told me all about you. He calls you the hippie boy in the rain forest."

Seth glanced at Leah and grinned slowly. "Yep, that's me. Not exactly at the top of Franklin's list of favorite people. You are, though, you know. You're right at the top of his list."

Leah ignored the comment and asked, "So what are you doing in Glenbrooke?"

Seth parked the van on Main Street in front of the *Glenbrooke Gazette*. He pulled off his sunglasses, and raising his eyebrows, he said to Leah with a sly grin, "I'm here to obtain the favor of Uncle Franklin so that when he dies he'll leave all his riches to me." With that he hopped out of the delivery van and hurried across Main Street with a large manila mailer in his hand.

Leah sat still, her eyebrows furrowed. *Was he serious? He couldn't be serious. Franklin doesn't have any riches. He lives in that old house and eats spaghetti and canned green beans. Seth had to be joking.*

Leah leaned back in the front seat of the delivery van and tried to remember what else Franklin had told her about this "hippie boy." She knew Franklin had mentioned Seth over the years because he was the only one of the clan who had done much traveling. She remembered three postcards Franklin had kept on his coffee table for several years. One was of the Austrian Alps, one of the Seine River in Paris, and one was of Venice. That was Leah's favorite. The postcard pictured a gondola docked by a red-and-white-striped pole. The gondolier, wearing a wide-brimmed straw hat with its blue ribbon hanging down the back, stood on the dock. He leaned casually against the pole and indicated with his hand that his gondola was available for the next rider.

Seth had sent those postcards.

Every time Leah had visited Franklin, she would study the cards, especially the one from Venice. And if Franklin wasn't watching, Leah would whisper to the gondolier, "Wait for me. One day I really will come ride in your gondola."

She hadn't yet made good on that promise. For years she

had dreamed of exotic travel adventures but could never pursue any such whims because of her obligation to her ailing parents.

A wash of insecurities came over Leah. If Franklin considered Seth the hippie in the rain forest, then how had Franklin spoken of her to Seth? Did Franklin consider her the matronly nurse, destined to make house calls offering charity to all the old people of Glenbrooke until she herself was too old to leave her rocking chair?

Just as she was beginning to feel overwhelmed with self-doubts, Seth returned with a grin on his face. "Kenton says hi," he said.

Leah looked out the van's windshield. She couldn't see into the front window of the newspaper office, but she could guess that Kenton Buchanan, the owner and editor of the paper was in there, watching her in the PDS van with Seth. Leah smiled and waved at the window, which, due to the sun's angle, only reflected the image of the delivery van.

"I suppose you figured out that Kenton and Kyle are brothers," Leah said. "The Buchanan boys."

"So he just told me. News travels fast around this burg, doesn't it?" Seth started the engine but kept his foot on the brake. "I asked Kyle about his dog last night, and he told me he has three puppies at home. I'm going there now to pick one. By any chance would you like to come with me?"

Leah nodded. "Sure." As long as the whole town knew she was spending her Thursday evening driving around with the new boy in town, she might as well show up at Kyle and Jessica's with him. After all, Seth had admitted he had asked Kyle about her. Why not give her friends something to speculate about? Especially since she was the one who was starting to speculate the most.

Chapter Four

*A*fter Seth dropped off the delivery van at the PDS main terminal, he and Leah climbed into his rusted Subaru station wagon and headed for Kyle and Jessica's Victorian mansion on the top of Madison Hill. Leah had lots of questions for Seth but couldn't ask them because Seth kept talking. He told her about how he had found a place to live in Edgefield, twenty miles away, and had moved in last week. He was hired for his job with PDS after answering an ad in the paper, and the car had been sitting on a used car lot a mile from his apartment, just waiting for him.

Leah still couldn't understand why he had left Costa Rica for this. She was sure that if she ever got away from Glenbrooke, Oregon, she would stay wherever she was as long as she could. Especially if it was some place as exotically romantic as Costa Rica.

"What did you do while you were in Costa Rica?"

"I worked for Real Planet Adventures. Have you ever heard of them?"

Leah shook her head.

"They run tours for young people's groups. We usually worked with high school students."

"So that explains your experience with snack lines."

"Exactly. We would take them through a three-week course: backpacking, kayaking, sometimes orienteering. We would give them a couple of matches and a bag of granola, and they would have three days to find their way out of the rain forest."

"Are you serious?"

"Maybe it wasn't exactly that severe, but you get the idea. The program was designed to develop leadership skills. The most interesting groups were the management teams sent to us by big corporations. We would have four days to build them into what the brochure called 'a harmonious team' before sending them back to the concrete jungle. Those groups were always the biggest challenge."

Leah could believe that. She could also believe that Seth had enough leadership skills to take on any group of students or corporate managers and handily shape them into a team.

So why is he delivering packages in this insignificant corner of the planet?

"Why did you leave?"

Seth glanced at her and looked surprised. It took him a moment before he said, "I turned twenty-nine last month."

Leah wasn't sure what that was supposed to mean, although it gave her a small sense of comfort to realize he was older than she was.

The grand, two-story Victorian mansion came into full view, and Seth stopped the car to take it all in before continuing up the driveway. "Wow! They sure fixed that place up. I only saw it once, when I was in eighth grade. We came to Glenbrooke for my great-aunt's funeral."

Leah hadn't gone to that funeral, but she remembered when Franklin's wife, Naomi, had passed away. She also remembered how creepy the old Madison Estate used to look when she was a child. It had been vacant since the '50s, and when Kyle and Jessica bought it almost seven years ago, it had taken months of extensive renovations before they could move in.

The gem of Madison Hill now glistened, creamy white and inviting. New life had been breathed into the old masterpiece of a house. A wide porch wrapped around the front, complete with a porch swing on the right and a set of wicker furniture on the left. Large, moss-lined baskets of Martha Washington geraniums hung at intervals across the porch's overhang. A rounded turret ran up the side of the house and was topped by a pointed spiral and a rooster weathervane. The gingerbread trim along the roofline had been repainted recently and made the house look fresh in the glow of another gorgeous spring evening.

"These Buchanans must have some money," Seth observed. "What does Kyle do when he's not coaching Little League teams?"

Leah didn't know how much to tell Seth. The truth was, the money came from Jessica. When Jessica married Kyle, she was a millionaire. However, Jessica didn't like people to know that, and she and Kyle had done a commendable job of settling in and living a fairly normal life in Glenbrooke. The initial shock and novelty of her wealth had worn off, and over the years it had become less and less of an issue to the townspeople.

"Kyle does a lot of things," Leah said. "They have some money."

Then, in an effort to redirect the conversation, she said, "I wonder why your great-uncle never moved into this mansion. You know it was built by his grandfather, Cameron Madison."

"Funny you should mention that. I asked Franklin just a few days ago." Seth slowed down as he neared the top of the driveway. "Cameron was bankrupt when he died. He put all his fortune into building this house and was so in debt by the time he died that the place was no longer his to will to anyone. I'll be honest," Seth said, parking the car. "I'm really curious to see inside."

"It's beautiful," Leah said.

The golden retriever that had been barking at them from the front porch now bounded down the steps to greet them. Travis, the Buchanans' oldest son, held open the screen door and called out, "Hi, Auntie Leah. Did you bring the eggs?"

"No, I haven't finished them yet. Are you looking forward to the big party on Saturday?"

Travis nodded and looked shyly at Seth.

"Travis, this is Seth Edwards. He's come to look at your puppies."

Travis's cherub face lit up. "I'll show them to you. They're in the laundry room."

Seth trailed behind Leah as they followed Travis into the house. Seth seemed to be taking in the hardwood floors, the spectacular staircase, and the evening sunlight coming in through the door's beveled glass. Travis led them down the hall-way into the kitchen where Jessica was clearing the dinner table.

The toddler of the family, Emma, squealed with delight when she saw Leah and hopped down from her chair to run into Leah's open arms. Leah kissed her soundly on the cheek and then proceeded to tickle her madly. As Emma tossed her curls and burst into giggles, Leah tried to introduce Seth to Jessica. Fortunately, Kyle stepped in from the back room and finished the introductions.

The Buchanans' youngest, Sara, sat in her highchair and pounded her spoon on the high chair tray, demanding some attention, too.

"I wasn't ignoring you, Sara Bunny," Leah said, going over to the high chair while Emma clung to her like a baby koala bear. Leah managed to release Sara from the high chair and scooped her up, holding a happy little girl on each hip. "Do you two want to show Seth your puppies?"

"I was going to show him," Travis said, standing in the doorway of the laundry room with his hands behind his back.

"I can hear them," Seth said. "Why don't you all show me?"

Kyle, a tall, good-looking man in his mid-thirties, stayed in the kitchen and slipped his arm around his wife, Jessica. She was a gentle-spirited woman and more of a big sister to Leah than any of her own sisters had been.

Jessica rested her fair-skinned cheek against Kyle's chest. "Let us know if you guys need any help, although I doubt you will. Travis is our resident expert on the puppies."

Leah followed Travis into the large laundry room. A separate area had been sectioned off by a board that was low enough for Lady, the young mother golden retriever, to step over. Lady lay comfortably curled up on top of what looked like a flat beanbag pillow. Leah had one, too, for her dog, Hula. The pillow was filled with cedar chips and was supposed to ward off fleas.

As Seth bent down, the three beautiful bundles of vanilla fluff yelped and tumbled over each other in an effort to climb out of their box and play with the visitors.

"They're silly puppies," little Emma said.

Sara patted Leah's cheek with a sticky hand.

"They have gotten so big since I was here last!" Leah said. "Look at that one."

The largest of the three fur balls romped toward them with

a strip of bed sheet tangled around his hind leg. He took a flying leap in an effort to jump over the board barricade. He would have made it, too, if one of his siblings hadn't been sitting on the other end of the sheet, halting his escape in midair. The confused pup hung halfway over the board with the sheet still holding him by the leg.

Seth reached for the daredevil and released his hind leg from the sheet. Lifting him up for a closer look, Seth said, "You're quite a little Bungee jumper, aren't you?"

"They never could jump that far before," Travis said with concern. "Daddy, come here."

Kyle entered, and Travis told the story of the flying puppy.

"Sounds like we better find a taller board," Kyle said.

"Or send this one home with me," Seth suggested. Then, in a tender gesture that made Leah smile, Seth squatted down to eye level with Travis and said, "What do you think? Is this puppy looking for a new home?" The pup licked Seth's chin as if right on cue.

"He likes you," Travis surmised.

"I like him," Seth said.

"They're all boys," Travis said. "The two girls already got sold."

"Do you think I should buy this one?" Seth asked.

Travis seemed to ponder the question deeply but only for a moment before saying, "I think you two are good for each other."

Leah pressed her lips together so she wouldn't break into too big of a smile. She loved all three of the Buchanan children. Whenever any of them did or said something especially endearing, Leah allowed herself to get all choked up. If she couldn't have her own children, she would funnel her motherly emotions into these three pixies every chance she had.

"It's a deal," Seth said, putting out his hand for Travis to shake. They shook vigorously, and the puppy yapped his approval.

Emma covered her ears. "Stop barking," she ordered.

Leah adjusted her precious cargo and realized how heavy Emma was getting. "I have to put you down, sweetie. Auntie Leah is getting to be an old lady, and she can't hold you as long as she used to."

As Leah bent at the knees, Emma got down and went right to her daddy, who effortlessly picked her up and slipped her around to his back so that her arms were around his neck and her legs around his middle.

"What are you going to name him?" Travis asked.

Without hesitation Seth said, "Bungee. I'm going to call him Bungee."

Travis laughed and repeated, "Bungee."

Leah doubted that Travis knew what a Bungee jumper was, although it was possible. He had surprised her more than once with his keen sense of observation. It was a fun word to say, and Travis repeated it. "Bungee."

"I better take this guy home so he can get used to his new house tonight," Seth said. Looking at Kyle he added, "Is it still okay if I write the check next week?"

"No problem," Kyle said. "Whenever it's convenient for you."

"You can give the money to me," Travis said. "It's for me to go to college."

"We'll make sure it goes into your college account, son," Kyle said. Then looking at Leah he asked, "Do you want to stay for a while? Have you had dinner yet?"

"We need to get going. My car decided to have a nervous breakdown this afternoon," Leah said. "I have to call Martin to see if he can tow it over to his station tonight."

"Do you need any help?" Kyle asked.

"I think I'm okay. Seth said he could drop me off back at my car."

"That is, after we make a stop at Dairy Queen so I can repay Leah for helping me out today," Seth said.

Kyle looked at Leah and then back at Seth. "I'll tell you what's even better than a fast-food dinner. You talk Leah into making you one of her spinach casseroles, and you'll be tempted to turn into a vegetarian."

"I am a vegetarian," Seth said. "I'm only into Dairy Queen for their shakes. I'm making up for lost time during the past four years in Costa Rica. So far I've only tried three of their flavors. I'm making my way down the list."

Leah caught Kyle's eye, and she knew what he was thinking. Leah happened to know that Kyle was a Dairy Queen Blizzard aficionado as well.

"Have you tried the Oreo yet?" Kyle asked.

"Not yet," Seth said.

"And did you know that Leah is a vegetarian, too?" Kyle added.

Seth smiled at Leah as the squirming puppy tried to crawl out of his arms. "No, I didn't know that. I think Leah and I are discovering quite a few things we have in common."

To Leah's surprise, she didn't blush at his comment. For some reason it didn't embarrass her. She felt natural standing here with Kyle and Seth and hearing Seth say such a thing. It was as if the two of them were long-lost classmates, getting caught up at an impromptu reunion. Seth was connected to Glenbrooke in a unique way: He was related to the man who had built the house they were standing in.

"If you're free on Saturday, Seth, you're welcome to come for our Easter egg hunt," Kyle said.

"And bring Bungee," Travis said, patting the puppy on the head. "He might want to visit his mommy."

"Will do," Seth said.

"We can go out the back here," Leah suggested, pointing to the screen door. It led to the back deck where Seth stopped to admire the sprawling backyard lawn bordered by ancient evergreens and cedars.

"You have a beautiful home," Seth said to Kyle. "It's really something, the way you've fixed it up."

"When you come back on Saturday we'll give you the grand tour," Kyle said, putting down Emma and taking Sara from Leah. Neither of the little girls liked being displaced, and both put up a fuss.

"I'll see you real soon," Leah said, blowing the girls a kiss. She and Seth left side by side.

"What should we do first?" Seth asked. "Eat, or take care of your car?"

"Either one. You pick." At that moment, Leah didn't care. She felt as if her wish upon Pluto or Venus was coming true. She was in the company of a charming man, and he happened to have a puppy under his arm.

Chapter Five

$\mathcal{J}$t does your heart good to see a real family like that, doesn't it?" Seth said, as the two of them got back in his car. "Mom, Dad, 2.5 kids, and a couple of dogs, living the American dream. I noticed they even had a hammock in the backyard."

"You didn't see a lot of those in Costa Rica?" Leah asked, holding Bungee on her lap.

"What, families or hammocks?"

"Either. Both."

"I saw very few families because of the kind of organization I was with. And I spied a few hammocks here and there. But I never had one I could call my own."

"And that's what you came to Glenbrooke for? A hammock of your own?" Leah asked, still trying to obtain a clearer understanding of why a man who had the world at his feet would give it up to move to Glenbrooke of all places.

Seth grinned as he headed down the driveway. Once again he avoided Leah's pointed question. Bungee sunk his pointed teeth into Leah's hand, and she pulled away with a cry. "Hey, no biting, Bungee."

"We can put him on the floor in the back, if you'd like," Seth suggested.

"No, he's okay," Leah said. "He's going to have to learn his manners sooner or later."

"Not necessarily at your expense." Seth stopped the car at the end of the driveway. He reached over and took Leah's hand in his, pulling it closer for an examination of the teeth marks. Leah noticed how rough and worn Seth's hands felt. She was used to holding hands with little girls and elderly friends. Compared to them, her hands always felt like the rough, dry, overworked ones. As they were cradled now in Seth's hand, she actually felt feminine. The sensation surprised her, and she pulled away.

"It's okay," she said. "Why don't we take care of my car first." She really didn't want her time with Seth to end, and she wasn't sure why she had suggested dealing with the car rather than eating.

Seth took her request to heart and drove toward Fourth Avenue. Silence nestled down between them for a full two minutes, and Leah didn't like it. She had enjoyed the way they had chatted freely. *I was too abrupt, pulling away like that. Why did I do that?*

"Or," Leah suggested tentatively, "we can swing by my place. I just happen to have a spinach casserole in the freezer. I could put it in the oven while we get my car, then we could eat at my home afterward."

"Sounds like a plan. Tell me how to get there," Seth said.

Leah directed him into one of Glenbrooke's older neighborhoods, less than half a mile from where she had left her car. They pulled up in front, and Seth said, "This is your house?"

Leah nodded and tried to evaluate her quaint bungalow from Seth's point of view. The house had a steep roof with a brick chimney that ran up the left side. The chimney was painted white, like the rest of the house. The front door was rounded at the top and had a leaded, stained glass window in the upper section. She had found the stained glass, which depicted a pale blue morning glory, at an estate sale and had it fitted into a new front door when she moved in almost six months ago. Her small front yard had been mowed recently, but she hadn't planted a lot of flowers or bedding plants yet. Two overgrown azalea bushes stood to the right of the front door like a pair of matronly sisters, heads bent close, sharing a bit of juicy gossip. They were both budding and about to cast a spray of white blossoms across their four-foot-wide bosoms.

"You're right," Seth said, eyeing the maple tree's trunk. "That tree is almost larger than your house."

"I might need to get it trimmed back one of these days."

"Great house!" Seth said.

"It needs a lot of work still." Leah thought of the long row of self-sticking notes on her refrigerator that listed all she planned to do to make her property and home look better. She had focused her efforts over the past few months inside, including installing a dishwasher, which she had managed by herself with no problem. "And it's really small inside. It wasn't as nice looking when I bought it. It was gray with a red-brick chimney, and the front door was painted red."

"Nice choice on the color and the new door. I envy your being a home owner."

"It's not all that great when you need a plumber in the middle of the night."

Seth laughed and opened his door. "Do you want me to leave Bungee in the car?"

"Of course not," Leah said, scooping him up. "He has to come in and meet my dog, Hula."

"Hula?" Seth asked as he took Bungee off Leah's hands. "Named after an exotic Hawaiian vacation?"

Leah opened her front door without a key.

"You don't lock your door?" Seth asked, stunned.

"Sometimes. I left it open today because my friend Lauren was coming over this morning to pick up some of the eggs for the Easter egg hunt Saturday. I volunteered to decorate more than I could handle."

Leah led Seth through a narrow entryway into a small kitchen. On the tile counter sat fifty hard-boiled eggs in their cartons, waiting to be decorated. Leah had left a note for Lauren on top of the first dozen.

"Looks like Lauren didn't make it over here." Leah turned to Seth, and with a cunning grin she said, "So, how do you feel about dyeing a couple dozen eggs tonight?"

Seth was examining her ceiling. "Did you put in the skylight? It looks new."

"Yes," Leah said looking up. "It was too dark in here. I put in the ceiling fan, too. It can get hot here in the summer." She reached over and stroked Bungee behind the ears. He was gnawing on Seth's thumb. "Do you want to meet Hula?"

"Of course."

Leah led Seth and Bungee only a few feet to a door off the kitchen.

"You keep her in the pantry?"

"This isn't a pantry," Leah said. "This is something I think you only find in old houses in the Northwest. It's a mudroom." She opened the door into a small room with a linoleum floor, a deep sink, and a metal baker's rack stacked with gardening pots and tools. A doggy door opened to cement steps that led to the backyard. Hula wasn't in the mudroom.

"She must be in the backyard," Leah said, opening the door and stepping outside. Hula had positioned herself comfortably at the bottom of the steps, basking in the last bit of sunlight that spilled through the gap between two large trees in the neighbor's yard.

"Hi, girl," Leah said as Hula slowly rose and came to check out the puppy in Seth's arms. "This is Bungee. What do you think?"

"Your yard isn't fenced, I see," Seth said. "I better not put Bungee down, or we might end up chasing him all over the neighborhood."

"He can stay in the mudroom, and we can put a board over the doggy door, if you want to leave him here. You don't mind, do you, Hula?"

Hula returned to her corner of sunlight as if to register her apathy.

"I'll stick the casserole in the oven and set the timer," Leah said. "I'll also call Martin to see if he can meet us at the car with his tow truck."

Leah made her call and placed the homemade spinach casserole in her not-so-clean oven while Seth situated Bungee in the mudroom.

"All set?" Leah asked, hanging up the phone.

"All set," Seth replied. He had washed his face, and a few beads of water still clung to his eyelashes.

"All I have in the mudroom are paper towels," Leah said apologetically. "Did you want a hand towel?"

"No, I'm fine. I like your house. It's really nice."

"You've just seen half of it. The clean half."

"Only one bedroom?"

"Yes," Leah said.

"I had hoped to get into a little house like this," Seth said as they made their way back to his car. "I had to settle for an apartment in Edgefield, at least for the time being."

"You're really set on the supposedly 'normal,' Middle-American lifestyle, aren't you?"

Seth closed the car door behind him and gave her a puzzled look. "Why does that keep surprising you?"

"Because," Leah spouted, shutting her door hard for emphasis. "It's so uneventful here."

"Costa Rica can be uneventful, too. So can Sweden. It's not the place; it's the people."

"Well, this is all I've ever known. I would think that some-one who has been to Europe and who has camped out in a tropical rain forest would find all this pretty blasé."

"If you're seventeen, maybe," Seth said, starting the car. "That's why I left the U.S. at that ripe, know-it-all age. I spent my senior year of high school as an exchange student in Sweden. Later I backpacked through Europe as far south as Greece."

"And you saw the Alps and Paris and Venice," Leah said.

Seth turned and gave her a humored expression as if Leah's three stated locations were all good guesses. "Yes, I saw a lot of Europe. A lot of wonderful places. And I met a lot of fascinat-ing people. But I returned to the U.S. for college. That's when I lived in Boulder. For the last four years 'home' has been a Quonset hut with a wide variety of roommates who have no idea what the terms 'privacy' and 'lights out' mean."

"Turn right at this corner," Leah said, motioning for him to keep talking.

"I've never had a place of my own, the way you do. I looked around one day and realized the incoming staff kept getting younger and younger. I was the oldest staff member except for Keegan and Marabella, who ran the program. And they're settled in for the long haul. They have their own cabin. They even have their own hammock."

Seth pulled up in front of Ida's house where Leah's car was parked.

"So you came to America in search of your own cabin and hammock," Leah surmised.

"Something like that."

"Boy, are we ever different," Leah said, leaning against her door. "Ever since I was fourteen I've dreamed of going places and seeing things. What I wouldn't give to live in a Quonset hut or hike the Alps or go dancing in the streets of a Greek fishing village."

Seth laughed. "It's not all like the movies."

Leah returned his smile. He had such a nice smile. "I know. But I always wanted to see for myself that it wasn't like the movies, you know?"

"Why didn't you?"

Leah looked down. She wanted to answer with the phrase that filled her mind at that moment and to admit to him what he obviously hadn't figured out yet. She wanted to say, "Because, behold, I'm Leah." That phrase had been enough to determine her destiny.

But Seth didn't know that. He didn't act as if her options were limited.

Leah lifted her head, and with a fresh breath of hope, she answered, "You know, maybe I will someday soon."

Chapter Six

Martin showed up with his tow truck before Seth could comment on Leah's statement, but that didn't matter. She felt brave and strong for having said what she did. And she meant it, too. Maybe she would take off and see the world someday. The freedom the very thought gave her was exhilarating.

Leah found it hard to keep from smiling as Martin checked under the hood for possible problems. At this moment she felt she didn't need a car to take her anywhere. She had something better. She had hope. And hope could take her places she hadn't been in a long time.

How strange that hope should have returned to my life after such a long, cold season of silence.

Leah glanced at Seth. He and Martin were engrossed in examining her car's engine. When Martin said he didn't see anything obvious that could cause the problem, he hooked up her Blazer to his tow truck and promised to have a look at it first thing in the morning.

Seth drove Leah home, but before they entered her front door, they could hear Bungee barking from the mudroom. They hurried to rescue the forlorn pup and remove the board from the doggie door so Hula could get in and have her dinner. Poor Hula looked offended that Leah had locked her out but had allowed the little pip-squeak to take over her domain.

Seth comforted Bungee in his arms while Leah checked on the spinach. The oven was turned off. "Oh no, don't tell me my oven is breaking down, too."

"Hey, I think your friend came by and took some of the eggs while we were gone," Seth said, nodding at the kitchen counter.

Leah noticed that half the eggs were gone. A note from Lauren replaced the note Leah had left on the counter. It read,

Sorry it took me all day to get over here. Molly Sue had her two-year-old checkup at the doctor's this afternoon. I turned off your oven because it smelled like something was burning. Hope I didn't ruin your dinner. See you tomorrow night at the Good Friday service.
    xoxox Wren

Leah checked the frozen state of the spinach and reset the oven. "Looks like it'll take another half an hour. Can your stomach wait that long?"

"You know, I was thinking I should probably head home and get this guy settled." Seth seemed to have turned self-conscious. He looked at the clock and then at Bungee in his arms. "I need to stop by the store on the way home and buy a few necessities for him. Thanks for the offer on dinner. Maybe another time."

Leah felt as if she was being rejected even though Seth

hadn't overtly indicated that. *What happened to my burst of hope? Where did those restored dreams fly off to without me?*

She felt the old, junky emotions rise to the surface. Familiar old thoughts. It was hard to make them go away.

"Let me ask you something," Seth said, hesitating on his way to the front door.

Leah's spirits rose. "Yes?"

"Do I turn right at the end of your street to get back to Main?"

"Yes, right at the corner."

"Thanks," he said. And then he was gone.

She stood silently for a few minutes, fighting back the disappointment. She had come so close to experiencing what she had longed for, the start of a new and rather promising friendship. But he left. Right on cue.

Did I sabotage the whole thing by continually asking why he had moved here? Why did I pull away when he took my hand? Why did he leave? Would he have stayed if I hadn't been so pushy?

Leah gave up on the spinach and settled for a Little League frozen bean burrito. She leaned against the kitchen counter trying to remember what Brad, one of her friends, had told her last summer when she went to him for counseling. She had slumped into a state of depression when her parents' house wasn't selling. The house she had wanted to buy was sold before she could make an offer, and nothing seemed to be moving forward in her life.

Brad had told her, "Blocked goals lead to anger, and blocked anger leads to depression. Readjust your goals and find healthy ways to express your anger or you're going to be one depressed little chickadee."

Brad's counseling methods weren't always conventional, but his words had helped her. She readjusted her goals regarding the house, and she confided her anger and frustration to Jessica, who listened without offering any advice other than "Let's pray about this some more together." Every Monday evening for four months, Leah had met with Jessica, and they prayed together.

Now Leah could look back and see how God had worked out everything better than her original plans. Her parents' house sold for less than she had hoped, but her sisters had had a change of heart and agreed Leah should have all the profit from the house's sale. The amount had been enough to buy this house outright, which meant she had no monthly mortgage payment. The house that fell through was twice the size and twice the price. If she had ended up with that other house, she would have been paying on it for at least fifteen years.

Leah had to admit God had been good to her. That didn't mean she was ready to trust him completely, though. Over the past few years it had become safer to keep God nearby but at a bit of a distance. She was one of his children. She knew that. She also knew she wasn't one of his favorites. It was best not to bother him too much but to take care of matters herself as much as possible.

With that in mind, Leah wondered if she should readjust her goals again.

Should I plan a trip to Europe? I don't exactly have enough money at the moment. I could start a special savings account and try to put away two hundred dollars a month. In six months I'd have… No, I'd have to put away more than that!

Leah set to work dyeing her mound of Easter eggs since she did her best thinking when she was busy on a project. She knew she didn't want to take off for Europe by herself; it would be much more fun to go with a friend.

But who?

Leaning against the counter with an egg in each hand, Leah

said to herself, "Go ahead; be honest. The only friendship you're interested in developing right now is with Seth Edwards. And you have no idea if he feels the same way."

In an effort to readjust some of her goals, Leah began to formulate a plan. First she decided she would make Seth feel welcomed in Glenbrooke by throwing a party at her home in his honor. Next she would make some cookies this weekend and surprise him at work on Monday.

Before she went to bed, Leah had a long mental list of wonderful things she could do for Seth. Giving was what Leah did best. It delighted her to fall asleep thinking of all the creative ways she could give to Seth.

The next morning, Leah caught a ride to work with her coworker, Mary. Mary showed up at 7:15 with a box of donuts on the passenger's seat. "Do you mind holding those?"

"Only if I can eat one on the way," Leah said.

"Sure. They're for the lunchroom. They're left over from my son's band performance at high school last night. What's wrong with your car?"

"Who knows?"

"Have you had your review yet?" Mary asked.

"No, I think I'm scheduled for next week."

"I had mine yesterday. No raise. The wage freeze is remaining in effect for another six months. I'm so upset I could spit! How do they expect us to keep up with the cost of living?"

Leah nodded but was glad she had a bite of old-fashioned buttermilk donut in her mouth. She didn't find her salary a hardship. She knew it had to be harder for Mary, who was trying to raise three teenagers by herself.

They were a block from the hospital when Leah spotted a PDS van. She perked up and leaned forward, trying to see who was driving.

"What are you looking for?" Mary asked.

"Oh, I just wondered if that was Harry," Leah said. The van turned in front of them. It was Harry, not Seth. Leah waved, and Harry waved back. "Nice guy, that Harry," Leah said awkwardly.

Mary gave her a strange look.

When Leah reached her desk, a note was waiting for her from Martin. She called him, and he said he had no idea what the problem had been the day before. The car started up for him on the first try, and everything checked out fine.

He told her to swing by after work to pick it up, which she did. After getting her car, Leah drove out to the PDS station and asked if Seth was around. One of the guys told her he was still on his route. She waited for half an hour and then left a note on his car's windshield since she knew she had better get going. The note read:

Hi, Seth.
I just stopped by to say thanks for giving me a ride last
night and to tell you my car is working fine now. As I see
it, I still owe you dinner as a way of thanking you.
  Leah

She stopped at home for a few minutes and then hurried on to church. It was Good Friday, and the special communion service was scheduled to begin at seven o'clock. However, Leah wasn't going to the communion service. She was working in the church nursery, as she did every Sunday. Several years ago, Leah had discovered the nursery was a safe place. She could keep going to church but didn't have to participate in the service, which only reminded her how distant she felt from God.

When Leah arrived, Jessica already was in the toddler nursery changing Sara's diaper. Leah told Jessica how the Blazer had refused to go last night but was running perfectly now.

Jessica stopped her task at hand and gave Leah a wide grin. "Do you know what I think?"

"No, what?"

"I think your guardian angel dislocated some wires just long enough for you to have to go around town with Seth."

Leah laughed. "Do you really believe that?"

"Why not? You remember Teri Allistar, don't you?"

"She used to be Teri Moreno, right?"

"Yes."

"Of course I remember her," Leah said. "She was my Spanish teacher my senior year. Is she still in Hawaii with her husband? What was his name?"

"Gordon. Yes, they're still in Hawaii. He pastors a church there."

"Oh, yes, Gordon. I liked him. He was a good match for her."

"I think so, too. She and Gordon and the boys are doing great. Teri was the first friend I made when I moved here," Jessica said. "She used to call unexplainable circumstances such as your experience with your car 'pockets of grace.' We don't control them. We just fall into them, and God catches us and directs us in ways we never imagined."

Leah had been raised with the philosophy that God helped those who helped themselves. She tended to be leery of the inexplicable being credited to angels or labeled miracles. "I think the car problem was a fluke, and it turned out okay. A loose wire or clogged something. I'm sure it was nothing more than that."

"I used to think that, too," Jessica said, finishing up with Sara and letting her crawl over to the play kitchen where Emma was making pies. "When I came to know the Lord, I started to see all those coincidences actually were his interventions. His 'pockets of grace.' I know now that he was doing those things to get me to turn to him and trust him. I remember one time, right after I moved to Glenbrooke, I came home and found groceries on my front doorstep."

Leah looked away, pretending to flick a speck of lint from her shirtsleeve. *That was my first secret delivery! I've never heard Jessica mention it before. She doesn't know I was the one who left the groceries, does she? Nah, she couldn't have known.*

"And in the bag," Jessica continued, "was a box of Dove ice cream bars. I love Dove bars. Nobody in Glenbrooke knew that."

Leah remembered how she had stood by the freezer section with the grocery cart already full with everything she thought this new teacher in town might need. Leah, who had worked as a volunteer at the hospital before being hired full-time, had been there the day Jessica was brought in after being run off the road by a logging truck. Leah still didn't know why she had progressed from May Day bouquets on Mr. Madison's porch to buying groceries. But she did know she had felt compelled to buy the Dove bars even though she didn't think she had enough money and was afraid the bars would melt. She had headed toward the checkout stand and then went back, returned the large package of peanut butter cookies, and bought the Dove bars instead. Leah remembered it all like it was yesterday.

"Teri was with me that afternoon," Jessica went on. "That's when she told me about God's pockets of grace. I know those groceries were a gift from God; his own little miracle to me because no one knew it, but I had no money and absolutely no food."

"You're kidding." Leah felt goosebumps run up her arms.

"No." Jessica shook her head and lowered her voice. "You know how I told you I left home secretly when I moved to Glenbrooke? I didn't have enough money with me, and I couldn't get any more until my first paycheck. For more than a week I lived on this giant zucchini from the garden and some noodles I found in the cupboard, left by whoever lived in the house before me."

All these years Leah had felt so foolish for taking groceries to Jessica after finding out how wealthy Jessica was. Now Leah felt as if she simply had been a delivery person for God. She leaned against the counter, stunned at the insight.

"Pride can make a person do very stupid things," Jessica said softly.

Leah could hardly move. Maybe a greater plan really was unfolding in people's lives. In *her* life. Why else would she have felt so compelled to give the groceries to Jessica and especially to go back and pick up the Dove bars? Leah wanted to blurt out that she had been the one God had used to cushion that little pocket of grace in Jessica's life. But it was better this way. Jessica didn't need to know.

A mother with two toddlers showed up at the nursery's half-door and greeted Jessica and Leah. Jessica gave Leah's arm a squeeze and rose to receive the toddlers. She said, "Trust me on this one, Leah. The car problem yesterday could have been orchestrated by God. I'm not saying that's how it was for sure, but just consider the possibility and be thankful."

"Thankful," Leah repeated under her breath.

For the next hour, Leah did what she loved to do. She played with the youngest citizens of Glenbrooke and let their innocence and whimsy fill her emotional well. Ever since Seth Edwards had walked into the Snack Shack two nights ago, Leah had felt as if her life was changing. Her routine was the same, but she wasn't the same. She was changing.

Maybe Jessica is right. Maybe I've just fallen into a pocket of God's grace. If I have, I don't think I want to get out.

Chapter Seven

The Good Friday service lasted an hour, and the parents came for their toddlers right away. Leah was almost finished cleaning up when she heard a voice at the open door say, "So here you are."

She turned to see Seth standing there in khaki slacks and a light blue oxford shirt with a button-down collar. He smiled at her, and she smiled back. Leah felt as if everything else around her blurred like the pastel background of a Monet painting. All that stayed in focus was Seth's clean-shaven face and his steady smile.

"I thought that was your car I saw in the parking lot," Seth said. "What was the problem with it?"

Leah couldn't stop smiling, thinking of Jessica's explanation. "Apparently it's a little miracle. It's running fine now."

"That's good," Seth said. "I got your note. You don't have to thank me. I was glad to help out. Anytime. Really."

Leah put down the basket of toys and walked over to Seth.

"I had an idea last night. I thought it would be fun to throw a welcome party for you. Nothing fancy. Just a little get-together at my house so you can meet other people from Glenbrooke."

"I don't know," Seth said. "I'm not big on social events. I appreciate the thought, but no thanks."

"Oh," Leah said, feeling a surge of rejection rising inside.

Seth leaned closer and said, "Actually, I was going to ask you something. This may be short notice, but do you have any plans for Easter Sunday?"

"I'll be here," Leah said. "I'm watching the toddlers."

"I mean early Easter Sunday. Sunrise, to be exact. The last few years in Costa Rica I went on a sunrise hike to the top of this hill behind our camp. I thought I'd try to keep up the tradition."

"Sounds great," Leah said. "I love to hike. When and where?"

"I was hoping you could help me figure out where."

Leah thought. "Only two hills are around here. Madison Hill, where Kyle and Jessica live. And a hill at the end of Camp Heather Brook. No one ever goes there, but I would guess some old logging roads lead at least partway up."

"Sounds like exactly what I was looking for. I knew you would know where to go."

"I could fix a picnic breakfast," Leah suggested. "Do you have any preference of what you like to eat?"

"You don't have to bring anything."

"You sure?"

"Yes. I'll pick you up nice and early. How does four sound?"

"Early," Leah said.

"I'll find a map, and we'll figure out how to get up that hill."

"We can ask Shelly and Jonathan," Leah said, gathering up a basket of plastic toys. She planned to take them home to wash and then bring them back Sunday. "The hill overlooks their camp property."

"Okay." Then with a grin he added, "I knew you would be interested in an adventure like this."

"Why do you say that?" She stopped and looked at him.

He came closer. "My great-uncle told me you have the makings of an Amelia Earhart."

"He said that?"

Seth nodded.

Leah turned out the lights and closed the door. Seth walked with her to her car.

"Amelia, huh? That's interesting. What else did Franklin tell you?"

"He said you visit him about once a month and that you've been doing that for years."

Leah unlocked the back and shoved in the basket of toys. "I like Franklin. He has the spirit of a twenty-year-old."

Seth leaned against the Blazer and looked at her curiously. "So what's in it for you?"

"What do you mean?"

"Why are you in Glenbrooke serving Sno-Kones and visiting old people and running the church nursery? Why aren't you flying off to parts unknown?"

Leah looked down at her hands. Her weathered, always busy, giving hands that never had experienced a manicure. "It's kind of a long story, Seth." This was the first time she had said his name aloud to him, and it warmed her to hear the way it sounded coming from her lips.

"I'm not doing anything the rest of the evening," Seth said. "Do you still need help to decorate those eggs?"

"No, the eggs are finished. But you're welcome to come over, if you would like."

"Yes, I'd like that."

"Do you want to follow me? Or do you remember how to get there?"

"I'd better follow just to be sure."

Leah climbed into her Blazer and subtly checked her reflection in the rearview mirror. Her cheeks weren't flushed red. She looked calm. She felt calm. This all seemed so natural. Did it really matter that Seth had left in a rush the night before? He was back. She didn't have to throw parties or bake cookies for him. Seth Edwards was pursuing her. This was nice. No, more than nice. It was amazing.

When they reached her house, Seth asked, "Are you a tea drinker or a coffee drinker?"

"It depends," Leah said. "If I make the coffee, I'm a coffee drinker. I usually don't care for other people's coffee. I like it darker and stronger than most people."

"It's never too strong for me. In Cost Rica, we used to brew true java—I don't know where we got those coffee beans, but they were the best. Where do you keep your coffee? I'll make you a cup 'Rica' style."

Leah opened the cupboard next to the oven and displayed her collection of coffee paraphernalia.

"Grinder, natural unbleached filters, perfect," Seth said, taking inventory. "Are these your bags of beans here? You look like you're running low."

"I don't drink that much coffee. It seems pointless to buy a lot that will sit for months. I'd rather buy the beans fresh every few weeks. You'll find a bag of decaf and a bag of regular in there. Which do you want?"

"Leaded, of course," Seth said. "I want to hear your whole story."

Leah smiled. "I don't think it's going drag on into the middle of the night."

"I'll be ready, just in case." Seth went to work preparing his gourmet coffee while Leah checked on Hula in the mudroom. She contentedly wagged her tail when Leah entered.

"You need some more water, girl," Leah said, filling the bowl. Then she went out the back door to her car and brought in the basket of toys so she could soak them in the basin sink.

Returning to the kitchen, she found Seth loading her dishwasher. "You don't have to do that. Come on, let's sit down in the other room. Is the coffee ready?"

The coffee was not only ready, but it also was the best Leah had tasted in a long time. "What did you do to make this so good?"

"Nothing special," he said. "You had good beans to work with."

At first Leah thought he said "good genes," and her sister's comment about her having "neither the frame nor frame of mind to attract a stable man" sprang to her mind. If she had good genes, then she would have inherited the "right frames," the ones her sisters had all inherited. Despite all that, she seemed to have attracted someone. A very appealing someone. He didn't have to be here, making coffee for her, loading her dishwasher, and inviting her to accompany him on sunrise hikes. She had done nothing to coerce or lure him.

Leah leaned back as Seth made himself comfortable on her denim blue loveseat. Actually, it was her parents' old avocado green loveseat, which had sat in the upstairs guestroom of their house and had very few visitors. Since it was such a sturdy piece of furniture, Leah had covered it with a denim slipcover that matched the blue in her recliner. It was the only furniture she had room for in her small sitting area, but it was all she needed. Instead of a coffee table, she had stacked two old brown suitcases she had found at a garage sale. The one on top still had the original antique travel stickers affixed and in good condition.

"Cairo," Seth said, reading the sticker nearest him before placing his coffee cup on a coaster on top of the suitcase. "Now there's a place I'd like to go someday."

"Me, too," Leah said.

"Where else would you like to go?"

"Anywhere."

"Tell me why you never took off with your Amelia spirit and left Glenbrooke behind."

Briefly, Leah told him about being the youngest of six daughters and how she ended up being the one to stay home and care for her parents.

"How did you finish college?" Seth asked.

"It took me seven years. All part-time. Driving back and forth to Edgefield. But that's the only place I went. Edgefield. Not Paris. Not…what is that one?" she said, tilting her head and reading the stickers. "Roma."

"Your parents have been gone a year, right?"

Leah nodded and sipped her coffee.

"Why don't you go to Rome now?"

"I don't know," she said after a pause. "I might go. Later. Not right away. I bought this house, and I have all kinds of commitments and obligations here. I don't think it's my turn to leave Glenbrooke."

"Or do you mean it's not your turn to leave Bedford Falls?"

Leah gave him a quizzical look. "Bedford Falls?"

"You know, in *It's a Wonderful Life*. Jimmy Stewart. Donna Reed. You sound to me like the female version of George Bailey."

It took Leah a moment to make the connection. When she did, she laughed. "You think I sound like George Bailey?"

"A little."

Leah shook her head. "I'm not that discouraged about my life in this small town. Just don't try telling me you're really my guardian angel, and I'm your ticket to a pair of wings."

Seth laughed. "I don't hear any bells ringing, do you?"

Leah laughed with him and felt captivated by the man sitting on her couch. Did he have any idea that *he* was the reason she wanted to stick around Glenbrooke?

Seth reached for his coffee cup and said, "I have a question for you."

"Yes?" Leah felt open and unguarded.

"Tell me about the Glenbrooke Zorro."

Chapter Eight

"he Glenbrooke Zorro?'" Leah repeated. "What about the Glenbrooke Zorro? I mean, what have you heard?"

"I've heard someone in town loves to give. And that someone is generous and random and—" he leaned forward for emphasis—"has managed to keep his or her identity a secret for many years."

"That's what I've heard, too," Leah said, pulling her coffee cup to her lips. She downed the last sip and stood up. "Is there more coffee?"

"Let me get it for you," Seth offered. "Would you like me to fix it the same as the first cup?"

"Yes," Leah said, fidgeting in her chair. All her happy, secure feelings had flown.

What is this man doing in my house? What does he want? It's one thing for me to entertain the thought of an innocent little crush on him. But it's something else for him to pry into my personal life.

Leah couldn't sit still. Hopping up, she joined Seth in the

kitchen. "I feel funny having you serve me. Why don't I get that?"

Seth was pouring the thick, dark brew into her cup. "Is it hard for you to let other people serve you?" he asked without looking at her.

"No," she answered immediately. "It's just that you're my guest. I should be serving you."

"All done," he said, holding a mug in each hand and heading back into the other room. "Come on."

"Would you like to watch a movie?" Leah asked, trying to sound casual.

"I'd rather talk. I want to hear your take on the Glenbrooke Zorro."

Leah sat down on the loveseat this time, thinking Seth would take the recliner. Instead he sat on the loveseat with her. She didn't know how she could feel so at ease with Seth one minute and so uncomfortable the next.

Sipping the fragrant brew and drawing up her courage, Leah decided she had no reason to be nervous. This was her house, her couch, her good coffee beans. This was her life he had stepped into, uninvited. She didn't have to make room for him. She could, should, and would stand her ground.

"Look," Leah said, "you obviously have a point you want to make. Go ahead and make it."

Seth looked surprised. But not too surprised. "Okay, here's my point. I think you are the Glenbrooke Zorro."

Leah looked at her coffee cup and ran her finger around the white ceramic mug's rim. She had met her match when it came to standing her ground. Lifting her eyes to meet his, she said, "Why do you say that?"

"Oh, no. Uh-uh. No," he said, shaking his head and giving her a subdued smile. "If I can't be coy with you, you can't be coy with me. Come on, George. Level with me."

"George?" she repeated. As soon as she said it, she realized he was making reference to their George Bailey-Wonderful Life conversation. *Did he just give me a nickname?*

The small gesture warmed Leah in an unexpected way. While she was growing up, she always wanted her dad to give her a nickname to prove his affection. She thought a boy's name would be the best because then she would know he had come to consider her equal to the son she should have been. But her father only called her Leah. Everyone only called her Leah. She didn't even have a middle name.

"You're the Glenbrooke Zorro, aren't you?" Seth pressed her again.

Leah impulsively decided to risk everything for the sake of being honest with this man. "Yes, I am."

Seth slapped his knee. "I thought so! I was almost positive."

"Why?" Leah asked. "Why do you even need to know? What does it matter?" It struck her that she had just confessed to him something she had never told anyone. Was this level of vulnerability the price she had to pay for a relationship with someone "stable"?

I don't know if I'm ready for this.

"Some guys were talking about it at work today. One of them said his sister just had a baby, and her husband had surgery a few days later. He said someone left groceries for them on their doorstep and that the Glenbrooke Zorro was back. That's when they gave me the history on this invisible superhero. Or should I say superheroine?"

Leah felt as if Seth, who was practically a stranger, had just run in and stolen something vital to the core of her identity. Her secret deliveries all these years had been her one private, silent source of delight. The secrecy allowed her to feel that even though she was only a "Leah" she could do noble things.

This is my secret. What is he doing sharing my secret?

"You probably feel pretty proud of yourself, don't you?" Leah said, pulling back and crossing her legs in the other direction to put a definite distance between them.

"Why?"

"Because no one else has figured it out. You come to town, and three days later," she snapped her fingers for emphasis, "you solve the mystery." Leah crossed her arms and gave him an angry look, which was not completely in jest.

"Oh, come on," Seth said, playfully tagging her shoulder. "Do you mean to tell me that no one has ever challenged the identity of this anonymous gift-giver?"

Leah shrugged. "I don't know."

Seth sat back and in a more serious tone said, "You know what? Your secret is safe with me. I promise I won't tell anyone."

Leah tried to relax. This was what she wanted: a close friendship with someone she could trust, someone with whom she could be open and honest. If self-disclosure and vulnerability were the price she had to pay, maybe it was a fair price.

"About a year ago," Leah began, leaning back, "Kenton at the *Glenbrooke Gazette* wrote an editorial. He was the one who used the term, 'Glenbrooke Zorro.'"

"Is that right?"

Leah nodded.

"And how did people react?"

"Everyone was talking about it and coming up with all these ridiculous speculations as to whom the Glenbrooke Zorro could be. I felt like telling some of the people at work that it was me, just so they would stop with the dumb guesses. I don't know if they would have believed me. Your great-uncle was one of the candidates. They said Franklin inherited a fortune from Cameron Madison and used his riches to help others."

"Was that in the paper?" Seth said, leaning forward.

"No, it was just what people said at work and at the grocery store. You and I both know your great-uncle is far from wealthy."

"Right," Seth said quickly.

"It was terrible around work and church for a couple of weeks," Leah continued. "Everyone assumed the phantom was a male. And then people started writing letters to the editor. You wouldn't have believed it. Actually, I kept some of the letters." Leah rose and went over to a bookshelf in the corner and picked up a photo box. She pulled out a few pictures and some newspaper clippings.

"Look at this one."

Seth read it aloud. "Dear Glenbrooke Zorro, Please bring me $447 so I can have my terrible leaking kitchen sink fixed. It keeps me awake at night."

He looked up. "Did you give her the $447?"

"No, I didn't do anything. I found out later that a guy from our church went over and fixed it for her for free."

"Cool," Seth said with a smile. "What's this one?" He read another newspaper clipping. "Dear Glenbrooke Zorro, I am a fifty-two-year-old gentleman through and through. I'm hoping you can send me a new wife." Seth burst out laughing.

Leah pointed to the clipping. "Read the rest of it."

"She must be a nonsmoker who likes to cook and do crossword puzzles. My preferences on height are over 5'6"; weight, under 130 pounds; brown hair and green eyes. No visible scars and no pets. Please have her contact me at the P.O. box number listed below. With appreciation, Mr. X."

Seth shook his head. "Mr. X. Now there's a real clever guy for you. Did he get his ideal wife?"

"Who knows!" Leah said. "I had nothing to do with it. I'm not Santa Claus. Or the Tooth Fairy. I'm not even Zorro! Wasn't Zorro a sword fighter? What does that have to do with giving?"

"What happened with all these letters?" Seth asked.

"I guess when none of their expectations from the Glenbrooke Zorro were fulfilled, they gave up. The letters to the editor dropped off after about two weeks."

"But you went back to giving."

"Eventually."

"May I make an observation here?" Seth asked.

Leah laughed. "As opposed to keeping your opinion to yourself as you've been doing the rest of this evening?"

Seth gave an open-armed shrug. "What can I say? I tend to be opinionated."

"Oh, really?"

"And it's my opinion that you have the gift of giving. Or maybe the gift of service. It's definitely a spiritual gift when you feel compelled to continue even though it isn't as easy or as uncomplicated as when you started."

Leah asked Seth what his spiritual gift was and that prompted a discussion on their spiritual journeys for the next hour. Leah found that she and Seth had similar backgrounds. Both of them were raised going to church and made decisions to ask Jesus into their hearts when they were in grade school. Seth described himself as being in a growing season in his relationship with the Lord. He paused, looking at Leah gently, as if waiting for her to express her view of her current walk with Christ.

"For me, everything with God has been the same for a long time," Leah said. "He's there, I'm here. I don't ask much of him. He doesn't seem to be asking too much of me. I think everything is okay." She didn't elaborate. She didn't need to. Seth was, in every way, right there with her.

"I'll tell you something," Seth said. "We all go through different seasons in relationships. Including our relationship with God. Things are rarely what we imagine them to be; our understanding is too limited."

Leah nodded.

"I say that because you definitely weren't what I imagined."

Leah waited for an explanation.

"When I was at my great-uncle's last weekend, he said I should meet you because I'd find you 'delightful.' That was his word. Delightful. He said, 'For twenty years she's been bringing me flowers on May Day.' With all those clues, I thought for sure this delightful woman he adored must be at least sixty, maybe seventy years old. Especially when he said your name was 'Leah.'"

Leah felt herself drawing inward.

"Hey, I'm trying to compliment you here. I'm saying you weren't an old lady like I thought you would be. Why did you pull back?"

Leah waved her hand for him to disregard her actions. "It was nothing."

"You're not a very good liar, you know. Obviously it was something. What did I say?"

Leah was beginning to learn that if this man wanted to drag the truth out of her, he could be rather convincing. She saw little point in trying to cover up what she felt.

"It wasn't anything you said. I mean, it was, but you didn't say anything wrong. It's just my name. I've never liked my name. And when you said that Leah sounded like the name of someone who was sixty, well, that's what I was reacting to."

Seth sat back and didn't say anything for a moment. He sipped his coffee and seemed to be considering Leah. She felt as if he were looking at her the way a painter sizes up his subject before attempting to tackle the task of transposing one reality into another form.

"The name Leah comes from the Bible, doesn't it?" Seth asked.

"Yes," Leah said sharply.

"So does my name."

"But Seth was a Bible hero, wasn't he?" Leah said.

"I suppose. He was Adam and Eve's third son. The blessing of God was on Seth and not on Cain. And of course, Abel was murdered. That left Seth to carry on the godly heritage. What do you know about the Leah in the Bible?"

"Enough," Leah said flatly.

"Tell me. I don't remember."

"Her father tricked Jacob into marrying her first, instead of Rachel, the one Jacob really loved."

"Is that all?"

"That's all I know about her." Leah didn't want to quote the verse that prompted her name, but it was fresh in her mind. The pain from it must have shown on her face because Seth reached over and took her hand. The gesture surprised her yet she didn't pull away as she had when he had taken her hand to check for doggy teeth marks.

The tender look on his tanned face reflected sincerity. "If you don't like the name Leah, then how about if I just call you George?"

Something inside Leah broke, and she burst into tears.

Chapter Nine

*A*nd then what happened?" Jessica asked Leah. The two of them were in the far corner of Jessica's huge backyard the next morning, tucking Easter eggs into the tufts of grass.

"I bawled like a baby for two minutes straight, and then I somehow turned off the tears. He said he should get going, and I apologized for falling apart. Of course he told me not to worry about it. Then he left, and I sat up half the night worrying about it."

Leah bent down, leaving a blue-and-green-striped egg next to a clump of wild daffodils. "I'm telling you, I was scared. I can't remember ever crying like that. And never in front of someone I hardly knew, all because he held my hand and called me, 'George.' Do you think I need counseling, Jess?"

Jessica left the last of her eggs and plucked several fresh, yellow daffodils. She linked her arm through Leah's, and the two women headed toward the house across the newly mowed, spring grass.

"I think the same thing I told you at church last night," Jessica said after a pause. "God has scooped you up and plopped you into a pocket of grace. You can't exactly control what happens."

"That's for sure," Leah said, gazing at the pastel streamers and balloons that adorned the back deck of Kyle and Jessica's Victorian home. Tall, canvas umbrellas were opened above the two patio tables. Curls of smoke rose from the covered barbecue where Kyle was cooking the first group of the two hundred shish kebabs Leah had helped him assemble earlier that morning.

"It's not as if I had control of my life before, but now I can't predict how I'm going to react!" Leah let go of Jessica's arm so she could pick up the tennis ball at her feet and toss it to one of the golden retriever puppies. Travis was keeping them corralled in the sandy play area under the jungle gym. Jessica and Leah hung back from the house and play area to finish their conversation.

"At least before in my life," Leah continued, "I knew what was expected of me, and I always did my best to fulfill those expectations. For years my life was on a controlled, tight schedule. Now, everything is tumbled around. I can't depend on myself for anything!"

Jessica chuckled. "You know that verse in Joel about how God says he will restore to you the years that the locusts have eaten?"

Leah didn't know that verse. "Are you trying to say my parents were locusts, and they ate up my best years?"

"Not exactly," Jessica said gently. "I was wondering if in some way God was restoring to you the feelings and experiences you might have had over the last decade, but those years were taken up in your giving and caring for others. Maybe some of those feelings had to be placed on hold. You had to act older than you were. You can be younger now."

Leah looked at Jessica, trying to absorb what she was saying. "Could be," Leah said with a sigh. "I don't know."

She paused to admire her friend in the shimmering brilliance of the late morning sunshine. Jessica wore a long, flowing, pastel pink-and-gray skirt with a matching pink sweater set. Her honeyblond hair was a darker shade than Leah's was and longer. It billowed from beneath the wide-brimmed straw hat Jessica wore every year for the Easter egg hunt. The hat had a circle of silk flowers around the band, and pink satin ribbons raced down the back, almost to Jessica's waist. It was the kind of hat that perfectly suited an Easter egg hunt, and it distinctly marked Jessica as the hostess of this grand event. Leah had on overalls and a plain white T-shirt because she knew she would be running in the grass with the little kids today. Leah didn't even own anything as soft and feminine as the outfit Jessica had on.

"I can't say I know exactly what God is doing in your life," Jessica said.

"That makes two of us," Leah muttered.

"But you know I'm always here for you, and I'm praying my little heart out."

"I know," Leah said. "And if you guys ever need anything, you know I'm here for you, too."

"We know that. You have given so much to us and to others, Leah. I know God is going to give abundantly back to you. You can't out-give God, you know. Maybe he's giving you back some of your emotions."

"And what exactly would someone like me do with more emotions?"

Jessica looked past Leah to the deck where Kyle had been stringing tiny white lights on the insides of the two patio umbrellas. Jessica stood there holding her fresh daffodils and smiling past Leah in a way that highlighted the half-moon scar on her upper lip. "Oh, I can think of one direction you might want to toss some of those emotions."

Leah turned and followed Jessica's line of sight. There on the deck, next to Kyle, stood Seth, holding Bungee under his arm. He had on shorts and a white, knit shirt, which accentuated his bronzed skin.

Leaning closer to Jessica, Leah murmured, "Does that man have any idea how good he looks in shorts?"

Jessica laughed. "No, but I think you and your revived emotions might find a way to tell him!"

Leah worked hard not to burst out laughing. Instead, she waved at the guys, and they both waved back.

Just then a loud wail came from the upstairs open nursery window.

"Sounds like Sara woke up," Jessica said.

"I'll get her," Leah volunteered.

"No, not this time. You have a guest to entertain."

Before Jessica and Leah made it to the deck, Kyle had gone inside to answer his daughter's cries. He had left Seth to turn the shish kebabs on the barbecue. Seth tied Bungee to the leg of a patio chair, and Jessica went to the play area to check on Travis, leaving Leah alone to greet Seth.

"How are you doing?" he asked before she was all the way up on the deck.

"Well. I'd like to apologize again for last night."

"You know, I have a philosophy about tears," Seth said. "Tears wash the windows of our souls, and afterward we can see ourselves more clearly."

"That's poetic," Leah said, smiling at him.

He smiled back. "You like it? I just made it up. It's yours."

The back door opened, and two-year-old Emma paraded out in a white Easter dress with pink sash, white shoes, and lacy anklets. On her head was a white straw Easter bonnet with an elastic string that tucked under her chin. She walked toward Leah as if she were the Princess of Just About Everything.

"Oh, look at you!" Leah said, putting her hands to her face with an exaggerated expression of amazement. "Who is this absolutely gorgeous little princess?"

Emma played right along, and with her chin in the air she said, "It's me!"

The backdoor opened again, and Kyle's brother, Kenton, and his wife, Lauren, appeared with their two-year-old, Molly Sue. Lauren wore her short hair tucked behind her ears. She recently had colored it a shade of cinnamon brown that was close to her daughter's hair color. Molly Sue wore a frilly Easter frock with a big pink bow in her hair.

"And look at you!" Leah said, making over Molly Sue with equal enthusiasm.

Lauren said hello to Leah and told her the eggs she had decorated were on the kitchen counter. Kenton introduced Lauren to Seth.

The four of them chatted a few minutes before Kenton asked if he should start to hide the eggs they had brought.

"I can do it," Leah said.

"Actually, I was kind of looking forward to it," Kenton said. "I have a few favorite spots where I hid them last year." Kenton resembled his brother with his strong jaw and dark hair, but he was a little heavier than Kyle and not quite as tall.

"Then I wouldn't want to spoil your fun," Leah said. "Jessica and I already hid a lot in the back section of the yard. You might want to put some around the sides of the house."

"Okay, got it," Kenton said, going inside for the eggs.

Lauren called over to Jessica, "Did you see your daughter here? We came early to help, but we've been inside the last fifteen minutes. I'm afraid we created a little peer pressure. When

Emma saw Molly Sue all dressed up, she wanted to wear her Easter dress, too. I hope it's okay that I let her change into her Easter outfit."

Jessica smiled at her little charmer. "You look beautiful, Miss Emma."

"You probably didn't want her to wear all this cute stuff until church tomorrow, did you?" Lauren asked.

"No, it's okay," Jessica said, joining them on the porch.

Lauren fussed with the ruffles on her daughter's dress. "I decided this morning that I'd put so much money into Molly's outfit I wanted her to get as much wear out of it as she could before she outgrows it."

"I agree," Jessica said. "As long as we have them in their finest, let's go out front and get a picture of these two cousins on the porch swing."

They all left, and Leah stood there with a big rip in her heart. She had never been anyone's little princess. She couldn't remember an Easter or any holiday when she had been dressed up and made a fuss over. It never had bothered her before. Why did it hurt so much now?

Seth was looking at her. Leah blinked and tried to sniff quietly. It didn't work.

"Do the windows of your soul need another cleaning today?" His voice was kind but also carried a pinch of teasing. That was enough to convince Leah to buck up and put her exasperating emotions back inside, somewhere deep, where they couldn't get out again and make her look foolish.

"No, I'm okay. Must be the smoke from the barbecue. It messes up my contacts." Leah quickly wiped her right eye. "Do you need any help there?"

"I think these are about done. Kyle told me to load them up in that tray and then put on another round."

"I'll get the next round. They're in the refrigerator."

When Leah entered the kitchen, Kyle was holding baby Sara and talking to his brother, Kenton, about the Little League game coming up on Tuesday.

"Is Seth ready for more kebabs?" Kyle asked when he saw Leah opening the refrigerator.

"I can get them," Leah said.

"Tell him I'll be right there after I change Sara. Jess wants her in her Easter dress, too, so she can take pictures on the porch."

"I'll trade you," Leah said to Kyle. "You can take the shish kebabs out, and I'll change Sara."

Kyle handed Sara over a little too willingly. "Jess wants the little bows in her hair," he said, admitting that wasn't his area of expertise. "I think Jess had to use Scotch tape the last time."

"I'll figure it out," Leah said, balancing the sleepy-eyed girl on her hip.

"And I better get these eggs hidden," Kenton said.

Leah talked softly to nine-month-old Sara all the way up the stairs. The nursery smelled like baby powder and lilacs mixed with a twinge of barbecue smoke. From below the open window came Kyle and Seth's voices with an occasional yap from Bungee.

Leah looked out the window, still holding Sara close. Sara nestled her head in the curve of Leah's neck and breathed with the calm, steady rhythm of a heart secure and at rest.

For several minutes Leah took in the closeness of her little Sara Bunny and the view out the nursery window, which consisted of rich grass bordered by deep woodlands and the fair, blue sky with a handful of fluffy clouds frolicking over the tops of the giant cedars like spring lambs at play. It all was beautiful.

Leah had lived in Glenbrooke all her life but never had the sky, the trees, or the birds' songs seemed as magnificent as they did this moment. If she ever did pack up her Amelia Earhart spirit and fly to the ends of the Earth, this was where she would want to come home. And these were the people she wanted to greet her when she returned.

This is where I belong.

Brad's counseling advice from last summer made even more sense now. For so long she had thought her parents were blocking her goal to see the world. Then, for years, she stuffed her anger inside and fought depression. Yet the truth was, when she no longer was bound by her obligations to her parents, what did she do? She had enough money to pay for a memorable trip. Instead, she bought a house and settled into Glenbrooke even more firmly.

This must really be where I belong.

Chapter Ten

*D*o you remember what Shelly said at the party yesterday?" Leah asked Seth, as his car bumped along the dirt logging road in the dark on Easter morning. "Didn't she say keep to the left off the side road at the end of the camp property?"

"I thought she said right," Seth said.

He had arrived punctually at four that morning to pick up Leah for their sunrise adventure. She had been ready twenty minutes early and had made a thermos of coffee, which they had given up on drinking as soon as the road turned bumpy. They also gave up trying to listen to the CD in Seth's portable player since it kept skipping. At the moment, drizzle covered the windshield. The wipers' steady swish filled the strained silence between Seth and Leah. Things weren't going the way she had thought they would.

The day before, at Kyle and Jessica's Easter party, the only time Seth and Leah had really talked to each other was their brief exchange right after he had arrived. Once she had dressed

Sara, other guests began to show up, and Leah ran around at her usual pace, doing everything she could to help with the event.

Seth left right after the egg hunt. He came up to Leah while she and Shelly were lacing the kids together for the three-legged race. "Four o'clock tomorrow okay for you?" he asked.

"Sure," she said. "Have you asked yet about the logging roads?"

"No."

"Well, Shelly here is the one to ask. Do you remember I told you she and her husband, Jonathan, run Camp Heather Brook? Shelly," Leah called to her recreation partner, "can you tell us how to get to the top of that hill behind the camp? Seth and I want to go there for an Easter sunrise view of the valley."

Shelly, who had been a flight attendant for many years before marrying her childhood sweetheart and moving to Glenbrooke, gave Seth directions. She pointed with two fingers the way a flight attendant indicates where the emergency exits are located on a plane.

Leah wished Shelly and her two efficient fingers were with them now in Seth's Subaru so she could point out the emergency exit on this dark, bumpy road.

"I'm almost positive Shelly said to turn this way," Leah said, holding on to her shoulder safety strap so it wouldn't press against the side of her neck with each bounce. "This road is really bad."

"Are you kidding? This would practically be a super highway in Costa Rica," Seth said, bringing the car to an abrupt halt. "Look, there's the cedar tree she told us about and the fork in the trail."

"You're right," Leah said, squinting into the light of his high beams at the obvious division in the trail.

"At this fork we go right," Seth said.

"Right," Leah agreed, and on they went, bouncing like crazy.

The road curved and led up a steep incline. Seth punched his way to the top and stopped with a jerk when the road suddenly ended.

"Looks like a moderate hike, from what I can see," Seth said, getting out of the car.

Leah was glad the rain had stopped as they began to hike. She had to hoof it fast to keep up with Seth. He held a large flashlight high to spread light for both of them. The earth beneath their feet was soft but not so muddy it slowed them down.

They hiked in silence for ten minutes before Seth said, "This looks like a worthy spot." He swung the light to the right and left. Leah could make out that they were standing on the knoll of the hill. Half a dozen sawed-off tree stumps revealed that this area had been the victim of a clear-cut decades ago. What lay beyond them and in the valley below remained to be seen.

"I'd put a bench right here, if I owned this mountain," Seth declared.

"It's not exactly a mountain," Leah stated, brushing off the top of mossy log before sitting down and removing her left boot. She shook it, and a tiny pebble fell out.

"Was that in there the whole time?" Seth asked.

"Yes, but I didn't want to stop." They were speaking in hushed voices, as if the rest of the world was still in a deep sleep. Their whispers carried far on the top of this windless hill. The moist scent of earth and decayed leaves filled the air.

Seth sat on the stump closest to hers. "You're the kind of camper we loved to have on our tours. The ones who didn't complain and could take a bit of inconvenience."

"That's me," Leah said. "The original happy camper."

"You know, it took us a lot less time to get to this lookout point than I thought it would," Seth said. "Are you cold? Do you want to walk around some? It's going to be awhile before we see the sun."

"I'm fine."

The low-hanging clouds served as a canopy, covering the stars and keeping the earth warmer than it would have been if the sky were wide open above them.

Seth flashed the light around. "It is pretty dark, isn't it? Not much chance of being mauled by a mountain lion here in the clear-cut, is there?"

"Oh, now, that's a nice thought," Leah said. She noticed for the first time that she could see her breath. Crossing her arms, she tucked her hands under her armpits to warm them.

"Tell me about your family," she suggested as an alternative to concocting spooky images in the darkness.

"My family?" Seth turned toward her. He placed the flashlight on the ground between them. The light shot upwards like a beacon. Its brilliance dispersed in the fine mist of the clouds.

"You said you grew up in Colorado, right?"

"Yes, the Boulder area. My parents are mild, law-abiding citizens. My dad is a financial consultant. I have one older sister, who lives in Canada with her husband and three kids. That's about it." Seth gazed into the vast night, preoccupied with his own thoughts.

It disappointed Leah that he wasn't acting more attentive to her. The closeness and warmth that had overpowered her on Friday night when he had called her George didn't seem to be with them in the damp chill of this early morning. She wanted that feeling back. She wanted him to say something tender and poetic like he had said yesterday about her tears washing the window of her soul.

Seth's thoughts obviously were elsewhere because he said, "Do you know an elderly woman named Ida?"

"Yes." Leah looked at Seth in the light of the flashlight beam. "Ida Dane. You met her. You delivered a package to her last week. My car stalled in front of her house."

"*That's* why she acted as if she knew me. The lemonade. She invited me to come back for lemonade the day I delivered a package to her."

"You should take her up on it," Leah said. "Ida makes terrific lemonade. She uses local summer berries and makes it in the blender."

"I did try some. She gave it to me at the Easter party yesterday."

"That's right," Leah said, "Ida did bring some yesterday, didn't she? My favorite is her marionberry lemonade."

"I think that's the one I had. It was great. Although when she started to talk to me, I didn't realize I'd already met her. Do you think Ida knows what she's talking about?"

"Most of the time. She gets fuzzy every now and then. Why?"

Seth stretched out his legs in front of him and stomped his right heel in the damp earth, dislodging a mud clod from the bottom of his boot. "When Ida found out I was Franklin's relative, she had all kinds of trivia to tell me. For instance, she said this hill and the surrounding 150 acres belonged to Cameron Madison, as well as another 50 acres on and around Madison Hill."

"That sounds about right," Leah said.

"Ida also said that Franklin inherited all two hundred acres."

"How could that be?"

"I don't know, but that's what she said."

"It doesn't make any sense." Leah paused. "I always heard

that Cameron was bankrupt when he died. How could he leave anything to Franklin? Or, if he did, then Franklin must have sold it all long before I was born."

"That's what I thought, too. But Ida got me curious. I went to the library when I left the party yesterday, and I tried to look up information on the area. I didn't get very far. It's quite a research project. I was thinking of asking Kenton if the newspaper has a reference system I could use to look up notices of land sales."

"Why don't you just ask Franklin?" Leah asked.

"Do you think he would tell me?"

"Why not? He's your great-uncle."

"Has he ever said anything to you about owning lots of land?"

Leah thought a moment before shaking her head. She was beginning to feel chilled. "No, the subject never has come up. And why would he discuss it with me, anyway?"

"Because…" Seth paused before finishing his answer. "I have a feeling you're in his will."

"Me? Why on earth would you say that?"

"He likes you a lot. He said something the other day about planning to reward you for all your decades of kindness to him. That's when I still thought you were his sixty-year-old girlfriend."

Leah shook her head. She felt like telling Seth he didn't know what he was talking about. "I'm sure Franklin's idea of rewarding me would be with a candy bar or tickets to the movies. He did that once when I was in high school. He called the theater in Edgefield and arranged for the manager to send me two passes."

"Do you think that's it?" Seth said. "A candy bar or a movie?"

Leah tried to make out Seth's expression in the hazy light.

"What? You think he's going to leave me his house when he dies? No thank you. It took me months to clean out my parents' house and get it ready to put on the market. I don't ever want to go through that again."

"Did you hear that?" Seth said, looking behind them. "We woke up the birds."

Leah listened to the melodic twittering and felt as if this chilly, barren hill had just warmed. With a lighter tone to her voice, she said, "Let me know if you find out anything interesting about this area and what Cameron Madison actually owned. I'd be curious to know."

Seth nodded.

She could see him more clearly now in the approaching light of the dawn. Leah wished she could read his thoughts.

What does Seth think of me? Am I merely a "happy camper" to him? Someone to keep him company? Or is he attracted to me the way I'm attracted to him?

Leah thought about how she had freely given Seth her secrets a few nights ago. Now Seth insinuated that Franklin also had secrets. Seth seemed to have an exceptional ability to uncover information. If Franklin had money, Seth would find out. And then what would happen?

Leah shivered, even though the morning sun was breaking through the clouds and pouring out a pale, golden glow across the valley.

I hope with all my heart that I can trust you, Seth Edwards.

Chapter Eleven

'*V*ery early on the first day of the week, they came to the tomb when the sun had risen,'" Seth read to Leah from his thin, leather-bound Bible that he had pulled from his coat's inside pocket.

He looked up and surveyed the valley before them, which was now flooded with light. "When the Son of God had risen," Seth said more to himself than to Leah. "The light of the world."

Snapping out of his private thoughts, Seth returned his attention to the passage in the Gospel of Mark and read the rest of the resurrection account.

Leah thought his voice was easy to listen to, and she enjoyed hearing the recounting of the first Easter and how the women went to the garden tomb early in the morning to seek Jesus. But Jesus wasn't in the grave. He was alive. Christ was resurrected and walking among them without their knowing it.

By the time Seth had finished reading, the world around

them was filled with a soft, diffused light. Thin clouds hung over their heads, making the golden sun on the horizon even more spectacular.

"Amen," Seth pronounced when he had finished reading. "Amen and amen! He is risen!" Seth stood and declared.

"He is risen indeed," Leah echoed, rising to her feet. She remembered answering with that phrase on Easter morning when she was a child. The children of Glenbrooke Community Church used to be invited to sit through the Easter morning service. When the pastor ended his short sermon with, "He is risen," all the children took their cue to jump to their feet and at the top of their voices answer, "He is risen indeed!" The opportunity to yell in church after sitting under the intoxicating influence of a hundred pungent Easter lilies always gave Leah a rush.

This morning the memory gave Leah the idea of bringing in a few Easter lilies for her toddlers class. The church no longer included the little ones in the service, which now ran an hour and a half instead of an hour. Her young friends would enjoy the chance to jump up and shout.

Leah noticed that Seth had set his face toward the valley below. They stood in silence, both taking in the vastness of the lush green spread before them. She stood close enough to him that he could have put his arm around her shoulders if he chose to, but he didn't.

"Can you imagine what old Cameron must have thought when he first gazed on this?" Seth asked.

"I can't imagine," Leah said. She was thinking how dearly she needed Seth to put his arm around her. Then she would know he was thinking of her as fondly as she was thinking of him. She would be able to trust him again.

"Look at that perfect blue ribbon," Seth said, lost in a world beyond the one where he and Leah now stood.

Leah drew in her vulnerable feelings and said, "That's Heather Creek. It's full this year because we had a wet winter. Over to the left, do you see that forest? A gorgeous waterfall lies just on the other side of those trees."

"Really? A waterfall?"

"Yes. You would never guess the land drops off enough for a large waterfall. And the meadow there in the middle is behind the main lodge of Camp Heather Brook. It's too far away to see the lodge, but it's there."

"What about the woodlands on the right?" Seth asked.

"That's a beautiful area," Leah said. "I've only been there once. The camp doesn't own it, but they want to buy it. Shelly told me they have plans to add a junior camp. What they want to do is make it a tree house camp. Isn't that a fun idea? I would have loved to spend the night in a tree house when I was in grade school."

"Who owns it?"

"I don't know. I'm not sure Jonathan and Shelly know. Actually, Kyle is the one who is handling buying the property. He and Jessica bought the land for Camp Heather Brook about five years ago."

"Really," Seth said, stroking his chin. "Interesting."

They lingered on the knoll only a few more minutes. Seth remained distant, preoccupied in a world of thoughts to which Leah didn't have a passport to enter.

She knew her emotions were too far out in front of reality. They needed to go away. And quickly. But in the same way that she had done nothing to bid them to take center stage in her life, she felt powerless to make them leave.

If Seth isn't going to reciprocate or indicate that he's interested in me, I should pull back. Now, before I get hurt.

"We probably should get going," Seth said, picking up the flashlight and bending to tie his boot laces.

"Right," Leah agreed.

They drove home with Seth lost in his thoughts and Leah struggling with her feelings. She noticed he held the steering wheel with his right arm fully extended. His knuckles were large, and his fingers were thick and rugged.

She wanted Seth to say something when he dropped her off at her house. Something promising like "When can I see you again?" or "I loved being with you this morning." But all he said was, "Don't forget your thermos."

In a way, it was a good thing she didn't linger to talk with Seth because Leah had just enough time to change for church, gather up the clean nursery toys, and dash out the door. When she arrived at the nursery, the first, dressed-up toddler already was there with his parents. He was clutching the head of a chocolate Easter bunny in his fist.

She had to forgo the fragrant Easter lilies, but she did get the fourteen children going with a rousing, "He is risen, indeed!" yelling session.

All her friends wished her a happy Easter, and she received three invitations for Easter dinner. But she turned each one down, waiting in the classroom until the church halls were empty. She kept hoping Seth would show up as he had Friday night.

When he didn't come sauntering down the hall, Leah closed up her room and went to the parking lot. Her car was the last one.

She ended up going to Kyle and Jessica's since she knew they wouldn't mind if she reconsidered their earlier invitation. She spent the afternoon, along with nine other guests, dining on ham, scalloped potatoes, green beans, and gourmet chocolate Easter eggs in the Buchanans' formal dining room. They all lingered at the table, telling stories, bouncing children on their knees, and laughing at Jessica every time she scolded Kyle for slipping table scraps to Lady and her last, unspoken-for puppy.

Travis called the puppy "Skipper." He was supposed to stay in the laundry room, but he kept mysteriously "skipping" into the dining room behind Lady, who knew that Kyle would be the soft touch when it came to table scraps.

Little Sara settled herself on Leah's lap and nodded off as the conversation continued around the table. The afternoon sunshine danced through the lace curtains, sprinkling Sara's back and Leah's legs with a delicate pattern of fairy light. Leah kissed the top of Sara's head and thought how perfect all this was. The only element missing was Seth. He would have enjoyed this. A real family. A big, holiday dinner. Where was he? With Franklin? By any chance was Seth thinking of her? She was mad at herself for not taking the initiative to invite him to Kyle and Jessica's. They gladly would have welcomed him. Why didn't she think of it sooner?

From Sunday afternoon until Leah saw Seth again on Tuesday, she went through a gigantic loopty-loop of emotions. She wanted to see Seth. Did he want to see her? Why hadn't he called? Should she call him?

On Monday she decided to make cookies for him. That would give her an excuse to stop by his work on Tuesday and see him. She didn't know exactly what she would say, but it would come to her. What guy didn't like receiving a batch of homemade cookies?

All the ingredients were lined up on her kitchen counter when Leah felt overwhelmed with feelings of rejection. If Seth wanted to see her again, he would have called her. How could she have been so foolish as to think he had been captivated by her the way she was captivated by him? She knew she had frivolously allowed herself to dream about Seth in the first place.

She was only setting herself up for defeat.

Leah bent over the sink and began to cry. She knew this feeling. It was anger. Anger at having her goals blocked. Her wishes would never come true nor would her prayers ever be answered. A man like Seth would never be interested in someone like her. She was mad that he had come into her house and sat on her couch and called her George. She was angry with herself for admitting her secret about being the Glenbrooke Zorro.

Hula padded into the kitchen and stood beside Leah, comforting her as her tears fell. "Why did I do it, Hula? Why did I let myself open up like that? Why?"

Leah didn't trust herself to make cookies in her emotional state. She didn't trust herself to do anything. She hated the power of her feelings. The only way to gain control over them was to shut them down, to allow the old tapes to play themselves over in her mind, reminding her that she "had neither the frame nor frame of mind to attract anyone stable." "Behold, it was Leah."

By the time Leah saw Seth again Tuesday night at the Little League game, she successfully had shut down all her feelings. The evening was cool and drizzly, and the bleachers were dotted with umbrellas. Definitely a smaller crowd had gathered for this game than had been there the week before. Seth showed up at the Snack Shack during the second inning and bought a hot chocolate.

"I guess you're not doing much of a Sno-Kone business tonight, are you?" Seth asked.

"No. You're my tenth hot chocolate order," Leah said.

"Is this pretty typical spring weather for this area?" he asked, while he stood there with his hands in his jeans pockets.

"Yes, sometimes the rain hangs on through June."

"What you're trying to tell me is that my first week here

was just a tease. It's usually not that sunny and nice."

You got that right, Leah thought, as she turned her back on him to stir the cocoa mix in the boiling water. *Your first week was just a tease for both of us.*

She handed him the cocoa and matter-of-factly said, "Be careful; it's hot. We don't print a warning on our cups, so I have to make sure you hear me say it's hot."

"Got it."

Leah thought he would turn to go, but he stood there under the metal awning, sipping his cocoa and not saying anything. Several other customers came up in search of something warm, and Leah made more hot chocolate and a few burritos.

"I spent Easter Sunday with Franklin," Seth offered after Leah had passed a cup of cocoa on to the last waiting customer. "We had a nice time. He wanted me to ask if you would come by to see him sometime this week."

"Is he okay?"

"He seems okay to me. He said he wanted to talk with you about something that couldn't wait until May Day when you came by with your annual bouquet."

"Did he say what it was about?"

"No. I didn't ask."

"Thanks for relaying the message," Leah said. "I'll check in on him this week." She went back to inventorying the candy bars, which is what she had been doing when Seth walked up.

"I guess you're not going to need help with the crowd after the game this week."

"No. Thanks anyway." Leah knew she sounded curt. Mild indifference was the only safe route for her. She refused to let her feelings rise to the surface.

"I guess I'll be on my way," Seth said. "I'll see you around."

"See you around."

As soon as Seth was gone, she felt depressed.

What did you think he was going to do? Ask you out to dinner? Invite you to sail off into the sunset on his private yacht? See what happens when you let your emotions get all gushy, and you start wishing on planets and opening yourself up? You set yourself up for failure, Leah. You set your course on a road that eventually will become a dead end. Why do that to yourself?

Leah suddenly realized the words playing in her head weren't her words. The phrases about setting herself up for failure and setting a course on a dead-end road were her father's words. He had used them in a lecture to her years ago when she first announced she wanted to go to college.

But look, Leah prompted herself, *I did go to college. And I finished! It wasn't a dead-end road for me. I didn't set myself up for failure.*

If she had a place to sit in the tiny Snack Shack, Leah would have let herself down with a thud. This was earth-shaking news. Not all of her father's predictions about her life were necessarily true. Perhaps the predictions her sister had made of her weren't true either. Could it be she wasn't destined to fulfill everyone else's expectations of her?

Leah stood still and whispered, "Could that be true?" Her question was directed at God, the heavenly Father with whom she had maintained a cordial distance.

Chapter Twelve

*L*eah didn't receive any thundering answers from the heavens about whether her family's prophecies regarding her destiny were all true. She didn't expect any thunder. But Glenbrooke did receive a sudden downpour of rain that caused the game to be called. She closed up the Snack Shack and ran to her car.

The rain continued through the night and was still coming down when she left for work the next morning. She didn't know if it was the darkness of the skies or the overpowering revelation she had discovered last night, but she felt sapped of energy. The week had been emotionally draining.

Leah sat at the front admissions desk, forcing herself to catch up on phone calls to fill out insurance forms. She dialed the number listed for a patient and was checking her notes on what missing information she needed, when a robust male voice on the other end of the line said, "WPZQ, where the hits just keep on coming. And your name?"

"Ah, this is Leah Hudson from Glenbrooke General Hos—"

Before she could explain for whom she was calling, the booming voice said, "Well, congratulations, Leah Hudson! You are caller number nine, and you have just won the WPZQ bonus jackpot!"

A chorus of chipmunk voices sang into her ear, "You won! You won! You really, really won!"

"That's right!" The enthusiastic radio announcer said. "Leah Hudson, you have just won an exciting cruise for yourself and a friend to—are you ready for this?—Alaska!"

The chipmunk voices sang out again. "You won! You won! You really, really won!"

"What do you have to say, Leah Hudson?"

Leah was speechless.

The announcer jumped in. "You're on the air, so go ahead and tell all the listeners what you think of the hottest station in the nation playing all the hits all the time."

"Um, I, ah, the number I dialed…it's…"

The announcer broke in with deep laughter. "I think our winner is in shock, folks. Winning the WPZQ jackpot can have that effect on a person. Nevertheless…"

The chorus chirped in with, "You won! You won! You really, really won!"

"But, you see—" Leah tried to explain.

"Now you just stay on the line," the announcer said, "and Tina will tell you all about the fabulous cruise you've won."

After two clicks, a female voice said, "May I have your name and phone number, please?"

"Actually…Tina, is it?"

"Yes."

"Tina, I was trying to call a patient from our hospital who left this as his phone number. But I think I misdialed the number."

After a pause Tina said, "What number did you think you dialed?"

Leah repeated the number she was trying to reach, and Tina verified that was the number for the radio station.

"What area code did you dial?" Tina asked. "This is 203."

Leah began to laugh. "Well, that explains it. I meant to dial 503 for Portland, Oregon. Sorry to have troubled you."

"No, wait!" Tina said. "Don't hang up. You won the cruise."

"But how could I? I don't even live…where is your station located, anyhow?"

"New Haven."

"New Haven what?" Leah asked.

"Connecticut," Tina said.

Mary, who had just returned from lunch, slid her purse in the bottom drawer of the desk, giving Leah a curious look as Leah echoed, "Connecticut?"

"Look, you won the cruise," Tina said. "We just announced you live on the air. We can't go back and say the last winner was a hoax. Nothing in our rules says you have to know you're entering the contest to win. Or that you have to be in Connecticut when you call. You were caller number nine. You won the cruise, whether you want it or not."

"I can't believe this," Leah said.

"Would you be so kind as to give me your name, phone number, and a fax number for your travel agent? We deal directly with travel agents for all our arrangements."

Leah figured she might as well give Tina the information. Reaching for the telephone book, Leah looked up the number for A Wing and a Prayer, the only travel agency in Glenbrooke.

Mary stepped closer to Leah's desk and mouthed the word "What?"

"Thank you," Tina said. Then sounding as if she was reading

from a card, Tina continued, "Congratulations, Leah Hudson, on winning the WPZQ jackpot. All prizes are for promotional consideration only and cannot be exchanged for cash value. We hope you will keep on listening to the hottest station in the nation, playing all the hits all the time. Enjoy your cruise."

Leah hung up the phone and turned to Mary, who asked, "What was all that?"

"I just won a cruise to Alaska. Via Connecticut."

Word of Leah's trip spread quickly at work, and everyone agreed Leah "deserved" the cruise. She didn't know how she "deserved" anything. She had dialed a wrong number. It was all pretty crazy in her opinion.

One of the ER nurses had been to Alaska, and she was eager to tell Leah all about it. The woman even went home on her lunch break and brought back four travel books on Alaska, a large photo album, and two home videos of her trip, which she told Leah to watch that night at home.

Leah left work at 4:30, as usual, and drove directly to the travel agency for her 4:45 appointment.

Alissa, the owner and only travel agent at A Wing and a Prayer, was on the phone when Leah entered. In Leah's opinion, Alissa was beautiful enough to be a model. She carried herself with a bit of a swish when she walked and always looked fresh, as if she had been born with naturally gorgeous hair, skin, and nails. Alissa and Brad had moved up from Southern California, and whenever the weather warmed, Alissa wore the classiest outfits in town. Today, however, Alissa was wearing gray, just like the sky.

Taking a seat on the couch by the window, Leah flipped through a travel magazine and gazed at pictures of the Bahamas.

Is it wrong for me to wish I'd won a cruise to the Bahamas instead of Alaska? I mean, I should be happy to go anywhere. But after seeing all those pictures of that frozen land, this picture of warm blue water sure looks appealing.

Alissa hung up the phone and turned to greet Leah. "Sorry to keep you waiting. I received the fax from the radio station this afternoon. This is pretty exciting, Leah!"

Leah rose and went to one of the chairs in front of Alissa's desk. "I have a question. Do you know if this cruise is transferable?"

Alissa looked down, carefully reading the fax paper in her hand. "The only conditions they list are that you can't work for the radio station or be related to anyone who does."

"No problem there. I don't even know anyone in Connecticut!"

Alissa smiled. "And you're limited on when you can go. It looks like you have to take the cruise offered from May 15 through 19."

"This year?" Leah asked.

Alissa nodded. "These limited promotional packages often tie into the lowest priced season, which I'd guess is the case here. But, no, it doesn't say anything about transferring to another person. I can call them to make sure. Did you want to try to sell the ticket?"

"No. No, I didn't mean transferring it to another person. I meant transferring the destination." She pointed to a poster behind Alissa of the Grand Canal in Venice. It showed a man and a woman lounging on a mound of pillows in a gondola. Behind them stood a dashing gondolier, who was doing all the work while they cuddled. "Now that's my idea of a real vacation. If I had my choice, I'd like to go someplace warm."

Alissa shook her head. "No, sorry. It's valid only for the Alaskan cruise."

Leah kept staring at the poster. The way the gondolier was positioned, he seemed to be singing. For some reason the thought of being sung to made her feel like crying. She tried hard to hold back the tears, but they welled up in her eyes and tumbled down her cheeks before she could stop them.

"I'm sorry," she said to Alissa, who was offering Leah a tissue and looking startled. "I've been like this a lot lately." Leah continued to stare at the poster.

Alissa turned around to see what Leah was fixated on.

"Jessica says my emotions are being released after being pent up for too long, or something like that. I think I'm slowly going crazy."

Alissa reached across her desk and gave Leah's hand a squeeze. "Maybe this cruise is exactly what you need. You've had an intense year, Leah. I've heard Brad say that sometimes people don't start to grieve until months or years after a shocking loss. It might do you a world of good to get away and completely relax."

Leah nodded.

"And you do know, don't you, that if you ever feel like talking to someone, my husband has a way of helping make sense of all the pieces. Brad would be happy to talk with you."

"Thanks," Leah said quietly. She took another tissue and wiped the last tear. "I appreciate it, but I'm okay. Really."

Leah rose to leave when Alissa said, "By the way, do you know anyone who needs a couch? It's in good shape. Brad had it in his duplex in Pasadena, and I've never liked it. We finally found a new one we could both agree on, but now I have to haul the old one to a donation center—unless you know someone who wants it."

Leah immediately thought of Seth. "I know someone who just moved into the area, but I don't know what his furniture situation is."

"If you talk to him, could you tell him it's available? And it's free," Alissa said.

"Thanks," Leah said. "And thanks for the Kleenex."

"Remember what I said about talking with Brad."

Leah nodded. "I will. Thanks again."

Leah left the travel agency and sat in her car a few minutes, trying to decide what to do. She was planning to visit Franklin next. She could ask him for Seth's phone number, and then she could call Seth, the way she would call any one of her friends and tell him about the couch. It didn't have to be awkward. Just because she had let her feelings get the better of her the first few days she was around him, that didn't mean they couldn't settle into a nice, everyday relationship like she had with so many other men in Glenbrooke.

Leah wondered what Brad, who had provided wise counsel for her in the past, would say about that. Was she repressing her true emotions? Maybe. But that had to be better than dreaming up some one-sided romance in which she was the only one doing the dreaming.

She closed her eyes, but all she could see was the poster of the gondola and the singing gondolier. She wished she was nestled in those cushions right now, floating down a canal instead of sitting in the middle of Main Street, hugging the steering wheel, alone in her car.

It's just so hard to admit to anyone that I have a problem. How could I tell Brad I'm confused by my feelings for Seth? Or that I've realized for the first time that my father's predictions of me weren't true? Or that I'm wondering if maybe I do have the right frame and frame of mind to attract someone stable after all? Would Brad tell me to grow up and start to act my age?

Leah drew in a deep breath.

No, Brad wouldn't do that. Brad would listen carefully, and he would have sound, caring advice. But then he would know the deep thoughts of my heart. I'd have to trust him to keep my thoughts and feelings private. It was hard enough opening my heart to Seth and telling him my secrets without any guarantee that he was trustworthy.

Leah wasn't in the habit of trusting anyone but herself. And now that she realized she couldn't trust herself to settle her own emotions and to make sense of the tumble of recent events in her life, she felt completely lost.

Opening her eyes, Leah turned the key in the ignition. That's when she noticed a note on her windshield, wrapped in what looked like a used plastic sandwich bag. Apparently it was supposed to keep the note dry. Leah retrieved the note, which was damp despite the plastic bag. The name at the bottom of the scrawled lines was "Seth."

Chapter Thirteen

*H*er heart began to pound as she read Seth's simple words on the note he must have left while she was in the travel agency.

I thought of you this morning when I read this verse: Song of Songs 6:11.
    Seth

Leah's spirits instantly rose. *He thought of me? But what does the verse say?*

Since Leah didn't have a Bible handy, she laid the note flat on the passenger's seat so Seth's words could dry out. Then she drove to the grocery story for a quick purchase and on to Franklin's house, as she originally had planned.

Seth thought of me.

Leah arrived with a smile on her face and found Franklin napping in his favorite recliner. The spry old man always left the door unlocked. He said it was so the "Cleaning House" people would know to come on in if he didn't hear them knock. Leah tried to tell him once, years ago, that the contest was run by the Publishers Clearing House. But Franklin still called them the "Cleaning House" people.

As far as Leah knew, Franklin sent in his entry form every time one came in the mail. He only subscribed to two magazines but that didn't stop those "Cleaning House" people from inviting him to enter every contest they had.

Leah called out from the entryway, "Franklin? Hello, it's Leah. I brought you a little something."

Franklin stirred in his old, brown recliner and immediately perked up. "Well, look at you! And with flowers to boot."

"Flowers and candy." Leah waved the bag of peppermint patties for him to see. She knew they were his favorite candies. Or at least they were the easiest candies for him to eat.

"It's not even my birthday," Franklin said, struggling to stand up with the help of his cane.

"Don't get up." She went over and gave the old gentleman a kiss on the cheek.

He settled comfortably back into the recliner.

"What have you been doing?" she asked.

"Making plans," Franklin said with a twinkle in his eyes. His glasses were so dirty Leah didn't know how he could see her.

"Here, let me clean your glasses, Franklin. I'm going into the kitchen to put these flowers in water. I'll be right back."

"Leave the candy here with me," he said, reaching for the bag.

"Yes, sir," she teased. "Don't eat them all before I come back."

"Just watch me try," Franklin quipped.

Mavis, the day nurse who cared for Franklin, was in the kitchen fixing chicken for dinner. She had a small television on the counter and was engrossed in an afternoon talk show. Leah helped herself to a vase for the daffodils and then washed and dried Franklin's glasses.

When she returned to the living room, Franklin had opened the bag of candy and was letting one of the mint patties melt in his mouth. She handed him his glasses.

"Oh, much better," Franklin said, adjusting them a bit. "You are much too kind to me, Leah darlin'. And that's why I've been making plans."

Leah slid over to the couch, where she sat down, wondering if Seth had been right about the will. Was Franklin going to announce he had left her his house? His old recliner? Or was Franklin going to declare he had bought her tickets to the movies?

"You know I enjoy visiting you and bringing you treats," Leah said. "You don't have to make any plans to do anything for me, Franklin. And you certainly don't have to give me anything."

"Who said I'm doing anything for you?" Franklin spouted. "I've been making plans for you to do something nice for me."

"Oh!" Leah felt her cheeks turn red. "What do you want me to do for you?"

"I want you to take me to Hamilton Lodge."

"Do you mean at Hamilton Hot Springs? That's more than four hours away. Why do you want me to take you there?"

"I haven't been there since Naomi passed on." He leaned back, and a tender look crossed his face the way it always did when he spoke of Naomi. "That used to be our favorite place. We were among the first customers to stay in their new facility. That was on our twenty-fifth wedding anniversary. After that, we went every other year. Like clockwork. It was our special place."

Leah quickly calculated and deduced that the new facility must have gone up in the sixties. This brought her an instant vision of a resort done up in harvest golds and avocado greens, just like the house she had grown up in.

"I'd like you to take me there," Franklin said. "You name the weekend."

"I—I don't know."

"You don't know what? You don't know if you want to take me, or you don't know which weekend?"

How could she say that the last place she wanted to go was a sixties-style hot springs resort? She knew she shouldn't be so picky, after complaining for years about never going anywhere. But this all seemed so strange. First the cruise to Alaska and now the hot springs. And both of them on tight time schedules so she had to make decisions right away.

That wasn't the only reason Leah hesitated. She didn't know how to tell Franklin she didn't want to be responsible to care for him for a weekend away. Visiting at his home and occasionally taking him out for a drive was one thing. Going all the way to Hamilton Hot Springs and caring for him for a weekend was asking a lot.

"Wouldn't you be more comfortable with someone else like Mavis?"

"Mavis deserves some time off," he said.

Leah knew the next obvious choice would be Seth. She had a funny feeling Franklin was waiting for her to ask about his nephew. "What about Seth?"

The glimmer was back in Franklin's eyes. "I have his picture right up there on the mantle."

"Yes." Leah noticed the photo of Seth was now front and center. The picture showed a much younger, less tan version of Seth with hair longer and darker than his current shade of sun-kissed blond. The smile was the same. Leah tried not to let her feelings show. Seth had such a nice smile.

"He turned out all right, didn't he? You know he had that crazy spell when he lived with the monkeys in the jungle. You know that, don't you?" Franklin paused, waiting for Leah's reaction.

"Wasn't it the rain forest in Costa Rica?"

Franklin feebly waved his hand as if to dismiss all the details he couldn't keep straight. "Point is, he turned out all right in the end, don't you think?"

Leah hesitated.

Franklin sat up a little straighter and answered for her. "Yes, he did. He turned out all right. And so did you. Now answer my question, Leah. Will you take me to the hot springs this weekend?"

"I can't go this weekend."

"Then how about the next weekend?"

"I don't think so." She was starting to feel bad about saying no.

"Why not?" Franklin persisted.

"It's May Day weekend, and I'm helping Shelly with the May Day event at the camp."

"Oh," Franklin looked down at his thin hands. "Then it was nice of you to bring me the May Day flowers early this year. I 'spect you'll be too busy on May Day to stop by. I understand." He lifted his gaze. "You've been good to me, Leah, honey. I wouldn't want to take you away from all your other friends."

Franklin was a sly one. Did he sound more frail than usual? Was he making his voice weak so she would take pity on him? Leah knew she would miss him when he was gone. It made her realize that once Franklin died, the last piece of her childhood would be gone. She didn't have parents or grandparents left to connect her with her early years. Only Franklin.

"Oh, all right, you ruthless trickster, you," Leah said, picking up a throw pillow and pretending she was going to toss it at Franklin.

"Good. Which weekend?" His voice seemed to have improved.

"The last weekend in May. Is that okay for you?"

"That's just fine. I'll make the reservations tomorrow."

"I don't know how you talked me into this," Leah said, sauntering over and snatching one of the candies from his bag. She also didn't know how she could go on the cruise and fit in a trip to the hot springs with Franklin.

"We'll have a grand time," Franklin said. "All three of us."

Leah stuck the candy in her mouth and froze before letting her teeth sink into the thin layer of chocolate. "And who would the third person be, Franklin?" she finally asked after swallowing the mint.

Franklin smiled smugly but said nothing. He just sat there smiling and chuckling to himself.

Chapter Fourteen

*I*nstead of driving home from Franklin's house, Leah drove straight to Kyle and Jessica's. Too much had been happening too fast for Leah. She needed perspective, and Jessica often had provided her with just that.

Travis answered the doorbell and said his mommy was upstairs with Sara. Leah asked, "Could you tell her I'm here and see if she needs any help?"

Travis took off up the stairs, and Leah called after him, "And ask her if she has a Bible nearby."

Leah thought she remembered seeing a Bible on the living room bookshelf so she meandered in and pulled the leather Bible off the shelf. Turning to Song of Songs 6:11, Leah eagerly read the special message Seth had left for her. "I went down into the garden of nuts to see the fruits of the valley, and to see whether the vine flourished, and the pomegranates budded."

She stared blankly at the wall. *"Garden of nuts"? "Fruits of the valley"? This verse reminded Seth of me?*

Jessica appeared holding Sara, who was bathed and in her pajamas. "Congratulations!" Jessica said.

"For what?"

"Alissa told me you won a cruise to Alaska. That's fantastic! When are you going?"

"May 15. Would you like to go with me?"

Jessica hesitated.

"I'm only kidding. You have your hands full." Leah put down the Bible and stood, reaching out for Sara. "Come here, my little Sara Bunny."

Sara went right to Leah and cuddled up.

"She's really tired," Jessica said. "We had an early dinner. All my kids need to get to bed early tonight. I think the weekend of parties and sugar took a toll on them."

"It has been a wild week," Leah said.

"Do you want to put Sara to bed, and I'll get the other two settled? Then we can talk. I want to hear all about this cruise. Kyle won't be home for a couple of hours so you and I can have a good, long visit."

Leah felt relieved. That was exactly what she needed to hear. Jessica had time to listen and hopefully to help Leah figure out what was going on in her life.

Just then Travis padded into the room with a heavy Bible in his hands. "Here you go, Auntie Leah. You can use my dad's Bible."

"Thank you," Leah said, taking the Bible from him. "You are such a great helper, Travis. How about if you and I help your mom tuck your sisters into bed?"

Travis slipped his hand in Leah's, and they followed Jessica up the stairs. It took almost an hour to settle all three of the kids into bed. Leah helped herself to some cheese and crackers and poured a large glass of orange juice. She and Jessica sat in the living room facing each other in comfy chairs by the window that looked out over the driveway.

"You know this pocket of grace you said I fell into?" Leah began their conversation. "Well, I don't think I want to be there any longer. It's way too crazy."

Jessica smiled. "Why do you say that? Don't you want to go on the cruise? I think it's another one of God's gifts to you. Do you remember what I said before? You can't outgive God."

"It's not the cruise," Leah said. "It's everything. A week ago Seth Edwards walked into my corner of the world—my little Snack Shack—and nothing has been the same since."

"You two seemed so comfortable around each other last week when you came to pick out a puppy. Have your feelings changed?"

"Changed?" Leah said. "Ever since I fell into this 'pocket of grace,' my feelings have changed every hour on the hour. Who knows how I feel about anything? I don't think I trust myself to answer any questions until I get my emotional equilibrium back."

Jessica laughed softly. "I have a funny feeling that might not happen for a while, my friend."

"Look at the note he left on my car today." Leah handed Jessica the note and then retrieved the Bible so she could read the crazy verse to Jessica. "Are you ready for this? This is what it says, 'I went down into the garden of nuts to see the fruits of the valley—'"

Jessica interrupted Leah's reading with a giggle. Then Jessica covered her lips with her fingers and said, "I'm sorry. Go ahead."

"The rest of it is, 'and to see whether the vine flourished, and the pomegranates budded.'"

Jessica raised her eyebrows and kept her fingers over her

smiling lips. "What is that supposed to mean?"

"That's exactly what I'd like to know." Leah couldn't help it; she had to laugh. Jessica's initial reaction was correct. This was laughable.

"'I went down into the garden of nuts to see the fruits of the valley,'" Leah repeated, laughing. "Do you think he's trying to tell me I'm one of the nuts or one of the fruits in this valley?"

Jessica released a ripple of laughter. "Oh, Leah, that is so funny!"

"To you, maybe, but I'm feeling desperate here. You know how on Saturday I told you I burst out crying when he called me 'George'? And you told me I was getting back all the emotions the locusts had eaten?"

"That was sort of what I said, yes."

"Well, right after that, I took Sara up to her room, and I decided I didn't want to see the world like I thought I did. I wanted to stay right here in Glenbrooke. I wanted to pursue a relationship with Seth. Then we went hiking Sunday, up that hill behind Camp Heather Brook. Seth barely noticed I was there. So I told myself my whacked-out feelings had gotten out of control. I could never hope for a relationship with someone like Seth, and I completely shut down."

Jessica's expression changed from mirth to concern.

"I know. It's not good when I swallow my feelings and hold them in. Don't worry, I've been crying like crazy. Last night I had this huge revelation at the Little League game that some of the things my father said about me years ago weren't true. It never occurred to me before. I started to wonder if all those other messages I've believed about myself are false, too."

The phone rang, but Jessica sat quietly, waiting for Leah to continue.

"Do you need to get that?"

"No, this is more important. If it's Kyle, he'll call back

immediately. Otherwise I can let our machine pick it up. Go on, you were saying you realized you had believed some things that weren't true."

The phone stopped on the fourth ring. Leah picked up her train of thought. "I gave up my old wish of wanting to travel and then, bing! I won this cruise. I gave up on Seth, and then I stopped by Franklin's today and bing! Franklin wants me to take him to Hamilton Lodge for the weekend, and he's invited another guest to go with us."

"Seth?" Jessica ventured.

Leah nodded. "It's all happened in a week, Jess! I don't know what I'm supposed to think or feel anymore. I hope this 'pocket of grace' is well padded because I feel as if I'm about to start bouncing off the walls!"

Jessica smiled.

Leah pointed at Seth's note Jessica still held in her hand. "See? Even Seth agrees. Fruits and nuts! Further proof I'm going wacky, and everyone else recognizes it."

Jessica chuckled and looked more closely at the paper. "Are you sure this is chapter 6 verse 11? This number looks like a two to me."

"Let me see," Leah took the paper and examined it more closely. The rain had smeared the letters so that all she saw was the loop of the number. She had assumed it was a six. Possibly Seth made loopy twos. Leah turned to Song of Songs 2:11. Jessica turned there as well in Kyle's Bible that Travis had brought downstairs for them.

"Oh, yes, I think this verse is the one he had in mind," Jessica said before Leah could read the whole verse herself. Jessica read aloud, "'See! The winter is past; the rains are over and gone. Flowers appear on the earth; the season of singing has come.'"

Leah looked up at her, feeling humbled. "That's a little different than the fruits and nuts verse."

"Yes, it is." Jessica smiled. "Much more fitting. I think Seth was trying to encourage you, Leah, by saying you're entering into a new season in your life. That's what I was saying on Saturday when I told you the verse about God restoring the years the locusts had eaten. You need to feel free to move on in your life."

"Move on to what?" Leah asked.

Jessica smiled and then hopped up from her chair. "It just so happens that now I'm the one who has a verse for you."

Leah knew where Jessica was going. She kept a stack of three-by-five-inch cards at the desk in her kitchen with various verses written on them. Those cards often ended up taped to bathroom mirrors or framed and placed above the kitchen sink. Jessica carried verses in her purse, she had them in the car, and Leah had even found them in Sara's diaper bag. Kyle referred to the verses as his wife's "spiritual snacks."

Jessica hadn't grown up going to church, and she didn't know a lot about the Bible when she and Kyle married. In an effort to get to know God's Word in the midst of her busy days, Jessica had written out dozens of these verse cards. More than once she had passed a card on to Leah. Leah usually stuck them in her Bible and didn't bother to really look at them.

Jessica returned with a card for Leah and handed it to her as it if were the key to a treasure chest. "This is it," she said, reciting the three verses from Psalm 37 from memory. "'Trust in the LORD and do good; dwell in the land and cultivate faithfulness. Delight yourself in the LORD; and He will give you the desires of your heart. Commit your way to the LORD, trust also in Him, and He will do it.'"

Leah looked at the card, hoping the words would instantly work some special blessing on her as they obviously had on Jessica, judging by the expression on Jessica's face.

"It's that middle verse you need to concentrate on right

now," Jessica said. "'Delight yourself in the LORD; and He will give you the desires of your heart.' Don't concentrate on figuring out what your heart's desires are. Concentrate on delighting yourself in the Lord. Then the rest will fall into place."

"You promise?" Leah asked.

"I don't have to promise. God is the one who made that promise."

When Leah looked skeptical, Jessica added, "He hasn't broken a single one of his promises yet, you know. I doubt he would start now."

Chapter Fifteen

$\mathcal{A}$t five the next morning Leah lay awake, unable to fall back asleep. She felt as if she had gone riding through the night on the tattered edges of midnight's dark, velvet cape. She knew emotionally she was going somewhere—and fast. But where?

When Leah realized she wasn't going to fall back to sleep, she reluctantly rose and shuffled into the kitchen for a drink of water. The stillness comforted her. The rain had stopped, and it was quiet outside. She stood at the window, sipping her glass of water and trying to see the sky, but it was still too dark.

On a whim, Leah reached for a blanket in the living room and went through the mudroom out to the back steps. Hula rose and padded after her, not fully awake but ever faithful. For a long while Leah sat on the cold, cement steps, wrapped in the blanket and with her arm around Hula. Leah stared into the deep, quiet darkness, waiting for the morning light to come.

Her thoughts were of God and trying to understand who

he was and what he expected of her in light of the conversation she had had with Jessica the night before. For so long Leah had pictured God as a cosmic motorcycle cop, hiding behind a billboard and pointing a radar gun at her. That's why she always followed the rules. As long as God couldn't catch her doing anything wrong, he wouldn't be mad at her. And if he wasn't mad at her, maybe he wouldn't mess up her life.

Until this point, that image of God had made sense to her. She never had mentioned it to anyone, but she was sure if she had it would have seemed right and not at all twisted. Now, just as she was recognizing other lies she had believed for years, Leah realized how inaccurate that image of God was.

God, you're not standing there, pointing a radar gun at my heart, are you? The inaccurate image immediately dissolved. *What do you want, God? What do you expect from me? How am I supposed to respond to you?*

For the first time since high school, Leah felt a hunger in her spirit. She wanted to know God. To hear how others viewed him and responded to him. Leah thought of Jessica as someone who had a deeper relationship with God than she did. Seth had seemed so much more connected with God when he read aloud the Easter account on their morning hike. It was all so real to him. Leah felt she was missing something. She had felt it for some time.

In the quiet of her intense contemplation, the morning came softly, a blessed contrast to the frenzy of the past few days. A chorus of birds greeted her from the treetops. Hula barked at a squirrel as it scampered across the lawn. Leah held Hula back from running after the intruder. The scent of the rain-soaked earth rose and circled Leah, inviting her to come into the garden.

Leah reached for a hoe in the mudroom and slipped her

bare feet into an old pair of wooden clogs she kept by the door. In the pristine morning light, she trotted into the yard in her flannel pajama bottoms and T-shirt with the blanket tied around her shoulders like a cape. She grinned at her impulsiveness. What did it matter? No one was up to see her, digging the hoe into the damp earth.

The previous owner had sectioned off a plot for a small vegetable garden, but Leah hadn't had a chance to do anything with it. Now, as she turned over each clod of dirt, she made plans for peas, carrots, tomatoes, and some sort of melon. Cantaloupe sounded good.

The rain-kissed earth turned for her like soft butter. She could have dug this garden with a spoon. Bending to grasp a handful of the mink-brown dirt, Leah rubbed it between her fingers and breathed in deeply its dark, spicy fragrance.

Gently, the words from Seth's verse came back to her. Not the verse about the fruits and nuts, but the verse about the rains being over and the flowers appearing. The season for singing had come.

Leah didn't sing. She barely breathed. Standing still in her blanket cape and flannel pj's, with her hand full of moist earth, she prayed. It had been a long time since she had really prayed.

"Lord God," she whispered, "You're here, aren't you? I mean, you're really, truly right here. And you're here in my heart, even though it's been so long since I've talked openly and intimately with you. You never left. I was the one who ignored you."

Leah let the dirt fall through her fingers. "The winter is over. The storms have ceased in my heart. You're trying to plow things up, aren't you? You want to plant something new." A gentle breeze lifted the feathery strands of her hair from her neck.

"I'm sorry I've been so resistant to you. Please forgive me. I want to learn how to delight myself in you because I honestly don't know how to do that."

The longer Leah stood in the morning chill, the more she shivered. She didn't want to move. One doesn't step away from holy ground too quickly. This place, this simple earth, this garden, had become holy to Leah. God had met her here. And she had responded.

"You want me to trust you, don't you?" Leah curled and uncurled her toes inside her wooden clogs. "You know how hard that is for me."

Feeling compelled to kneel in the moist earth, Leah went down slowly. First on her right knee and then on her left. "Okay," she whispered. "I promise. I'll trust you."

A full five minutes later, Leah returned to the house with Hula beside her. Kicking off the muddy clogs, Leah scampered barefooted into the bathroom where she jumped into a warm shower. The soothing water washed over her, refreshing her. Her spirit had never felt so clean.

Leah wrote on a yellow sticky note to buy some three-by-five cards. She wanted to start writing down verses the way Jessica did. It was time to plant some new seeds in her life.

It was also time to plant seeds in her vegetable garden, now that the earth was ready. She began a list of the vegetables she had decided on while she was hoeing. She could go buy the seeds on her lunch break and then plant them as soon as she got home from work. The thought made Leah smile. This was her home. Her garden. It was a small blessing, one she hadn't fully appreciated until now.

Leah entered the hospital with a light step and greeted everyone she saw on her way in. On her desk sat another tour book of Alaska.

"Did you see the memo on vacation time yet?" Mary asked

as Leah settled in her chair. "I'm taking off the third week of May because my sister's coming to visit."

"That should be fun," Leah said.

Mary shook her head. "I don't know about that. We're not going anywhere. It's her fiftieth birthday, and she's pretty depressed about it. I'm not sure what I can do to cheer her up."

Leah turned and looked at Mary. "Why don't you take her on a cruise?"

"Yeah, right."

"Take her on the cruise to Alaska," Leah said. "The two of you can use the free tickets. It's the week she's coming, and I don't know who I would go with."

Mary stopped and stared. "Are you serious?"

"Yes, I'm completely serious. This would be good for you and for your sister. You haven't been on a vacation in years, Mary."

"Neither have you, Leah. You're the one who always wants to go somewhere exciting. This is your trip."

Leah laughed. "It was my fluke. My goofed-up dialing. I didn't do anything to win the trip."

"But it's your trip," Mary protested.

"Okay, it's my trip, and I can do what I want with it. And what I choose to do is give it to you and your sister." Leah began to dial the phone number for A Wing and a Prayer.

Mary sat down on the edge of the desk. "Are you sure?"

Leah smiled. "Very sure. Hi, Alissa? This is Leah. Hey, you know how you said those tickets were transferable to another person? Well, I'd like to transfer them. Here's Mary. She'll give you all the information."

Mary took the phone and relayed the details to Alissa and agreed to go by the travel agency at lunch to pick up the papers. When Mary finished the call, she leaned over and hugged Leah.

"You have no idea how much I appreciate this." Mary began to cry. Leah guessed those tears had come often, quick and silent like that, during the last five years since her husband had left with a woman who worked at the gas station on the outskirts of town. Mary had worked hard to rebuild her life with her three kids. This would be a nice break for her.

Leah handed the Alaska tour book to Mary. "Here, you're the one who needs to read this. And I have a couple of home videos of Alaska in my car you can watch, too."

They both chuckled, and Mary dried her tears. Settling in with the stack of patient folders before her, Leah felt good. Very good. Better than she had felt in a long time. The anxiety of the day before, when she had gone to Jessica's, had subsided. Leah's heart was more at peace with God than it had been in years.

One of her coworkers handed Leah a bunch of papers and said, "Are you ready to be impressed? This is the list of day surgeries for tomorrow and all of next week. Are we getting organized around here or what?"

"I'm impressed," Leah said, flipping through the pages. Tuesday was the lightest schedule. Friday of next week was the fullest. A name on the list for Friday caught her eye and caused Leah's heart to skip a beat.

The name on the list was Seth Edwards. And the description of the procedure was underlined in red, which meant one thing to all hospital employees: cancer.

Chapter Sixteen

*H*i, Jack, this is Leah Hudson. Could you please leave a message for Seth? Ask him to call me when he returns from his route. Let me give you all my numbers." Leah gave Jack, the clerk at the PDS station, her work number, home number, and cell phone number.

"Did you try him on his cell phone?" Jack asked.

"No, I don't know the number."

"Well, we're not supposed to give them out, but since it's you, Leah, I'll tell you what it is."

Leah was using her cell phone as she drove to the hardware store on her lunch break. She was determined to buy her garden seeds so she could get right to work when she arrived at home. Punching in the numbers for Seth's cell phone, she felt relieved when he answered after the second ring.

"Hi, it's Leah."

"How did you get this number?"

"Jack at the PDS office. He used to go out with one of my sisters."

"Oh. So what's up?"

"Yesterday Alissa told me she and Brad have a couch they would like to give away. I didn't know if you needed a couch, but I thought I'd let you know."

"I do need a couch. Thanks for telling me. Do you have a number for them?"

"Alissa runs the travel agency on Main Street. It's A Wing and a Prayer. You can't miss it. It's next door to the Wallflower Cafe and across the street from the Glenbrooke Gazette."

"I'm about three blocks from there now. I'll stop in and talk to Alissa about it. Thanks."

"Sure." Leah knew she could end the call then, but she didn't want to. The last time she had talked to Seth, at the rained-out Little League game, she had been cool and reserved. That was before her spirit had been plowed up. Everything in her life was fresh now. That was also before she had read Seth's name on the day surgery form next to the procedure listed as "L5-S1: removal of melanoma and surrounding lymph nodes."

"I'm headed downtown, too," Leah said. "Any chance you would like to meet for some lunch?"

Seth hesitated only a moment before saying, "Sure. Where do you suggest?"

"The Wallflower Cafe is close and easy."

"Okay. I'll see you there in a few minutes."

Leah hung up and turned left on Main, parking four doors down from the Wallflower Cafe. The vegetable seeds could wait until after work.

The small diner had once been a charming, favorite spot to stop for a sandwich or cup of soup on a rainy day. Today the sun was shining, which made the many flaws of the Wallflower stand out. The real flowers in the planters on the walls above the booths had been replaced years ago with plastic red and orange ones. The vinyl seats had too many lumps to be comfortable to sit on for long, and the menu had decreased in variety. Last year the café owners had put a for sale sign in the window, but after receiving no offers in two months, they took down the sign and compromised by trimming their menu and shop hours.

Leah greeted Hazel, the waitress at the counter, and decided to sit at the window seat so she could watch for Seth.

"Coffee?" Hazel asked, walking toward Leah with the coffee-pot in her hand.

"No, thanks. What's your soup today?"

"Vegetable barley," Hazel said.

"I'd like some soup and a large orange juice."

"Coming right up," Hazel said. She shuffled past the four customers who sat at a table in the center of the cafe and filled their coffee mugs.

One of the customers was Collin Radcliffe. He was ignoring Leah, which was typical of him since their days growing up together in Glenbrooke. Collin had gone off to college and become a lawyer. He had been in California until the first of this year when rumor had it that he had returned to Glenbrooke to take over his father's law practice. Radcliffe Sr. had announced his retirement at the end of this year.

Leah looked down and noticed that her hands were shaking. She refused to think that being around Collin made her nervous. So what if he was a big, important, successful classmate who had gone out into the world and had made something of himself? He still ignored her. Leah was certain that the nervousness was because of Seth.

What am I going to say to him when he walks in? Do I tell him I know about the surgery right away or do I wait to see if he tells me?

She knew better than to make assumptions about the severity of the cancer until after the test results from the surgery. But she had been around enough to know melanoma could be life-threatening.

Does Seth understand how serious this is? Is this the real reason he came back to the States, but he hasn't told anyone? I wonder if Franklin knows?

Seth drove past the window just then. When he spotted Leah, he waved to her. She guessed he would have to drive around the block to find a place to park the delivery truck. While she waited, she tried to calm herself. It wouldn't do any good for her newly discovered emotions to overwhelm her again.

Her soup and orange juice arrived before Seth did. When he did enter the café with his casual grin lighting up his tan face, Leah saw his tan differently than before. *Didn't he realize how damaging the sun could be? Sunscreen is no guarantee against skin cancer. How could he not realize that?*

"Hope I didn't keep you waiting long. I checked in with Alissa next door, and it looks like I'm going to take their couch. Thanks for letting me know about it."

"I'm glad it worked out," Leah said. It seemed to her that Seth was saying all the right words, but he was acting reserved. It was the same way she had treated him last time she had seen him.

Hazel walked over with the coffeepot and asked if Seth wanted any.

"No, thanks. I'd like the same thing she's having. Soup and orange juice. And do you have any bread?"

Hazel nodded and returned to the counter. Seth looked at Leah and said, "I understand you went to see Franklin the other day."

"Yes, I did."

"He said you agreed to take him to some hot springs for the last weekend of May."

"Yes, I did."

"I don't know if it's such a good idea for him to make a trip like that. He told me it's been more than a year since he broke his hip, but he's still not very strong. Doesn't he seem frail to you?"

"He's an elderly man," Leah said, feeling her defenses rising. "I agree that he is frail, but this trip seems important to him."

Seth leaned back. "I just don't think it's a great idea."

"Did Franklin ask you to go on the trip, too?"

"Yes, of course. And I told him I didn't think May was the best time for him to go. So the old fox turns around and asks you."

Hazel placed a soup bowl in front of Seth as well as a breadbasket and a glass of orange juice. "Are you Franklin Madison's grandson?" she asked him.

"No, I'm a great-nephew."

Leah couldn't help but take advantage of Seth's line. "Well, if you really were a 'great' nephew, you would see how important this is to Franklin. And you would give the elderly gentleman a chance to do what he wants to do." She knew her emotions were unraveling again, and the frayed edges were showing.

Seth looked down at his soup bowl. She couldn't tell if he was praying or trying to control himself so he wouldn't snap back with an answer.

"Can I get you two anything else?" Hazel asked.

"No, thanks. Just the check," Leah said.

Seth looked up. He appeared calm. "I don't think I can go along with this. In my opinion, Franklin isn't strong enough to make such a long trip."

"What about you?" Leah asked. "Would you be strong

enough to make the trip in a few weeks?"

"Of course," Seth said. He definitely looked offended now. "Why would you ask that?"

Leah swished the last bit of orange juice around in the bottom of her glass. "I work at the hospital, you know. I see all the paperwork. I know you're scheduled for surgery next Friday."

Seth looked at her steadily but didn't say anything.

"I think I know what you're feeling right now," Leah said, lowering her voice and leaning closer. "I felt the same way when you asked me about being the…" She looked over her shoulder to make sure no one was listening. Then in a whisper she said, "the Glenbrooke Zorro. You told me I could trust you to keep my secret. I'm inviting you to trust me in the same way."

Seth drew his soupspoon to his mouth and took his time before speaking. "I had a mole removed in Costa Rica. When the results came back positive for melanoma, I decided to move back to the States. A guy I knew in Costa Rica recommended a specialist in skin cancer who retired and moved to Glenbrooke. Only this specialist didn't completely retire. He still sees occasional patients at Glenbrooke General."

"Dr. Norton," Leah said. "He and his wife moved here five months ago from Palm Springs."

Seth nodded. "I knew my great-uncle was here in Glenbrooke so I had a convenient connection. A reason to move here. I haven't told anyone since there's nothing specific to tell."

"The doctor in Costa Rica might have gotten it all," Leah said. "It's best when they find and remove it early."

"Yes, but Dr. Norton said the results from the Costa Rican lab weren't as specific as what he sees on reports from U.S. hospitals. He told me to be prepared for a lengthy surgery on Friday. He'll remove some of the surrounding tissue. If they find any cancer cells, he plans to remove a large section that day and go all the way to the bone. They'll do a skin graft if necessary."

"That's pretty standard," Leah said. "And Dr. Norton is the best. He's very thorough. I'm surprised he listed you as day surgery. It's more likely you'll be staying overnight."

Seth pushed away his soup. "If the area tests out clean after the surrounding samples are examined, then I can go home."

"And a lot of people do," Leah said, trying to be encouraging. "I see this often. We had two patients last month who came from out of state to see Dr. Norton. He tends to paint the worst case scenario just to prepare patients for what could happen. With both of those patients it was treatable."

"Let's hope that will be true in my situation," Seth said quietly. He looked as if it had taken a lot out of him to confide in Leah.

As she would with any friend, Leah reached across the table and took Seth's hand in hers and gave it an encouraging squeeze. She realized he had made the same gesture toward her twice before, and both times she had pulled away. Now Seth was the one who pulled away.

"I should get back on my route. I have a lot of deliveries today." He took some money from his pocket and left it on the table. "I'll see you later."

"Okay," Leah said, trying to sound cheerful, even though she felt as if she had been rejected. "Let me know if you need any help with the couch."

"No, I have it covered." Seth headed for the door. Then he turned and walked back to the table. "I still don't think it's a good idea for Franklin to go anywhere. Will you at least reconsider your answer to him before he makes a lot of plans?"

"Okay, I'll think about it." She waited until Seth was gone before she pulled out the remaining amount due and placed it on top of the bill along with Seth's contribution. She slid across the seat and was about to rise when Collin Radcliffe came across the room and stopped by her table.

"Leah?" he asked.

"Yes."

"Leah Hudson, right?"

"Yes."

"So good to see you," Collin said in a professional tone. He stuck out his hand to shake Leah's. With his other hand he pulled a business card from the pocket of his expensive-looking jacket. "You probably don't remember me. Collin Radcliffe. We went to school together."

How could I forget you? Leah thought. Collin was her first gradeschool crush and a disastrous disappointment. She found this attention from Collin almost humorous. In third grade she had saved her best valentine for him and bravely wrote the word "love" on the back. He had somehow managed to return it to her valentine box before the school day was over. Only, instead of a mutual, secret message of admiration, Collin had torn the valentine into two pieces and x-ed out the word "love." That was Leah's most vivid memory of Collin Radcliffe. This polite, professional version was a surprise to her.

"I was sorry to hear about your parents."

"Thank you, Collin."

"Perhaps you've heard that I'll be taking over my father's practice. If you have need of any legal advice, you feel free to call me."

Leah took his business card and then looked up at his face, just to make sure this was the same Collin she knew so many years ago. He was a nice-looking man, with rich, dark hair and dark eyebrows. He was also tall, which meant Leah had to look up to him, in the literal and figurative sense. And that was something Leah didn't do well with men.

"I'll be sure to call you if the need ever arises," Leah said politely. "But I doubt it will. Thanks anyway."

She left before Marcus Shelton, the insurance agent dining with Collin, could corner her and ask about her current life insurance policy. She had enough challenges on her plate at the moment.

Chapter Seventeen

$\mathcal{A}$s Leah planted her garden that evening, she thought about Seth and how life offers no guarantees. Before going to bed, she wrote out her verses on three-by-five cards, first the verses from Seth about the winter being over and the flowers appearing. Then she wrote out the three verses from Jessica about trusting in the Lord and delighting in Him.

Leah crawled into bed tired and sore from her gardening. She prayed aloud into the stillness of her room, "Lord, I don't know how to delight myself in you, and I don't know how to trust you. I think Jessica's right. These are important steps for me to take. So please teach me how to trust in you and delight in you. Plant these new seeds in my heart."

Not until she was on her way to Camp Heather Brook the next morning did Leah realize how easily she had been talking to God ever since her early morning rendezvous with him in the garden. Everything in her life felt fresh, just like the clear, spring morning that greeted her as she drove along the country road to Glenbrooke's outskirts.

I hope the weather is this nice next weekend for the May Day event.

All the other women on the May Day planning committee were saying the same thing when Leah arrived at Camp Heather Brook. Jessica and Lauren already were seated next to Shelly in the lounge area of the camp's main meeting hall. Shelly had the chairs and leather couch pulled close in a circle by the window where the morning sun poured in and troupes of dust ballerinas danced on the sunbeams.

On a thick wooden coffee table sat trays of muffins and a carafe of coffee. Hot water stood ready in a teapot covered by a quilted white cozy, and stuffed in several small baskets were tea bags, sugar, and powdered coffee creamer. The party napkins, decorated with sleek, white swans, were fanned across the front of the table. Teacups and saucers were stacked two high across the back. It looked like a picture from a magazine.

"You sure have a knack for this sort of thing," Leah told Shelly as she reached carefully for a teacup.

"I wasn't sure about sitting in the direct sun," Shelly said, surveying the room.

"It's so inviting." Lauren opened an Irish Breakfast tea bag and dipped it in her cup of hot water. "I'm ready for some more sun after all the rain we had last week."

"If we get too warm, we can move to the center of the room," Shelly suggested.

The ladies settled in with their beverages and muffins, and Shelly said, "I have a handout of the schedule." She was efficient and organized but not bossy. Leah enjoyed working on projects with Shelly.

The May Day event was Shelly's idea two years ago. At the

time, Mother's Day was approaching, and she was going through fertility tests at the hospital. She and Jonathan had been married for four years and had hoped to have children right away, but Shelly was having difficulty conceiving. That made Mother's Day a painful event for her so she decided to host a celebration that would encompass all the women of Glenbrooke, whether they were mothers or not. Leah liked the idea right away since it included her as a single woman.

"We need two greeters at the main door," Shelly was saying now.

Jessica and Lauren simultaneously signaled that they would volunteer.

"Okay, good." Shelly held up a packet of seeds. "This year I thought it would be fun if we used these for name tags. The permanent markers work well on the front and that way the women can take the seeds home and plant them. I got a great deal on the packets. They're mostly flowers, but I have some vegetables as well."

"I love it!" Lauren said, taking the sample packet from Shelly and examining it more closely. "How many women are we expecting this year?"

"Around two hundred."

"And only the four of us to run it?" Lauren asked.

"My mom and my sister Meredith are coming for the weekend. I know they'll pitch in and help us."

"How's Meredith feeling?" Jessica asked.

"Better. She thinks she's over the morning sickness now that she's out of the first trimester."

Leah wondered if Shelly found it hard to talk about her younger sister's pregnancy—especially since Meredith had gotten pregnant only a few months after she and Jake were married. Leah tried to imagine how Shelly must feel about not having children when all her married friends and sisters seemed to have no problem getting pregnant. Considering Shelly's situation made Leah realize everyone has her unique challenge in life.

"Is that okay with you, Leah?" Shelly asked, drawing Leah back to the meeting.

"I'm sorry. What did you say?"

"I asked if you would be willing to oversee the maypole event like you have the past two years."

"Sure," Leah said. "Is Jonathan going to have it up the day before?"

"We'll have it up at least the day before," Shelly said.

"Good, because I think some of the vinyl streamers tore last year when those kids were hanging on them. I'll check it out and see if we need to replace any of them."

"That would be great," Shelly said. She continued through to the end of the list and asked if anyone had questions.

"The food?" Leah asked, noticing there was no list like last year's of what everyone was supposed to bring.

"We were able to have the event catered this year," Shelly said. "Some of you may have met Genevieve Ahrens and her daughters at church on Easter. They just moved here, and Genevieve is starting up a catering business from her home. She's going to take care of all the food for us."

Leah guessed that Genevieve's daughters weren't toddlers, otherwise Leah would have had them in her Sunday school group.

"That's a huge relief," Lauren said. "Remember all those egg salad sandwiches we made last year?"

"And the fruit cups?" Jessica added. "I think Kyle and I were up until midnight filling those little pastry shells with pudding and fruit cocktail."

"Those were a big hit," Lauren said. "Are we having those again?"

"I don't know," Shelly said. "I'm leaving it all in Genevieve's capable hands. Her talent in the kitchen is surpassed only by her talent in the garden."

"That reminds me," Lauren said. "Do you want us to bring in cut flowers like we did last year?"

Shelly went over the instructions for the cut flowers, the craft table that offered a glue-it-together birdhouse or a clay pot for each guest to paint and to plant the seeds from inside her name tag. That brought them to the end of the list.

"Are you sure you don't need to delegate anything else to the rest of us?" Leah asked.

"I believe that's it," Shelly said, checking her list one last time. "Why don't we pray together about all this before you go?"

Shelly led them in a heartfelt prayer, thanking God for the opportunity to have a day they could celebrate together. She asked for his blessing on the event and asked that the time would encourage many of the Glenbrooke women.

As Leah listened to Shelly's prayer, she felt as if she were praying every word with her. Leah was no longer an outsider, listening and observing while others communicated with God. She felt connected. The sensation was overwhelming, and she found uninvited tears tumbling down her cheeks as Shelly said amen.

"Are you okay?" Jessica asked, reaching over and giving Leah's arm a squeeze.

"You guys," Leah said, encompassing Lauren and Shelly in her answer to Jessica, "I have something I want to tell you."

The three women waited in a united silence.

"Jessica knows part of this, but I wanted to tell all three of you what's been happening in my life lately." The tears kept coming, but Leah didn't care. They were like a gentle spring rain and seemed necessary to water the fresh seeds God had been planting in her heart.

She let out a breathy laugh and wiped her cheeks with her

fingers. "Seth told me that tears wash the windows of our souls, helping us to see ourselves more clearly. I think the windows of my soul must have needed a lot of cleaning because I've been crying more these past few weeks than I've cried in years."

Her three friends all looked at her with understanding smiles.

"The thing is," Leah continued, "I don't know if I'm seeing myself more clearly, but I'm definitely seeing God more clearly. Is it possible to be a Christian for a long time and then suddenly have this breakthrough, and you feel as if it's all brand new, and all you want is to know God more deeply and completely?"

All three women nodded with shared understanding.

"I experienced a huge change in my life about five years ago," Shelly said. "I was supposed to be helping with food service at a woman's retreat, but my sister tricked me into going to the chapel and listening to the speaker. I think Meri knew I needed to get my heart set back on the Lord. Do you feel as if God is pursuing you?"

"Yes," Leah said, straightening up in her chair. "That's exactly what I feel."

"Your soul is mingling with God's," Lauren said. "Don't hold back. Let your heart echo back to him all the messages of love he's sending you."

"Okay," Leah said, absorbing Lauren's advice.

"God is the relentless lover," Shelly said with a knowing smile. "You're his first love. He will never stop pursuing you because he wants you back."

Leah nodded.

"'Delight yourself in the Lord.'" Jessica quoted the Scripture softly. "'See! The winter is past…the season of singing has come.'"

Chapter Eighteen

$\mathcal{L}$eah didn't sing a lot during the next week. But she found herself humming. And praying. She prayed more often and more openly than she remembered ever praying before.

At work every day that week Mary talked about the cruise and thanked Leah for giving her the tickets. She kept telling Leah how excited her sister was about going.

On Wednesday night, the Glenbrooke Rangers won their game, and even though Seth wasn't there to help her out in the Snack Shack, Leah felt content. She had posted several of her three-by-five cards inside the small building, and in between customers she was absorbing verses from 1 Corinthians 13 and 1 John. Any and all passages she could find on God's love seemed to feed her soul.

She ran into Seth on Thursday afternoon when she went past Ida's house to pick up her muffin tins. He was standing on Ida's front steps, politely sipping a glass of her lemonade while the delivery van was double-parked with the motor running.

When Ida ducked back into her house to get Leah's muffin tins, Leah told Seth, "I've been praying for you every day this week. I wanted you to know that. I've been praying that God would give you strength and that he would be merciful and heal you."

Seth smiled appreciatively at Leah. "Thank you. Ida was just telling me that you won a cruise to Alaska and that you gave the trip away to a friend at work." He tilted his head and looked at her closely. "What happened to the Amelia I met two weeks ago who was going to take off to see the world?"

Before Leah could answer, Ida appeared with the muffin tins and a glass of iced lemonade for Leah. Ida was chuckling to herself as she said, "And here I thought the Glenbrooke Zorro had left these muffin tins for me."

Seth and Leah exchanged a quick look and then both began to speak at the same time.

"I need to get going," Seth said.

"Thanks for the lemonade," Leah said. She took a gulp as Seth nodded his good-bye to both the women and hurried to his truck.

"Such a fine young man," Ida said. "I'm not surprised Franklin changed his will last week."

Leah lowered her lemonade glass and turned to Ida.

"Mavis told me," Ida said. "She's been a might concerned about him lately. Seems Franklin has it in his mind to go to Hamilton Hot Springs for some reason."

"It was a special place for him and Naomi," Leah said, defending her old friend. "He probably wants to relive some of the memories."

Ida shook her head. "He's a crazy old man. With his poor health, he has no business traveling. I told Seth that, and he agrees with me. He said he wouldn't be taking Franklin to the hot springs and that was that."

"I might take him," Leah said. "He asked me to. If Seth won't, then maybe I will. If I were ninety-two and wanted to go somewhere, I'd like to think I had a friend who would take me."

Ida blinked, showing her surprise. "Why, Leah Hudson! I'd never expect such brashness from you. Mavis said that Franklin called a lawyer last week, and he came to the house and charged Franklin a good deal of money to change his will." Ida stood her ground as if she had just made a bold declaration, and Leah should be shocked by the news.

Leah finished her lemonade and said, "I'm sure Franklin has the right to change his will whenever he wants."

Ida squinted at Leah and said, "Doesn't it make you a tad suspicious that he changed it right after that amiable young nephew came to town?"

Leah knew it wasn't her place to tell Ida that Seth had another reason for coming to Glenbrooke besides finding a way to appear in his great-uncle's will, not that Ida knew any of the specifics of how the will had been changed. Ida, of all people, didn't need to know about Seth's scheduled surgery with Dr. Norton.

Handing Ida the emptied glass, Leah said, "You certainly make the best lemonade in town, Ida. One of these days you'll have to tell me your secret ingredient."

"It's the fresh fruit, of course," Ida said with a snap in her voice. "I told you that before. Six fresh lemons and just a squeeze of fresh lime. Not too much sugar."

"It sure is good. Thanks. I need to be going," Leah said before Ida realized that she had been sidetracked from the conversation about the lawyer and Franklin's will.

"Your irises are beautiful this year," Leah said, as she headed down the front steps.

"I'm overrun with them in the backyard. Why don't you cut some and take them home with you?" Ida said.

"We could sure use them for the May Day event," Leah said. "Would you mind if I came over early Saturday morning? That way the flowers would be fresh."

"Heavens, no, I don't mind! Cut all you want. And help yourself to tulips by the back door. They need to be thinned out something awful. I don't seem to be getting all my gardening done as quickly as I should this year."

"I'll come by around 7:30 Saturday morning. If you would like a ride to Camp Heather Brook, I'd be glad to take you."

"That would be wonderful."

Leah hurried to her car, glad that she had successfully diverted Ida's attention off Franklin's will. It occurred to Leah that she was the only one who thought Franklin should take his trip. She hadn't been in favor of it when he first asked her, but now she felt as if she was his only advocate.

Instead of turning right on Pine and heading for her house, Leah turned left and drove to Franklin's. She let herself in and called out her usual greeting, but Franklin wasn't in his recliner. Mavis met Leah in the entryway and said Franklin was lying down in his bedroom.

"Is he feeling okay?" Leah asked.

"He's running a slight fever," Mavis said. "I think he's been overdoing it the last few days. He's had company nearly every day this week, and it takes a lot out of him."

"Do you think I should pop my head in or let him rest?" Leah asked.

"It's up to you. You always cheer him up. Might be just what he needs today."

Leah followed Mavis into Franklin's bedroom. He was

sound asleep on top of the bedspread with a patchwork quilt pulled up over him. Leah slipped into the chair beside his bed and held his frail, wrinkled hand. "Hi, Franklin. It's Leah. I stopped by to see you for a few minutes."

The old man's eyelids fluttered, but he didn't perk up the way he usually did when she caught him napping in his recliner. He smiled when he saw her and said in a clear voice, "I've made all the plans, Leah."

"Good," she said, giving his hand a gentle squeeze. "Mavis told me you've had a busy week. Why don't you sleep, and we'll talk another time."

Franklin didn't let go of her hand. "You know," he said in a weakened voice, "it's the blessing of the Lord." His eyelids fluttered closed, and he said, "That's all it is."

Leah wasn't sure what he meant. "You rest up, Franklin. I'll come see you later." She leaned over and kissed his warm cheek. A smile came to Franklin's thin lips, and the steady sound of his deep breathing returned.

"He said the same thing after the lawyer left the other day," Mavis told Leah on her way out. "He said, 'The blessing of the Lord makes you rich.' Now what do you suppose he means by that?"

"Maybe it's a verse," Leah ventured.

"That's not a verse I've ever heard preached about," Mavis said.

Leah opened the front door and said, "Let me know if he needs anything or if his fever goes higher. I'd be glad to help out if you need me."

"I'll let you know," Mavis said, sounding as if she had everything under control as usual.

Leah thought about Franklin all evening as she was doing laundry and cleaning up her neglected kitchen. The bottom of her oven was sprinkled with charred pizza dough crumbs.

That explained why Lauren had turned off the oven the night Leah was trying to bake the spinach for Seth and herself.

As she scrubbed, Leah thought about Seth. She wondered how he was feeling about his surgery tomorrow. Her emotional response to that man had changed so much in the past two weeks. But one thing remained the same from the start: She felt drawn to him. Connected with him. He held her secret, she held his. Leah wondered if she would feel the same way about a brother going in for cancer surgery. Since she didn't have a brother, she didn't know. It felt different from how she had handled concern for sisters and friends, young and old, who had gone in for some type of surgery. And Leah had seen them all. This time, with Seth, she wanted to be there for him in anyway she could. She didn't know exactly what that meant, but she knew she could pray, and she did.

Chapter Nineteen

On Friday Seth arrived at the hospital at ten o'clock for his surgery. Leah treated him as she would any other patient she admitted for day surgery. Seth responded as any other patient would. A little nervous. A little self-conscious.

Leah didn't leave the hospital for lunch. She wanted to hear the results as soon as they were available, and she let Shirley, the nurse in charge of day surgeries, know that she was waiting for news. By one o'clock there hadn't been any news. Dr. Norton had been with Seth for almost two hours. It didn't look like a good sign.

At 1:15, Shirley called Leah's desk to tell her Dr. Norton had completed the diagnostic check of Seth's back where the previous procedure had been performed. Those samples had been sent to the lab. Three other areas, however, appeared suspicious, and Dr. Norton was testing them as well.

Her heart racing, Leah said thanks to Shirley and hung up.

Leah sat at her desk numbly staring at the phone. This was not good. She knew that, if Dr. Norton had found so many suspicious areas, the chances of the melanoma spreading were greater than Seth may have suspected.

After trying unsuccessfully for almost an hour to catch up on her paperwork, Leah finally told Mary, "I'm going upstairs to day surgery. I need to check on something. Call me up there if you need me."

"Sure," Mary said. "Could you take this file up to Shirley? She called about it a little while ago, and I told her I didn't have it, but it was buried on my desk."

Leah took the file and went to the elevator where a number of people already were waiting. She decided to take the stairs and dashed up them as if she needed to beat the elevator. The urge to do something to help felt overpowering and yet there was so little she could do.

Shirley gave Leah a curious look after she breathlessly handed Shirley the file. "You didn't have to bring it up," Shirley said.

"I wanted to check on Seth Edwards. You said Dr. Norton was exploring several suspicious areas."

"Yes. The lab results won't be back for awhile. Did you need to check with the patient on something? He's still heavily sedated. I don't think he'll be able to answer any questions."

"I'll check back," Leah said. "Could you let me know when the lab results come in?"

"Sure," Shirley said. "I'll call you right away."

"Thanks." Leah returned to the elevator and pushed the button three times. The brutal inevitability of disease and death angered Leah. She thought of how she dealt with death every day. She filed the papers for death certificates and directed grieving family members to the hospital chapel. When her own parents had passed away, Leah was so immune to the sting of death and so conditioned to handling it as a step-by-step paperwork procedure that she had made all the arrangements for her parents with barely a tear.

The tears seemed to have been catching up with her the past few weeks and now they came again, rushing up her throat and fleeing her system through her eyes. Covering her face with her hand as she stood in the elevator, Leah tried to make it appear as if she had something in her contact. Which she did. Tears. An ocean of them.

When the elevator door opened, all the other people left the elevator, but Leah stayed inside. She pushed the button for the fourth floor and quietly made her way to the chapel where she grabbed a handful of tissues from the box by the door and then went straight to the front pew.

The chapel was empty. She sat down and prayed for Seth. "Please be merciful to him, Father. Spare his life. Don't take him yet. Let him live so he can serve you."

Leah opened her eyes and realized she had jumped way ahead in her conclusions regarding Seth's condition. Much could be done to treat cancer. Even if his melanoma had advanced, he had plenty of chances to survive and make a full recovery.

Her tears subsided. The sense of panic dissipated. She rode the elevator back to the first floor where she returned to her desk.

Mary had the phone to her ear and motioned for Leah to pick up line two.

"This is Leah," she said.

"Leah, we just received the results back on Seth Edwards," Shirley said. "Dr. Norton is right here. Would you like him to go over the specifics with you?"

"Could you ask him to wait?" Leah asked. "I'm coming

right up." She dashed up the stairs and, out of breath, met Dr. Norton at the desk.

"That was fast," Dr. Norton said, appearing amused. "Shirley said you needed information on Seth Edwards."

Leah nodded, still catching her breath. She motioned to an empty couch in the waiting area. "Mind if we sit down?"

"Not at all." Dr. Norton followed Leah to the couch.

"What are the lab results?" Leah asked, trying hard to appear professional.

"Good news," Dr. Norton said firmly. "The original area was clean, and all other areas were benign. No further melanoma."

"Does Seth know yet?"

"No. He's still sedated. We sent him to recovery. It will be a while before he's fully cognizant. I'd like to do a recheck in six months." Dr. Norton stood, tucking his skilled hands into the pockets of his white coat. "This is the kind of case I like to see. Always best when it's caught early. He'll be relieved."

"Yes, he will," Leah said. "Thanks, Dr. Norton."

"Why don't you go check on him? And let whoever is driving him home know he's ready to go."

Leah's relieved smile expressed everything that was on her heart when she stood next to Seth in the recovery room. He appeared to be awake since his eyes were open, but Leah could tell he was still floating from the sedatives.

"Good news," Leah told him, giving his arm a squeeze. "The tests all came back negative."

Seth gave her a dazed look, as if he wasn't sure what that meant.

"There's no more evidence of cancer in the original area or the other areas the doctor checked. It's great news, Seth! You can relax now."

"Okay," he answered compliantly. "I'll relax now." Seth closed his eyes.

"Wait! Before you fall asleep," Leah said, gently patting his hand, "did you make arrangements for anyone to drive you home?"

"No," Seth answered without opening his eyes. "I thought I was staying overnight."

"No, you can go home now. I'm sure you'll sleep better there. Would you like me to drive you, since you didn't make other arrangements?"

"Okay."

"I'll be back in a few minutes."

"Okay."

Leah hurried downstairs to her workstation and told Mary she needed to leave early.

"What's going on with you today?" Mary asked. "You've hardly been here when you've been here."

"I'm taking a patient home who doesn't have a ride." Leah didn't expect Mary to question that. Leah had done the same favor for other patients in the past.

"It's Seth Edwards, isn't it?" Mary asked.

"Yes, why?"

"Shirley told me you were asking about him. Did you know his insurance isn't up-to-date?"

"What do you mean?"

"I have his complete file here, and his insurance from his current employer doesn't go into effect yet because he hasn't worked there long enough."

"Okay," Leah said, not sure why that should concern her.

"It looks like we'll have to file this with his previous insurance, if it's still in effect, since it appears to be a preexisting condition."

"Right," Leah agreed. "It sounds like standard procedure to me."

"Well, there is part of it that's not standard." Mary turned

Seth's file in Leah's direction so she could see the paperwork Mary seemed so concerned about. "Look at this. There's no way to even tell if he had prior insurance."

Leah took one look and understood why Mary was worried. The paperwork was all in Spanish. "We've had those before," Leah said.

"We have?"

"It was before you started in this department. We had some medical forms in French. Or maybe it was Dutch. I don't remember. We have an agency that translates it and negotiates for us. It's not a problem."

"Oh, well, if you say it's not a problem then I guess it's not a problem."

Leah felt relieved that Mary's concern over Seth hadn't been something serious, such as a mistake on the diagnosis of all clear.

"I'll take care of it tomorrow," Leah said, grabbing her purse. "You can leave the file on my desk." She copied down Seth's address in case he was too woozy to remember. Hurrying back up to the day surgery unit, Leah found that Shirley had Seth in a wheelchair, ready to go.

When Seth saw Leah, his face lit up, as if she were the only one in the room.

"Hi," Leah said, giving Seth a smile that equaled his in warmth. "Are you ready to go home?"

"That depends."

"On what?"

"Am I driving?"

Leah's smile broadened. "No, I'm driving."

"Good." Seth leaned back in the wheelchair.

Shirley said, "Remember, Leah, he's still under the influence of the Versed, and we gave him Vicoden for the pain. He'll be able to move fine and respond to you, but he may not remember the ride home after the medication wears off. He had a little more than normal since the procedure went longer than expected."

Shirley handed Leah a list of post-op instructions. "Make sure he eats something. Vicoden can be pretty rough on an empty stomach."

Leah nodded. She knew all that. She also knew that Shirley was just doing her job in relaying the information to Leah.

"Don't worry. I've done this a few times," Leah told Shirley, as she wheeled Seth to the elevator. What she didn't tell Shirley was that never before had she wanted to care for a patient as much as she wanted to care for this one.

Chapter Twenty

*Y*ou know, I'm sure I can walk," Seth said when the elevator landed on the first floor. His voice sounded higher than normal, and his expression was much peppier than Leah had seen before.

"Hospital policy," Leah told him. "All patients must leave in wheelchairs."

As soon as she had Seth wheeled out front and settled in her Blazer, he became more talkative.

"I have to say that this is so very, very extra kind of you." He sounded normal but with more of an enthusiastic twist than the situation called for.

"I'm glad to do it. Would you like something to eat now? Or when we get to Edgefield?"

"You mean I get to eat? Oh, good! I haven't had anything since last night because they make you fast after midnight, you know. How about a jumbo shake. Doesn't that sound good? A nice, big, jumbo milkshake. I could really go for a shake."

Leah pressed her lips together so Seth wouldn't see her smiling at his energetic dialogue. The medication obviously had made him loopy.

"Okay, I'll stop at Dairy Queen," Leah said.

"Oh, perfect! Dairy Queen! How did you know? You're amazing. Absolutely amazing. Did I ever tell you you're amazing?"

Leah didn't answer. She pulled into the small parking area in front of the Dairy Queen and said, "You can wait here, if you like. I'll get your shake."

"Oh, I don't want to wait," Seth said, opening his door. "I think it would do me good to stretch my legs."

Leah hopped out and ran around to the passenger's side just in case his legs turned to jelly. Seth slowly climbed out of the car.

"Whoa!" he said. "It feels like a big bubble is all around my head."

"You're doing fine." She held out her hand in case he needed it to steady himself.

Seth took a few steps without assistance and then stopped and swayed slightly. "Whoa! Did you feel that? We're having an earthquake."

"No, it's okay," Leah said quietly. "It's not an earthquake."

Several people were watching Seth, including a group of teenagers at one of the picnic tables. His voice was louder than it needed to be, and his actions were drawing attention to him.

"Maybe you should wait in the car," Leah suggested.

"No, it's okay. I'm okay. We're okay. You're okay." Seth took a few more steps with improved balance. "See? I've got it. I've got it. I've got it." Then he sang the words. "I've got it. Oh, yeah, I've got it."

Leah didn't recognize the tune. She doubted it was an actual song. But that didn't stop Seth from singing as if it were a catchy commercial jingle. "I've got it. I've got it. Oh, yeah, I've got it. Baby, you know I've got it."

They stepped up to the order window, and all eyes were on Seth.

"May I help you?" the waitress asked, looking dubiously at Leah.

"A large shake to go, please," Leah said.

"What flavor?" the waitress asked.

"What flavors do you have?" Seth asked in a singsong voice with a wide grin.

"Um, they're all listed on that sign," the waitress said.

Seth looked over her head and began to read each flavor listed. After "strawberry" he slipped into singing the flavors.

The teenaged waitress leaned over and asked Leah, "Is he drunk? Because if he is, we're supposed to ask him to leave, and if he doesn't leave, then we have to call the police."

"No," Leah said, "he's not drunk."

Seth kept singing. He was merrily going through the list of burgers now.

"He's just on drugs."

The waitress's eyes widened.

"No!" Leah spouted. "That wasn't what I meant to say. He's on medication. He's just come from the hospital, and the anesthesia and painkillers haven't worn off yet. He needs something to eat."

Seth was beginning to sing the shop hours and the posted policy on bounced checks.

Leah gave the waitress a desperate look. "Please, just give him a large vanilla shake. I don't think he'll know the difference."

"One large vanilla shake," the waitress called over her shoulder. Another employee jumped right on the task of preparing the order.

Seth suddenly stopped singing and turned to Leah. "Hey, what do you know? That's exactly just the same thing as what I'm having. And what are you having?"

"I already ate," Leah said. "The shake is for you." She pulled some money from her pocket and paid for it.

"Did you just pay for my shake?"

"Yes."

"Does that mean we're on a date?"

"No, I'm taking you home," Leah said, loud enough for those around to hear. "Do you remember you had surgery today? You need to get home and sleep off the effects of the anesthesia."

"We don't have to go right home, do we?" Seth asked, leaning against the counter as if his knees were turning wobbly on him. "I mean, if you're paying, then why don't we make an evening of it? We could go to the movies. I wouldn't mind seeing a movie right now. How about it?"

"I think we better get you home," Leah said, taking the shake and motioning with her other hand for the waitress to keep the change as a tip. "How are your legs feeling? Could you use a little help getting back to the car?"

"I think I've got it," Seth said. But as soon as he leaned away from the counter, he wobbled way too far to the left.

"Here," Leah said, quickly slipping her strong shoulder under his right arm. "Lean on me."

It was the wrong phrase to use because those three words sparked Seth on to another song. He sang it with wild abandon as Leah helped him to the car, with his arm around her shoulder and her arm around his waist.

Several teenagers, who had been watching the whole fiasco,

joined Seth in singing. Two of the girls who had been sitting on top of the picnic table stood with their arms around each other and, in between their playful laughter, matched Seth's lounge lizard voice note for note.

I can't believe this is happening! I've been transported into the middle of a Muppet movie.

Yanking open the passenger's door, Leah all but shoved Seth into the cab. But he wouldn't get in all the way. Instead, he hoisted himself up on the running board and held on to the top of the open door. He faced the teen girls and held out the last note with his right arm lifted high. Then, with a conductor-like swish of his hand, he directed the concluding note, and the girls stopped right on cue.

A burst of laughter, whistling, and applause followed from the Dairy Queen audience.

"Thank you. Thank you. Thank you very much," Seth obliged them with an Elvis accent. "You've been a great audience."

"Seth!" Leah said, pulling on his arm. "Come on! You need to get in the car."

"I gotta go," he told his laughing fans. Pointing his finger at them with his thumb up, he said, "Stay sweet, girls."

Lowering himself with a controlled tumble, Seth landed in the seat, and Leah closed the door. She went around the back of the car to get in her side.

"Here," Leah said, holding the shake out for him to take. "This is for you."

He didn't take the shake. Seth sat perfectly still with a larger than necessary grin on his face.

"Are you okay?" Leah asked.

Without a flinch or any change to his life-of-the-party expression, Seth said, "You know what? I think I'm gonna hurl."

Chapter Twenty-one

$\mathcal{L}$eah squealed the car's back tires, as she pulled out of the Dairy Queen parking area. She knew it wouldn't do Seth any good to lose his cookies in front of his fan club. She didn't take the time to look for a plastic bag for him or to drive slowly to avoid motion sickness. She knew that Seth wouldn't remember any of this in the morning, but those high schoolers would never forget it.

A block away from the Dairy Queen, Leah pulled to the side of the road where tall grass rose from an irrigation ditch in front of an automotive store. "Do you need to get out?"

Seth had broken into a sweat and had closed his eyes. "No," he said after a moment. "I think I'm okay. Could you put on the air? It seems pretty hot all of a sudden."

Leah turned on the air conditioner and left the window down on his side, just in case. "Do you want to try drinking any of this?" She handed him the shake that she had jammed into the cup holder before her maniac exit from the Dairy Queen.

"Sure. It might help." He took the shake and drank slowly, turning his face to the stream of cool, blowing air. "Oh, yeah," he said a moment later. "This is much better."

"Good. Do you think it's okay if I drive now? Or would it help to sit for a few more minutes?"

"I'm fine," Seth said. "We can go." He drank some more of his shake. "Boy, this is a good shake. It tastes really, really good."

Leah pulled back onto the road and drove slowly toward Edgefield.

"So where are we going?" Seth asked.

"I'm taking you home. You need to rest."

"I feel much better now. This is a really good shake."

"So you said."

"I was pretty hungry."

"I can imagine."

"This is awful nice of you to take me home."

"No problem."

"You know what I think?"

"No, what do you think?"

"I think you're beautiful."

Leah wasn't ready for that statement. She glanced at him and then turned her attention back to the road. His expression was sincere. He was no longer perspiring. He looked normal.

"I mean it," Seth said. "I thought you were beautiful from the very first time I saw you. You were in that little hot dog shack, and you were cheering your heart out for those guys on the…" he paused. "What's the name of their team?"

"The Rangers."

"Yeah, that's right. The Rangers. You were in there cheering for those Rangers, and the sun was coming through the side of that hot dog shack, and it was shining on your face and making your hair look like the flame on a candle. All glowy and warm. And I looked at you, and I said to myself, 'Now, there is one beautiful woman.'"

Leah could barely breathe. The tears rushed to her eyes, and she blinked quickly to hold them back.

"Oh," Seth said tenderly, touching her shoulder. "Are you okay? You look like you're crying."

Leah blinked and wiped her cheek under her right eye. "Just washing the windows of my soul. I seem to be doing that a lot lately." She glanced at Seth. His expression remained one of concern, and he didn't seem to recognize his own line about washing the windows of the soul.

"You know what?" Leah said. "You're not going to remember this conversation tomorrow so I'm going to tell you something. The reason I'm crying is because no one ever," she drew in a breath and repeated the word with emphasis, "ever, has told me I was beautiful. You're the first one. And it doesn't really matter if you mean it or not. I'm going to take your compliment and hold it in my heart always."

"But I do mean it," Seth said, reaching over and fingering the ends of her wispy, blond hair. "Your hair is like honey. Like fine strands of pure honey spun into gold. And your face is open and honest and clean."

Leah found herself laughing nervously at his description. "Clean?" she repeated, as he touched her round, blushing cheek with his work-worn fingers.

"Yeah, clean. It's like you look the same up close as you do from a distance. There are no surprises."

Seth withdrew his hand and went back to drinking more of his shake, as if he were caught up in serious contemplation.

Leah took the moment to calm herself and to banish any more of her relentless tears. She was glad she had driven this route to Edgefield so many times. Because she could drive it in her sleep, she had the freedom to process what was happening with Seth.

The guy is on drugs, she reminded herself. *He doesn't know what he's saying.*

"I wanted something to work out between us, but I guess that's not how you felt." Seth sounded as if he were talking to himself. He was looking straight ahead. The breeze from the air conditioner ruffled his hair in the front. "Could you turn this down?" he asked. "It's getting cold in here."

Leah adjusted the temperature and went back to his previous statement. "Why did you say that's not how I felt?"

"Hmm?" Seth asked, looking at her with the shake straw in his mouth.

"You said you wanted something to work out between us. What did you mean by that?"

Seth put down the shake. "I thought it was obvious. I'm attracted to you. I feel connected somehow. I like you. I want to spend time with you. My great-uncle Franklin…oh, yeah, you know him. Franklin. Franklin said you were the key to what I was looking for. But you obviously don't feel the same way about me, and I can't do anything to change that, I don't think."

"What do you mean I don't feel the same way? I do! I was attracted to you from the beginning, too. I just didn't think you could ever be interested in me."

Seth stared at her with his eyebrows pushed together in an expression of disbelief. "How did you ever get that idea?"

"I don't know," Leah said in an effort to drop the subject. This conversation was becoming painful. If she let herself believe what Seth was saying, it would change her whole life.

But how could she be sure he would remember any of it? She felt sneaky. It was as if unsuspecting Seth had been injected with truth serum, and she was extracting as much information as she could before the effects wore off. It didn't seem fair to either of them. He wouldn't remember what he had said in the morning, and she wouldn't be able to forget.

"I'm serious, here!" Seth said, raising his voice. "You are essential to my future happiness."

Leah smiled at his flowery words and the depth of his sincerity. Yet something in her cautioned her to pull back. She couldn't tell if it was the old recordings, reminding her that she wasn't worthy of such a man. Or if it was the new, gentle persistence of her heavenly Father who had been making it clear that he wanted Leah to delight herself in him, not in the tantalizing possibilities of a romance.

All she knew was that she couldn't continue this conversation. "Can we put this topic on hold? If it comes up another time, I think it would be better." She didn't want to mention that he was euphoric and vulnerable at the moment and that it had been too easy for her to plunder the feelings of his heart.

Seth pressed his head against the headrest and closed his eyes. "That's okay. We can talk another time. I'd like to talk another time. I think it would be good to talk with each other sometime. You and me." His voice trailed off, and he seemed to drop off to sleep—or at least to shut down his amped-up system—for the last ten minutes of the ride to Edgefield.

Leah found the apartment using the address she had written down. She parked the car, and as soon as the motor stopped, Seth looked up. "Are we here?"

"Yes, we're at your apartment."

"Good, because I am really fried."

"Your legs might feel wobbly so let me know if I can help you up the stairs."

Seth slowly climbed out of the Blazer. The vim and vigor from half an hour ago at the Dairy Queen had dissipated. Leah went to his side and helped him up the stairs.

"My legs feel so heavy," was all he said, as Leah propped him up by the front door and went through his plastic bag of personal belongings Shirley had turned over to Leah. She found the keys at the bottom, and as soon as she turned the doorknob, she could hear Bungee yelping with delight.

"Someone is glad you're home," Leah said.

"That's Bungee. My Bungee. He's my dog."

"Yes, I know," Leah said, helping Seth through the front door. She shouldn't have been surprised by the sparseness of Seth's apartment, but she was. If he hadn't gotten the couch from Brad and Alissa, which now filled the wall on the right, the only piece of furniture in the living room would have been a folding beach chair.

"Do you want to go to the couch or to your bed?" Leah asked.

"The couch," Seth said, lowering himself with a grimace.

Leah guessed the painkillers were wearing off.

"Why don't you make yourself comfortable?" Leah suggested. "What can I get you? A blanket? Some water?" She pulled the list of instructions from the bag along with the prescription painkillers. "It says here every four hours on the medicine. Shirley wrote down the time she gave you the first one and," Leah checked her watch. "Yep, you're ready for another one."

Seth stretched out on the couch and called to Bungee, who was barricaded in the kitchen where Leah noticed he had had an accident on the linoleum floor.

"I'll take care of Bungee," Leah said. "You settle yourself on the couch, okay?"

With her usual flare for jumping in and organizing things, Leah took care of Bungee and Seth. She found only one blanket in the whole apartment and that was on Seth's "bed," which was an inflatable air mattress. He had one brightly colored beach towel in the bathroom and no sheets. Now she understood why Seth had thought her house was pretty special. It made even more sense that he had been overwhelmed with Kyle and Jessica's mansion. The guy had been living with bare minimum for a long time. No wonder he was enamored with the idea of owning a house and a hammock at the same time.

"I'm going to go now," Leah said after she had fixed him a mug of soup from the meager supply of cans she found in the kitchen cupboard. She found more food to choose from in the refrigerator but only brought him juice and water. The phone was on the floor in front of the couch, and she pulled the kitchen trashcan near, just in case he felt sick.

"Thanks so much for doing all this," Seth said with a woozy slur to his words.

Bungee kept barking sharp, staccato yelps. Leah couldn't imagine how Seth could get any sleep.

"How about if I take Bungee home with me? He needs some attention, and you need some rest."

"Okay," Seth said, without opening his eyes.

Leah had to smile. For the first time, she saw a slight resemblance between Seth and Franklin when they had their eyes closed and were about to fall asleep. They both maintained beguiling little grins, even when they were nearly unconscious.

She couldn't help it; she had to lean over and kiss Seth good-bye the way she kissed Franklin. Seth didn't stir.

"Bye," she whispered, tiptoeing over to the kitchen where she reached down and picked up the hyper ball of fluff. "Come on, Bungee. You're coming with me."

To show his appreciation, Bungee lunged toward her and slobbered a big kiss on her cheek.

"Oh, you little Romeo, you. You know the way to a girl's heart, don't you?" she murmured.

Just as Leah was about to close the apartment door behind her, she heard Seth call out, "Good night, Bungee. Good night, George."

Chapter Twenty-two

*A*nd then he called me 'George,'" Leah told Jessica when they saw each other the next morning before the May Day event began. They were working quickly to arrange all the cut flowers in vases for the tables in Camp Heather Brook's dining room.

"How did you react to that?" Jessica asked, snipping the end of the deep purple iris that Leah had cut at Ida's earlier that morning.

"I didn't say anything. I left." If they had had more time, Leah would have liked to keep the conversation going. But just then Shelly entered the dining room with her mom and sister. Leah and Jessica greeted them, and Leah thought pretty, energetic Meredith didn't look as if she were pregnant. The three new arrivals had their arms full of food trays, and Shelly and Meredith's mom was fussing at Meredith about carrying too much.

"I can help carry stuff in," Leah said. "Jess and I were almost finished with the flowers."

"Good," Shelly said. "Genevieve needs all kinds of help bringing in the food. She's running behind because her electricity went out this morning. If you can carry the rest in, I'll fire up the ovens."

Leah hurried out to help Genevieve unload the food, and from that moment on, she ran all morning doing what she did best—helping. Despite Genevieve's electricity failure, the food was ready right on time, and it was a big hit with the 237 women and girls who showed up for the event.

As usual, the maypole dance was a favorite with the little girls. Shelly had arranged for Christian praise music to play while each girl took a vinyl ribbon and danced around the maypole in the meadow outside the camp dining room. The clouds that had covered the sky earlier that morning blew away. The gentle breeze, which had cleared the way for the sun to attend this gala event, decided to stick around as well, creating an afternoon of perfect weather.

Leah and Ida stayed to help clean up. As they were clearing the tables, Leah decided to gather the flowers into several big buckets. She had planned to stop at Franklin's on her way home with a bouquet of May Day flowers from the grocery store, but a bucket of flowers was better. Two buckets on his doorstep would be grand!

It was nearly three o'clock when Leah and Ida pulled out of the conference grounds with their flower wagon. "Would you like me to take you home first?" Leah asked.

"Oh, no! I'd like to see the look on Franklin's face when he discovers what you're bringing him this year," Ida said with a cluck of her tongue. "And just where is that poor man supposed to put all these flowers?"

"All over!" Leah said. "Aren't they wonderful? Take a deep breath."

Ida rolled down her window halfway. "It's overwhelming. And overdoing it, if you ask me. Why must you lavish so much attention on Franklin?"

"I don't know. I like to. Nobody else seems to." Leah pulled up in front of Franklin's house and opened the back of the Blazer. She carried a bucket in each arm up to the front door while Ida waited in the car. Placing them on the doormat, Leah rang the doorbell and dashed around to the side of the house just as she used to when she was a kid. She expected Mavis to come tottering to the door, but she didn't.

Leah went back to the door and rang the doorbell again. This time she waited. When Mavis didn't answer, Leah tried the doorknob, planning to let herself in. But the door was locked.

This is a first. Leah knocked and called out. Still no answer. She peered in the front window. Franklin's recliner was in clear view, but no one was in the room.

Returning to her car, Leah reached inside for her cell phone.

"No one home?" Ida asked.

"I'm not sure. No one came to the door, and it's locked." Leah dialed Franklin's phone number and let it ring ten times before she hung up.

"Where do you suppose he is?" Ida asked.

Leah paused before answering. She had a sick feeling in the pit of her stomach. With a hesitant finger, Leah punched in the number to the hospital emergency desk.

"Annie? Hi, it's Leah. By any chance was Franklin Madison admitted today?"

"He arrived about an hour ago," Annie told her. "I don't

know the status. Would you like me to check?"

"No, I'm coming right over." Leah hung up and jumped in the car, leaving the flowers on the doorstep.

"The hospital?" Ida asked, as Leah's car lurched onto the street and sped toward downtown.

"Yes. About an hour ago. Do you mind going with me, Ida?"

"Of course not. Watch how you're driving, Leah!" Ida was clutching the door and seat with her thin hands. "It won't do to get us in a wreck on the way there!"

Leah slowed down, but inside her heart was still racing. She was blaming herself for not taking her May Day bouquet to Franklin that morning before picking up Ida and going to Camp Heather Brook. That meant she would have been ringing his doorbell before 7:30 that morning, but at least he would have been there.

When Leah pulled into the emergency parking lot, Ida had her seatbelt unbuckled and her door open before Leah did. But Leah had to slow her steps so Ida could keep up with her. The two approached the emergency desk with flushed faces.

"How is he?" Leah asked Annie.

Annie glanced at Ida and then back at Leah as if she weren't sure what to say. "You can go on back, Leah. Dr. Schlipperd is on duty. Ida, perhaps you should wait here."

"I have a right to see Franklin," Ida spouted.

Patting wiry Ida on the shoulder, Leah said calmly, "I'll come right back after I've checked on him. Then we'll see about letting you visit him as well, okay?"

Ida looked worried. "You come right back, now."

"I will," Leah said, leading Ida to a chair in the nearly vacant emergency waiting room. "You wait right here for me."

"I'm not going anywhere," Ida said.

Leah headed for the back emergency area, and Annie rose

to follow her. When they were out of Ida's view and hearing, Annie reached over and laid her hand on Leah's arm.

Leah froze and forced herself to look at Annie and to read the message in Annie's expression.

"I'm sorry," Annie said. "He was dead on arrival, but I didn't know that when you called. I wasn't sure what to tell you with Ida standing there. You can talk with Dr. Schlipperd if you want, but the cause of death was cardiac arrest."

"Do you know anything else?" Leah asked, trying to remain calm as she always had in the past when bad news came her way. She refused to let herself feel anything.

"Mavis left only a few minutes ago. She called the ambulance. She said he didn't respond when she brought him his lunch. He wasn't in any pain. She said he was sitting in his recliner and appeared to be napping."

"And he slipped into heaven on a dream cloud," Leah said, quoting a line from an old poem her mother used to say.

"He was an old man," Annie said in a comforting voice. "His heart simply stopped."

Leah drew in a deep breath. "He was a very special old man." To her surprise, no tears came. "Has anyone notified his relatives?"

"Mavis probably will. I don't know. She was going back to his house."

"Okay," Leah said, her mind beginning to line up all the details. "I'll tell Ida and take her home. She can make some calls around town. I'll check on Mavis, and then I'll call Seth." As soon as she said his name, Leah slapped her forehead, remembering that Seth didn't have his car with him. It was still in the hospital parking lot since she had driven him home last night.

"Thanks, Annie," she said, giving the attendant a quick hug.

"Are you okay?"

"Sure."

Leah sat down next to Ida and spoke to her the way she had spoken with dozens of people in the hospital waiting room. She calmly explained the situation and immediately gave a direction so the stunned recipient of the news would have something to do while the news sunk in.

"I'll take you home first," Leah told Ida. "And then would you mind making a few calls? Let Pastor Mike know and Kyle and Jessica."

"All right. Yes, I can do that." Ida rose and started toward the parking lot. "It shouldn't be a surprise, you know. He was an elderly man."

"Yes," Leah agreed, offering Ida her arm as they stepped down from the emergency room entrance curb into the parking lot. "He was a very special elderly man."

They were quiet on the drive to Ida's. Right before Leah pulled up in front of the house, Ida said, "You know, when I go, I think that's the way I'd like to go. In my sleep."

Leah nodded. As soon as Ida was safely in her front door, Leah called Mavis on her cell phone and heard the details Annie had told her repeated. Right before Leah hung up, Mavis said, "He would have liked all the flowers. This morning he asked if you had come yet."

Leah felt her throat tighten. "I should have come before the event out at Camp Heather Brook."

"No, no," Mavis said gently. "I told him you were coming after the May Day party, and he said he would wait in his recliner. He knew you were coming. But bless his soul, he just couldn't wait."

Leah drove the few blocks to her house. She was eager to burst through the front door and let her tears have a private place to fall before she went out to Seth's apartment and drove him back to pick up his car. That is, if he was well enough to drive.

Unlocking her front door and stepping in, with the tears clinging to the edge of her eyelids, Leah stopped short at the sight that greeted her. One frolicking ball of vanilla fluff with an eager yelp came bounding up to her. Somehow Bungee had managed to knock down the barricade she had put up to keep him in the mudroom with Hula. Bungee had shredded a stack of magazines and dragged the pieces all through the living room. He had knocked the trash can over, and garbage trailed across the kitchen floor. Half a bag of flour that she had thrown in the trash last night when she spotted little bugs in it was now torn open. A white trail of buggy flour dust streaked across the floor in loops, as if Bungee had sunk his teeth into the bag and turned around in half a dozen prancing circles, trying to make as big a mess as possible.

And the little scoot had succeeded right down to the flour on his nose and the barbecue sauce on his front paws. Evidence of where he had romped after he stepped in the nearly empty trash led through the house to Leah's bedroom. There she found one of her slippers gnawed to a slimy pulp. The matching slipper appeared to be MIA.

With a filthy Bungee under her arm, Leah marched to the mudroom. Poor Hula hunkered back in the corner on her beanbag bed. She lifted her head when she saw Leah and looked at her with pleading eyes as if to say, "Please, take that rabble rouser away from here and leave me in peace!"

"I really didn't need this today, Bungee," Leah said, placing the culprit in the deep basin sink. "You're getting a bath, and then you're going home!"

Hula thumped her tail against the wall.

"I know, Hula. It's been a trying day for both of us. But you didn't just lose one of your oldest and dearest friends." Leah's quick tears tumbled into the sink, mixing with Bungee's bath water. Hula rose and came to Leah's side, pressing against her leg.

"Franklin is gone, Hula. And I'm going to miss him."

Chapter Twenty-three

*L*eah decided it was pointless to start cleaning up her destroyed house until after the pesky Bungee was far, far away.

After she had washed him and allowed her tears to dry up, she found a large box in her side garage and planted Bungee in the box on the car's backseat. She returned to the house to pick up a few items to take to Seth's and decided to grab the frozen spinach. With an apologetic pat on the head for Hula, who refused to move from her bed, Leah hurried to the car only to find Bungee had tipped over the box. He was on the floor, gnawing on the backside of the passenger's seat.

"You are amazing!" she said scooping up the rambunctious boy. "Come on. Let's try this again—with you in the front seat where I can keep an eye on you."

Leah moved the passenger's seat all the way back, wedged the box in between the seat and the dashboard, and settled Bungee in his cell. He yelped at first. Then the car's motion on the open highway and the soft jazz radio station lulled him to sleep.

The lack of distraction from Bungee allowed Leah to make several phone calls to locate a number for Seth's apartment. When she finally reached him, he answered on the first ring.

"Oh, good, Leah, it's you. Did you get my messages?"

"No, I didn't listen to my machine. I was only home for a few minutes." She decided not to mention the disaster that had met her at her house.

"Mavis called about forty minutes ago," Seth said. "Where are you now?"

"I'm on my way to your place with your little pal. I thought you might want a ride back to the hospital to pick up your car. By the way, how are you?"

"I think I'm in shock. How are you?"

"I'm okay. How's your shoulder and back feeling?"

"They're not bad. I'm taking the painkillers so it might be worse than I think. I don't know. The doctor did say everything checked out clear, didn't he? I'm a little fuzzy on what actually happened yesterday after they took me into the operating room."

"Yes, it's all good news for you. The original spot was clean so he didn't have to go all the way to the bone. He found several other suspicious places, which he removed and tested, and they were all negative as well."

"I thought that's what I remembered. I wanted to make sure."

"I'll be there in about twenty minutes."

"Good. I'll be ready when you get here."

Bungee slept the whole way like an adorable angel. When Leah stopped the car, she had to lift him out of the box and carry him to Seth's apartment while he was still conked out.

"Oh, sure, you're a tired fellow, aren't you? Well, you just wait until I clean up my house tonight. I'm going to be more tired than you!"

Leah knocked on the door, and Seth met her with his hair still wet from the shower. "Come in. I need to grab my shoes." He scratched Bungee under his chin and said, "Boy, I wish he'd sleep like that for me!"

Leah bit her tongue and shook her head.

While Seth went to put on his shoes, Leah settled Bungee in his bed in the barricaded kitchen. She remembered the spinach and told Seth she would be right back. When she returned, Seth was ready to go, and Bungee was wide awake and ready to play.

"I brought you a spinach casserole," she said. "Should I leave it in your freezer, or do you want it to thaw out in the refrigerator?"

Seth looked surprised. "You didn't have to do that. Thanks. Here. I'll put it in the refrigerator."

Leah noticed that the living room was all picked up, not that there was much to straighten. The kitchen was clean as well. She remembered how Seth had automatically begun doing her dishes when he was at her house. Tidiness was a trait she admired.

Maybe you can teach Bungee a few tips!

"You're feeling okay, then?" Leah asked once they were in her car and on the way back to Glenbrooke.

"Yes, I'm doing okay. I'm supposed to take another pain pill in half an hour, but I don't think I should since I'll be driving."

"Wise choice."

They traveled in silence for awhile before Seth said, "I can't believe he's gone. I only knew him for these few short weeks. He was quite a character, wasn't he?"

"He was." Leah swallowed. With Franklin's passing she had lost a major connection to her childhood. Since she was already in the midst of an identity crisis these past few weeks, this loss added to her awareness that she was on her own. Not all alone, since God had made his presence so evident in her life, but fewer and fewer people were defining who she was and how others perceived her.

Seth reached over and began to massage Leah's neck with his left hand. "You sure you're doing okay? You were much closer to Franklin than I was."

"I'm going to miss him."

Seth pulled away his hand. She glanced at him and realized that the motion of stretching his arm out like that must have made him aware of how sore he was.

"What would be easiest for you?" Leah asked. "Would you like to go to Franklin's house or to the hospital to pick up your car?"

"To be honest, I'm not sure what I should do. I've never gone through this before."

Leah explained that Mavis was making phone calls. Arrangements needed to be decided on, and people needed to be met with, such as the funeral home director and the pastor. She offered to help in any way she could.

"If you have the time, could you stick with me and walk me through all this?" Seth asked.

"Of course." The last thing she wanted to do was go home to her domestic disaster, and besides, this would help her to grapple with Franklin being gone.

One of the great things about the people in Glenbrooke was that they knew how to gather around and support one another in tough times. Everyone they talked to offered to help in one way or another. Leah told all of them there was nothing to do. She and Seth had it taken care of, and no, no one needed to bring food to the house because Mavis was fine, and she and Seth were just leaving.

By the time Leah drove to the hospital to pick up Seth's car, it was nearly seven o'clock. They said an awkward good-bye to each other. Seth looked exhausted and in pain. He was going home to a rowdy puppy and hopefully, somehow, a good night's sleep. Leah was going home to a mess. She wanted to be angry about it, but she wasn't sure whom to blame. Bungee, for getting out? Herself, for volunteering to take Bungee home and for not making the barricade more durable? Or Seth, for having the puppy in the first place?

When she came up with that accusation, Leah knew she wasn't thinking clearly. She needed to tackle the mess, clean it up, and forget about it. However, it took Leah almost three hours to return her house to normal. She fell into bed exhausted.

The next morning she went through her Sunday school time with the toddlers in a fog. She wished she were in the service instead. It had been a long time since she had gone to the worship service. She hadn't missed it before, but now she did.

She did have a chance to sit in a pew at church that week. It was at Franklin's memorial service on Wednesday.

Collin Radcliffe called Leah that morning at work and asked if she would like him to escort her to the memorial service.

"No, thanks," Leah told him.

"I wanted to express my condolences. I know you and Franklin were close. It would mean a lot to me if I could help in any way. If you don't need a ride to the service, then please let me know if there's anything else I can do for you."

"Thanks, Collin, but I'm fine."

He sounded sincere. Leah couldn't figure out why Collin was suddenly being so attentive. When she saw him at the church, he was standing by the front door. He solemnly walked in with her as if they had arranged to meet there and sit together.

The pastor gave a wonderful tribute to Franklin Madison, a man who had lived nearly a century in Glenbrooke and who had quietly, steadfastly trusted God through many seasons.

The church was packed. Seth sat in the aisle in front of Leah, next to his parents, who had come from Boulder. After the service, Collin followed Leah out of the church. She turned to him and said, "Thanks for showing support to me, Collin, but really, I'm fine. I don't need anything. At all." The edge in her voice made it clear she wanted him to stop following her around.

Collin looked a little hurt yet he controlled his emotions well. Leah couldn't help but feel a twinge of victory as she thought, *There! How do you like having your sincere effort torn in two and the spirit of "love" crossed out?*

As soon as she thought that, she felt guilty. It was her habit to encourage people and give to them, not hurt them and take away their dignity.

Collin mumbled good-bye and turned to go. Leah reached out and stopped him with a brief touch on his arm. "I apologize for sounding so abrupt. I appreciate your concern, Collin. Thank you."

His eyes met hers, and a look of confidence washed across his face. "It's my pleasure, Leah. And please know that my expression of concern is genuine."

Leah nodded. She didn't know what to say. He had such a calming voice and such a commanding presence. She felt guilty all over again for doubting his sincerity. After all, this was Glenbrooke. Glenbrooke people stuck together in hard times. It didn't matter that he had been gone for so long. He had Glenbrooke ways in his blood. Leah knew she should trust Collin, but trusting anyone had always been a challenge for her.

Collin reached over and gave Leah's elbow a gentle squeeze. "I'll see you around, Leah."

She nodded again. "See you around, Collin."

Collin headed for his Mercedes with another glance at Leah over his shoulder and a friendly wave. She waved back and thought, *Why couldn't Collin, or any guy, have been that nice to me in high school? Does it take an extra decade to turn these local boys into men? Or was I as off-putting and porcupine-like in high school as my sisters kept telling me I was?*

Seth exited the church with his mother and father. He came over to Leah and introduced her to his parents as "this is the one I told you about."

His mother appeared to be an outgoing woman, even in the somberness of the occasion. His father resembled Seth in many ways, including his engaging smile.

"Seth tells us he would have been lost without you these past few weeks," Mr. Edwards said, as he shook Leah's hand.

She felt herself blushing and shrugged off the comment. "I didn't do much."

"You're coming to the house, aren't you?" Seth's mom asked.

"Yes, I'll be there."

Leah had arranged for all the food at the family gathering in Franklin's house. She had expected around fifty people, but nearly seventy guests came. Collin wasn't among them, which didn't surprise Leah. The invitation had circulated among close friends and family. She didn't know how close Franklin was to his lawyer. Leah did notice that Franklin's physician came as well as several home care nurses who had tended to Franklin over the years.

Despite Leah's immediate fears when she walked into the house and saw more than fifty people present, there was plenty of food to go around. And typical of Glenbrooke gatherings, there were even more stories to go around, as old-time folks recounted their favorite memories of Franklin.

"You know," one of the older gentlemen said, "a little neighbor girl used to bring Franklin flowers every year on May Day. I guess she must have done it for years because he told me once that May Day was his favorite holiday."

Leah looked down.

"That was Leah," Ida stated. "Leah Hudson. You know Leah. Why, she's standing right there in the corner. Tell him, Leah. Tell him how we brought the flowers this year, but it was too late."

All eyes turned to Leah. "I should have brought the flowers in the morning," she said quietly. The tears she had so effectively held back for days apparently had reached their limit and suddenly began to spill out. Leah felt an arm around her shoulder, and thinking it was Pastor Mike, she turned and let herself cry on his sports coat.

"Go ahead. Let the windows of your soul have a good cleaning."

Leah looked up and swallowed her tears. Everyone in the room was watching Seth comfort her. In the past, she would have pulled away from his sympathetic touch. Not this time. She buried her face in his shoulder and cried her eyes out, not caring who was watching or what they thought.

Seth wrapped both his arms around her and tenderly whispered in her ear, "Come on. Let's go in the other room."

Chapter Twenty-four

Seth led Leah into the kitchen and offered her a napkin to dry her eyes. "You're not somehow feeling responsible for Franklin's passing away, are you?" He let go of her and leaned back to give her some space.

"I don't know. I guess it all caught up with me."

"Go ahead and cry if it helps. You're always there for everyone else. This time, let me be there for you."

"Thanks, Seth." She looked up at him through bleary eyes. "I really appreciate it."

"Any time, George," he said warmly.

George! Does he have any idea how that nickname comforts me?

Leah wasn't sure she could believe what was happening. Seth wasn't teasing her. He wasn't on drugs. He was there, with her, by choice. In front of a crowd of people, he had willingly put his arm around her and drawn her aside to comfort her. He had called her George. Leah's tears began to subside.

"You know, you've become someone very special to me," Seth said, reaching over and catching the last of her tears as it coursed down her cheek. "Franklin told me you were the key I was looking for. I think he was right."

Leah felt her heart pounding. His confession to her in the car on the way home from the hospital hadn't been a cruel joke. He had meant it, whether he remembered all of it or not. She knew she had to decide whether she believed him. If she believed him, that meant she needed to believe something new about herself. She was of the right frame and frame of mind.

"Do you really mean that, Seth?"

"Yes, I do."

Just then Ida walked into the kitchen. "Don't mind me, you two. I'm after some more napkins."

"Right there on the counter," Seth said.

"So they are," Ida said. She seemed to search Leah's expression, trying to discern what was going on with them. "I'll just have a look in the refrigerator and see if anything else needs to be put out on the table."

Leah and Seth waited quietly until Ida was gone.

"Would you like to go somewhere?" Seth asked.

"Where? I mean, I'm supposed to clean up after everyone leaves."

"Why don't you let someone else do that for a change?" Seth suggested. "Let's go for a ride. It'll give you a chance to clear your thoughts."

"Okay," Leah heard herself say. "I'll go ask Jessica if—"

"I'll ask her," Seth volunteered. "And I'm sure my mom will be glad to help, too. You always take care of everyone else. It's time you let someone take care of you."

Leah stood in the kitchen, stunned at what was happening

with Seth. He returned after a few minutes and told her everything was set. Then he motioned to the back door and suggested they avoid walking through the crowd.

Fortunately, Seth had parked down the street so he had no problem pulling out of his parking spot. They drove past the house and took the road that led out of town.

"Where are we going?" Leah asked.

"I thought we would just drive. It's a beautiful afternoon. What happened to all that rain you said would hang around until June?"

"Don't worry. It will be back. They don't call this area the 'Great North-Wet' for nothing," Leah joked.

"I like it here," Seth said.

"You still want to stay even though you don't need to be here to be treated by Dr. Norton?"

Seth glanced at her and then back at the road. "Yes, of course I want to stay here. This is where I want to settle. Why, did you think I'd leave now that I've been given a clean bill of health?"

"Well…" Leah stalled. That was exactly what she had been thinking. More precisely, it was what she feared. She thought Seth would announce he was going back to Costa Rica. "The thought did cross my mind."

"No," Seth said decidedly. "This is where I want to be. I told my parents that last night when they tried to convince me I should go back to Boulder with them."

"Why did they want you to go to Boulder?"

Seth shrugged. "My dad thought I could find a better job there. My mom thinks the doctors are better there. I told them about the melanoma. They were pretty upset that I hadn't told them sooner. You know how it is when you're the youngest. It doesn't matter how old you are, they still think they have to take care of you."

"Not always," Leah said softy. She was the youngest, but her experience had been the opposite of Seth's.

"That's right, your situation was a little different, wasn't it?"

"But I know what you mean. Even though I was the responsible one toward the end, I still felt my parents didn't trust me to figure things out or to do things the right way. The day before my mother passed away, she asked me if I had filed my income taxes yet because April 15 was just around the corner."

"And had you worked on your taxes yet?"

Leah nodded. "I had done mine and theirs by February 15."

"My mom would have been impressed. As a matter of fact, I'm impressed. It's taken me a while to feel independent of my parents."

"I thought you said you've been on your own since high school, when you went to Sweden."

"I tried to pretend I was on my own. My mom sent me underwear in Sweden." Seth glanced at Leah with a grin.

She laughed. "Did she think they didn't sell underwear in Sweden?"

"Something like that. But we had a good talk last night. I think my parents understand why I'd like to stay here and turn the next corner of my life." Then, as if on cue, Seth turned the steering wheel and headed down a narrow, country road. Leah recognized it. It ran along the perimeter of Camp Heather Brook. She hadn't driven on that road for years, and she was amazed when they came around a bend and were met with a row of trees in full bloom.

"Look at those trees!" Leah exclaimed. "I don't know what kind they are, do you?"

"I have no idea." Seth slowed the car and looked out his window.

"They're gorgeous! And so old. Look at the blossoms. They're almost a pale lilac."

"Really? I'd call that a light pink." Seth stopped the car. "Come on, let's check them out."

Leah clambered out of the car and walked over to one of the trees. She reached up and pulled down a low branch to sniff the blossoms. It gave off the faint scent of vanilla. "This is beautiful," she said.

"Come on," Seth invited. "Let's explore some more."

"On foot?" Leah asked, when Seth took off walking into the woods behind the blooming trees.

Seth stopped and looked back at her. She had worn a black skirt with a white cotton blouse and black linen blazer to the memorial service. It wasn't her nicest outfit, but for her it was dressy. She wore practical, flat shoes simply because she always wore practical, flat shoes. That's all she owned. They were suitable for a jaunt in the woods.

Seth had on dark slacks and a light blue Oxford shirt with a tie, which he had loosened but left on. Nothing was fancy about his shoes, either.

"Aren't we a little dressed up for a hike?" Leah asked.

Seth looked at his outfit. "I thought maybe our professional appearance would frighten away the bears. They're only used to scruffy looking campers. They won't know what to do with us."

Leah laughed. This man was like medicine for her. He didn't care about dress clothes getting dirty; he always was up for an adventure; he cared about her enough to take her away from Franklin's house so she could breathe again and stop being responsible for everything. Suddenly she felt natural and easy following this man into the woods—and anywhere else he wanted to lead her.

He wasn't able to lead her very far because they hit a huge patch of what Seth called "blasted brambles."

"They're wild berries," Leah told him. "Probably blackberries, but they could be raspberries. I don't know my early spring berry brambles very well."

"Or your blooming trees," Seth added.

"Or my blooming trees," Leah repeated with a laugh.

"Why don't we venture on down the road and see if we can find a trail?" Seth suggested.

They returned to the car and drove for a long while down the bumpy road until they came to a turnaround at a dead end. Instead of heading back, Seth stopped the car and got out again.

"That looks like a trail to me," he said, leading Leah to a place where the tall spring grasses were flattened slightly. A trail did appear to lead into the woods.

"A deer trail," Leah said.

"Let's see where it leads." Seth pulled back some low branches of a cedar tree and welcomed Leah to go first.

"Since when did I become the trailblazer?" Leah asked, standing her ground with her hand on her hip.

"Fine, I'll go first." Seth let the branch sway back, just missing Leah by a fraction of an inch.

"Thanks a lot!" she spouted.

"Well, what's it going to be? Do you want to make the first move, or should I?"

Leah couldn't help but wonder if his question had a double meaning. "You," she said quickly. "You make the first move."

Seth smiled at her. "Okay. Got it. This way, if you please." He took off at his brisk hiking pace, and Leah had to work her short legs hard to keep up with him. She had left her jacket in the car this time and was glad because she warmed up quickly.

"Hey, aren't you supposed to take it easy after your surgery?" Leah asked.

"I'm feeling okay. The stitches give me grief every now and

then when I turn the wrong way. But I'm doing pretty well."

"So where are we going?"

"Onward," was Seth's answer.

They followed the narrow trail through the heart of the ancient woods. The new leaves on the trees formed a fragrant, lime green canopy over their heads. Then they came into an open area where the sunlight shot through the trees like iridescent, bronze javelins thrown from the heavens.

Seth stopped. "Here," he said. He stood in the center of the woodlands, with his hands on his hips, face toward the sky, daring the golden javelins of sunlight to spear him through the chest.

Leah drew in the fragrance of the wild violets that laced the air around them. "This is amazing!" At her feet lay an endless carpet of rich lapis-shaded bluebells and deep green moss. High overhead, brightly-colored blue jays squawked at the intruders in their enchanted world. Two squirrels sprinted across the ground about ten feet from Leah and Seth and then scampered up a tree, with their fluffy gray tails waving good-bye.

"Let's build a house right here," Seth said after several long, silent minutes.

Leah chuckled. "On our Easter hike you only wanted to build a bench at the top of the hill. Today it's a whole house! Next hike you'll envision an entire resort."

Seth stood still, studying her. Finally he said, "Exactly what is it that you don't like about me?"

Chapter Twenty-five

Leah was stunned by Seth's question. Was it true that she was standing in the woods with this wonderful man and that he was telling her he wanted her to like him? "I like everything about you," she assured him.

Seth studied her expression. "I have something to tell you." He moved over to a fallen log and sat down. Patting the space next to him, he invited Leah to sit beside him. The rotted log provided a soft, level seat. She drew near but not too close.

"I looked up your name in the Bible," Seth said. "I read everything I could find on Leah."

She felt a pinch in her stomach. "So you know I'm named after a woman who was a big disappointment."

Seth frowned and paused. "Oh, you mean how Jacob ended up marrying Leah first when he thought he was getting Rachel?"

"Genesis 29:25. 'Behold, it was Leah,'" she repeated

solemnly. "My father used to say that was the saddest verse in the Bible."

Seth looked down and rubbed his eyebrow. "That's only one small part of a verse. Many verses talk about Leah. She gave Jacob six sons and a daughter. And you know those sons became six of the twelve tribes of Israel."

Leah didn't know that. She probably should have. But, as a child, she had tuned out any Sunday school lesson when Leah was mentioned. She hadn't thought the biblical Leah had ever amounted to anything.

"The fourth son of Leah and Jacob caught my attention as I was reading," Seth went on. He reached over and took Leah's hand, intertwining his fingers with hers. This time she didn't pull away.

"Their fourth son was Judah. Leah named him that because Judah means 'praise.' The line of Christ comes through Judah, you know."

Leah nodded and thought about this revelation. All her life she had thought of her biblical namesake as unwanted, unloved, and unimportant in the great scheme of things. Yet Leah, the wife of Jacob, was a great, great, many times over great-grandmother of Jesus Christ. And Leah's more desired sister, Rachel, wasn't.

"I found out something else I thought was pretty interesting when I was reading," Seth said.

She didn't know if she could process any more. The sensation of his holding her hand and speaking to her with confidence was overpowering. Leah found herself ready to believe anything he said.

Seth continued, "Leah's first three sons were all named to reflect the state of her relationship with Jacob at the time they were born. Each time she was hoping she would gain her husband's favor because she had given him a son."

"What do you mean?"

"For instance, Levi means 'attached.' When Levi was born Leah said, 'Now my husband will be attached to me because I have borne him three sons.'"

Leah knew all too well what it was like to try hard to win the approval and favor of others. She understood what the biblical Leah must have been feeling.

Seth held Leah's hand tighter. "Then something must have happened in Leah's heart because when her fourth son was born, all she said was, 'Now I will praise the Lord.' It was as if she stopped striving and started praising God and being thankful. And that was the son on whom God chose to place his blessing. Not the firstborn son, or the second or the third. But the one Leah named 'Praise.' The lion of Judah."

Leah had so many thoughts at once. She wanted to tell Seth about her early morning encounter with God last week, how the verse Seth had left on her windshield had showed her the winter was past, and how God had been plowing up her heart to plant new seeds.

This fresh account of the biblical Leah resonated deeply within her.

"I needed to hear all this," she said softly.

A hint of bashfulness washed over Seth's face. "I hoped you wouldn't think I was lecturing you."

"No, of course not. Not at all. I want my life to change like that, too. I want to start praising God and being thankful for what he brings into my life. I've spent too many years trying to prove myself."

Seth drew her hand to his lips and kissed her fingers softly. "You don't ever have to prove anything to me, Leah."

After all Leah's tearful outbursts in the past few weeks, she was startled to find that now, when she really wanted to cry, she had no tears. Only amazement.

"Seth, I don't know what's happening, but something definitely is changing inside me. It's as if you marched into the garden of my heart, and with one mighty slash of your truth sword, you've slain the dragon that has breathed down my neck my entire life."

Now Seth looked as if he might cry. With a catch in his voice, he said, "I've never been anyone's dragon slayer before."

Leah smiled. Overhead a blue jay let out a series of sharp, squawking calls.

"Someone doesn't like us being here," she said.

"I suppose we should get back before my mother decides to send out a search party." Seth rose and drew up Leah with him.

Since she didn't consider herself to be good with words, she impulsively decided to express what she was feeling with actions. She wrapped her arms around Seth's middle and gave him a hug.

"I meant it when I said something is happening in my life. In my heart. Thanks, Seth."

He circled her with his arms. Leah let her head rest on his chest, and he drew her close. Never in her life had she felt like this.

"You know," Seth murmured, his lips lost in her hair. "You don't have to do anything for me. You don't have to give me anything. Just be who you are and let me get close to you."

"Okay," she whispered. "I will."

"I mean it," he said. "This is for real. I'm not playing games with you, Leah."

"I know. And I don't want to play games with you. It's just that it's hard for me to believe you truly could be interested in me."

Seth pulled away so they could look at each other. Leah let go. His expression was tender. "I am very interested in you."

"Why?" Leah said. "I mean—"

"Do you want a list?"

Leah shrugged.

"First, you have a long-standing relationship with the Lord, and you're interested in that relationship growing. Second, you attract me. You're beautiful."

"No, I'm not," Leah said quickly.

"Hey, this is my list. Do you mind? According to what I find attractive and desirable in a woman, you are so high, you're off the chart. Your hair is beautiful. You're just the right height. You have a great laugh. I've never gone hiking with a woman who could keep up with me. Not only do you keep up with me, but you also seem to enjoy the hike as much as I do. You fit me, Leah. You're just right in every way."

Leah felt as if her insides had turned to mush. "I think you're just right in every way, too."

Seth reached over and tilted Leah's chin up. "I've been meaning to tell you that you left something at my house the other day." A mischievous twinkle appeared in his eye. It reminded Leah of Franklin's look when he said he was making plans.

"The spinach pan? You can get that back to me any time."

"No. This was something you left on Friday after you brought me home from the hospital."

"Really?" Leah said, finding herself swimming in his deep blue eyes. "I didn't think you would remember anything that happened on Friday."

"Oh, I remember this. You left it on my cheek."

With that Seth leaned over and offered a tender, first kiss to Leah's unsuspecting lips.

Chapter Twenty-six

*F*loating? *No, that's not it. Exhilarated? Maybe. Soaring? Yes, that's it. Soaring.*

Leah was trying to describe to herself how she felt as she and Seth drove back to Franklin's house. After Seth kissed her, he said he guessed she was changing her mind about always pulling away. Leah blushed, but she didn't mind a bit. If Seth wanted to get to know her, this was part of her—the ever-blushing, candy apple cheeks.

They had lingered for a few more minutes in a warm hug before Seth uncurled his arms from her. Then he offered Leah his hand, and they began their hike back to the car. She could feel her bare legs itching from bug bites she had received while they sat on the log—bugs and mosquitoes seemed to like to nibble on her. She forced herself not to scratch the bites with a vengeance once she was seated in the passenger's seat of Seth's Subaru station wagon.

"If I still had my letterman's jacket from high school, I'd give it to you," Seth said. "Then we officially would be going together, wouldn't we?"

"What did you letter in?"

"Track. The 440 was my specialty."

A smile played across Leah's lips. "I still have my letterman's jacket. Should I give you my jacket?"

Seth laughed. "And what did you letter in?"

"You're going to laugh," Leah warned him.

"I'm already laughing."

"Discus. But mind you, it wasn't a very competitive event for our school or our state, for that matter. Especially for the women's event."

"Discus, huh? Remind me to keep my distance if you ever decide to throw things."

"Don't worry. I'm not the tantrum throwing sort."

"Would you be interested in going out to dinner with my folks when we get back? I'd sure like for them to have some more time with you."

"I'd be honored," Leah said. "How long will your parents be here?"

"They fly out in the morning. I had hoped they would be able to stay for the reading of the will, but the lawyer is out of town until Friday."

Leah wasn't sure why, but she felt a little uncomfortable when Seth mentioned the will. She remembered Ida's saying that Franklin had changed his will less than two weeks ago. It made Leah wonder if Franklin knew his life was coming to a close. She dismissed that thought when she remembered that he had planned for her to take him to the hot springs in three weeks.

A wash of remorse came over her again, the way it had at

the house when she said she wished she had brought the flowers by in the morning. Now she wished she had taken Franklin to the hot springs the very day he had asked her. Her argument to others all along was that she wanted to make an old man happy. Now it was too late. She wouldn't take Franklin anywhere ever again.

"I wish I could have taken Franklin to the hot springs," Leah said, as Seth pulled up in front of Franklin's home. Only a few cars remained out front.

"It wasn't meant to be," Seth said. He took her hand as they walked up to the front door. "You were more considerate than I was. At least you were willing to take him. I knew he was frail, though."

"And you were right. The trip would have been too much for him."

"At least he knew you were willing to take him," Seth said, opening the front door and letting go of Leah's hand so she could go in first.

"Is that you, Leah?" Ida asked as they entered. She was busying herself around the living room with a feather duster, which Leah thought was comical. The company was all gone, and no one would live in this house for a while. How funny that Ida felt she was helping by dusting. Or was she finding a way to kill time until Seth and Leah returned?

"Are you all right, Leah?" Ida asked.

"I'm fine."

Seth slipped his arm around her shoulders, as if offering a show of moral support.

Seth's mom came into the living room from the kitchen and appeared slightly surprised to see her son with his arm around Leah. She smiled at Leah and said, "We're almost finished up here. Jessica is helping Mavis put away the last of the dishes. Seth, your father went on to the hotel in Edgefield. He asked us to meet him there at six for dinner. You will be able to take me, won't you?"

"Of course. I invited Leah to come with us as well."

"Good," Mrs. Edwards said with a warm smile for Leah.

Jessica exited the kitchen with a dishtowel in her hand. "I think that's everything. Oh, Leah, you're back. Good. I'm about ready to head home. Ida, would you like me to drive you home?"

Ida looked at Leah, who had been her ride to the memorial service and then to Franklin's house. With a snap of her eyelids, Ida turned to Jessica and said, "It looks as if I will be needing a ride, thank you."

"Are you ready to go?" Jessica asked.

"I suppose."

The two of them returned to the kitchen—Jessica to put the dish towel away and Ida to stow the feather duster. It all seemed so natural to Leah, being in Franklin's house with her friends and feeling Seth's arm around her shoulders while he made small talk with his mother. Yet, at the same time, it was all so unreal. Franklin was gone. A wonderful man was showering her with attention and affection. Leah felt as if she had stepped into a parallel reality and wondered how long the two worlds could overlap. Would the dream continue and take over? Or would the old reality return and leave her alone with Hula and a handful of flowers next May Day but no doorstep to leave them on?

Seth ushered his mom and Leah to the car. Out of respect, Leah opened the door to the backseat so Mrs. Edwards could sit in the front.

"Oh, no, please, Leah," Mrs. Edwards said. "You sit in the front. I'll be comfortable in the back."

"I wouldn't," Leah said.

Seth and his mom stopped short and stared at Leah after her abrupt response.

"What I mean is, I wouldn't feel comfortable in the front seat if you were in the back. Honest. You're Seth's mom. I was raised this way. Sorry I turned this into something awkward. I'd just feel better if you sat in the front, Mrs. Edwards."

The generous smile and spontaneous hug that Seth's mom gave Leah told her she was liked and had done the right thing, even though the remark had come out bumpy.

"Please, call me Bonnie." Mrs. Edwards gave Seth a grin that reflected her definite approval of Leah. They got in the car, with Leah in the backseat and Bonnie Edwards in the front.

Leah had never been one to carry a makeup bag in her purse, but she wished she had one now. After the tromp through the forest, she felt she could use a little freshening up before meeting Seth's dad for dinner. But all she had was a comb, which she used on her hair. What she really wanted was some eye drops. The pollen in the air had gotten to her. She would love to pop out her contacts, rinse them and her eyes, and then put the contacts back in. As it was, she kept blinking in hopes of cleaning them enough to see clearly.

The conversation on the way to Edgefield was light. Mrs. Edwards was curious to learn about Leah's family and her long history in Glenbrooke. Seth glanced at Leah several times in the rearview mirror, and each time, his eyes smiled at her.

Dinner with the Edwardses turned out to be a casual affair, for which Leah was grateful. They dined in the hotel coffee shop, and she rinsed out her contacts in the restroom. She also applied a cold paper towel to the red bites on her bare legs. The beauty regime was simple, but it was enough to make her feel more comfortable with Seth's parents.

The conversation flowed easily, and Leah enjoyed Seth's parents. They both indicated they approved of her for their son, and Seth seemed proud of her.

It wasn't until the drive home with just her and Seth that she allowed herself to believe all this was really happening. She was curious about so many things, and as soon as Seth stopped talking about how much his parents liked her, Leah asked her first question. "Did you take many of your girlfriends home to meet your parents?"

"What makes you think I had a lot of girlfriends?"

"Oh, come on! I'm not that naive. Do you want me to guess which number I am? Maybe girlfriend number thirty-two? No, more like forty-seven, right?"

Seth shook his head. "How about maybe three and a half."

Leah studied his profile. "Three and a half? Am I the half?"

"No, the half was Tiffany Andrews. She was my date to the junior prom, but she asked me, and we never went out again so I'd say she was a half."

"And the other two?"

Seth extended his arm on the top of the steering wheel and casually responded, "There was Fiona in Sweden my senior year. We were together for all of three weeks before her previous boyfriend came home from the university. She told me she was getting back together with him because they 'spoke the same language,' which was, of course, true in more ways than one."

"That must have been a heartbreaker," Leah said.

"Better than a bone breaker." A sly grin crept up the edge of Seth's mouth. "Her boyfriend was huge! He could have snapped me like a dog biscuit and tossed me off some fiord. I still think Fiona made the wrong choice getting back together with him. He dominated her life, and she was this free-spirited, creative woman. I have no idea what happened to her. I always hoped she met some musician. She could have written lyrics for him."

Leah liked the way Seth spoke of this woman with such respect. "And number two?" she asked.

"Ah, number two. That would be Tessa. She's the one who broke my heart." Seth paused.

Leah didn't know if she had the right to probe. The sad truth was that she had no comparable stories to tell him. She had never had a guy return her interest in him.

"You don't have to tell me anything if you don't want to," Leah said.

"No, I don't mind. It's funny how it still hurts a little. I really fell for Tessa my senior year at college in Boulder. I thought she was the one. She had long, blond hair and was homecoming queen that year. It took me two weeks to work up the courage to ask her out. I couldn't believe it when she said yes. We went to dinner and seemed to hit it off. So I asked her out again. We went out six times. No, actually seven times. Then one of the guys I played racquetball with took me aside and told me she had spent the night in his dorm room and had slept with his roommate the night before."

Seth shook his head. "Here I'd just taken her to a movie and kissed her good night at her door. As soon as I left, she went to be with this other guy. I asked her about it, and she said I was the kind of guy she wanted to marry. But since she wasn't ready to get serious yet, she still wanted to have some fun."

"I can imagine how much that must have hurt," Leah said.

"Hurt me enough to make me boycott women for several years."

"And now? You've obviously ended your boycott."

"I settled my heart with God the last few years in Costa Rica. I knew what I wanted in a woman, in a relationship with an equal partner. That's why I was so amazed when I saw you the first time at the Little League game. It was as if God took my wish list for the perfect woman and put it all together, and there you were."

"Your wish list, huh?" Leah asked with a smile.

"You don't have a wish list?"

"Not really. But I have been known to wish upon Pluto."

"And what exactly happens when you wish upon Pluto?"

Leah turned to Seth and with a grin said, "You, I guess."

Chapter Twenty-seven

$\mathcal{M}$e, huh?" Seth said, as he stopped the car in front of Leah's house. "You wished upon Pluto, and you got me, huh? What would have happened if you wished upon Neptune?"

Leah shrugged playfully and said, "A guy who carries around a forked spear and likes seafood?"

Seth let out a deep laugh. "I hope that doesn't mean my being connected with your wish on Pluto is your way of telling me I'm a dog?" Seth got out of his side of the car and motioned for Leah to stay where she was so he could come around and open the door for her.

As he offered her a hand out, Leah answered him with, "No, but I noticed you came with a dog, or at least you got a dog the first time we did something together."

"Yes, and by the way, how was Bungee the night you had him?"

"Oh, he was great during the night," Leah said carefully, as she unlocked her front door and led Seth into the kitchen. "I took him for a long walk around the block, and he was good and tired when he went to bed."

"He sure needs a lot more attention than I've been able to give him. I've felt bad about leaving him alone in the apartment so much. And he needs a yard to run in."

"That's for sure," Leah said.

Seth went to the cupboard and pulled out Leah's coffee beans and filters as if they already had discussed his staying for coffee. They hadn't, but Leah had hoped he would come in. And here he was, in her kitchen, making coffee.

"Did I detect a hint of sarcasm there?" Seth asked. "Where does that come from?"

"I might as well tell you, your little Bungee Boy tore down the barricade I left up in the mudroom and had a free-for-all in my house."

Seth glanced around. "Anything broken?"

"No."

"Looks like you managed to clean it all up."

"It only took me three hours," Leah said dramatically. She opened her dishwasher and pulled out two coffee mugs.

"Why didn't you close the door?" Seth asked.

"I wanted Hula to be able to get away from Bungee since I had to block off the doggy door to the backyard. I thought Hula might want her space. As it was, she stayed huddled in the mudroom, and Bungee had the run of the place."

"Did he ruin anything?"

Leah had to wait a minute before answering because Seth was grinding the coffee beans. As soon as he spooned them into the filter, she could smell the rich aroma. "Not really. He just made a gigantic mess."

"I'm sorry, Leah."

"No need to apologize. I should have known Bungee is fast growing beyond the sleepy puppy stage. And I should have put up a bigger barricade."

Seth poured water into the coffeemaker and pushed the start button. It was quiet for a moment between them as they stood facing each other by the kitchen counter. Seth reached over and lightly fingered the ends of her hair. "Did I ever tell you how much I like your hair?"

"As a matter of fact, you did. More than once. However, the first time, you were slightly spacey so I wasn't sure how much of what you said was true."

"Really? What did I say?"

Leah felt her cheeks blushing.

"That good, huh?" Seth said, touching his fingers to her rosy cheeks. "What else did I say?"

"Nothing much." Leah looked down. "Just enough to let me know you were interested in me."

"And you didn't believe me, did you?"

"Well…" She hesitated, not sure if she should tell him of his mini-concert at the Dairy Queen. Any woman would question what a man said immediately after he had sung a list of hamburgers.

"Come here," Seth said, drawing Leah to him in a hug. He held her close. "Believe me, Leah. Trust me."

She wanted to. But something made her hesitate. It suddenly struck her that everything had happened so quickly and had seemed a little too perfect. Things didn't go along the lines of "perfect" or "smooth" in her life unless she did lots of preparing and planning. None of this was planned.

Leah didn't pull away from Seth on the outside; yet on the inside she began to put up a barricade. The feelings she had were similar to how she felt about Bungee. He could be in her house but only within the limits she set for him. She felt frightened to think Seth might break through and have the run of her heart. She hadn't had time to think all this through yet.

Leah guessed that Seth sensed her reluctance. He released her from his hug and held her at arm's length. "You haven't told me my number yet."

"Your number?"

"My number. Which boyfriend am I? Which number? Forty-seven? Ninety-three?"

Leah pressed her lips together and looked into his deep blue eyes. Seth seemed so sincere, so open to her. She knew she shouldn't be skittish. She had trusted him with her secret about the Glenbrooke Zorro. She could trust him with this truth.

"Seth, you're the first and only."

"Oh, come on, I find that hard to believe."

"I've never led much of a social life. Surely you guessed that."

"You know everyone in this town. They all adore you. I can't believe none of the guys I've met has come knocking on your door."

"Believe it, Seth. I've always been everyone's pal and never anyone's girlfriend."

"Their loss is my gain." He drew her close again, and Leah had the distinct impression he was about to kiss her. She turned her head, and his nose ended up in her ear. Seth let her go.

"Am I coming on too strong?" he asked gently.

"Yes," Leah said. "I mean, no. I mean…I don't know. I know you're going to say I'm too much of a skeptic, but I still can't get used to the idea that you're interested in me."

Seth took two steps back and crossed his arms in front of him. "What can I do to convince you?"

"Nothing. You don't need to do anything. I guess I need a little more time to get used to all this."

"Okay," Seth said, unfolding his arms and reaching for the coffeepot. "I'm in no hurry. We can take it as slow as you want."

Leah held up her cup, and he began to pour the coffee very slowly. "Is this slow enough for you?" he teased.

"That's perfect."

They shuffled into the living room with their coffee and a bag of cookies Leah pulled out of the cupboard. Seth sat on the recliner, and she stretched out on the couch. For the next hour and a half they talked about a dozen different topics. Leah began to feel more at ease. She scolded herself for being so paranoid about giving herself to a relationship with Seth. She guessed it was her lack of experience that made her hesitant.

When Seth left, he kept his word about taking things slowly, and he didn't kiss her good night. He promised to call her the next day at work and asked if she wanted to plan on dinner and a movie on Friday night.

Leah went to bed dreaming of Seth's kiss in the woods. The sensation of being circled in his embrace and feeling his lips on hers was intoxicating. The only thing she could compare it to was the way she had felt as a child on Easter Sunday when the pungent fragrance of lilies filled the sanctuary, and she was allowed to stand up in church and shout.

Tonight, in the stillness of her room, she felt the intoxication of Seth's touch as strongly as she remembered the scent of those Easter lilies. However, something was keeping her from standing up on the inside and shouting her declarations about Seth.

The next day Seth called her twice. First he phoned before she left for work just to say good morning and to give her the list of movies playing so she could choose which one she wanted to see Friday night.

The second time he called was late afternoon, right before she left work. He said the lawyer had phoned, asking if they could meet Monday morning for the reading of the will. Seth told Leah the lawyer would be calling her as well.

"Why?" she asked.

"You're mentioned in the will, obviously."

"What time Monday morning?"

"Nine o'clock. Do you think it will be a problem for you?"

"No, I can make arrangements."

"Good," Seth said. "I'm sure looking forward to seeing you tomorrow night."

"Me, too," Leah said and then hung up. Leah had to do some fancy schedule changing with two other employees before she could arrange to be gone for an hour Monday morning.

Seth called again on Friday afternoon and said he would pick her up at 6:30.

"I was thinking about that," she said. "Why don't I drive to your place or meet you at the restaurant in Edgefield? It would be a lot easier than your driving home after work, then driving all the way here, and then we turn around and go back to Edgefield."

Seth paused. "Are you sure? Because I don't mind coming to get you. If you wanted, I could pick you up right at work, and we could go to an early movie and then to dinner."

"No, I'd rather change out of my work clothes," Leah said. "I'll just come to Edgefield at 6:30. Where should I meet you?"

"My place, I guess. Oh, and I've been meaning to tell you, the spinach was fantastic."

"Good. I'll make you another one."

Seth chuckled. "You don't need to make me another one. I simply wanted you to know I enjoyed it."

As Leah hurried home from work Friday, she wondered if

she was overdoing it with Seth. Offering to make him spinach, insisting on driving so he wouldn't have to.

It reminded her of something Shelly had said several months ago. "Leah, you seem like the kind of woman who is only comfortable when you're in charge of things. Every once in a while it's good if you let someone else take control. Let others give to you for a change."

The comment had come during the practice for the annual church Christmas pageant when Leah was doing everything from sewing wise men costumes to coaching kids on their lines to showing up early at the performance to making sure enough chairs were set up.

Leah wondered if she actually could let herself relax with Seth tonight on this, their first official date. Could she stop being in charge?

In an effort to get herself started on the right foot, Leah decided to take a bath. It wasn't a long bath, but then she wasn't given to such luxuries so the twelve minutes she soaked in the warm tub were restful for her. Then she made liberal use of her only bottle of hand lotion. The bug bites on her legs had turned to small, red dots. Not that it mattered; she planned to wear jeans. She always wore jeans.

Leah began to dress but then wondered if her chinos might be a little nicer. She didn't know what kind of restaurant Seth planned to take her to.

What if it's formal attire only? No, Seth wouldn't like a place where he had to wear a coat and tie. I was surprised he even owned a coat and tie to wear to the memorial service. I wonder if he bought them just for the funeral?

Leah looked in her closet and decided it wouldn't hurt her to do a little shopping one of these days, too. She couldn't remember the last time she had bought herself anything other than work apparel or new tennis shoes.

She finally decided on a white cotton shirt, which she ironed vigorously so the collar would stay in place. The final vote on the pants was the jeans because the chinos looked wrinkled to her, and she didn't want to take the time to iron them. When she slipped on her black linen blazer, she thought it looked pretty good. Some sort of jewelry would improve the outfit, but her selection was limited and none of it seemed right.

While brushing her hair, which had air-dried after her bath, Leah decided to pull the top part back in a single clip. She didn't usually do anything with her hair so this seemed like a fancy change. She wondered if Seth would like it.

Her makeup routine was simple and the same every day. Tonight she experimented with some blush, which she rarely used since, in her opinion, her cheeks blushed enough on their own. The extra minutes with the mascara wand and the extra detailed flossing and brushing of her teeth all seemed to have a good effect. She felt pretty, and that was as important as anything else.

With a squirt of her only fragrance, which was a gift-sized bottle of Fresh Ocean Breeze, Leah called her good-byes to Hula and opened her front door.

There stood Collin Radcliffe, just about to ring her doorbell.

Chapter Twenty-eight

*C*ollin, you startled me," Leah said, catching her balance.

"Good evening, Leah. My, don't you look nice. Are you going out?"

"As a matter of fact, I was just leaving," she said, checking her watch. It was five minutes before six.

"That's a pity." Collin had on one of his expensive business suits and looked as if he had just come from the office.

"Is there something wrong?" Leah asked.

"I was hoping I might have a word with you before you met with my father Monday for the reading of Mr. Madison's will. Did you get my message?"

"No, I haven't listened to my machine yet."

"Would there be a convenient time for me to stop by tomorrow?" Collin asked.

"Tomorrow? I guess so."

"I don't want to hold you up," he said smoothly. "Here's my

card. Would you call me in the morning after nine and let me know a time that would work for you?"

"Sure." Leah took the embossed business card from him. "I'll call you."

"Good. May I walk you to your car?"

Leah found his superb manners once again put her on the defensive. This time, instead of resisting his assistance, she held her tongue and let Collin reach over and open the car door for her. She thought again of Shelly's observation that Leah only was comfortable when she was the one in control. This seemed as good a time as any for her to practice relinquishing control. Collin seemed as determined to do things for her as she was determined to do things for others.

"You'll call me tomorrow then?" he asked.

"Yes, I'll call you." She smiled at him before she drove off. Not a flirty, inviting smile, but one that expressed her decision not to resist Collin or his sudden involvement in her life. It was her way of saying, "Okay, I'll stop being the edgy, poor-me girl you knew in high school. This is the new me, the Leah who is learning to like who she is and is accepting her life as it is."

Her drive to Edgefield seemed to take only ten minutes instead of the actual thirty. She was lost in her thoughts—or more accurately, in her dreams. She saw her response to Collin as a major step in the right direction. She could be free and open in her relationships instead of controlling. It didn't matter to her at the moment if Collin wanted to talk about business or Franklin or—maybe he was considering running for mayor and wanted her support. She was a strong woman learning to soften up around the edges. And she was on her way to have a date with the most wonderful man in the world who had captured her heart. How could she possibly allow herself to enter this evening as the old, driven, misunderstood Leah?

She found herself praying aloud the last few blocks to Seth's apartment. She wanted God's blessing on her life. On this evening. On her relationship with Seth.

Parking in one of the three visitor parking spaces, Leah looked at the sticky note on her dashboard that had the Psalm 37 verses printed on it. She read the last verse aloud, "'Commit your way to the LORD, trust also in Him, and He will do it.'"

Trust in him, trust in him, Leah repeated to herself as she headed for Seth's apartment. *I'm trying, God!*

The moment she knocked on the door, it swung open, and Seth held out a bouquet of daisies.

Leah laughed. "How pretty! For me?"

"For you," he said. "I have to admit it would have felt more natural if I were the one ringing your doorbell and you were the one opening the door."

"We can try it that way," she said, playfully handing him back the flowers and pulling him outside. She went into his apartment and closed the door on him. Bungee yelped and barked and begged for Leah to come rescue him from the kitchen.

"Just a minute, Bungee Boy. I'm having a little fun with your master."

The doorbell rang. Leah deliberately waited. The doorbell rang again. "Who is it?" she called out sweetly.

"Open the door and find out," Seth said. His voice didn't sound quite as joking as she had intended this exercise to be.

She opened the door, and Seth stood there, looking more embarrassed than jovial. He held out the flowers without saying anything. His eyebrows were raised as if to say, "Are we done with this game?" Leah noticed three of his neighbors standing in the parking area. They had been loading a self-rent moving van when she had pulled up. Now all three men had stopped working and were elbowing each other and watching Seth.

"Thanks," Leah said quietly, as Seth entered the apartment and closed the door. "Sorry I sent you out the door like that. I don't know what I was thinking."

"Beginning relationship jitters?" Seth suggested.

Leah nodded. "Mind if I leave these here in water? I'll get them when we come back."

"Sure."

Leah felt awful. She had done it again. She had seized the opportunity to be the one who controlled the situation. *Why couldn't I just say thank you and take the flowers while we were both in a happy mood and excited to see each other?*

She stepped into the kitchen and greeted Bungee with enthusiasm that matched his excitement.

"Does it matter to you what I use for a vase?" she called out to Seth.

"No," he said, standing in the living room, watching her. "A bucket is under the sink, glasses are in the cupboard. I don't know which would work best for you."

Leah opted for the bucket because it was easy. Then she joined Seth on the couch.

"I don't know why I did that," she said. "I'm sorry. It was supposed to be a joke, but it didn't end up funny."

"Forget it; it's okay."

"No, it's not really okay," Leah continued. "I don't want to be like that."

"Like what?" Seth leaned back and folded his hands behind his neck, listening to her. He looked open and understanding, not upset, like he did earlier.

Leah decided not to make such a big issue out of apologizing. "I guess God is working on this one area of my life, and I keep noticing ways I need to change. It's humbling."

Seth nodded, as if he understood what she was saying.

"Shelly says I'm only comfortable in a relationship if I'm the one in control."

"Do you think that's true?" Seth asked.

"I'm sure there's some truth to it. I could make up all kinds of excuses about how I had to be that way to survive with five older sisters and in the role I played with my parents for so long. Only thing is, I don't want to go through life apologizing for who I am. I've done that far too long."

Seth's tender expression invited her to continue.

"You helped me to see that, you know," Leah said. She hadn't planned to say any of this. It was all coming up as if an underground cistern had been exposed, and she couldn't hold back the water from flowing out. "When you told me about the biblical Leah and how she started praising God instead of always trying to prove her value to others, I thought a lot about that. I've thought about how her son was the one who received the blessing. I've started to esteem my namesake more highly, and I think it's affecting how I think about myself."

"Actually," Seth said, "I think it's all in the voice inflection when you get to verse 25. You say it as if it's, 'Boo, hiss, behold, it's Leah.' I prefer to think of it this way." Seth stood and struck a pose in front of Leah like a regal town crier. He had one arm bent behind him and one bent in the front. With his chin up, he raised his left arm and dramatically announced, "Behold! It's Leah!"

Leah grinned. "You make it sound as if I've been chosen to attend a royal ball."

"Not a royal ball," Seth said, offering her his hand. "Just fish fajitas at Del Rey, and our reservation is in five minutes. Shall we?"

Leah took his hand and let him usher her out the door and to his car. She couldn't believe how easily Seth made her feel relaxed and as if her personality flaws didn't bother him. It wasn't that he didn't notice them nor have a dislike for some of them. It was more as if he had a goal, and nothing else seemed important enough to deter him from it. He was a man on a mission, Leah decided. And if his mission was to win her heart and soul, he had succeeded. She just didn't know if he realized that yet, or if she would have to find a way to express her heart to him.

As the evening progressed, Leah realized she didn't need to spell out anything for Seth. They talked and laughed freely over dinner at the Mexican restaurant Seth called his home away from home. He estimated that he had eaten there twelve times in less than a month. It was close to his apartment, inexpensive, and offered plenty of variety for a fish-eating vegetarian.

The movie they had decided on turned out to be a good choice. While they sat in the fifth row—a mutual, spontaneous decision based on both of them liking to feel as if they were part of what was happening on the screen—Seth and Leah held hands and shared a large tub of buttered popcorn.

By the time they arrived back at his apartment, the last thing Leah wanted to do was go home. She wanted to settle in with a fresh pot of coffee and sit up all night talking. However, Seth had other plans.

Chapter Twenty-nine

*L*ingering in his car in the apartment parking area, Seth nodded at the moving van now parked in front of the complex. "I promised one of my neighbors I'd help him move tomorrow."

"Did you get your stitches removed already?" Leah asked.

"No, which is why I couldn't help them load the van. I volunteered to drive instead."

"Oh." Leah had been dreaming of fun things they could do together on Saturday. "Where is he moving to?"

"Walnut Creek."

"Where is that?"

"Near San Francisco."

Leah looked at him with disbelief. "It'll take you all day to get there."

"So I've been told. I didn't know exactly where he was moving until after I volunteered to drive the van. We're leaving at two in the morning and driving straight through. I don't imagine I'll be back until Sunday evening."

Leah made an exaggerated pout. "I'll miss you. I was hoping we could spend some more time together this weekend."

"Me too," Seth said. "I'm glad we had tonight together. My neighbor wanted to pull out this evening as soon as he had the van loaded, but I told him I had an important meeting I couldn't cancel."

Leah thought back on how she had sent Seth out the door with his daisies in hand. The movers must have surmised quickly that his "important meeting" was with a woman who had a strange sense of humor. She wished she hadn't done that.

"I hope you understand," Seth said. "I'd invite you in for some really superb coffee, but I think I need a little sleep before I start driving."

"Definitely," Leah agreed. "I'll just run in, grab my flowers, and be on my way."

"Oh, that's right, your daisies."

"And my good-night kiss," Leah added.

Seth looked surprised. "Your good-night kiss, huh? What makes you think we were going to share a good-night kiss?"

"Just a prediction."

"Wow," Seth teased as he got out of the car, "you must be psychic."

Psychotic is more like it! she thought as he came around to open her door. *Why did I say that? My knowledge of dating etiquette is atrocious!*

They walked to his front door with an arm around each other's waist. Seth leaned his chin against her hair and said, "I suppose I'm going to have to kiss you twice tonight. Once for good night and once to soften you up extra for the huge favor I'm going to ask of you."

Leah smiled. She wouldn't mind two kisses. Not one bit.

Seth unlocked the door to his apartment, and Leah asked, "What's the favor? Or do you think you should kiss me first before you lay the tough request on me?"

Seth leaned over and kissed her on the cheek before she realized he was going to do it. She immediately felt disappointed. The first of her two kisses had been used up just like that.

"I better ask you now, and then you can decide if you still want to kiss me good night." Seth flipped on the light, and they immediately heard Bungee scampering across the linoleum floor and letting out a happy bark.

"Wait. Let me guess. You want me to baby-sit Bungee while you're gone."

Seth looked at her sheepishly. "Would you mind? I know he was a problem last time, but I bought him a long leash. I thought maybe you could anchor him in the backyard, and he could get a little exercise."

"Sure," Leah said.

"Are you positive?"

"Yes. I'll check that the barricade is strong enough to keep him in the mudroom this time, and I'll even take him for a walk or two. I'd be glad to take him for the weekend."

Seth took Leah by the elbows and pulled her close, showing her his appreciation in his kiss, which was considerably longer than the first and not on her cheek. They drew apart slowly, and Seth said, "You know, I think we're getting better at this each time."

Leah let out a nervous chuckle. "You have to consider that when you kiss someone who has as little experience as I have, there's plenty of room for improvement."

"As little experience as both of us," Seth corrected her. "I may have had two and a half girlfriends before you, but there's plenty of room for improvement in my kisses."

"That's not my opinion. I like your kisses just the way they are." She wrapped her arms around Seth in a warm hug. He held her for a minute before giving her a kiss on the side of her forehead, right where her eyebrow met her temple. "And I like yours just the way they are," he whispered.

They drew apart and smiled at each other. Neither of them initiated another kiss. It seemed to Leah that everything was right and balanced the way it was. She didn't want to do anything to disrupt the wonderful, overwhelming sense of falling in love.

"Your flowers," Seth said after a moment.

"My flowers." Leah stepped into the kitchen. "I'll take them home in the bucket, if you won't miss it."

"No, I definitely won't miss my bucket this weekend," Seth said with a laugh. He scooped up Bungee and added, "Your lasagna pan is in the cupboard there. I'll get Bungee's leash."

Leah opened the first cupboard and saw only bowls, plates, and cups. The next cupboard held papers and file folders. She was impressed Seth was so organized. For fun, she flipped through the files to see if they were alphabetized. They weren't. A file labeled Madison Property was the first file, and it came before the one labeled Car Insurance.

At least I know he's not perfect, Leah thought. She checked the lower cupboard and found her spinach casserole dish just as Seth returned with Bungee on his leash.

"You don't know how much I appreciate this," Seth said.

"I think Bungee is going to appreciate it more than you." Leah bent to greet the happy-to-be-going-anywhere puppy. "And you can show me your appreciation, Mr. B., by following the house rules this time."

"He will," Seth said. "At least I hope he will. I see you

found the pan. Would you like me to carry the flowers?"

"No, I can get them if you have the hyper-hound there."

Seth walked Leah to her car with Bungee leading the way. They settled him on the floor in front and gave each other a quick hug.

"I'll see you Monday," Seth said. "Monday morning at the reading of the will."

"Oh, that's right. Do you want to come to my house for dinner Monday night?"

"That would be great. And if you don't mind having Bungee that long, I'll pick him up then."

"That's fine. Have a safe trip." She waved good-bye, and all the way back to Glenbrooke, she planned what she would make for dinner Monday night.

When she arrived home with Bungee under her arm, sleepy Hula woke and gave Leah a look as if to say, "Oh, no, please, anything but that troublemaker again. Don't do this to me!"

"Oh, don't look at me like that, Hula! You and Bungee need to work out your differences and become good friends. You two will most likely be seeing a lot of each other in the weeks ahead. Work it out, okay? And you," she said, pulling Bungee close, "you behave!"

Bungee licked her chin. Leah closed off the doggy door and closed the door to the mudroom. "Now good night and not a peep out of either of you."

Three hours later, Leah wished they were only peeping. Bungee had taken to barking continuously when his whimpering didn't produce any results. He barked and barked until she thought his throat must be hoarse. Twice, she yelled out, "Go to sleep!" through her closed bedroom door. Then she pulled the pillow over her head and tried to ignore the ruckus.

She didn't remember falling asleep, but she did remember checking her bedside clock at three. All she knew was that once Bungee finally quieted down, she crashed.

Leah was up again at 5:30 to take Bungee outside and then plopped back into bed. She had forgotten how much work a puppy could be.

She finally woke up at nine o'clock and went to check on the dogs. They seemed fine, as if it hadn't been such a rough night for either of them. Hula was eager to get out the doggy door. Leah let her out and then fastened Bungee's leash and let him lead her down the steps and out to her backyard. With careful calculation, Leah fastened the end of Bungee's leash to the metal rail that ran along the back steps. He had enough leash to get into the mudroom if he wanted and enough to frolic on the grass, but not enough leash to reach her garden.

After providing fresh food and water for both dogs, Leah played with Bungee, giving him praise and attention. That seemed to calm him down, and she wondered why she hadn't thought to comfort him the night before. She remembered how long it had taken Hula to get used to her new surroundings when Leah had brought her home. And here poor little Bungee had been bounced between Leah's house and Seth's apartment. No wonder the little fellow was confused.

The dogs taken care of, Leah decided against what she really wanted to do, which was to go back to bed. Instead, she turned on some music and started breakfast.

A nightmare met her when she opened her lower cupboard and reached for a bag of granola-style cereal. The bag had a hole in the bottom, and on closer examination, Leah was certain a mouse had nibbled it.

"I will find you and destroy you, you destructive rodent," she muttered, getting on her hands and knees and pulling out the cupboard's contents. The plastic bag of organic, steel-cut oatmeal had an even bigger hole in it and left a trail as she pulled it out.

"Hmm, this is serious." Leah went to the bedroom and put on her glasses since she didn't want to take time to put in her contacts. She pulled up her hair and fastened it with the clip she still had in from when she had fixed her hair with such care last night. She left on her pajamas, which were flannel shorts and a long T-shirt, since she didn't care if they got ruined. To complete the ensemble, Leah slipped on a pair of garden gloves, just in case the varmint tried to chomp into one of her fingers while she was pulling everything out. A huge mess awaited her in the back of the cupboard, and she ended up throwing out everything that showed evidence of being nibbled on. She even threw away a box of graham crackers because the box hadn't been closed properly when she put it away, and she didn't know if the mouse—or mice, whichever the case might be—had managed to get into the crackers.

Once the cupboard was empty, she found neither culprits nor an obvious point of entry. Using Seth's bucket, she prepared warm, disinfected water, and still wearing the garden gloves, she grabbed a sponge and began to scrub the shelves.

The doorbell rang in the middle of her vigorous cleaning. "Come around the back," she called out. "I'm in the kitchen."

Sticking her head in the cupboard and reaching as far to the back as she could, Leah wiped down the last section of the shelf. She heard the back door close and called out, "I'm in here. Enter at your own risk."

"Doing a little spring cleaning?" a cultured voice asked behind her.

Leah bumped her head trying to get out of the cupboard fast enough to see if her suspicion was correct. It was. Her morning visitor was Collin Radcliffe. And there she sat on the kitchen floor, her glasses crooked, her hair sticking straight up from the clip in back, her garden gloves and rag-bag quality pajamas her only attire, and the fragrance of pine-scented disinfectant permeating the air.

And there stood Collin, every hair in place, wearing khaki shorts and a polo shirt. He looked as if he had just posed for pictures before the start of the U.S. Open golf tournament and was now ready to tee off.

Leah caught the sudden drip coming out her nose with the back of a garden- gloved hand and tried her best to greet Collin with a smile. There was no mistaking the look on his face. The poor man was in shock at the sight of her.

Chapter Thirty

"Mouse," Leah said simply, by way of explanation.

"Mouse?" Collin repeated.

"This is a mouse-mess. And you know what? I never expected my visitor to be you, or I wouldn't have exposed you to such a terrifying sight." She looked down and caught another drip from her nose with the back of her gloved hand.

Collin stood his ground, undaunted. "I should have called. The apology is mine. I was on my way to brunch at the country club in Baker's Grove and discovered the battery had gone out on my cell phone. I thought if you had been trying to call me this morning, you wouldn't have been able to reach me."

Leah had forgotten all about saying she would call Collin after nine that morning. "I hadn't tried yet. This took priority. How about if I call you this afternoon?"

"If that's convenient for you," Collin said. "Or, if you prefer, I'd like to invite you to join me for brunch at the country club."

Leah couldn't help but find his invitation laughable. "Okay, Collin, sure. Would you like me to go like this? Or should I maybe change into something more suitable?"

Collin didn't laugh with her. "I don't mind waiting."

"Okay," Leah answered after studying his expression for a moment. She scrunched up her nose and continued to poke fun at herself. "Why don't I just go freshen up a bit. Maybe powder my nose."

Collin still didn't laugh.

Leah slipped into her bedroom and called out, "Please help yourself to whatever you can find in the refrigerator to drink. I'm sure the mouse didn't find his way in there. Magazines are in the living room. You can change the music, if you prefer something else."

"No, I'm fine, thanks," Collin answered.

Leah was glad her bathroom had an extra door that connected to her bedroom. She could shower, wash her hair, put in her contacts, and apply some makeup before slipping into her bedroom and pulling on a pair of black, linen shorts with a belt. She chose a light blue knit shirt with collar and sleeves, just to be in the same apparel range as Collin's outfit. However, her knit shirt didn't have a pocket, let alone a fancy embroidered designer logo like Collin's.

As she buckled her watch, Leah noticed she had only been keeping him waiting for twenty minutes. That wasn't bad. Somehow she expected this all to be some kind of crazy joke and Collin would be gone when she emerged from her room.

But he was there, comfortably situated in the living room watching the sports channel. "You look terrific," he said when she joined him.

"I'd imagine anything would be an improvement over the sight you saw in the kitchen."

Collin smiled only slightly. "Shall we go?"

"Sure."

Leah wondered if she had agreed to go with Collin because she liked the idea of breakfast at the country club twenty minutes away in Baker's Grove. Or was it Collin? Was she overwhelmed with his presence in her home? His invitation for her to join him? It couldn't be because she was looking for someone to go out with. She had Seth. She was sure she was falling in love with Seth, even though she hadn't verbalized that yet.

As they sped down the road in Collin's comfortable Mercedes, he told Leah about how he had run into an old classmate of theirs when he lived in California and all the details of that person's life. Leah made the appropriate nods and "oh, reallys?" but her mind was in another place.

Is it possible Collin considers this more of a social call than a business call? Or am I delusional and pretending that all kinds of men find me attractive and want to spend time with me simply because I'm starting to feel good about myself? But Collin couldn't be interested in me. Not after the way he found me this morning on my mouse hunt! He must want something from me. Be on your guard, Leah.

"And you?" Collin was asking as Leah pulled herself out of her deep thoughts. "Are you still planning to stay in Glenbrooke, now that your folks are gone?"

"Yes, I'm pretty settled here."

"Any plans to marry soon?" Collin asked, glancing at her with his dark eyes, as he turned into the long driveway that led to the country club.

"Marry? No," Leah said cautiously. She felt as if the question was a hot potato, and she tossed it back to Collin immediately. "What about you?"

"I married almost six years ago," Collin answered.

"Oh." She didn't remember hearing about that in the local grapevine.

"But I'm currently not married."

Leah assumed he was divorced, even though he didn't offer an explanation. They were almost to the front of the impressive entrance to the country club, and Collin seemed to be concentrating on the car in front of them that was apparently going too slow for his taste.

Leah had never been here before. Classmates had gone to this country club for the prom, but she hadn't attended. A friend from work held her wedding reception here, but it was the week after Leah's father's funeral, and she couldn't leave her mother alone for the afternoon.

Leah didn't want to feel as smug as she did at this moment, but she couldn't help it. In a silly way, this was one of her high school dreams finally coming true—only better. She was riding in an expensive automobile to the white portico where uniformed valets were ready to open her door, and Collin Radcliffe was about to treat her to brunch.

Wait a minute! This isn't the prom, Leah. This is your present life. Remember? You…Seth…kisses in the woods…. God's planting new seeds in your heart. What are you doing here with Collin?

They came to a stop while waiting for the car in front of them to unload its passengers and for the valet to attend to them. Leah adjusted her posture so she was sitting up as straight as possible. Her mind was busy forming a list of questions for Collin about his motives. If he failed to answer any of them to her satisfaction, she simply would march into the country club and call a cab.

Before she could ask the first question, Collin turned to her and said, "I should tell you that my wife was in a fatal car accident two years ago in Los Angeles. She was five months pregnant at the time. I lost both of them."

The valet opened Leah's door and offered her a hand out. But she slumped against the leather seat, stunned. "I'm so sorry, Collin. I hadn't heard. I didn't know."

He shook his head and looked away. "Not many people do. I knew you would understand because of the loss you suffered with both your parents. It takes a while to recover, doesn't it?"

"Yes," Leah said simply.

The valet waited until she turned and began to get out of the car. Leah felt all her defenses lowering. Collin was someone she had known since she was a girl, just as she had known Franklin since her childhood. Collin had endured a deep and terrible blow. She did understand. She walked beside this distinguished classmate on the plush, green carpet runner, past the huge terra-cotta planters spilling over with bright flowers, and up to the entrance. It was all she could do to keep herself from slipping her arm through his and giving him several comforting pats to let him know she felt for him.

The door of the country club opened automatically, and Leah entered first, at Collin's gentlemanly gesture. They proceeded silently to the restaurant at the back of the club where the Saturday morning brunch was in full swing. Collin asked for a window seat, and they were ushered to what Leah considered the best seat in the house. Two prominent colors filled the view from the window: the crisp blue of the sky and the emerald of the golfing greens.

"Do you play golf?" Collin asked, as Leah stared out the window, taking in the serene beauty.

"No, I never have. Do you?"

"Every chance I get. You know, you're dressed the part. If you would like, we could take in nine holes after we eat."

"I might need to walk nine holes after I eat everything I saw offered on the buffet."

"We would use a cart," Collin said graciously.

"How much exercise is that?" Leah teased.

"You would be surprised." Collin smiled at her, and she found herself wanting to stare. He looked so different from Seth. Seth still had a youthful look, especially when he wore his baseball cap like the night she first saw him. Collin was a man. Suave, confident, and established. The contrast between the two was strong.

"Good morning," the waiter said. "Will you be having the buffet? Or would you like to order off the menu?"

"The buffet would be fine," Leah said, trying to match the gracious tone in the waiter's voice. Last night at the Del Rey Mexican restaurant, the waitress had a squeak when she laughed. Leah doubted anyone at the country club was allowed to squeak for any reason.

"I'll have the buffet as well," Collin answered.

The rest of their brunch progressed with continued smoothness. They talked about lots of the people they grew up with and what all of them were doing now. Leah felt as if she were with an old friend, even though she and Collin hadn't associated much while they were growing up.

"It's such a pity we're so narrowly focused as teenagers," Collin said. "If I'd known you were going to turn out this gorgeous and this much fun, I would have snatched you up our freshman year of high school and never let you go."

"Oh," was all Leah could say. She felt herself blushing and quickly buried her nose in her coffee mug, even though only a sip was left.

Gorgeous?

She knew Collin didn't mean "gorgeous." She wasn't gorgeous. Collin was a flatterer. A smoothtalker. This wasn't the simple, freckle-faced Collin she slugged in seventh grade when he said her bike was a "wimpy girlie bike." This was Collin, the lawyer from LA who drank Pelligrino sparkling water with a twist of lime.

For a brief moment, Leah allowed herself to float back to that imaginary place in her past when she was seventeen. She toyed with the idea of what it would have been like if she really were gorgeous and were dining at the country club with Collin on a date.

What would my sisters have thought of that?

Leah imagined how different the last ten years of her life would have been—and what a different person she would have been if Collin had "snatched her up."

Wait! What am I thinking? I'm becoming a different person now. I like who I am.

An image of her blue-eyed dragon slayer came to mind. Simple, earthy, living-on-a-shoestring Seth. That's the person she wanted to be snatched up by.

Leah broke off a corner of her croissant and busied herself buttering it because she didn't want to look up at Collin. She found this past week it had become increasingly difficult to make a distinction between the real and the fantasy parts of her life. Some of her realities with Seth had been more wonderful than any fantasy she ever had dared to dream up.

What am I doing here with Collin? Why am I allowing myself to think these crazy things?

Leah didn't like the feeling, as if she were losing her balance. She especially didn't like that her mind could play these kinds of games with her emotions.

"Excuse me," she said, pushing back her chair. Collin rose slightly as she stood. "I'll be right back."

As Leah asked directions to the restroom, she could almost feel Collin watching her. Had he noticed that she was short with muscular legs and a straight torso? She imagined Collin had married a tall, thin woman with a twenty-inch waist. It was still shocking to think he had lost his wife and unborn baby in a car accident.

Leah took a good look at herself in the restroom mirror. She stared at her reflection until arriving at the conclusion that she didn't know who she was. None of the old, recorded messages fit any longer. She wasn't the big failure her father and sisters had insinuated she was. Few expectations of others weighed upon her the way they used to. The soil of her soul had all been turned over. Some seeds had been planted right away. Now it was as if Leah held several bags of mixed seeds, and it was up to her to decide which ones to plant.

Do I think I'm in love with Seth simply because he was my only option? I mean, what if Collin could actually be interested in me? Is that crazy?

Leah knew she should get back to the table. Drawing in a deep breath, she decided she was going right back to her chair, sit down, and look Collin in the eye. She would ask him why he had initiated this meeting. And she wouldn't leave that chair until she knew exactly what this man's motivation was.

Chapter Thirty-one

*L*eah returned to the table and asked Collin her first question. "You indicated yesterday that you had something you wanted to discuss with me before the reading of the will Monday. Would this be a good time to talk about it?"

Collin leaned back in his chair and seemed to consider her question a little too long, which made her uncomfortable. Finally he said, "I think I've reconsidered. I was going to discuss a matter with you that is of the strictest confidence. However, after spending this very enjoyable time with you, I'd prefer to postpone that conversation until after the reading of the will. I'm confident my words will make more sense then."

"Are you saying you're not sure you can trust me with the confidential information?"

"Oh, no, not at all. I believe you're completely reliable."

"How is it that the urgency of your message can change simply because we've shared a meal together?"

Scratching his forehead, right between his eyebrows, Collin said, "You aren't making this easy for me." The look he gave her was the way he used to look at her on the Little League field when he pitched to her for Ranger practice games. She always could hit just about anything he tossed over the plate at her. Now she was the one pitching the fast ones over the breakfast plates.

"And exactly what is it I'm not making easy for you, Collin?"

The grown-up, cosmopolitan part of Collin took over, and he opened his hands to her in an earnest appeal. "Leah, I want you to understand I approached this case originally as a lawyer approaching a client. However, now that we've had some time together, I feel more as if this is a friend-to-friend issue. I value your friendship more than I value the prospect of gaining a new client."

Leah didn't want to play with the grown-up Collin. She wanted him to go back to being feisty, not engaging. "That's what this is?" Leah challenged. "An attempt to rustle up some business, and you thought of me as a potential client? Sorry. I don't need a lawyer."

Collin folded his arms and quietly said, "That may all change on Monday."

After that statement, Leah shut down in every way she could. If she could have figuratively taken her ball and marched home, she would have. But Collin had positioned himself as a cool, calm, civilized professional, and she knew she needed to respond in kind.

He signed for the tab and asked if she wanted to take in nine holes of golf. She declined, saying she had too big of a project with the cupboards waiting for her at home. Besides that, she had left Bungee in the backyard, and she felt she should get home to check on him.

They drove along the country road with the music from his car stereo softening the air between them. Collin spoke briefly of his credentials and listed a few of the big cases he had handled in California. None of it impressed Leah. She had no intention of feeding her imagination anything that would have dazzled a seventeen-year-old. She was fully her age and at full capacity in her ability to think rationally, with no intention of allowing herself to revert to a ridiculous fantasy world.

When they arrived at her house, Collin said he thought he was doing what was best for her. Then he said one line that nearly toppled her over the edge of frustration. "I need you to trust me on this, Leah. Everything will make sense Monday. We'll talk then, okay?"

Leah simply answered, "I'll see you at your father's office at nine on Monday."

Stomping into the backyard, she found Bungee contentedly gnawing on a doggy chew that he must have retrieved from the mudroom. Hula was stretched out in the shade, apparently catching up on the sleep she had lost the night before. That didn't sound like such a bad idea to Leah, but she had a major mess waiting for her in the kitchen.

She spent the rest of the day organizing her cupboards. She had to go to the store to buy some mousetraps, and while she was in the checkout line, she overheard two women in the line next to hers. One was saying she was on her way to pick up her new car. Leah gathered from the conversation that the woman had been in an accident. She was raving about how much she received in the settlement and how great her lawyer was.

"Did you go through a law firm in Eugene?" the other woman asked.

"No, right here in Glenbrooke. Radcliffe and Sloane. My lawyer was the younger Radcliffe. The son who recently moved here. He's really terrific."

"Did they charge you an outrageous fee?" the other woman asked.

"Only fifty dollars, which he said was for processing some papers."

The other woman went on to say what a bargain that was and all about how high the lawyer fees had been for her cousin when he was in an accident.

Leah left the grocery store wondering if Collin Radcliffe was really the dashing hero this woman had made him out to be. Was it possible he *was* out to protect Leah's rights and did have her best interests in mind?

She didn't want to think about it. She wished Seth were home. He would help her make sense of everything. By nine o'clock Sunday night, Leah still hadn't heard from Seth. She tried to call him several times, but when he didn't answer, she tried not to worry about something having gone wrong on his trip. It was more likely that it took him longer to drive back than he had estimated. Or perhaps he was sleeping and not answering the phone because he was so exhausted.

Whatever the reason, all she could hope was that Seth would show up at the lawyer's office Monday morning. She didn't want to face Collin Radcliffe alone. If Seth were there, she felt certain it would be easy to stay focused and not start thinking crazy thoughts about Collin being interested in her.

On Monday morning, Leah wore a nice skirt and jacket. It was the same outfit she had worn to Franklin's memorial service. She decided she needed to go shopping that week because her wardrobe was far too limited for this crazy life that had fallen into her lap. Women in California no doubt arrived at their lawyer's office wearing silk dresses with their nails done in a color that matched. Leah knew she would never go that far, but it wouldn't hurt her to own a decent-looking outfit.

When she entered the efficient, air-conditioned office, Andrea Brown met her at the front desk. Andrea's son was the tallest of the Glenbrooke Rangers. The two women chatted comfortably for a few moments before Andrea offered Leah some coffee.

"No thanks. Am I early?"

Andrea checked her watch. "Only by a few minutes. Why don't you go on into Mr. Radcliffe's office."

Knocking twice and then opening the polished wood door, Andrea ushered Leah into a large office and invited her to take a seat on the leather sofa. Collin, who was seated in one of the four wingback chairs, rose politely as she entered. He held an open file of papers in his hand.

"Sure you don't want any coffee?" Andrea asked.

"No thanks."

Andrea left, closing the door behind her.

Collin smiled at Leah and asked about her kitchen cleaning.

"I caught the mouse yesterday," she said. "Let's hope he doesn't have any pals."

"Yes," Collin said politely.

Leah felt certain that Collin Radcliffe had never lived where rodent infestation was a problem.

Fortunately, someone knocked on the door so she didn't have to come up with any more small talk. Collin's father, whom everyone called "Radcliffe Senior," walked in. A large, striking man with white hair and a white moustache, he shook Leah's hand and placed a large file on the edge of the desk.

"Franklin and I went back for years," the distinguished gentleman said. "He will certainly be missed in this community."

Leah thought that was an odd thing for Radcliffe Senior to

say since Franklin had led such a quiet life. He had very few visitors aside from Leah and had never been involved in local politics or civic events. Perhaps he simply represented the last living tie to Cameron Madison and the founding of Glenbrooke.

"We're going to wait for Mr. Edwards before we begin," Radcliffe Senior explained.

"Do you mean no other relatives are coming?" Leah asked.

"No," Radcliffe Senior said.

"That surprises me."

"Does it?" the white-haired gentleman asked, pulling one of the wingback chairs closer. "Why so?"

"Several of his relatives came to the memorial service from out of town. I thought this would be an important meeting for them as well."

"No, only you and Mr. Edwards."

Collin added to his father's comment, "It's unfortunate so few of those relatives came from out of town to see Mr. Madison before the memorial service."

Leah was beginning to feel uncomfortable. She had imagined several people would attend the meeting. Unless, of course, Franklin had nothing to will to anyone, and they all knew it. She wasn't sure why she was here. And it concerned her that Seth hadn't arrived yet.

"Could I get a drink of water?" she asked.

Collin immediately rose. "I'll get it for you."

She smiled nervously at Radcliffe Senior. She felt as if she had been called to the principal's office and was waiting to find out what she had done wrong.

"Collin told me he had an enjoyable time with you on Saturday," Radcliffe Senior said. He looked cool, calm, confident. After all, this was his domain. She was the fish out of water here.

"Yes, it was nice. I hadn't been to the country club before." As soon as she said it, Leah realized how much of a hick that made her sound like. "The brunch was scrumptious," she added, trying to sound a little more sophisticated.

Oh, brother! "Scrumptious"? Where did I pick up that cutesy word?

Just then the door opened, and Andrea appeared with Seth beside her. Leah felt like springing up and running into his arms. He apologized for being late and greeted Leah as formally as he greeted Radcliffe Senior.

Leah noticed Seth was in his PDS uniform, and she guessed he was slipping this meeting in between deliveries. She also noticed he looked extremely tired.

"Here you are, Ms. Hudson," Collin said, handing her a cold bottle of sparkling mineral water. "May I bring you anything, Mr. Edwards?"

Seth held up his hand. "I'm fine." He smiled warmly at Leah but then sat in one of the wingback chairs, leaving Leah alone on the couch and feeling deserted.

"Let's get down to business," Radcliffe Senior said. He began to read through the papers in the file. It all sounded like blurry double-talk to Leah. When he finished the first page, Radcliffe Senior looked up and said, "Are you with me so far?"

Leah glanced at Seth and then back at Radcliffe Senior. "I'm sorry, but I'm not catching a lot of this. Would it be possible for us to follow along on copies of what you're reading?" Leah navigated complicated lab reports and monstrous stacks of insurance forms on a regular basis, but she always had the words to look at, not just listen to.

"I would like that as well," Seth said.

"Basically, I just read you some of the preliminary information with respect to the estate of Franklin R. Madison," Radcliffe Senior said. "In an effort to save time, perhaps you would allow me to continue. Andrea has prepared copies, and she will present them to you before you leave."

"But if the copies are already prepared," Leah stated, "I don't see why—"

"Actually, Dad," Collin interrupted. He leaned forward and granted Leah a gracious expression of apology for cutting her off. "I think we can tell these two the bottom-line of the will. We're among friends here."

Radcliffe Senior looked at his son with startled disfavor. It appeared he was a man of the old school who always went by the book, line by line.

Without waiting for his father's blessing, Collin said, "Leah, you are to receive the contents of Franklin's safe-deposit box, which has been kept sealed at the bank. Mr. Edwards, you are to receive the rest of Franklin's estate, which includes his house, fifty acres of woodlands, and $250,000 in treasury bills."

Leah turned to Seth. He looked as if he was in shock. She couldn't blame him. Fifty acres, a house, and a quarter of a million dollars was quite a fortune, especially when no one suspected Franklin still had such holdings.

"However," Collin continued, his voice going up a notch in volume. "There is one stipulation. Franklin Madison made it clear when he changed his will earlier this month, that the only way Mr. Edwards could receive his inheritance was under one condition."

Seth seemed to have lost his voice, but Collin was pausing and dramatically waiting for the inevitable question.

Leah jumped in. "What condition?"

Collin stood and turned to his father, as if inviting Radcliffe Senior the privilege of delivering the punch line. It seemed as if the two lawyers had choreographed the meeting to elicit the maximum shock from Seth and Leah.

"The condition," Radcliffe Senior began, "simply put, is that you, Seth Edwards, must legally marry Leah Hudson before the property, house, and funds are transferred to your name."

Chapter Thirty-two

$\mathcal{L}$eah and Seth exchanged stunned glances.

"The estate will be held in trust for a year," Collin explained. "If, at the end of that time, you and Ms. Hudson are not legally married, the entire estate will be donated to the Glenbrooke Historical Society."

Leah couldn't move. What was Franklin thinking? Why would he make such a condition? Did the old fox even consider that he was making plans for other people and controlling their lives without including them in the decision?

"Leah, are you all right?" The voice was coming from Seth, but it sounded far away.

She turned and saw he was still in the chair, less than three feet from her. "Yes. Are you okay?"

Seth nodded. "Did you know about any of this?"

"No, I had no idea."

"This is the first I've heard any of this," Seth said.

"That's how Franklin wanted it," Radcliffe Senior said. "You'll find all the details in the document, Mr. Edwards. Andrea has prepared a copy for you. Now you can see why I didn't want you looking at the papers until after we had a chance to go over them with you."

"Thank you," Seth said with a nod. He was still looking at Leah. His face had turned pale. With his right hand he kept rubbing his jaw line.

"Do you have any questions?" Radcliffe Senior asked.

"A dozen," Seth answered numbly. "But perhaps I should read the papers for myself and then set up another appointment with you."

"That would be fine. Andrea can make the appointment for you."

Radcliffe Senior stood next to Collin, who was still standing from when he rose to make the shocking announcement. It appeared that Leah and Seth were being dismissed.

Seth caught the cue and stood. Leah rose as well, but Collin stepped closer to her and said, "I wonder if you might stay a few more minutes, Leah. We need to give you the key to the safe-deposit box and discuss a few other items."

"All right."

"I'll see you later," Seth said, walking slowly to the door. "I'll call you."

"Okay," Leah said, trying hard to give him a smile. It seemed all her smiles were buried under an avalanche of stunned emotions. The best she could offer was a simple raised hand in a parting wave.

Seth exited the office, and Radcliffe Senior followed him out, closing the door behind him. Collin sat down and leaned forward, as if he were about to offer Leah confidential information. "Perhaps you realize that Franklin Madison listed you in his will many years ago."

Leah shook her head and began to speak quickly, as if she had to defend herself. "No, I didn't know. We never talked about it. I never expected anything. To be honest, I was convinced he didn't own anything besides his house. I had no idea about the treasury bills or the property."

"He did in fact own some property," Collin said.

"Where is the property? Here in Glenbrooke? Is it from Cameron Madison's original landholdings? Because Seth thought Franklin might still own land, but I didn't think so."

Leah noticed that Collin's eyebrows rose on her last statement. "What else did Mr. Edwards have to say about Franklin's estate?"

"Nothing." Leah felt the need to slow down and watch her words. "I'm sure Seth is just as shocked as I am that Franklin had so much."

"Leah," Collin leaned toward her and rubbed his hands together. "This is what I wanted to discuss with you the other day. You see, I don't think you realize it, but all of this was in your name in Franklin's will until a few short weeks ago."

"In my name?"

"After Naomi passed away, Franklin changed his will. We have all the paperwork in his file. He willed everything he had to you."

"But why?"

"I asked my father, and he said Franklin's reasons were private. We may never know. Or perhaps the safe-deposit box holds an explanation for you. Regardless of the reason, for nearly twenty years, you were heir to his entire estate. Don't you agree that it's suspicious that a distant nephew would come into town and suddenly the will is changed?"

Leah wasn't ready to accuse Seth of anything. "Were you the one who went to Franklin's house two weeks ago to change his will?"

"No, unfortunately, my father was out of town. Franklin met with my father's partner, Mr. Sloane. Their meeting was strictly professional with no explanations given. Franklin might have offered more of an explanation if my father had been the lawyer he was working with since the two of them had known each other for so long. I thought you might have some insight because I don't understand why everything was changed to Seth's name."

"I think that should be obvious," Leah said. "He's a relative. Franklin liked him. Seth has very little. He would benefit greatly from such an inheritance."

Collin looked at Leah, his eyes level with hers. "And you don't find this a bit suspicious?"

"No."

"Don't you see that all this would have been yours?"

Leah shrugged. It hadn't sunk in yet, but she didn't see why this was such a big issue. Leah was more eager to receive the key and get out of there so she could find out what was in the safe-deposit box.

"I'd like to represent you in this case," Collin said, reaching into his suit coat pocket to pull out one of his business cards.

"I have several of your cards, Collin," Leah said impatiently. "And I don't have a case."

"Oh, but you do, Leah. If we can prove that Seth influenced Franklin unduly to change his will, or if we can prove that Franklin wasn't in his right mind when he made the change, then the estate will revert back to you."

"But I don't want Franklin's estate!"

Collin leaned back in the chair and pressed his fingers

together. He drew the index fingers to his lips as if in deep contemplation.

Leah rose to her feet and said, "If that's all, I think I should get back to work."

Collin rose and looked down on Leah. His voice was calm. "I apologize, Leah. This is what I was making reference to on Saturday. You're not like other women, and I'm approaching this the wrong way. Would you be so kind as to sit for just another moment? I feel there's something important for you to know."

Leah sat down but not very quickly.

Collin took a seat next to Leah on the couch. He seemed to be searching for the right words. When he met her gaze, his expression was sincere and concerned. "Leah, you know me. I'm from here. You were with me when I fell off the boulders at Heather Creek and broke my arm."

"That's right," Leah said, a smile creeping across her lips. "We went fishing together that one time."

Collin nodded and smiled. He seemed pleased finally to have initiated a shared memory that brought a smile to Leah's face. "We were fishing for frogs," Collin corrected her. "The creek was thick with them that year, remember?"

"Oh, yeah. I got in trouble for leaving my dad's bucket at the creek when I took off on my bike to go for help. Do you remember how I told you to stay there and put your feet up?"

Collin chuckled.

"I don't know where I got the idea that if you thought your arm was broken you should raise your feet. How old were we? Nine?"

"At least nine. Maybe ten."

"I'd forgotten all about that," Leah said.

"It was a little harder for me to forget," Collin said, leaning forward. "This is exactly the point I wanted to make, Leah. We go back quite a few years. I trusted you to go for help that day, and now I'm asking you to trust me. I can help you with this."

Leah felt herself calming. It was easy to melt into the softness of the leather couch under Collin's dark gaze.

"I didn't want to have to disclose this to you," Collin continued, "but it seems the only way to help you understand. We have reason to believe that Seth Edwards is, for lack of a better word, an opportunist. We ran a check on him last week, and I'm afraid the results weren't very promising." Collin reached for the file he had left on the coffee table. He opened it to the first page and showed it to Leah.

The paper was a credit report showing that Seth Edwards had filed bankruptcy and backed out of almost $30,000 in credit card debt.

"But he was in Costa Rica for the last four years."

"Are you sure?"

Leah thought quickly. She didn't have any proof. The melanoma and the tan skin were the closest she could come to proving he had been in the tropics.

"This paper details his police record with the Colorado police. As you can see, it's for possession of illegal drugs."

"Police record? Colorado? Collin, you must have the wrong Seth Edwards. Where did you get this information?"

"From a very reliable service we've used for years." Collin closed the file. "I see I don't have to subject you to the rest of the information listed here. The question for you is whether you truly know Seth Edwards or not. Is he reliable? Has he been telling you the truth?"

Leah sat back in stunned silence.

"Let me help you consider the facts," Collin said. "As a friend. You've only known Seth Edwards for a few weeks. I'm sure he's told you exactly what he wanted you to believe. As I see it, he'll be eager to marry you, but once the estate is his,

Franklin added no provision for cancellation on any grounds. In other words, Seth could very well marry you, take everything, and disappear."

Collin reached over and took Leah's hand in his. "We go way back, Leah. I would hate to see any man do that to you. Especially if one of the most precious treasures he takes with him is your heart."

Leah needed air. She couldn't breath. She couldn't think. Pulling her hand away from Collin's, she stood up and said, "I need to get back to work, Collin."

He stood beside her and said, "You can see why I didn't want to drop all this on you on Saturday. I was enjoying being with you too much. Please call me." He began to reach into his pocket and then stopped and pulled out his hand. "That's right, you already have my card. Consider me a friend, Leah. That's all. A friend who cares and can help you through this. I'm sure a woman like you could find good use for a quarter of a million dollars."

Leah all but fled the law office. She drove like a crazy person toward the hospital and then realized she couldn't work in her state of mind. She needed to think. Suddenly, she knew where she could go.

Turning at the next corner, Leah put her foot to the accelerator pedal and headed for the Victorian mansion on the top of Madison Hill.

Chapter Thirty-three

"I can see how you would feel that way," Jessica said sympathetically, as she and Leah slowly rocked together in the porch swing. "That was an awful lot of information to take in."

"Maybe I don't exactly feel like I'm going crazy," Leah said, retracting her previous statement with a sigh. "That might have been an exaggeration. I'm overwhelmed; that's more accurate. I feel overwhelmed, and I don't know who to trust."

"You have to trust God," Jessica said simply.

"I know, but I mean, I don't know if Collin is telling me the truth about Seth."

"That's my point," Jessica said. Her smile accentuated the faint, half-moon scar on her upper lip. "God knows which one is trustworthy. Let him reveal it to you. Trust him."

"That's much easier said than done," Leah muttered, taking a sip from her iced tea glass. "I saw the credit report. The name was definitely Seth Edwards."

Jessica didn't comment. Leah had hoped Jessica would say something like, "There has to be more than one Seth Edwards in the world. They must have gotten the wrong one." But Jessica just closed her eyes, and Leah had the impression her friend was praying for her. Leah didn't know why Jessica hadn't invited her to pray aloud the way they had when, months ago, they had prayed together regularly.

Leah slowly drank her iced tea and forced herself to breathe deeply. She felt herself calming down and a sense of peace coming over her. Forming her own, silent prayer, Leah asked God for wisdom and direction. She told him she wanted to trust him but was having a hard time, in case he hadn't noticed.

Jessica opened her eyes and smiled at Leah. "I have a very good lawyer in Los Angeles. Greg Fletcher. If it would be of any help, I'd be glad to forward the papers to him and ask him to check into the situation for you."

"Do you mean forward Franklin's will or the file on Seth?"

"Do you have the file on Seth?"

"No."

"Then just the will," Jessica said. "Maybe Greg won't see anything in it. I don't know. I'm not sure how Greg could help, but if you think you would like me to contact him, I'd be glad to."

"I would. It's my right to obtain a second opinion. We encourage patients to do that all the time with doctors."

"I'll get his number," Jessica said. "If you tell his secretary you're my friend, she'll make sure he calls you as soon as possible."

Jessica went inside and left Leah alone in the swing. The late morning sky was stuffed with clouds. Only remnants of blue showed through. It was warm, not hot. The hanging geraniums were still dripping from when Jessica had watered them just as Leah pulled into the driveway and frantically ran up the steps.

This house on Madison Hill has become such a place of comfort and blessed retreat in my life. Then Leah recognized an ironic twist. *How strange that it was built by the man who started all this property-ownership, land-rights, inheritance business. Never in a million years would I have guessed I would be linked to this property in such a bizarre way.*

The air was filled with the scent of coming rain. Everything was still except for the sound of a slow moving honeybee, drunk on the sweetness of his cargo. Leah spotted the bee in the hydrangea bush and felt sympathetic for his dilemma. He had so many blossoms from which to choose. The flowers were adorned in their finest, soft pink gowns like enticing belles of the ball, torturing the one bewildered bee with their wild-scented pollen.

Suddenly a thought came to Leah with clarity and strength. If she did have the money from Franklin's estate, she could live in a house like this. A quarter of a million dollars could buy a lot of beauty and peace. Not to mention how incredible it would be for the Glenbrooke Zorro to have such resources available. Leah felt certain she could make good use of the money. And if the fifty acres were the woodlands she thought they were, the land that bordered Camp Heather Brook, Leah could give that land to Shelly and Jonathan, and they could build their tree house camp. As far as Franklin's house was concerned, she could fix it up and rent it out. Glenbrooke had few rentals in that neighborhood.

The opportunities seemed as bountiful as the blossoms available to that bewildered honeybee. Leah hadn't seen it from this angle at the lawyer's office, but it was beginning to make sense. Maybe this was something worth fighting for, on the off-chance Seth really was a rogue. Franklin never would have put such a qualification in the will if he had known what his nephew really was like.

"Wait a minute," Leah said to herself. "What am I saying?" She pressed the cold, iced tea glass to her cheek in an effort to shock herself into thinking more clearly.

How can I even think of Seth that way? What if Collin ran the report on the wrong Seth Edwards? What if Seth truly loves me and is an honest, God-fearing man? If we marry, the inheritance will be mine as well. I don't need to pull it away from Seth and claim it all for myself.

The front door opened, and Jessica appeared with one of her ubiquitous three-by-five note cards. "Greg's number," she said, handing it to Leah. "And a verse for the day to give you some encouragement."

Leah looked at the reference. When she saw it was Psalm 37:4, she said, "You gave me this one before. I've even memorized it. 'Delight yourself in the LORD; and He will give you the desires of your heart.'"

"I thought it might be a good reminder to you in the midst of all the confusion."

"Thanks," Leah said, rising to go. "And thanks for being here for me. I don't know what I'd do without you."

Jessica hugged her. "Keep me updated, okay? I'll be praying my little heart out for you."

As Leah drove to work, she thought about how much she depended on Jessica's prayers. It was astounding to think that Jessica might very well be the only person in the world who prayed for her. Where would she be if Jessica hadn't been praying all this time?

The realization prompted Leah to pray herself. And she had plenty to pray about. Her biggest concern was what she should do that night when Seth showed up at her house for dinner. Should she come right out and ask him about the credit and police reports? What would he say? If Seth had managed to lie so convincingly to her for these past few weeks, wouldn't he continue to lie and convince her of whatever he wanted?

When Leah arrived at work, she pushed all thoughts of the intense morning from her mind. She had to. The hospital was busy, and she was half a day behind with no backup support from Mary.

Of the many phone messages her coworker from ER had taken while covering Leah's desk that morning were messages from Alissa, Seth, and Collin. Leah chose not to return either man's calls, but on the way home, she dialed Alissa's number on the cell phone.

"A Wing and a Prayer Travel," Alissa answered the phone.

"Hi, it's Leah. I received a message that you called earlier today."

"Yes, I have good news for you. Or interesting news. Before I tell you what it is, I want to remind you that you gave away the last vacation package that fell in your lap. You might want to reconsider this one."

"What? Did the radio call you to say I'd won their grand drawing? Around the world for two?"

"Not quite that glamorous. The trip I'm talking about is to Hamilton Hot Springs for the weekend. They called today since I had made the arrangements for Franklin, and this was the phone number listed. They wanted to know if any of the party of three wanted to schedule a massage. I tried to cancel the whole reservation, but they said they required two weeks' notification, and since it's for this weekend, they couldn't refund the money."

"What do you mean this weekend? I was supposed to take Franklin the last weekend in May."

"Really? The last weekend? He told me it was this weekend when he set up the reservations. I wonder if he was confused."

Leah's heart began to pound. This was exactly the kind of evidence Collin was looking for to build a case against Franklin's changing the will.

"Are you still there?" Alissa asked.

"Yes, I'm here. Go ahead. What were you saying?"

"I was saying, the trip is paid for. It's in your name. Why don't you go up for the weekend and treat yourself for once? It's not too late for me to schedule a massage for you."

"A massage? I don't need a massage."

"But you could use some time away," Alissa said.

Leah couldn't argue with that. "Okay, tell me what I need to do."

"Just show up at the hot springs on Friday, any time after three. I have a brochure and a map, if you need it."

"Yes, I need a map. I'll come by tomorrow to pick it up."

"Good for you," Alissa said. "I think Franklin wanted this for you even more than he wanted it for himself."

Yeah, well, I know what he really wanted. He wanted to play matchmaker with Seth and me in the same place where he shared romantic memories with Naomi.

"You have two rooms reserved, so why not take some friends, if you don't feel like being by yourself."

"Can't you cancel one room if I keep the reservation on the other?"

"Possibly but not likely. The second room still is listed in Franklin's and Seth's names. Franklin was hopeful when he made the reservation that Seth would go with you, although Franklin told me Seth wasn't sure he wanted to go."

Leah sighed. "No, he didn't want to go. Seth didn't think Franklin should go either. Nothing is ever easy, is it? Let's drop the whole topic of Seth going. I'll go. That's that."

Alissa paused on her end of the line, apparently not sure what to make of Leah's comment.

"I'll see you tomorrow," Leah said. "Thanks for letting me know about this, Alissa. You're right. I should get away now."

Leah pushed the End button on her cell phone. When she turned the corner to her street, the first thing she saw was a PDS truck parked in front of her house.

Chapter Thirty-four

eah turned off the car's engine and sat in front of her house looking for the PDS truck's driver. She didn't see anyone at her front door. Seth might have gone around the back of the house to pick up Bungee. Maybe he was avoiding her after the meeting this morning. She wondered if he needed time to sort out this turn of events as much as she did.

Leah realized how awkward it would be to see Seth, now that they suddenly were expected to get married. Before today she hadn't even allowed herself the luxury of daydreaming about such an outcome to their growing relationship, but now it was set, established by someone who hadn't asked them what they thought of the idea.

Ironic, Leah thought as she compared the similarity between this situation and the account of Jacob and Leah in Genesis. To obtain Rachel, Jacob had to take Leah. For Seth to inherit the estate, he had to take Leah. She didn't like the comparison one bit.

What concerned her even more, as she sat in her car, alone with her tormenting thoughts, was the possibility that Collin was right. What if Seth had known all along that the original will was in Leah's name? What if he had been romancing her to gain all that Franklin had left to her? What if Seth never cared for her, and it was all a lie? He could hire his own lawyer to refute the conditions, find a way to cut the marriage clause out of the will, and take the entire estate for himself.

Leah didn't know what to think or who to believe. She successfully had pushed it all away at work, but now that she was home the situation's complexities came rushing at her with a fresh urgency. She needed some answers.

Leah punched the phone number for Jessica's lawyer into her cell phone. She reached a voice mail message inviting her to dial a pager or leave a message. Leah left a brief message and then dialed the pager as well, giving her home phone number.

She knew that, if she ate something, her energy level might be restored. That's when she saw Jack from PDS crossing the street and jogging back to his truck. The older couple across the street were waving good-bye to him. Jack called out a cheerful hello to Leah and drove off down the street.

You can now enter your home safely, Leah. Seth is not lurking in the backyard ready to spring on you.

Once in the house, the first thing Leah did was change into shorts and a T-shirt. Then she went into the backyard to check on Bungee and Hula. She found Hula in the mudroom, lapping up the few drops left in the bottom of her water dish.

"Poor girl. I should have realized you were sharing your water. Would you like some dinner, too? It looks like Bungee cleaned you out."

As Leah filled the water and food dishes, she called for Bungee to come in through the doggy door. A moment later a very dirty bundle of fun came bounding in.

"I thought you might come when the word 'dinner' was mentioned." Leah roughed him up behind the ears. "How did you get so dirty, Bowser?" She looked out the window and felt relieved to see her garden was still intact. He must have been digging along the side of the house to have such a snootful of dirt.

Leaving the dogs to their dinner, Leah went out the back door and located where Bungee had been digging. He had made a royal mess, but it was just dirt along the side of the house, and he hadn't disturbed anything. If he had to dig, that was a good place to do it. Leah turned on the hose to water her garden. The sight of tiny green sprouts sticking up in straight, neat rows made her smile.

Maybe I don't want a big mansion on a hill. Maybe this is all I need to feed my soul. A little place of my own. A little garden.

Leah turned the hose onto the grass and began to water the lawn. The tormenting thoughts of Seth, Collin, and Franklin's estate had followed her to the garden sanctuary, and they didn't seem eager to leave. Leah knew the main conflict was deciding whom she was going to believe. It still seemed impossible to her that Seth could have filed bankruptcy and had a police record. She preferred to believe the research was incorrect. A different Seth Edwards had shown up on Collin's report. It had to be.

Still, there was the nagging thought that women more intelligent and less trusting than Leah had been duped by men before. She could have fallen into a great big trap.

What have I fallen into, God? A trap? Or a pocket of grace? What do I do now?

Oddly, all Leah could think about was the poster behind Alissa's desk of the gondola in Venice. *Yes, I would like to run away and float down a serene canal right now. Is that what you're telling me, God? I should buy a one-way ticket to Italy? Say the word, and I'm there! Ciao, baby!*

Leah thought of how pleasant it would be to sit back in that gondola and let someone else do the navigating through these challenging canals before her. She felt as if she was doing all the rowing and steering, which had been her pattern in the past. But this time she had no idea where she was going. Only uncharted waters lay ahead.

Bungee began to wrestle with the dripping garden hose, delighted with the spray of water that soaked his underside.

"Not a bad idea, Bungee. Come here. I'm going to hose you down and get all that mud off you before Seth comes for you."

Leah held Bungee down and washed him off. Once all the mud was gone, she unfastened the leash, picked him up, and took him inside to towel him off. Blocking the doggy door, she then instructed Bungee to stay put and stay clean while she changed and started dinner.

Closing the door to the mudroom, she turned to see Seth standing in her kitchen with a bouquet of red roses.

"The front door was unlocked," he said. "I guess you didn't hear me knock."

Without saying a word, Leah examined everything about Seth in an effort to determine if he was trustworthy. He looked stable. Sincere. Honest. Could he really be out to deceive her?

"I, um…" Leah felt weak and unable to respond to Seth and the gorgeous bouquet. "I'm all wet," she finally managed to say. "Let me go change. I'll be right back."

She fled to her bedroom, closed the door, and crumpled onto her bed. There she cried what seemed like a thousand salty tears. It was all such a cruel joke. A guy, who was perfect for her in every way, was standing in her kitchen waiting for her with a bouquet of red roses. It was the dream she had given up long ago when she realized all "the good ones" were taken.

Who am I supposed to believe? Which canal do I paddle down?

The fear of the unknown paralyzed Leah. If it weren't for her cold, soggy T-shirt, she might have stayed in that position a lot longer. Pulling herself to her feet, she drew on the strength and determination that had been her banner traits in demanding situations. She took a deep breath and changed her clothes. Then, washing her face and quickly brushing her hair, Leah returned to the kitchen.

Seth had managed to find Leah's one and only large vase and had arranged the flowers for her. They dominated the kitchen counter. The daisies he had given her on Friday were still fresh and filled a jar on her small kitchen table.

"How are you doing?" Seth asked cautiously, as Leah stood staring at the roses.

When she didn't answer, he took several steps closer to her with his arms open, inviting a hug.

Leah pulled back and put up her hand. "I'm still processing all this, Seth."

"Tell me about it." Seth scratched his forehead. "It's unbelievable, isn't it?"

"Yes." Leah cautiously made her way past Seth to the small kitchen table where she lowered herself onto a chair. "It's pretty overwhelming, all right."

Seth joined her at the table and moved the daisies so they could see each other more clearly. "Can I get you something to drink, Leah?"

"No. I mean, I should be getting you something to drink." She hopped up and went to the refrigerator. "Juice? Milk? Water?"

"Just water," Seth said. He had gotten up and was standing

beside her. "I can get it. Are you sure you're okay?"

"Yes, I'm okay." Leah heard the edge in her own voice and headed into the living room, as if the soft furniture would offer her comfort at this moment of confusion. Part of her wanted to order Seth to leave her house. Another part of her wanted to fall into his arms and beg him never to let go.

Seth joined her with two glasses of water, both with ice. He placed them on the coasters on top of the suitcase coffee table. Then, as if he sensed Leah's need for a little breathing space, he sat in the recliner, letting her have the love seat to herself.

They sat for several long minutes without speaking. Seth sipped his water.

"Seth," she said at last, "I have to ask you something. Did you know that you weren't in Franklin's will until he changed it two weeks ago?"

"No, I had no idea. I told you at the law offices. I didn't even know he changed the will."

"Did you know what was in his will before he changed it?"

Seth hesitated and looked down. He gazed up at Leah. "Yes, I did. Franklin told me. I didn't ask. He told me. On Easter."

A random phrase Seth had used several days ago suddenly came back to Leah. Franklin said you are the key to my future happiness.

"So you knew he had a large estate."

"No, I didn't. I thought it was just the house and the land. I didn't know about the treasury bills."

"The land?" Leah echoed. "You knew about the land?"

Seth leaned back and rubbed his hand across his jaw line. "I was going to tell you when the time was right, but it got a little awkward."

"A little awkward?" Leah repeated. Her memory flashed on the file folders she had seen in Seth's cupboard. She remembered now that the first rather full file had been labeled Madison Property. At the time, she hadn't made the connection.

"I hired a person to run a title search, and all the papers came in right after Franklin passed away. It felt awkward for me to tell you the results of my research on the heels of his death. I was going to tell you the day of his memorial service. I had studied the map, and I thought I'd take you to the property and tell you there."

"The woodlands," Leah whispered.

Seth nodded. "Once we got there, you were still pretty distraught. It was such a beautiful place. What you and I shared that day was so intimate and incredible to me that I felt it would ruin the moment if I started to talk about Franklin's estate. I knew we were meeting with the lawyer Monday, and I thought it best to wait until then."

Leah let his words sink in. Something still felt unbalanced. "You knew about the land, but you didn't tell me."

Seth nodded. "I should have. Then it wouldn't have come as such a surprise to you at the law office."

"And you knew I was listed as heir to Franklin's estate."

Seth nodded again.

"Why didn't you tell me that? You knew I didn't know anything about it."

Seth shrugged. "I don't know, Leah. I guess a few other dimensions of our relationship seemed more important to me. Not to mention that the melanoma surgery pretty much occupied my attention for awhile. To be honest, I was waiting for you to bring it up so it would feel more natural."

Leah felt her lower lip curve inward. "None of this feels natural to me."

"I know," Seth said. "I understand this is all surprising. It's surprising for both of us. But, Leah, I've thought about it all day, and I think Franklin had the right idea. His methods were a little wacky, but Franklin knew that you and I were really good for each other."

Leah studied his expression, trying to determine if she could trust his words.

"Not only that," Seth continued, "but I think the conditions of the will are... well, they're good."

"Good?" Leah repeated.

Seth readjusted his position and leaned forward with his hands folded. "I know this has to be the world's most backward, crazy, unromantic proposal in history, but Leah, honey, I think we should get married."

Chapter Thirty-five

*L*eah stared at Seth in disbelief. All of Collin's cautions about Seth's eagerness to marry her and to take possession of the inheritance came rushing back. She couldn't believe Collin's predictions had come true before the sun had even set that day.

Seth rose with a timid expression on his face. He opened his arms, welcoming Leah to come to him and to accept his proposal.

Leah couldn't move. "Seth, I have to ask you a question. And you have to promise me you will answer honestly."

"Of course." He lowered his arms and sat next to Leah on the love seat.

She looked him in the eye. "Seth, is it true that you filed bankruptcy with a credit-card debt in excess of $30,000?"

Seth's mouth dropped open. "Where did you hear that?"

"Just answer me. Yes or no."

Seth's eyes widened, as if he felt terror at her discovering this information. He swallowed and in a low voice said, "Yes, but—"

"And do you have a record with the Colorado police for illegal drug possession?"

"Well," Seth hesitated. "Kind of, but, you see…"

Leah felt her cheeks turning a fiery red as all the pieces began to come together. "You originally told me you came to Glenbrooke to seek the favor of your great-uncle so you could inherit—"

"I was only kidding, Leah! I didn't think Franklin owned anything."

"But now you know the inheritance is substantial. And I'm your only obstacle to obtaining it, aren't I?" Leah couldn't make herself wait to hear his answer. She sprang from the love seat, marched to the mudroom, and scooped up Bungee and his leash.

"Leah, it's not like that!" Seth called out as he followed her.

Shaking all over, Leah plowed her way back into the kitchen where Seth stood looking pale.

"Let me explain," he pled.

Yanking the roses from the vase, she thrust the flowers and the puppy into Seth's arms.

"Please leave," she growled.

"Leah, wait!"

"I mean it, Seth. Leave me alone!" She began to push him toward the front door.

"But, Leah, you have to let me explain!"

"No, I don't!" Leah shouted, yanking open the door and pushing Seth outside. "And I don't have to trust you, either!"

She knew her hand hit the spot on his back where the stitches had been because he winced and pulled away.

"Leah, this isn't fair!"

"No, it's not!" she cried, as the tears cascaded down her cheeks. "Just go!"

With a slam that rattled the morning-glory stained glass window, Leah locked the door and locked her heart to Seth Edwards. She leaned her back against the door while her heart raced and her lungs painfully pushed out great gasps of air.

Just then two steady knocks sounded on the door. She felt their vibrations against her back. "I said go away, and I mean it!"

"Leah," the smooth, professional voice called from the other side of the door. "Leah, it's Collin. May I come in?"

Leah hesitated before unlocking the door and opening it cautiously. Behind Collin she could see Seth standing beside his car with Bungee squirming in his arms and the roses spilling onto the street. Seth looked dumbfounded.

"Are you all right?" Collin asked.

Leah looked away. "I don't know."

"May I come in?"

Leah didn't know how to respond. She really wanted to be alone. Before she could think of what to say, Seth called out, "Is this where you got the information, Leah?" He still held Bungee under his arm, but the roses were now strewn on the ground.

"It doesn't appear that my client is interested in discussing this with you at the moment, Mr. Edwards." Collin stood between Leah and Seth, pulling his frame to its full height and speaking louder than was necessary in a quiet neighborhood like Leah's.

"What else did he tell you, Leah?" Seth persisted, his voice-level matching Collin's. Bungee started to bark. "Don't you see what's happening here? He's trying to turn you against me, Leah. Why are you believing him?"

Bungee kept barking.

Leah peered around Collin's broad frame and was about to

state that she had seen the evidence herself. But Collin spoke even more firmly than the first time. "I have to ask you to leave the premises, Mr. Edwards, unless you wish for my client to add harassment to the case she already has against you."

"What case against me?" Seth shouted. Bungee barked louder.

"Good night, Mr. Edwards," Collin stated, taking Leah by the elbow and ushering her into the house.

Leah didn't protest. Nor did she try to stop Collin when he firmly closed the door on Seth and Bungee.

"Come sit down," Collin said, leading Leah to the love seat. "May I get you something to drink?"

Leah sank onto the seat, shaking her head wearily. Something inside her urged her to run to the front door and let Seth back in. Maybe they could straighten everything out if the three of them could talk calmly. But Leah was not calm. She felt overwhelmed with weakness and vulnerability. She couldn't stand up and walk all the way to the front door if her life depended on it. All this was out of character for her. She knew how to be strong in any situation. She had proved that over the years. Now, she felt only weakness.

Collin lowered his large frame next to hers and put his arm along the back of the sofa. She didn't like Collin's taking her under his wing; yet she felt powerless to do anything at the moment.

"I'm sorry you had to find this out, Leah. Although I'm certain it's better to find out now than later."

Leah lowered her head into her hands, breathing deeply.

"This is too big for you to handle alone," Collin continued smoothly. "You need to give yourself some time. Then, when you're ready, I'm here for you. I can prepare the case to have the inheritance returned to you. You will only have to be involved at a minimal level. I can take care of everything."

"I don't care about the money, Collin, or the land, or any of it. I just feel so confused."

"I know," Collin said, placing his hand on her shoulder. "Unfortunately, I see this all too often in my line of work. You'll be glad later that it came out in the open so soon."

Leah wanted to cry, but no tears came.

"Is there any way you can get away for a few days?" Collin asked. "It would be good for you to separate yourself from all this. Let me start handling the case."

Leah told him about the reservations Franklin had made at the hot springs and how she was planning to go on Friday.

"Would it be possible for you to leave earlier?"

"I don't think so. Alissa wasn't able to cancel the reservations."

"The reservations can't be cancelled, but are they transferable?"

"I wouldn't know."

"It's easy enough to find out." Collin pulled an incredibly small cell phone from his breast pocket and asked information to connect him with Hamilton Hot Springs.

Leah wasn't sure why, but she liked the idea of leaving town for a few days. She felt too overwhelmed to stay here. She needed to be alone to think and pray.

"What you're telling me is that you can transfer the reservations?" Collin said into the phone. "Yes, I'd like to transfer the reservation for Leah Hudson to tonight."

"Tonight!" Leah squeaked out.

Collin put up his hand to silence her. "Right," he said into the phone. "She will arrive close to eleven tonight."

"I can't go tonight," Leah told Collin as soon as he hung up. "I have to make arrangements at work and...I don't know. I have to pack."

"You start to pack. I'll make a few calls."

"But work," Leah protested. "I can't call in sick."

"Have you ever?"

"No."

"Have you ever used all your sick days or vacation days?" Collin asked.

"No."

Collin reached over and placed his large hand on her forehead. "You feel feverish," he declared. "As your legal advisor, I'm recommending that you consider the next few days as sick days due to stress and fatigue. You need to take some time to recover. I can make the calls for you. I know several people in hospital administration. Now go. Start to pack."

Leah numbly obeyed. In some ways, it all made perfect sense. She pulled a battered suitcase from the back of her closet and began to fill it with everything her foggy brain thought she might need at a resort. She had nothing especially nice to pack, but then, what did that matter? She was going to be alone and to soak in the mineral pools. It wasn't as if this were a cruise to Alaska or anything.

Collin tapped on her closed bedroom door just as she threw in her toothpaste and a bottle of contact lens solution.

"I'm almost ready," she called out, lugging the ugly old suitcase to the front door. Collin stood there, holding out an envelope to her.

"I forgot, and I do apologize. This is the key to the safe-deposit box. I failed to give it to you this morning at my office. That's why I came over this evening."

Leah had nearly forgotten about the safe-deposit box. "It doesn't matter. The bank is probably closed by now."

"I made a few calls," Collin said. "Robert is still there. He said he would wait for us if we came over in the next few minutes. Here, let me carry that for you."

Leah handed Collin her suitcase and made a quick check

on Hula, giving her more food and water and a calm talking to as she hugged the dog around its neck. Then, locking her front door, Leah headed for her car only to find that Collin was loading her suitcase into his Mercedes' trunk.

Chapter Thirty-six

*W*hat are you doing?" Leah asked Collin, as he closed the Mercedes' trunk with her suitcase tucked inside.

"I'm driving you to Hamilton."

"It's four hours one way."

"I reserved a room for myself," Collin said. "I'll drive back in the morning. When you're ready to come home in a few days, you can call me, and I'll come pick you up. It's not a problem, Leah."

Without protesting, Leah got in his car, and the two of them drove to the bank. The truth was, Leah didn't know what to think of anything anymore. Her life had become a frantically twirling carousel, and all she could do was hold on tight as the ride went up and down and round and round faster and faster.

Robert, the bank president, and two tellers who were still doing paperwork were the bank's only occupants. Robert led Leah and Collin to the vault where Collin handed Leah the key and indicated he would wait for her in the bank's lobby so she could open the box in private.

Leah thought of how she would rather have waited until after her retreat at the hot springs to retrieve whatever was in the safe-deposit box. She wasn't ready for any more surprises. For all she knew, a check for a million dollars drawn on a secret Swiss bank account could be waiting for her. Or two tickets to the movies.

However, Collin was steering her life at the moment, and so she entered the bank vault holding in her hand the sum total of what she had inherited from Franklin Madison—a key.

Robert took Leah's key and used one of his own to open door of the safe-deposit box. Inside was a long, metal box with a handle. Robert pulled out the box and handed it to her. "You can open it in this room here," he said, pointing to a small private room she hadn't noticed before. He then quietly left.

As she opened the box's lid, inside she saw a plain, eight-by-ten manila envelope, folded in half and wedged into the flat, narrow box. Leah lifted the envelope. It was fairly light. And thin. She pinched the metal tabs on the back and was about to open the envelope when something stopped her.

She stood for a silent moment in the privacy of the room. *I don't want to know. Not yet. I want to give my heart a chance to settle.*

She folded the envelope and tucked it in her purse. As she walked back into the vault, Robert appeared and put the box into its slot, using his key and hers to lock it in place.

"Everything okay?" Collin asked when she joined him in the bank lobby.

Leah interpreted his question to mean, "What was in the box, and is there anything I should know about, now that I'm your attorney?"

"Everything is fine. Thank you."

Collin and Leah thanked the bank president and walked to Collin's Mercedes in silence.

"Any surprises?" Collin asked, as he opened Leah's car door for her.

She slid in without answering.

Collin got in and started the engine. "Not that you have to tell me. It is private, of course. You do know that I'm available if you need consultation on anything you found in the safe-deposit box. Franklin has turned out to be a man of surprises, and I want to make sure he didn't overwhelm you with another one."

Leah smiled to herself. Collin's voice carried the same tone of the little boy she had once left on the boulders at Heather Creek with his feet propped up.

"Collin, I don't know what was in the box." Leah decided that honesty was the best way to handle his questions. Especially considering this web she found herself caught in.

"It was empty?" Collin surmised.

"No, there was an envelope. But I didn't open it. I want to wait until after I've had time to clear my thoughts. I want to be prepared for whatever I find."

Collin nodded slowly, as he pulled the car onto the main highway. "Sounds wise."

For almost a mile neither of them spoke. Then Collin said, in the same tone as the freckled face boy Leah once had a crush on, "I suppose you're one of those people who actually can wait until Christmas morning to open her presents."

"Of course," Leah said. "Why? Can't you?"

"Nope. Never have been able to." With a chuckle Collin added, "The first Christmas we were married, my wife put three presents under the tree a week before Christmas. First chance I had, I unwrapped all three, saw what they were, and taped them back up."

"Did you get caught?"

Collin nodded and grinned. "And was she ever mad! Every year after that she hid my presents at her friend's house and refused to bring the gifts home until Christmas morning. Christmas was *her* holiday, and she wasn't going to let me spoil her fun."

Leah smiled and felt herself beginning to relax. "You must miss her a lot. Especially at Christmas."

Collin shot her a quick, startled look as if Leah had over-stepped a boundary. "Yes," he said. Then, with a lopsided tone to his voice, he added, "When do you miss your parents the most?"

Leah had to think about that for a moment. "I'm not sure. For so many years my life revolved around being available to meet their needs. It might sound heartless, but I don't miss that part. I miss funny little things like reading the Sunday comics together and the way my mom used to hum to herself when she was cooking dinner."

"The loss of special people in our lives changes us, doesn't it?" Collin's voice had switched back to the wise-advisor tone.

Leah felt a tight lump in her throat. "Yes, it does." She was thinking of Seth. *Ever since he stepped into my life I was changing for the better. Was it all a hoax? How will I change now that he's gone?*

They reached the freeway, and Collin headed north. "Would you mind, Leah, if I put on some music?"

"No, please do." She would be glad for the focus to be off their conversation. It felt as if she might lose her emotional equilibrium at any moment.

Collin pressed a few buttons, and suddenly they were sur-rounded by the magnificent voice of an Italian tenor. Leah leaned back in the plush leather seat and closed her eyes. What filled her ears was the most romantic, heart-stirring music she had ever heard.

And once again, the image of the gondola in Venice came to mind. Leah imagined she was settled in the soft cushions while the rich voice of this passionate Italian tenor sang over her. She didn't have to steer or direct or decide which canal to go down. All she had to do was nestle in this pocket of grace.

Casually opening one eye slightly, Leah glanced at Collin's profile as he drove. *Is he the gondolier I've been waiting for and dreaming of?* Leah snapped her eyes shut. *Where did that thought come from?*

A wave of confusion washed over her stronger than ever. She suddenly wasn't sure why she going anywhere with Collin Radcliffe. Leah wanted to rest in this pocket of grace, but somehow it wasn't right.

Collin shouldn't be directing and controlling which way I go, should he?

A sense of remorse over losing Seth hit her with force. Leah squeezed her eyes shut and turned her face to the window. While the Italian tenor sang his heart out, Leah cried silently, refusing to think of this exercise as "washing the windows of her soul."

Chapter Thirty-seven

When Leah awoke the next morning in her luxurious room at Hamilton Hot Springs, she blinked several times to make sure this wasn't part of a long, bizarre dream she had been floating in and out of. Even without her glasses on, she knew the fireplace set into the far wall was real. She could feel the extra fluffy down comforter. That was real, too. So was the silken, sheer canopy draped over the four-poster bed. She was at Hamilton Hot Springs, and there wasn't a fleck of avocado green or harvest gold in sight. Franklin's resort was a luxury spa.

This was all so foreign. She might as well have been dropped on Mars. Leah had no idea what to do in this place. She decided to dress and go downstairs to the restaurant for breakfast. As she pulled her clothes from her suitcase, Leah remembered how smoothly everything had happened last night. Collin drove for several hours while she silently cried herself to sleep under the spell of the Italian tenor's luxurious sounds. When Collin stopped for gas, Leah woke, and they ate at a drive-through restaurant. The rest of the way they talked about sports, music, and Collin's mother, who recently had sold one of her oil paintings to a museum in Minneapolis.

Collin didn't ask anything of Leah. He didn't bring up the topic of the safe-deposit box. He didn't talk business at all. After he saw Leah to her room at the resort, he said good night and asked her if she needed his number so she could call in a few days when she was ready to return home.

Leah sheepishly had to admit that she didn't have any of his business cards with her. Collin instantly produced a card from his pocket and disappeared down the hallway.

As Leah dressed this morning, she guessed that Collin already had left to drive home. She supposed he hadn't called her room to tell her he was leaving so that she could sleep in. It made her think of the sacrifices Collin was making on her behalf.

With bittersweet irony, Leah thought of the verse Seth had left on her windshield. The one she had thought was the valley of nuts. Leah was certain that if Collin hadn't intervened, she would have tumbled into that valley of nuts by now.

It was good to be here. Alone. Away from it all.

Leah checked her purse to make sure the envelope from Franklin's safe-deposit box was still there. She didn't feel ready to open it. Not yet.

Throwing a few things into the backpack she had brought with her, Leah decided to go for a walk. She stopped at the restaurant downstairs and asked if she could order a sandwich to go.

"Certainly," the hostess said. "Any particular kind of sandwich?"

"Wheat bread, no meat, lots of lettuce and tomato."

"We have a vegetarian special on a toasted basil and garlic bagel," the hostess offered.

"Perfect. And whatever kind of juice you have that comes in a bottle."

As Leah waited on the bench just inside the restaurant, she thumbed through a brochure that described the various mineral pools at the Hamilton spa. She already could imagine how good those therapy pools were going to feel when she returned from her hike. On the backside of the brochure was a map of a two-mile loop that led through the woodlands down to a small lake.

Leah took off on her hike with zest. Right away she noticed that she was hiking at a pace faster than she normally went. Her two hikes with Seth evidently had affected her hiking speed.

How could I have allowed myself to so easily fall in love with Seth? Weren't there hints along the way that he was setting me up?

Leah couldn't think of any. Everything about him had appeared genuine, even down to the lack of furniture in his apartment. She remembered the insurance papers Mary had showed her in Seth's file that were all in Spanish. Those documents couldn't have been false. Collin had suggested Seth had lied to her about being in Costa Rica, but Leah had seen the doctor's report on letterhead from a Costa Rican hospital.

Okay, so Seth isn't a complete liar. He was in Costa Rica. But maybe Collin was right. Maybe Seth had to flee the country because of the drug charges.

Leah picked up her pace as the trail led through an open meadow, laced with tiny blue wildflowers and tall white field daisies. They reminded her of the daisies Seth had given her last Friday, and how she had pushed him outside his own apartment and made him stand there, ringing the doorbell. Yesterday she had shoved the roses back at him. It occurred to Leah that both gestures were expressions of a woman who was trying to be in control. She winced; that wasn't the kind of person she wanted to be.

Hiking past the meadow, Leah entered a cool, green woodland. With only the company of the sound of twigs crunching under her feet as she marched onward, Leah silently asked forgiveness again for trying to control her life instead of allowing God to be at the helm.

Suddenly she stopped walking. She drew in a deep draught of the moist earth and the mossy trees. Woodlands were so soothing and restorative. The faint scent of wild violets rose to circle her, reminding her of the day Seth had held her in his arms in the woodland. She thought back on how he had talked of building a house on the very spot where the sun poured through the trees.

And to think that Seth took me to the fifty acres of woodland that Franklin owned, and that he kissed me there, knowing all along the significance of that plot of earth we stood on. And yet he didn't tell me. Did he really expect me to believe that our time together was more important than the information he had on the property and the will?

Pushing herself onward, Leah thought about how she would include that bit of information in her next talk with Collin so he could use it in the case he would build against Seth.

Am I sure I want to build a case against Seth?

She knew Collin probably could win the case if she gave him the right information. Then all of Franklin's money and land would revert to her.

And then what? I build myself a castle in the woodland and live there all by myself for the rest of my life? What kind of reward is that?

A wooden bench appeared on the trail ahead, just at the

woods' edge. Leah sat down so she could remove her shoe and shake out a pebble. The gesture reminded her again of Seth and their Easter morning hike.

"Okay, enough of the memories of Seth!" she said aloud. Overhead several birds sang out, and Leah listened. Theirs was a song of springtime.

See! The winter has past…the season of singing has come.

Sitting quietly for some time, Leah rehearsed the past month's events. Yes, the winter season of her life had passed. Yes, she was close to the Lord again and feeling sensitive to his Spirit. Her heart felt clean. No unconfessed junk to clog it up.

Yet I don't feel right. This is supposed to be the season of singing, but I don't have a song to sing. I want to enter into the season of Judah, of praise, like Leah in the Bible when she started to praise God instead of trying to prove herself, and yet I don't know how to do that.

Leah cleared her throat and attempted to sing. It was a noble effort, although not a successful one. She gave up and let the birds do the singing.

By the time she reached the lake, she felt emotionally exhausted and more than ready for her lunch. Several ducks floated on the placid, blue-gray waters of the kidney-shaped body of water before her. One of them headed her way when he saw her sitting down with food in her hand. Leah tore off a pinch of her bagel and tossed it to the friendly local. That was all his cronies needed to feel they had been invited to a company picnic.

With great honking and comical waddling, the army of freeloading ducks came after Leah. She relinquished the top half of her bagel, standing and tearing it up piece by piece. She tried to eat as much as she could while sharing the bottom of her falling apart sandwich. As soon as the bagel was gone, it began to rain.

Without a single "thank you" honk, the line of waddling tails hotfooted it back into the lake and frolicked in the rain.

Leah pulled down her baseball cap and began to tromp uphill in the rain. The hike back was much more difficult than the walk that had sloped downward to the lake. All the way, as she huffed along, she heard birds singing.

Singing in the rain, she thought with a grin. *Wish I could sing. I just don't have a song. Maybe the season of singing hasn't come to me yet. Why not? What's missing?*

Leah stomped her boots on the front mat before entering the lobby of the resort. She was chilled and wet and eager to soak in one of the mineral pools. Hurrying to her room, she pulled on her bathing suit and covered up with the luxurious robe provided in her room. The elevator at the end of the hall took her to the mineral pools where a resort staff member offered her a towel and pointed out the specifics of each pool.

Leah chose the bubbling hot tub of 103-degrees and slowly lowered herself into the inviting cauldron. All her tension melted, as instantly she was warmed and soothed after her hike in the rain.

She didn't want to think about anything. She wished her mind could shut down and float for a while the way her body was floating in the relaxing spa. But jumbled thoughts kept popping up in her mind. Thoughts of Seth. Thoughts of Collin. Thoughts of Jessica's description of being nestled in a pocket of grace.

Leah's eyelids flew open. *Jessica! I called her lawyer yesterday, and he's expecting me to call him back.* Leah knew she didn't have to call him, but she also knew it would nag at her since she had said she would. She would call and leave a message that she no longer needed a second opinion.

Feeling sufficiently poached, Leah decided to get out of the steaming spa and ask the resort assistant on duty if she could use a phone in the pool area. She knew that if she got that call off her mind, she could relax some more.

Rising from the hot mineral water, Leah was about to reach for her towel on a nearby lounge chair when someone held it out to her. She looked up to see Collin Radcliffe offering her the towel with a pleasant smile on his face.

Chapter Thirty-eight

*W*hat are you doing here? I thought you had gone home."
Leah quickly wrapped the thick, white towel around herself.

Collin shrugged. "When I woke up this morning, I thought
about how long it's been since I've given myself a vacation. So
I made a few calls, did a little shopping for some clothes, and
decided to take it easy for a day or two." He was wearing a spa
robe, and his hair was wet. "Have you tried the steam sauna
yet? It's exceptionally good for the sinuses."

Leah felt deceived. Collin had just as much right to be here
as she did; yet her private space was being invaded. She didn't
know why she felt such a strong sense of distrust for Collin
after all he had done for her, but she did.

"No, I, ah…" Leah reached for her robe. "I haven't been in
the sauna yet, but I need to go back to my room right now."
She felt awkward admitting she was going to call another
lawyer so she added, "I forgot to do something."

"Well, I'll be here." Collin settled in a lounge chair and smoothed back his wet hair with a hand towel. "If you feel like coming back to the pools, that is."

"Okay," Leah mumbled.

"And if you don't have any plans for dinner, I'd love to have you join me. I made reservations at The Loft for six o'clock. Their specialty is prime rib."

"I don't eat red meat."

"Oh. Salad bar, perhaps?"

"I'll let you know," Leah said after a pause.

"Okay. Good. I'll call your room later to see what works best for you."

"Thanks." Leah turned to go.

"Oh, Leah?"

She looked over her shoulder at him.

"Any surprises with the contents of Franklin's envelope?"

Leah felt her jaw clenching. "I don't know."

Collin raised his hands in a gesture of apology. He didn't offer any more comments.

As Leah walked briskly to the elevator, her emotions ran at a frenzied pace. The moment she entered her room, the phone was ringing.

Come on, Collin, give me a little space here!

Opting for a warm shower to remove the scent of the mineral pools before calling Jessica's lawyer, Leah let the phone ring and turned the water on full force.

Once she had showered, changed, and dried her hair, she felt more centered. She called Jessica and wrote down the number for her lawyer. She also told Jessica what had happened with Seth and that she was at the hot springs. Leah thought it best not to mention Collin was there as well.

"I spoke with my lawyer today," Jessica said. "Greg said he

tried to call you several times and that people at work told him you had taken a few sick days. I was concerned about you. I'm glad you called."

"I'm going to call Mr. Fletcher now," Leah said. "I didn't think I needed a second lawyer's opinion, but maybe I do."

"Sounds wise," Jessica said. "Are you sure you're okay?"

"I think so. I went for a hike this morning, and that helped to clear my thoughts. Only you know what? I tried to sing, and I don't have a song."

Jessica paused. "What do you mean?"

"You know, 'See! The winter is passed…the season of singing has come.' I know that winter has passed. God has done amazing springtime planting in my life, but I'm not singing yet."

After another pause Jessica said slowly, "Well, I don't know if you're the one who is supposed to be singing."

Before Leah could process that comment, she heard a knock on the door. "I have to go, Jess. I'll call you later."

Leah hung up and hurried to the door, certain Collin would be standing there. She didn't want to talk to him. Not yet.

"Room service," the voice behind the door called out.

Leah opened the door and smiled at the uniformed woman. "I've already had my room cleaned, thank you."

"I'm here to restock the minibar," the woman said.

"I haven't even opened it."

"Okay. Thank you."

Just then the phone rang again, and once again, Leah let it ring. "I'm not ready for you to smooth talk me, Collin," she muttered. "Let me have some space."

She flipped the gas lighter switch on the wall, and instantly the logs in the fireplace began to heat up, taking the chill off the room.

Leah checked the clock. 4:20. She dialed the number for Gregory Fletcher, and his assistant answered.

"Yes, Leah," the assistant said. "Mr. Fletcher is available. He asked that I put you through if you called."

"Leah, hello, this is Greg Fletcher."

"I'm sorry you had to make several calls today trying to track me down. I just spoke with Jessica, and she told me."

"No problem," Greg said. "How can I help you?"

"I'm not exactly sure," Leah said, adjusting her position on the end of the bed. "I have a lawyer who is helping me with an inheritance situation, but I'm thinking I might need a second opinion."

"Yes, Jessica told me your lawyer was Collin Radcliffe."

"That's right."

Mr. Fletcher paused.

Leah sensed something in his silence. "Do you know Collin?"

"Yes. His office used to be in the same building as mine. As a matter of fact, one of my clients married his first wife."

"Collin told me about her," Leah said. "It was tragic the way he lost her and their child in the car accident."

"Their child?" Greg echoed.

"Yes, Collin said his wife was five months pregnant at the time of the accident."

"His wife?"

"Yes." Leah didn't like the tone in Greg's voice. "She was his wife, wasn't she? I mean they were married, right?"

"Actually, Collin and DeeDee had been divorced for two years before she married my friend, Bryan. She was carrying Bryan's child when she died."

Leah could only think of one response. "Oh. I'm so sorry."

"Yes. Well, Collin is a competent lawyer. He tends to get what he goes after so I'm sure he'll work hard for you."

Now Leah was the one pausing. "Mr. Fletcher, would it be

all right if I called you back? I think I need a little time to pull my thoughts together."

"Certainly. You have my numbers. Feel free to call me when you're ready to talk."

"You've already helped me more than you can know."

Leah sat on the edge of the bed staring into the fire that danced in the fireplace.

Collin lied. He slanted the details so I'd feel sympathy for him. I can't trust him. If he lied about his "wife," he also could have lied about Seth and Seth's records.

Leah felt her heart racing. She might have condemned Seth unfairly. *But why did Seth admit to the bankruptcy and the police record?*

Suddenly she felt very sure that Collin had slanted the facts in Seth's file to manipulate her opinion of Seth. She had been brutally unfair not to let Seth explain.

How could I have been so blind? For all I know, Collin is the one scheming to marry me after I claim Franklin's fortune and then dump me and take it all. What was it Mr. Fletcher just said? "Collin tends to get what he goes after."

"Well, he's not getting me!" Leah spouted, jumping up and heading for the door. She planned to march down to the mineral pools and tell Collin exactly what she thought of him. However, an urgent knock on the door caused her to pause for a moment.

So much the better! I'm ready for you now, Collin! Leah's fingers flew to unclasp the locks, and she yanked open the door, spewing out the first thing that came to her. "I don't take it very well when people lie to me!"

"So I noticed." The man at her door stood with his arms covering his face as if expecting Leah to throw something at him. "But I haven't lied to you about anything." He lowered his arms.

"Seth!" Leah rushed to him and threw her arms around him. "Seth, I can't believe you're here. Will you forgive me? I'm so sorry. Please forgive me."

"Of course I forgive you," he said. "Now will you forgive me?"

"Forgive you? For what?"

"For not telling you what you wanted to know when you wanted to know it."

"You didn't do anything wrong. I was the one who had it all mixed up. I misunderstood everything." Leah pulled back and looked up at his unshaven face and his red eyes. "Seth, you look exhausted. Come in. How did you know I was here?"

Seth went over to a chair by the fireplace. "I called you last night a dozen times. Then I called you again this morning at work. They told me you were out sick. I went by your house, and when you weren't there I guessed that if I could find Collin, I'd find you since you were with him last night."

Leah sat on the raised hearth and reached over to take Seth's hands in hers.

"Collin's secretary told me he was staying here. I called the front desk, and they said you were registered here, too. I know people at work must think I'm a maniac, but I turned in my truck at noon and said I had to leave on an emergency. I drove straight here, and when I arrived, I tried to call your room from the lobby."

"I thought it was Collin. That's why I didn't answer."

"I think the hotel operator slipped up when she told me there was no answer in room 145. That's how I found out your room number. I hope you don't mind my barging in on you like this. I was so concerned."

"I'm glad you're here, Seth."

His expression softened. "I'm glad I'm here, too. Leah, I apologize for handling everything so poorly yesterday. The roses and the suggestion that we get married.... I can imagine how that must have looked to you. I don't know why it seemed like a good idea."

Leah searched his expression for the deeper meaning behind his words.

"No, no! I don't mean that marrying you isn't a good idea. I mean coming on so strong like that after we've only known each other a few weeks. I can see how it would seem as if I were reacting to the condition of the will. I didn't realize that at the time. I didn't understand why you were so upset. And then all that information you had about the bankruptcy and the police record. How did you find out about that?"

"Collin."

Seth's expression turned grim. "What else did he tell you?"

"He has a whole file on you, but that was all he showed me."

Seth let go of Leah's hand. He began to pace the floor. "Man, that is really the lowest. Let me guess. He wanted to find a way to get the will switched back into your name only."

Leah nodded. "Tell me about the police record, Seth."

"It was in college. I had three roommates my senior year. One of the guys I didn't know until he moved into our apartment. He borrowed my car on a pretty consistent basis, which was fine. We all helped each other out. But then, because of Warren's excessive parking violations, my car was impounded, and the police found some drug paraphernalia under the seat. Warren said he was holding it for a friend, but it was all recorded in my name because it was my car."

Leah shook her head. "That's awful." She felt worse than ever for doubting Seth.

"And the bankruptcy issue is a very painful subject for me."

"You don't have to tell me about it if you don't want to,

Seth. I trust you." Leah was surprised to hear those last three words come out of her mouth. Trust was such an issue to her she might as well have just said, "I love you."

"No, I don't mind telling you. It was stupidity on my part. I received a credit card in the mail my last year of college. You know how they do those promotional deals. I activated it, but then I never used it. I kept it in my desk drawer at the apartment. When I moved out, I didn't notice it was missing. That is, until a credit bureau tracked me down in Costa Rica and said I'd run up debt of more than $28,000 plus more than a year's interest at 22 percent."

Leah let out a low whistle.

"I told them my card had been stolen, but I had nothing to stand on because I hadn't reported it lost or stolen. I had no way of paying it off. I had nothing. I followed my dad's lawyer's advice and filed bankruptcy."

"Seth, I'm so sorry. I'm sorry I doubted you and jumped to conclusions."

He moved over to the hearth beside Leah and drew her close. His voice mellowed. "What matters now is that we've cleared all this up. We're together. I couldn't sleep last night thinking I'd lost you, Leah."

"I trust you, Seth," Leah said firmly.

He drew away and looked into her eyes. She knew he understood the deeper meaning behind her words. "And I love you," he answered.

"I'll never let someone else influence my opinion of you again."

"Speaking of 'someone else,'" Seth said. "Is he still here at the hotel?"

"Yes, he's at the mineral pools now."

"I'd like to have a word with him," Seth said sharply.

"So would I. It just so happens I've learned that Collin has been manipulating all kinds of facts."

The phone's ringing interrupted Leah. She knew Collin was calling to see if she would take him up on his dinner invitation. "Seth, do you trust me?"

Seth's clear blue eyes opened wide. "Yes."

"Then don't say anything when I answer the phone. I have an idea."

Chapter Thirty-nine

*L*eah hung up the phone and said to Seth, "We have an appointment to meet Collin for dinner at six o'clock."

"What did he say when you asked him to change the reservations to three people instead of two?"

"Nothing. I think it confused him, but I don't think he suspects you're the third party."

Seth checked his watch. "It's five o'clock now. I have some clothes in my car. I should probably change before dinner."

"Why don't you use my shower, and I'll go downstairs? A library is on the other side of the gift shop. I saw in the brochure that they serve tea in the library until six."

"You don't mind my taking over your space?"

Leah couldn't help but think how different it felt to have Seth in her "space" compared to Collin crowding in on her.

"No, I like having you here. You feel like you belong in my space."

Seth smiled. "And you belong in my space. In my galaxy. In my universe."

Leah laughed. "Does this mean we've ended up on Pluto together?"

Seth kissed her on the end of her nose. "And who says wishes don't come true?"

Leah's heart felt full. She knew what needed to come next for her. Grabbing her purse, she gave the room key to Seth. "I'll be in the library. I have some reading to do."

"I'll walk you down so I can get the stuff from my car."

Hand in hand, Leah and Seth headed for the elevator. Seth let go and pushed the down button. Then he put his arm around Leah's shoulders. "Did I ever tell you that you're exactly the right height?"

Leah put her arm around Seth's middle and said, "We do fit together nicely, don't we?"

"Perfectly." He leaned over and gave Leah a tender kiss on the lips.

The elevator door opened, and Leah shyly pulled away. Then she froze. Before them stood Collin Radcliffe in the elevator.

"Seth," Collin said with a nod. "Leah."

Neither Seth nor Leah responded right away.

The door began to close, and Collin stepped out, dressed in his poolside apparel. "I take it this is our mystery guest for dinner." Collin's voice was anything but friendly.

"If you want to cancel dinner, that's fine," Leah said. "We both wanted to talk a few things through with you." For good measure, she added, "Before we drive home together this evening."

Collin straightened his shoulders. "Fine." The smooth, professional tone had returned to his voice. "You have to eat anyway; might as well eat before you hit the road. It's a long drive."

"Yes, it is," Seth agreed. "But I'm sure the ride home for me will be much less stressful than the journey here."

Leah caught Seth's deeper meaning and gave his side a squeeze since her arm was still around his middle.

"I'll see you both at six," Collin said, excusing himself and walking past them.

Seth pushed the elevator button again, and the door opened. They entered and rode to the lower level in silence.

"I'm not afraid of him," Leah said, as Seth walked her to the library. "I don't trust him."

"You don't have to trust Collin. The only one you have to trust completely is Christ. I know that's been hard for you over the years, but he's the only one who won't ever let you down." Seth gave Leah's shoulder a squeeze and headed through the lobby for the parking lot.

Leah watched him go and then entered the small library through the thick wooden doors. She was the only one there. A crackling fire rose from the large fireplace, which was lined with gray and brown river rock. Built-in bookshelves ran from the floor to the ceiling on the two opposite walls. In front of Leah stood a long marble-top table decked out with a silver platter of tiny sandwiches, strawberries dipped in white chocolate, and sugar cookies in the shape of flowers with light pink and purple frosting.

Shelly would love this. So would Lauren. And Jessica.

Leah poured herself a cup of tea from the brass urn in the center of the table. It felt strange to be the only one in the library and the only one at this tea. But this was good. She wanted to be alone with the fire, a soothing cup of tea, and the envelope from Franklin's safe-deposit box.

She settled herself on the comfortable, forest green sofa that faced the fireplace. After eating two strawberries and taking a sip of tea, she pulled the folded manila envelope from her purse. The nervous fear of the unknown had left her. The confusion over how to respond to so many surprises no longer hung over her. Leah knew that whatever was in the envelope was something Franklin had wanted her to have, and that alone made it special.

Reaching her hand into the flat envelope, Leah pulled out three postcards. One was of the Austrian Alps, the second of the Seine River in Paris, and the third of a gondola docked against a red-and-white-striped pole. The gondolier stood on the dock, complete with a wide-brimmed straw hat with a blue ribbon hanging down its back. He leaned casually against the pole and indicated with his hand that his gondola was available for the next rider.

Seth's postcards. A nostalgic smile danced across Leah's lips. She thought of all the times she had held those postcards at Franklin's house and how she had whispered to the gondolier that one day she would ride in his gondola.

Leah flipped over the cards. If she had read them before, she didn't remember any of Seth's messages to his great-uncle. The postcard from Paris held three scribbled lines: one about the weather, one about the Mona Lisa in the Louvre, and a final line about the weather again.

The postcard from the Austria Alps read,

Thanks so much for the money you wired me in Munich. My mom wrote and said you were going to send me some traveling money. It came at just the right time because I was down to my last two deutsche marks. I'm going to Italy tomorrow. They say it's cheaper to eat there.

Leah smiled broadly as she read the back of the postcard from Venice.

I looked up the verse you sent with the money, and I've thought about it a lot. I agree. It is the blessing of the Lord that makes us rich, and He adds no sorrow to it.

Leah gazed into the cheery fire and tried to remember where she had heard that phrase before. It wasn't from one of Jessica's three-by-five cards. For some reason, she could hear Mavis's voice when she thought of the verse.

Then she remembered. It was the last thing Franklin had said to Leah the day she visited him before he passed away. Mavis had noted he had been saying it ever since the lawyer had come to change the will.

"The blessing of the Lord makes us rich, and He adds no sorrow to it," Leah whispered into the firelight. "I agree with that." She felt a settled confidence that Seth believed that as well. His life so far was evidence that he had not lived to gain riches. Seth impressed her as someone who was living for God's blessing, not man's. That was certainly how Franklin had lived.

Leah read the last lines of the postcard.

Thanks again for the money. Here's one of my favorite verses for you to look up. Zeph. 3:1.
    Seth

The double doors of the library opened, and Leah turned to see Seth entering. He was clean-shaven and wearing fresh clothes. She smiled as he grabbed a strawberry before coming over to sit beside her on the couch.

"What do you have there?" he asked.

"Do you recognize these?" Leah held up the postcards.

It took Seth a moment. He turned one over and viewed his own handwriting. A smile came across his face. "Where did you get them?"

"Franklin's safe-deposit box."

"Those were in his safe-deposit box?"

"Yes, that's all that was in it. He kept these on his coffee table for years, and I would always stare at them. I had a private conversation going with this gondolier." She handed Seth the postcard.

He read the back. "'The blessing of the Lord makes us rich.' So that's where I first heard that verse."

"And what's the verse in Zephaniah?" Leah asked.

"That's been my favorite since I was a kid. You probably know it, too. 'The LORD thy God in the midst of thee is mighty, he will save, he will rejoice over thee with joy, he will rest in his love, he will joy over thee with singing.'"

Leah didn't know that verse. "Wait, what was the last part again?"

"'He will joy over thee with singing.'"

Leah took the postcard from Seth and stared at the picture of the gondolier. She felt her lungs squeeze and the pulse pound in her throat.

"Are you okay?" Seth asked.

"I'm not supposed to sing," she said in a whisper. "That's what Jessica said today. I'm not supposed to be the one singing."

"I don't follow you."

Tears rushed to Leah's eyes, as she held the postcard for Seth and tried to explain what had just become so clear. "The gondolier. It's the Lord. He's been inviting me to rest in this pocket of grace for so long, but I've been the one doing all the steering. My whole life I had to be in control, even if I didn't know which canal to go down."

Seth reached over and wiped away a tear. He looked at her compassionately; yet his expression showed he didn't have a clue what she was rambling on about.

"It's from your verse, Seth. 'The winter is past and the season of singing has come.' Only I'm not the one who's supposed to do the singing. Jesus is the Gondolier of my life. He wants me to rest in his pocket of grace while he decides which canal to take me down."

The tears came in a steady cascade. "Do you understand what I'm saying at all? It's my season of Judah. I choose to praise God instead of trying to prove myself good enough for him. I finally get it! I don't have to steer the boat and sing the songs and do everything. Jesus is the Gondolier. I rest. Here." She pointed at the pillows cushioning the gondola. "He steers, he leads, and he sings over me. That's what I never understood. He's the one who does the singing."

Seth opened his arms, and Leah leaned against his chest, sobbing. She felt so free. Pulling away, with a ripple of laughter, she said, "Honest, Seth, I never in my life have cried as much as I have this last month."

"You know how I feel about your tears." Seth stroked her hair.

"It's just that I never understood before. Not the way I understand now. He sings over me!"

Chapter Forty

*L*eah wasn't sure if Seth completely understood what she was saying. It didn't matter. She understood. And her relationship with the Lord would never be the same.

Drying her tears and composing herself, Leah tucked the postcards back into her purse and tried another sip of her tea, which had cooled too much for her to drink.

Seth checked his watch. "Almost six."

"I'm ready," Leah said.

She and Seth strolled to The Loft restaurant with their arms around each other. Collin was already seated.

Leah resisted the urge to control the conversation. She sat back in her chair and opened her menu, as if this were just dinner with two friends.

Collin waited until they had ordered before saying, "I don't know that much needs to be said at this point. It's obvious, Leah, you've made some choices about whom to trust."

Leah remembered Seth's words from earlier in the lobby. "Collin, I've learned a few things today. One is that Christ is the only one I can trust completely. He's the only one who won't ever let me down. Humans make mistakes all the time."

Collin's expression registered his surprise. "Perhaps as a professional advisor, I should mention it can be risky to trust your future to people who have made mistakes in the past."

"I think it's even riskier to trust people who manipulate the truth."

Collin looked intrigued.

"I don't want to play any games, Collin. I just need to say that I felt it was unfair of you to try to gain my sympathy by telling me that your wife had been killed in a car accident. I happen to know you had been divorced for two years when she died, and the child she was carrying wasn't yours."

Collin squinted at Leah as if he couldn't believe she had detective powers that could uncover such information. Seth appeared equally surprised.

"I'm sure it was still a very painful experience for you," Leah continued. "But if you plan to stay in Glenbrooke and continue your father's practice, I think it would help you to know that the people your father has served for years are honest people who expect the truth. That's all, Collin, just tell the truth."

Collin paused, studying Leah. "You are an exceptional woman, Leah Hudson. I said it before, and I'll say it again. It's my loss I didn't recognize that when we were in high school."

Leah felt her candy apple cheeks doing what they loved to do. Yet she didn't try to hide their blushing. She looked openly at Collin and said, "I don't think I knew who I was in high school. But I know who I am now, and I hope we can be friends. I'd like the three of us to be friends."

Collin's appearance softened. "I'd like that as well, Leah."

Seth spoke up. "Before I'd be real comfortable with that, I think you and I have a few things to settle. First, I understand you have a file on me. I'm sure it's legal or else you wouldn't have it."

Glancing at Leah, Seth continued, "I told Leah everything, and I would like you to know that I have nothing to hide. Everything I said in your office yesterday was true. I didn't know the will had been changed. I didn't come to Glenbrooke in search of my great-uncle's fortune. I came here for medical reasons. I agree with Leah that I, like all the other people of Glenbrooke, expect honesty and decency from a man in your position. I look forward to your display of those qualities as we continue to do business together."

Collin looked at Leah and then back at Seth. He hesitated before saying, "My apologies. To both of you."

The waiter arrived with their food, and Seth asked if he could offer a prayer.

They ate quietly for a few minutes before Collin said, "If I might add my own swan song here, I'd like to say a few things. I moved back to Glenbrooke looking for something. I think you've both helped me to see what that was. I missed the honesty and integrity I grew up with. I guess some of my old business ways followed me back home. Consider your words taken to heart. I appreciate your honesty. Both of you. I'd highly value a friendship with you."

Leah felt relieved. She also was impressed that Collin had responded so well.

After that the conversation flowed more easily and freely. Collin agreed to destroy the file he had on Seth. Then, because Leah knew Collin was still probably dying to know, she told him about the postcards being the only treasure in the safe-deposit box. She pulled them from her purse and showed them to him.

"'It's the blessing of the Lord that makes us rich,'" Collin read. "I remember hearing Franklin say that once when I went with my father to pay him a visit."

"'And He adds no sorrow to it,'" Seth added.

Collin nodded somberly, turning over the postcards and examining each of the pictures. Leah couldn't help but smile when he studied the postcard from Venice. She knew that no one else would ever see what she saw in that picture. She already had plans to frame it so she would always remember what had become so clear to her today, that the Gondolier daily invites her to ride with him while he does all the work and chooses the right canals. And most importantly, that he expresses his delight by singing over her.

"So you two are heading back to Glenbrooke tonight?" Collin asked.

Seth and Leah both nodded.

"Is there anything I can do for either of you?"

Seth said, "No, thanks."

Leah was about to echo the same answer, but then she had a thought. "Actually, Collin, you could do one thing for me."

"Name it."

Twenty minutes later, Seth and Leah were on the road in his Subaru station wagon, heading south for Glenbrooke.

"Ready for this?" Leah asked.

Seth nodded. Leah held Seth's portable CD player in her lap and inserted the CD she had borrowed from Collin. Into the air floated the rich, romantic voice of an Italian tenor, singing his heart out.

Leah pulled the paper insert from the CD case and told Seth, "This says the title of this song in English is 'I'll Go with You.'"

Seth smiled at her. "It's true, George. I will go with you."

"And I'll go with you," Leah said, reaching over and slipping her hand into his.

Leah leaned back and closed her eyes. She could clearly picture a charming cottage tucked away in the clearing of a certain woodland where the sunbeams shot through the trees like bronzed javelins thrust from the heavens. She reveled in thoughts of Seth's kisses in the golden light of those woodlands. Bungee would have a yard to play in.

Leah looked over at Seth, wondering what he was thinking. She couldn't keep back the smile that had broken out as she studied the profile of the man with whom she knew she would spend the rest of her life.

"I was thinking," Seth said, glancing at Leah.

"Yes?"

"You don't have to say anything right away. Take all the time you want to think about it."

"Yes?" Leah waited for Seth to finish. She felt as if the Gondolier was steering their course home to Glenbrooke, and she and Seth had fallen together into this pocket of grace. As the soaring notes of the Italian love song showered over them, Leah whispered under her breath, "Oh, Lion of Judah, keep singing over us. Sing over us with joy!"

"I was wondering," Seth said. "What would you think of a honeymoon in Venice?"

Dear Reader,

During my teen years, which were spent in southern California, every Fourth of July my family visited friends at the beach. The summer I was fourteen, I was sitting on the beach watching the waves when "Uncle" Bob leaned over and said, "You do know, don't you, that the Lord sings over you?"

I had no idea what he was talking about. I did know that Bob was full of surprises. He wrote clever poetry, and his wife, Madelyn, decorated their beachfront home with his original oil paintings of their favorite Hawaiian locations. He had hung a swing from their vaulted ceiling for their three children. And he was one of the first God-lovers I ever met.

As the summer sun poured over us that July afternoon, I squinted at Uncle Bob in response to his remark. He added with a nod, "It's true. The Lord sings over you, Robin. It's in the Bible so I know it's true." He quoted Zephaniah 3:17, "He will joy over thee with singing."

I felt as if I had been handed a secret key that unlocked one of the mysteries of God. The Lord sings over me!

That knowledge became sweeter than just knowing that God loved me. It was deeper than believing Christ had died for me. It was more promising than trusting that one day Christ would return and take me to be with him.

The Lord sings over me! God takes delight in being with me!

My soul's response was to promise to always take delight in him. His singing over me became evidence that God liked me. He was the eternal romancer. The relentless lover. The one who always wants me back.

As I wrote about Leah, I felt she represented so many women I know who haven't yet realized God takes delight in them simply because they are his daughters. I wanted Leah to discover this truth and to realize it wasn't up to her to direct her life down each "canal" she came to. I like the way she yielded to the Gondolier and finally settled into his pocket of grace. I want to live like that every day.

My friend, you do know, don't you, that the Lord rejoices over you with singing? It says so in his Book so I know it's true.

Always,

Robin Jones Gunn

Write to Robin Jones Gunn, c/o Multnomah Publishers
P.O. Box 1720, Sisters, Oregon 97759

My son decided he liked spinach when he was in third grade. The school's cafeteria served spinach once a week, and none of the other kids could believe my son actually ate it. He came home one day with a story about how he not only ate all his spinach, but he also powered down most of the other kids' servings. They hailed him as having performed some kind of inhuman feat. (In third grade, I guess we all take whatever fame we can get.)

I asked my son what made the school spinach so good, and he said it was "all mixed up with cheese in in." I began to experiment with a spinach soufflé recipe until he said it was just as good as the cafeteria spinach. It's still his favorite. I make it every Thanksgiving, Christmas, and a dozen other times during the year. And, I have to say, it doesn't feel like a feat at all to pack away a considerable amount of spinach—even if no third-graders are surrounding you and cheering you on.

I think Leah would have come up with the same recipe, which is why I call it "Leah's Spinach."

I must tell you I really goofed on this easy recipe once. We were having company for dinner, and in my haste, I bought frozen collard greens instead of spinach. It wasn't until our poor company dug in and took the first bite that I realized something was wrong. I'll never forget the look on that poor guy's face! So whatever you do, don't substitute chopped collard greens. It makes for a bitter surprise.

LEAH'S SPINACH

6 boxes frozen, chopped spinach (10-ounce size)
6 large eggs
1 cup monterey jack cheese, grated
3 slices bread, crumbled into crumbs
few pats of butter
salt and pepper

Thaw the spinach and drain excess water. Place spinach in oven-safe soufflé bowl (or casserole dish). Mix in the grated cheese. Add a few shakes of salt and pepper. In a separate bowl, beat all six eggs and pour over spinach and cheese and mix together. Cover mixture with breadcrumbs and dot with a few pats of butter. Bake for 30 minutes in a 350-degree oven.

IDA'S LEMONADE

Berries are plentiful in the Northwest each summer so it's easy to think of creative ways to include berries in our summer menu. Here's a recipe for fresh lemonade with berries, one of Ida's secret ingredients.

1 1/2 cups berries, washed and hulled
1 cup fresh-squeezed lemon juice (about 6 lemons)
3/4 cup sugar
4 cups cold water

Combine the berries, lemon juice, and sugar in a blender or food processor. Blend until smooth. Pour into a large pitcher. Add cold water and squeeze half a lime over the top. Stir well and add ice. Ah, the joys of summer!

THE GLENBROOKE SERIES
by Robin Jones Gunn

Come to Glenbrooke...a quiet place where souls are refreshed

1-57673-420-X

1-57673-648-2

Secrets

ROBIN
JONES
GUNN

Whispers

ROBIN
JONES
GUNN

Secrets—book 1

Jessica Morgan tries to conceal her mysterious past from the citizens of Glenbrooke, including a compassionate paramedic and a jealous woman. Will Jessica ever find peace and stop hiding the truth?

Whispers—book 2

Invited to Maui by a handsome biologist, Teri is also attracted to an old crush and an endearing Australian with a wild past. Swept up by feelings, will she respond to God's gentle urgings?

THE GLENBROOKE SERIES
by Robin Jones Gunn

Come to Glenbrooke...a quiet place where souls are refreshed

1-57673-488-9

1-57673-619-9

Clouds—book 5

When Shelly's job as a flight attendant takes her to Germany, she unexpectedly meets up with her childhood sweetheart. Then she learns he's engaged. Shelly manages to hide her feelings from everyone but herself. Will she ever have the chance to tell Jonathan the truth?

Waterfalls—book 6

Meredith Graham has never had a problem holding her own, until she meets movie star Jacob Wilde and loses her characteristic cool. Jacob isn't impressed with Meri—until a twist of events makes him see her in a different light. Now he's discovering what it's like to be starstruck himself!

THE GLENBROOKE SERIES
by Robin Jones Gunn

Come to Glenbrooke...a quiet place where souls are refreshed

Woodlands

ROBIN
JONES
GUNN

1-57673-503-6

ROBIN'S NEWEST RELEASE

Woodlands—book 7

An unexpected inheritance—and the attentions
of Seth Edwards—throw Leah Hudson's life
into chaos. What will it take for her to be
able to hear the true song of this
springtime of her life?